I0461148

FAIRY

THIEF

BOOK 2
THE FAIRY CIRCLE SERIES

johanna Frappier

Copyright 2011 Johanna Frappier

Edited by Donna L. Bobbs

All rights reserved.

ISBN: 0983886121

ISBN-13: 978-0983886129

To my editor Donna L Bobbs

I gave you rocks and you gave me diamonds

I'm so thankful we found each other.

:D

Chapter 1

It was ten minutes past midnight. He had called her over forty times. Maybe Saffron was ignoring him, but no, Markis was going with his gut. Something was wrong. He didn't have the number to reach her mother and Derek. She had never given him that number, and it wasn't listed. His foot caught on his hockey stick, which sent him hopping across a pile of dirty clothes and tripping out into the hall. His parents were in the living room, watching TV. Mrs. Bryant was sitting up as straight as a schoolgirl on the edge of the couch, carding alpaca fiber that she had bought from Saffron's mother. His father was slumped in the La-Z-Boy, almost asleep.

"Hey, I'm going to Saffron's — something's not right."

His father grunted. His mother turned down the volume on the TV, and put the carders in a basket by her feet. "What do you mean? It's past midnight, Markis...."

"Yeah, I know...but, I don't know." He tugged his ear, looked at the door, and looked back at his mother.

"Oh, Markis, maybe you shouldn't do this anymore...." His mother's words and guarded voice brought him up short. She gathered her long, black hair in one hand, and fingered the pendant on her squash necklace with the other. The necklace had been in her family for over a hundred years, made by her own great-grandfather, Turtle Walker. "Maybe you should give Saffron some space."

Markis looked down as the tips of his ears tinged redder than his father's hair. Markis' own hair was dark and curly, and it covered is burning ears.

His mother could tell he felt ashamed from the way he hung his head. "Markis, I don't want to see you get hurt. She doesn't return your phone calls...."

"Yes, she does; it's just today she hasn't."

"When you came slamming in the door the other night, you said she ended the party early, then she went up to her room to get ready to go out..."

Markis rolled his eyes. *Why* had he confided in his mother about the other night? He had been so pissed when he got home from Saffron's, after seeing her up there through her bedroom window, so obviously not going to bed. She was supposedly sick from her party — on champagne she never drank. He saw her there, sitting at her vanity table and doing her hair up as if she was about to go out! When he got home he was so mad — and his mother was there, and usually she didn't say much about her opinion, and, well, he had told his mother.

"You've become a different person with this girl." She leaned forward and placed her elbows on her knees. Her hair swished with her. "It's like you're obsessed, Markis, and that's not healthy."

"Oh, my God, Mom, are you kidding me?" Markis folded his arms across his chest and stared hard at a phone commercial on the TV. "We're just friends. I'm concerned. That's all. I'm going to check her out — I'm going to check the *situation* out."

Mrs. Bryant stood and held up her hand to stop him from professing any more. She gathered a half-tipped bowl of salt and vinegar chips off her husband's lap, and went to the kitchen.

Markis put on his motorcycle boots and went tromping out into the still, summer night. He rammed his helmet on his head, straddled his bike, and gunned the engine. It was cool that he and Saffron were friends. He was just going to make sure she was okay. There was nothing wrong with that. It's what friends did for each other. He heeled the kickstand so hard the bike almost tipped over. He swore as he circled the thing around and sped out of his driveway. It wasn't too far to Coco's parents' place. As he pulled onto their cobbled drive he saw the lights were on. All four floors of the Georgian-style mansion were lit up with the glow of recessed lighting. It poured out of every immaculate, maid-cleaned window. He hoped her parents weren't having one of their all-snoot-review parties or a mine-is-bigger-than-yours benefit.

Coco's father, Reginald Gabrielli, answered the door in his power-suit. He commonly worked nineteen-hour business days. He probably slept in his suit. "Good evening, Markis!" Mr. Gabrielli was a real-estate developer who often helicoptered home on weekends to his expensive-smelling wife, and little-black-lamb of a daughter. Or, he was a drug lord; Markis and Coco weren't sure. Mr. Reginald Gabrielli felt everyone was a potential client and should be treated as such — even Coco's friend who showed up frantic on his doorstep in torn jeans after midnight. Even toddlers, Jehovah's Witnesses, and small dogs — Mr. Reggie Gabrielli orated at everyone with the same, I'm-greeting-you-with-respect/buy-something-from-me, voice.

With a sweep of his hand, Mr. Reggie ushered Markis over the threshold, then went strolling off to his office whistling a snappy tune. It didn't matter that Markis looked stressed out. It didn't matter that it was almost one in the morning.

Coco's mother paid Markis more attention. She was sitting on a plush carpet that had to be at least thirty by fifty feet. There was a crate in front of her, and bits of dry, grassy, packing material at her bare feet. She asked Markis questions as she inspected the insides of the crate, and the objet d'art therein. She was a great collector, even had landscapes that Saffron's mother, Audrey, had done years ago. Gabrielle Gabrielli had hit on Derek, the man that lived with Saffron and Audrey, and tried to collect him away from Audrey. GG still wouldn't accept that she didn't suit Derek's tastes. No one knew that, but Gabrielle and Derek — and Audrey — because the whole thing was too hysterical for Derek not to repeat. He wanted Audrey to protect him; he was a little nervous of Gabrielle's cat-like advances.

"What are you doing here so late, Markis?"

"Just came to get Coco."

"Need any money?"

Markis glanced at her sideways. "No, thanks."

"Could you hand me that trash bag, please? I'm going to get packing material all over the Aubusson."

Markis brought her the trash bag, then trotted to the curving staircase. He took the steps two at a time, then ran down an impossibly long hallway covered in carpet so thick, he never made a sound. He rapped on Coco's door. It was painted black and hanging a little crooked in the jamb — as if she hung on the top of it and swung like a monkey. She had painted the door herself — with nail polish.

"What?" Coco hacked out.

"It's Markis."

"Yeah, come in."

He opened the door. "Jesus Christ!" and swung it shut again. "Will you get some pants on?

"You're gonna see worse than a thong when I get my freaken' job," she yelled and didn't move. She was on her stomach, her legs bent at the knee, her ankles crossed and swaying back and forth, slow as a slave-run palm fan. She flipped the page of her People magazine.

"Coco," he pinched the bridge of his nose, "this is an emergency.

You're right. Something is wrong with Saffron." He scratched at some of the bumpy, black paint on her door.

Coco turned her head and considered Markis behind the door. Her glossy, black hair, freshly-washed, hung like spider's legs over her shoulders. "Oh, you gonna listen to me now?"

"I was listening to you yesterday, Coco. I know she's been freaky — I just didn't know what to do about it."

There was silence for several moments. Finally, Coco's door flew open and Markis jumped back. She whisked by him — jeans on, socks on, and spray-painted hiking boots in hand.

Before they were out the front door, Coco's mother swooped down on them. "Oh, Coco, have you made up your mind? Please, will you help me out at the brunch tomorrow?"

Coco looked out the door into the black and starless night. "I'm not wearing a dress or anything the color of babies, sunsets, or a warm spring day."

Gabrielle fussed with the fuzzy hair of what looked like a shrunken head. "Of course not, dear!" She grabbed Coco's shoulder and gave her an air kiss on each cheek while Coco looked heavenward.

Coco grunted as she hauled the great, oak, front-entry door shut behind her and Markis. "Ya know, I coulda done you on that hundred-thousand dollar rug — handmade by French dwarves — and the only thing she would've done about it would be to bring a towel so we wouldn't stain.

"Eeeew!" Markis winced. "Coco, you are really the grossest girl I've ever met."

She punched him in the shoulder. "Then get out more. Lots of gross girls in the world. Besides, you love it." And after a deep breath..."Let's go rescue your fair and mental princess."

When they arrived at Saffron's house, the lights were on downstairs in the kitchen. Markis and Coco were met at the screened door by Audrey and Derek, who stood dumfounded and disheveled in their nightclothes.

"What are you guys doing up?" Coco walked past them, and checked to see if there was any coffee left in the pot. Audrey put her chin down and frowned. Markis cleared his throat and walked away Coco occupied, trying to draw Audrey's attention to himself. When Markis explained their concerns, Audrey, who was already crying, shot Derek a traumatized look.

"But it's not the full moon." Audrey's voice was weak.

Coco winced. She stopped sniffing the coffee pot and slowly placed it back on its burner. Her eyes snapped from Audrey to Derek to Markis. She looked like a much younger girl under her smudged, black eyeliner. "Wha'da'ya mean — 'full moon'?"

Derek slapped his hands together, which made them all jump. He cleared his throat. "Don't worry about it, honey; you all just stay there, and I'll go get Saffron." He squeezed Audrey's arm. "We need to talk to her anyway. She needs to know about your mum...."

"Wha...?" Coco pulled a chair over to the table, sat down, and laid half her body across the surface — even though it was sprinkled with toast crumbs, empty envelopes and junk mail. "What's up, Mrs. Keller?"

Audrey stared at the dishwasher and gave a bittersweet smile. "My mother died. We just found out. We called 911." She shrugged. "They're on their...." Her voice broke as she brought her hand up to cover her mouth, as if she were trying to stop the noises that were slipping out.

Markis leaned back against the counter in front of the kitchen sink and stared open-mouthed at Mrs. Keller. He folded his arms across his chest, realized he was staring at her, and looked down to stare at his boots instead.

Coco bent her elbow and buried her face in the crook of her arm. "Oh, no. I'm so sorry, Mrs. Keller." Her voice was muffled.

Derek was all business. It was hard sometimes, being brave for Audrey. Saffron could be really freaky, like that Carrie chick at her prom. He shivered as he mounted the stairs, and shivered again as he passed the room where granny's body would hopefully not arise and eat them before the ambulance came. Of course, Audrey had fought with him about calling the ambulance; maybe she thought her mother would change her mind and come back.

He knocked on Saffron's door, then, after a moment of silence, knocked a little louder. There was no sound within her room. Derek opened her door about six inches and called her name. No answer. He threw the door open, causing a breeze to ruffle his turquoise, Chinese pajama-bottoms. With quick head-moves, he looked from her bed, to her floor, to behind her door. She wasn't in the room. Movement by the window caught his attention, but it was just the curtain — a long panel of sheer fabric caught up and blown in by the breeze. He ran down the stairs, two at a time, and reported to the others. As a group they marched up the stairs, past grandmother's room (both Markis and Coco blanched fish-belly pale when they saw her body on the bed), and spilled into Saffron's airy, empty bedroom — just to confirm what Derek had already told them.

They split up and searched inside the entire house. After Coco had gone through all the closets and under all the beds, she repeated her actions, as if Saffron was a naughty three-year-old playing hide-and-seek and changing her position. Coco bitched under her breath and tried to control her breathing as she slapped dust clumps from her hair.

Markis was outside. He came around the corner of the house from the backyard, crossed the gravel driveway, and looked up at Saffron's window just above the roof of the porch. His eyebrows were drawn together and his teeth were clamped. His steps silenced as he left the gravel and stepped onto the soft, wet grass. He held to the shaft of the apple tree and heard Mrs. Keller calling sharply from further away, near the ocean cliff. He backed up a little, into the light cast from Saffron's window.

Far to the right, at the edge of the roofline, in dark shadow, was something hanging over the roof. He focused on it. Then he walked over to the far corner of the house and looked up — two fingers. For a couple of seconds, he was unable to figure out this strange phenomenon. Then all at once, he realized, Saffron must be *out on her roof.* When they were in her room they all saw her opened window, but, in a panic, nobody had thought to look outside the window!

Markis began yelling, and quickly, Audrey, Derek, and Coco came running to his side. He pointed at the fingers, and again, as a group, they ran up to Saffron's room. Derek stuck his head out of Saffron's open window and looked all the way to his left. He squinted, and Coco felt his back stiffen under her hand as she leaned over him to get a look, too.

Markis pulled his hair with both of his fists. "I'll go out there! I'll go through the other window." He knocked over the chair that held Saffron's panda as he spun around and lumbered out into the hall. He looked to the right.

"Don't bother going that way, Markis. That's the guest bedroom.

That window is painted shut. You can use the window in my mother's room." Audrey's neck was red as she kept pulling at her throat.

Markis went to the left and into the adjacent bedroom. He passed the old lady who was dead on her bed. He hopped out of the old lady's window and onto the roof of the farmer's porch, skittered down the length of it, and prayed that the heebie-jeebies wouldn't cause him to lose his balance. "I can hardly see out here!" he screamed.

Derek smacked his ear on the window frame as he yanked his head back in. He ran out of Saffron's room, raced to the two other bedrooms down the hall, and put on every light he could find. He tried to open the window in the guest bedroom, but it wouldn't give. He took a Swiss Army knife out of his pocket and worked at the paint.

Coco and Audrey looked out Saffron's window, brought their heads in simultaneously as Markis passed, then rushed into the guest room to help Derek. Audrey pushed him aside when the panes swung free, and almost launched herself out the window. Derek grabbed her and held her still. It wasn't safe for too many of them to be out on that roof.

There was Saffron, leaning against the house and sitting so close to the edge of the roof that her hand hung over the side. She wasn't conscious.

Markis was huddled over her, touching her face. "I already tried to find her pulse...I couldn't...but that doesn't mean..."

Audrey pushed back from the window and gasped, knocking Derek off his feet. She pointed to Coco. "Go call 911."

"You already did, Mrs. Keller. Remember? Your mother...."

Audrey started crying. "Well, update them!"

Coco back-pedaled from the guest room, ran to Saffron's room, found the phone and slapped it off its base when she made a grab for it. "Shit," she hissed and grabbed at it again. She dialed as she hurried back to the guest room.

"Let me see the phone, Ma!"

Coco halted like she hit a brick wall. She frowned and looked at Mrs. Keller who held her hand out to take the phone. Audrey shook her hand, demanding the phone be given to her. Coco shook her head, 'no,' and watched as, right in front of her, Saffron's mother's eyes rolled back into her head.

Derek caught Audrey before she hit the floor. Hands under her armpits, he dragged her to the guest bed and sat with her on the quilt. He smoothed the hair back from her forehead. "Oh, dilly-girl. I need your help here...." Then his tears finally flowed over, too.

Coco could see how terrified he really was — his skin dull and yellow as cheese, his pupils dilating. He was shock-bound himself.

Audrey opened her eyes and sat docile in Derek's arms. She watched Coco talk with an emergency response person (when did they get there?). She decided she didn't need to ask Coco for the phone anymore.

Coco eyed Mrs. Keller – she looked super-duper-out-of-it. She hoped Mrs. Keller didn't call her "Ma," again. Coco took the paramedic's hand and pointed to Saffron's mother. "She called me "Ma," and passed out."

Audrey watched Coco point at her. That Coco was so confident for such a young girl — so unlike Saffron. Audrey sighed. She sat slumped and fussed with the borders of Saffron's quilt, feeling like she had tunnel vision and tunnel hearing and tunnel thinking. And when *had* the paramedics gotten there? What had she missed? What was Markis saying? Why was everyone's voice garbled? How had Markis known something was wrong? *Hmmmm*, she wondered. *I'll have to ask later.*

Derek encouraged Audrey to settle more comfortably on the pillows. He looked at her and sighed; she had grown awfully quiet. He stood up and walked to the window. "Listen, were you guys doing drugs tonight or something? Sniffing dairy products or whatever it is kids experiment with? I mean, this would be the time to tell me. We need to know."

Markis, still outside with Saffron, looked inside and shot a dirty look at the snippy man who was accusing him and Coco. "Dude, we weren't even with her tonight!" he spat.

"Yeah, *dude,* and we don't do any of that shit." Coco crossed her arms and sidled up to Derek with murder in her eyes.

Derek huffed and walked away from her, rightly assuming she'd bite.

Drugs! Well, that makes me mad. That's just insulting. Saffron might do a lot of wacky things — but drugs...? I need to tell Derek to get a grip. Audrey gently folded her hands on her stomach and stared at the ceiling. Was she dreaming? The movement of the paramedics as they raced around the room seemed impossibly slow, like an underwater ballet. She saw their mouths moving but she couldn't hear them speak. *Wow,* she thought, *I must be going deaf now. That sucks.* Oh, and here was Saffron. She did look pretty bad. She was on a stretcher and her eyes were closed. Her face was so, so white. *Ooooh,* thought Audrey, *I should tell them to get her a warm cloth to place on her face and bring her color back.* "When did you get here?" And now why was he answering her like she was a toddler? She said nothing more. The EMT was in her face. He was still talking to her. He was rubbing her arm. She smiled at him. He looked over to Derek, who he rightly and wrongly assumed was the man of the house. Derek shook his head very slowly and spoke quietly. "Her mother — in the other room — poor girl."

The medic motioned to his partner. The partner guided Audrey down to the ambulance and onto one of the tiny beds inside the truck.

Oh, good, I'm right next to Saffron. Audrey felt such a rush of relief, she fainted dead away.

Chapter 2

Saffron didn't wake up. She lay still and quiet in her hospital bed. Her pulse had been thready that first night, but was somewhat stronger now. Her other vital signs were not where the nurses would have liked, but they were holding steady.

Audrey was treated for shock and released. Days passed. She and Derek held a memorial for Saffron's grandmother. Audrey camped out at the hospital. She ate, slept, and read by her daughter's bedside. She sang *Jamaica Farewell* to Saffron, as if she was still a baby sleeping in her crib.

Audrey and Derek hounded Markis and Coco. They tortured Saffron's friends with their never-ending questions. There was nothing Coco or Markis could say to satisfy them and make them feel better. So, Audrey and Derek asked more questions. Coco and Markis were tired, anguished. They just didn't know.

One night, as Coco and Markis were sitting on a rub-worn wooden bench that contained benefactor's names on tarnished plates, Coco told Markis about the first time she really thought Saffron was going whacked. It was that night she put her to bed on the cardboard boxes in the store. Saffron had told her she was having sex with a fairy, and it was making her crazy. Markis slapped his knees, beyond perturbed, got up, and walked away from her. They didn't see each other until the next afternoon, and from that point on, they kept their vigils in silence.

Audrey interrogated the doctors. She nipped at the heels of the nurses. What the hell was going on? Why, again, exactly, were they giving Saffron a blood transfusion? Why, exactly, did they monitor Saffron's fluid intake with such scrutiny? Was she in danger? Was she going to die? Audrey felt the answers she was given were vague and insufficient. She was told to please be patient — satisfactory answers were forthcoming, but more information must be gathered. If Saffron's mother could please be a little more helpful, by being a little more tolerant, maybe the answers could be found.

"We're sorry – we're doing all we can," said the doctors.

"Please be patient," begged the nurses.

"We are seeking outside advice," admitted the doctors.

"We know this is very difficult for you," confided the nurses.

"We have never seen a case quite like this," claimed the doctors.

"We just don't know."

"We just don't know."

Markis wanted to be with Saffron every minute. Every day, he watched groups of important-looking men and women enter the room and ask him to leave for a short time. When he came back into the room, he stared mesmerized at the vitals monitor while it bleep, bleep, bleeped, and assumed his position – slumped and dejected in the uncomfortable, vinyl chair. He didn't like being there in the hospital, but he sat firm and held Saffron's hand.

He had known she was sick! He had known *something* was wrong with her! He told the doctors and nurses of her strange behavior before it all happened. But his observances seemed to do little for their theories. Their eyes clouded over as he spoke. They said, "Ah-huh, ah-huh," but they weren't really listening to him, and he knew it. Anger sat on his shoulders like a grotesque gargoyle. Never again would he trust doctors to know it all – or to know much, for that matter.

They asked him strange questions like, 'Has she been exposed to the cold?' Head tilted, he had stared at them. Huh? They made him irate — so much so that, when something miraculous happened in the middle of the night, he mentioned it to no one. He had wished Saffron goodnight, and rested his head on her arm, then fell into a light doze. He roused some time later, when he heard Saffron say, "I love you. I love you." He sat bolt-upright and whispered, "Saffron?" But, there was no response, and he wondered if she had really said anything at all. Maybe he had dreamed it.

When the hospital staff asked Saffron's mother to leave the room so they could talk about Saffron in private, Markis felt so bad for her. Audrey looked defeated. Her mother had just died, and now, what was up with her daughter? *Dy-ing*? Markis had never felt so awful in his entire life. He didn't want to lose Saffron. He felt like he just couldn't lose her, like he wouldn't make it if…. He absently massaged the ever-present pain in his chest. He had never felt so strongly about anyone outside of his family. Then again, he never had a friend come so close to death before. Maybe that just brought out weird feelings, he reasoned. He talked to his parents about it. They tried to console him as best they could. But mostly, they were at a loss for words. What could anyone say to make anything better?

And the questions from the doctors! They didn't stop! Over and over and over, Audrey, Markis, Derek, and Coco had to repeat their stories of what happened that night, that day, the week before….

"Are you sure?" they were asked. "Are you quite sure that is all you remember?" Then again, "Was she exposed to cold at all? No cold at all? Perhaps you own a walk-in refrigerator or freezer? Perhaps she was exposed in some other way?"

"No!" Saffron's mother had finally screamed. She had had enough.

The cold. The cold! What were they trying to get at? She told them, they all told them a million times, that Saffron had been in her room, then suddenly they found her on the roof – just sitting there, lifeless. No cold — end of story! It was June, for God's sake. It was *humid!* These past few nights it had been in the 80s! Cold?!

One night, over trays of turkey, cold mashed potatoes, jellied gravy, and warm cranberry sauce, Audrey and Derek sat talking. Dr. Udele came into the room, moved magazines and playing cards from a chair, sat, and took Audrey's hand. The feel of his warm grasp shocked her, and immediately she started to knead her throat with her other hand.

"I'm sorry, Audrey, I didn't mean to startle you. I was wondering if you and Derek could join me now, in my office." His smile was warm but not confident. His eyes were bloodshot. They knew he worked hard for Saffron. They saw him here, in the halls, day and night. They had gone to his office a few times before, and his nose was always buried in some great big medical tome or glued to the computer.

Audrey and Derek stood, joined hands, and followed the little man with tufts of hair down the echoing hall. It was just approaching midnight, and the only sounds were the hushed voices of nurses and the blip-bleeps of the various machines in the Critical Care Unit.

"I took the liberty of getting us some real coffee." Dr. Udele motioned to the steaming cups on his desk. They were from the trendy shop down the street. "Please, have a seat and make yourselves comfortable. Again."

Audrey stared dully at the coffee cups. Two smells she never again wanted to mingle in her nostrils — coffee and antiseptic.

Dr. Udele did not make his way around to the other side of his desk and into his plush leather chair. Instead, he pulled another chair through the thick carpeting from the corner of the room. He seated himself directly across from Audrey and Derek, so that the three of them were almost touching knee-to-knee. He reached back, grabbed the coffees off his desk, and handed them over. Audrey murmured her thanks, then went for her neck with the other hand. Derek nodded and stared at Dr. Udele's rumpled shirt.

The doctor looked like he was going to attempt a smile, but his face faltered. He took a deep breath, put the tips of his fingers together, separated them, grabbed the seat of his chair, and shifted around a bit. He ran his fingers through his hair, and raised the bits had been lying flat. Audrey and Derek exchanged weary glances.

"No, please, don't worry. I just don't know how to start this. I have never been in this situation before, as you'll soon understand. Let me get on with it now."

Audrey stared at him blankly. Derek's eyes filled with unbidden tears. He used both of his bear-paw fists to push them out of his eyes.

"To begin simply, let me make three statements. We, my colleagues and I, have come to the conclusion that Saffron is suffering from Paroxysmal Cold Hemoglobinuria." Audrey leaned forward, ready to let the questions flood forth.

"Please, please, let me go on, and I will try to cover most questions even before you ask." He raised his cup to his lips and pulled long and hard on the coffee. The old-fashioned mantel clock on his desk ticked loudly. "Second, from what we know currently, it is medically impossible that Saffron is suffering from Paroxysmal Cold Hemoglobinuria. And third," he rushed on, seeing the denial in their eyes and the welling anger, "we think the transfusion has helped in her case. Others like her have been saved by blood transfusion. Let me tell you a little about Paroxysmal Cold Hemoglobinuria. It is a very rare, swift, and potentially dangerous disorder. Personally, this is the first time I have ever seen it, for that matter, this is the first time anyone in this hospital has seen it — or anyone in this county...."

Audrey gasped.

"That is why we have chosen to seek outside council. PCH is characterized by the premature destruction of healthy red blood cells minutes to hours after exposure to cold. It is an autoimmune, hemolytic disorder — these diseases occur when the body's natural defenses against invading organisms destroy healthy tissue for unknown reasons."

He saw their faces contort and struggle with this new information. "This is a rare *childhood* disease, although a few adult cases have been documented. The problem is this...PCH doesn't just occur out of the blue." He paused and stared at the ceiling. He searched for the most basic explanation. "PCH sets in after the onset of infection — Saffron has had absolutely no recent infections that we know of, and you claim she has no other files — so we have no idea how she could possibly be suffering from this disease. But you must know, the tests have been done, it is, without a doubt, Paroxysmal Cold Hemoglobinuria. Idiopathic PCH is extremely rare, but not unheard of."

Audrey had been fast-bouncing her knee, but now her entire body froze.

"Idiopathic, Audrey," Dr. Udele took her hand away from her throat and squeezed, "it means the disease arose spontaneously from an obscure or unknown cause." She snatched her hand back.

He raised his eyebrows high and shrugged his shoulders. How he hated this — he felt so incompetent. But so did the handful of physicians he had met with this afternoon for the final briefing on his lovely, young patient with the bad haircut. It was unanimous — she had PCH, but nobody could fathom how. He clenched his teeth and stared at Audrey and Derek, waiting for the onslaught of questions.

They said nothing.

"The good news is, if all goes well over the next few days — if the blood transfusion is accepted — she will be cured of this disease and should have no further trouble with it." He tugged his right ear.

A mask of doubt and suspicion covered Audrey's fresh, bohemian looks. She watched the doctor without blinking. He was still keeping something back, she could feel it, and Dr. Udele knew she knew it. The energy from the futile hostility that ran between her and Derek almost arched over their heads.

The physician cleared his throat once again. He had lost three nights of sleep over this very strange case. He told himself he would lose three more, however, if it would help. Dr. Udele told himself to get on with it, even if Audrey did physically attack him like it looked like she would. The tic started in his eyelid again, the same eye that throbbed with the recurring migraine.

"Saffron…is in a coma, as you know. She…. There is no physical reason for this coma. It is not related to the Paroxysmal Cold Hemoglobinuria…."

"Which you also can't explain!" Audrey's voice peaked shrilly. Derek took her hand and held it tight to his chest.

"I'm so sorry Audrey, Derek — I can't begin to imagine your anguish, I'm sure. But you must believe me — we are doing everything we can. The very good news is that her condition is now stable, and the only thing we need is for that girl to come out of her coma. We just need her to wake up. Talk to her! I think we're in the homestretch here! We don't have answers as to why this occurred, but let's all try hard to wake her up. Then we can ask *her*."

Chapter 3

After Saffron left her grandmother in the glass boat, she sailed through black space for a short while, then slid into her body. When she opened her eyes, she wasn't on her roof, and she wasn't alone. She was on an island, sitting on its sandy shore. A monstrous wave was coming towards her. She squealed, put her hands down, lifted her bum and crab-walked backwards just in time. The wave broke and its froth slid over her feet. Another wave followed, then another. The crash and boom was almost deafening. While the sound of the waves pummeled her ears, the sunshine seared her eyes. She stood up and brushed sugary-looking sand from her pants. Behind her, there was shade under some palms. She walked into the cool of the green and sat beside the bushy fronds.

She felt him all around her, and knew without a doubt, he was watching her. "Ny!" *What is this? Where am I?* Suddenly, her thoughts were repeated, out loud, in the air all around her — as if there were invisible speakers broadcasting whatever came to her mind..."What is this? Where am I?"

No way.

"No way."

Saffron jumped when, again, her thoughts reverberated down the beach. She bit her bottom lip.

Damn!

"Damn!"

She realized she wouldn't have any secrets here. She kicked at the sand and twisted her ankle — the pain was quick and excruciating.

Her thoughts kept coming like a horrible recording she couldn't shut off. This wasn't a dream.

What is *this?*

"What *is* this?"

The monotonous waves missed a beat. They had been crashing, crashing, crashing all along, when suddenly there was a vacuumed silence, then the waves were crashing again.

"So what, Ny — it doesn't matter. You can hear every thought that goes on in my head. You don't *have* to eavesdrop, you know! I'll tell you everything! Do you hear me?! I know you hear me, I know you're near — so why don't you just come out and face me!" Her shrill words were met only by the soothing sights and sounds of paradise. Two long-legged egrets with snowy white feathers walked in the undergrowth just behind her. She jumped when, out of the corner of her eye, she caught their puckish movement. They stilled and looked at her sideways, then lifted their twiggy legs high to continue onto the beach. Saffron rested her elbows on her knees and laid her chin on her hands. She looked at the ocean and frowned.

This ocean was not like the ocean near her house. Her ocean was boding-grey — dark, jade-green on the brightest day, as was normal for the ocean of the Northeast. She'd been to Jamaica with her family. That ocean was bathwater-warm and a hypnotic aqua blue. But if nothing else, this ocean pounding before her was convincing enough to let her know she was in an unreal place. This ocean *glowed.* The lime-green water hummed like a neon sign. The dark, sapphire sky grew darker and darker, until it melded into a vibrant, purple horizon. The sand was so bright-white, Saffron thought she'd go blind, and the palm tree above her was dressed in sparkling emerald fronds. Saffron stared with naked wonder, then frowned again.

Where am I?

"Where am I?"

She gritted her teeth as pictures of this life and of her other lives began to scroll across the sky. There were lots of pathetic, groveling scenes — she at Ny's feet — as if he was that irresistible. She pushed herself up off the ground, bunched her fists, then screamed at the radiant sky. "If there is any way I can kill you — I will! How dare you do this to me! How dare you trick me! Again! When the hell will you stop? Where *are* you?"

Seabirds cried, waves lapped, a crab clicked his big claw as he scuttled across a flat of damp sand.

She sat down hard, and with a huff, on the blanket that appeared in the sand. Thump! A coconut fell next to her. She picked it up and hurled it at the sea. The waves were calm now, and barely tall enough to make a curl. In the canopy of fronds and vines above her head, birds squawked and peeped. A small monkey came to sit beside her and nibbled a date as he eyed her. Saffron couldn't help smiling at him. She closed her eyes and smelled ripened fruit warmed by the sun and the clean smell of the ocean.

How had the stupid blanket appeared? She screwed her eyes shut tighter and willed a mansion to appear. Nothing. Then, after a few more moments, she found herself suddenly sitting in a small bungalow — on the deck of the bungalow to be exact — swinging in a hammock. Her hair was long, too. Too long. She didn't know why it didn't occur to her before, but now that she thought about it — her hair was even longer than before! It swirled in endless crimson waves all the way down her back, and as she swung in the hammock, the ends of it slid back and forth across the floorboards.

Oh, that's just great!

"Oh, that's just great!"

"A *shack* is not quite like a mansion, Ny! Try again! And — I cut my hair for a reason — and that reason certainly wasn't so I could make *you* happy!"

No answer.

Food appeared before her on a small, dark table etched with dancing figures that looked very Balinese. She ate, and felt soothed. The bright colors, the different textures, the smell of spices and seared meat lulled her just like a Christmas meal at home. When she grew bored of sitting around in the little house, she took walks on the shore. On one particularly long hike, she walked for what seemed like miles, looking at shells and bits of sea glass. She enjoyed the warm water on her feet and the warm sun on her back. Suddenly, she stopped and turned to face the ocean.

What if I jumped in right now? What if I jumped in and swam away?

As soon as the words came to mind, she heard them in the space around her. Suddenly, the sea grew turbulent. The waves no longer rolled to shore, but crashed upon the sand with such force that it looked as though the sand had been bombed. More and more waves were forming out at sea – some of them built to one-hundred foot swells. One monster tidal wave kept growing and, as she ran down the beach to escape, it paralleled her movement. Her ragged screams were drowned out by the thunder of the water. She spun to the left and tripped up the beach towards the jungle and the little shack – both had suddenly appeared and were a hundred feet away. She was too terrified to wonder how they just appeared there. She stomped onto the front porch and grabbed one of the roof support beams. She looked back at the ocean as she struggled for breath.

The water was calm. A fiery sunset lit up the back of the lime-green, jellowy sea as it silently quivered.

"NY!" she screamed. "Where are you?" Her throat was raw from screaming, her nerves frayed by panic. She sat on the little porch in a heap and cried long into the night. At one point, when it was almost dawn, she crawled inside and nestled into a low bed that was piled high with soft, down-stuffed pillows. Several feathered and furred blankets kept the damp, night air at bay.

The first thing she was aware of when she woke up was the sound of the jungle. Then came the muffled crash of the sea, then came the soft kisses that were being placed on her forehead, each temple, her ears, and her eyelids. She longed for the kisses to reach her lips, and with her eyes still closed, she turned her head towards the kisser. He sighed and traced his fingers down her arm. Her blood began to boil and her skin tingled with exquisite, electric pain.

"I love you. I love you." She moaned and refused to open her eyes.

"I know. Now tell me you want me. Tell me you want me to kiss your lips." His fingers traced farther down, and around one of her jutting pelvic bones. Her eyes rolled back under her closed lids.

He whispered. "Let go of all of your thoughts. Come back to me and I will take you in such a way, no one on earth has ever quite fathomed." His finger traveled beneath her camisole to circle her belly button. "I can help you let go. Tell me you want me."

Saffron's eyes shot open. All at once, she sat up and gathered the blankets to cover herself. Her thoughts came in rapid fire, piecing together a puzzle that should have been so obvious. "Oh, my God. You tried to kill me."

Ny smiled. "I couldn't kill you Saffron. Come, come now, what is this?" He lay alongside her, balanced on his side, his long powerful thighs close to hers.

"The full moon...me sleepwalking towards cliffs...all those times. *I* wasn't a nut! It was you! You were trying to kill me!"

His eyes flashed with glee. "I have no idea what you're talking about."

She shriveled away from him and his predatory finger. "You tried to kill me!"

One of Ny's eyebrows shot up in acute irritation. "Yes, yes. Must you be so melodramatic? You're not dead after all."

Saffron backed off the bed and stood on shaky legs. She held one hand out before her, blocking Ny's face, and smooshed the blanket to her chest with the other hand, as if that were enough to keep him away from her.

Something was strange....

She slapped her other hand to the back of her neck and the blanket fell away, leaving her exposed in a shift of filmy lawn. No long hair. She panicked momentarily as her mind drew a compulsive, frightening conclusion. Had he taken her hair away to punish her now? She slapped all around her head and breathed a sigh of relief. No, her hair was still there — all of it — including the couple of feet he had added. It was all just piled on top of her head. Her neck was left exposed, of course. A swift rage flew through her, which made the hairs on her neck stand on end. Immediately, she started pulling at her hair, releasing it, and letting it fall over her shoulders and down her back.

"You like my hair up, do you? *That's* why I hacked it off, Ny! That's why I'll never, as long as I live, *never,* style my hair in any way remotely resembling that! "And what the hell am I wearing? If you want a nympho maiden from King Arthur's court, go get one! I don't wear this kinda shit!" This was said through gritted teeth as she continued to free the rest of her hair. It was no small attempt — it was *a lot* of hair. There was silence between them until finally, Saffron had released every single, little strand of red. She sat glaring at Ny in a pool of ravaged hair, pristine white sheets, and her gauzy see-through top.

"You can't keep me here forever, Ny." Her eyes skittered sideways. "Wherever we are."

"You are right." He seemed a little deflated now. He stared at her hair as if someone had just died. Then he perked up. "If you will not die, then we will have plenty of time here, alone, together. Then, when your human body expires, we will go back to the fairyland and be together there. After *a while,* we will choose new human lives, *together,* this time," he waggled his finger at her as if she had been a naughty girl, "and things will go back to normal. We will live our lives as we once did. How could you have done this to me, Saffron? I have been in agony without you!"

She ignored his question. "What do you mean, 'we have plenty of time here'?"

"Nobody can reach us. I can hardly believe my luck. Who knew this would happen when I slipped inside your mind?" He wiggled his eyebrows mischievously and tapped his temple. "Who knew? Your body was empty — you were visiting your grandmother — so I hopped right in. It is the very reason astral projection is not recommended." He stretched his arms wide, "This is fabulous!" Do you know I can feel you here?" He licked his lips as his eyes traveled all over her. "It's not like being human...but I can use your dream senses to feel you...." He grinned like a schoolboy, his big eyes blazing like blue fire under the fringe of tossled black bangs.

"How can we exist in my mind for 'plenty of time'? If I were dead, we couldn't be in my mind. But I'm obviously not alive because this sure isn't Earth!"

Ny smiled slyly. "Surely you can figure what is happening here, Saffron. Surely you can tell what it is that is giving us this, the greatest chance of all time, to be alone and become the lovers we once were."

Saffron narrowed her eyes and frowned. She stared at Ny.

"You are in a coma, Saffron! We can just lounge around in your mind for the next fifty years! Fifty years is but a drop in the well compared to our fairy lives, but we will just call this a vacation, shall we? A small escape from the daily humdrum and nagging voices of our peers."

Comprehension dawned. A coma. She pictured her body lying in the hospital for the next fifty years, being cared for, washed, by hospital staff. She pictured her mother.... She saw her mother coming in, week after week, her condition unchanged, until eventually Audrey would die, and then what? Saffron blinked. They pulled the plug.

"MONSTER!"

Saffron launched herself at him, her fingers rigid and ready to scratch his eyes out. She just wanted to get her hands on him. She gritted her teeth and followed him as he ran out of the hut and flew into a tree.

"Stop that, Saffron. You just stop that now!" He was greatly miffed with her and embarrassed by the way he had to flee into tree limbs to escape attack. What a shrew she had become in this life! She was almost nothing like the girl he had known for the last several millennia. Why, when she was Rosemary, he was allowed to do anything he wanted — anything! At one point, he even started bringing women back to their country home. It took him forever to encourage Rosemary/Saffron to join in the romps, if not with a little morbid docility. Still, she did it. He smiled at the fond memories. Yes, she was still, most definitely, his girl in the most important ways.

Even now, as she stood grunting and screeching, trying to climb the palm to reach him, he saw passion flaring in her eyes. It excited him. He imagined a hammock for himself right there, high in the tree, and swung lazily as Saffron gathered coconuts to fling at him. When her pile was big enough, she commenced firing. But, alas, she was far from strong enough to throw the husk so high. She flung one up. It reached its zenith, then made a quick downward trip — straight for her face. She let out a small squeak of fright, and dove for cover in the bushes. With a plop, it landed in the sand where she had just stood. She came tripping out of the bushes, twigs in her impossibly long, red hair, and stood beneath the tree. She glared up at her former lover. "Come down here, Ny, so I can kill you."

Ny was munching on a slice of pineapple. He took several moments to clean his teeth of the stringy fruit with his tongue. "Do you know? I can actually taste this! I can feel this on my tongue while we're here together. Come on, let me touch you. I cannot believe I can actually feel you here, without resorting to eating living creatures!"

"I want to feel your windpipe under my thumbs."

Ny frowned. One of the pineapple strings just wouldn't come out. He picked at it with his neatly trimmed fingernail. "You can't kill me. How long do you plan on keeping this act up? However long, I can pursue you longer."

"Come down here, Ny, so I can at least try and kill you."

Ny shrugged. "Time will tell what you will do when you finally lay your hands on my body." He guffawed. "I can actually feel now!" He stroked himself. He actually ran his hands down his thighs, cupped his groin, then stretched lazily and yawned. He drifted off to sleep.

For three days and three nights, Ny stayed at the top of the palm tree and Saffron sat by the trunk. Sometimes they slept. Sometimes they were awake and having a conversation, and sometimes they were awake and looking silently out to sea. He begged her to come back to him — she raged at him. He ordered her to come back to him — she begged him to let her go. He raged at her to come back to him — she firmly told him that it would never happen — she was done with him. And the conversation went on.

She cried.

He wept dramatically. "Why do you do this, Saffron? You must know I love you. I wouldn't chase you to the ends of your mind if I didn't love you...."

"Ny, you freak. Whatever you feel for me...you're always feeling for a million other women.... And I hate that! No thanks!"

"But I love *you*, Saffron — doesn't that mean anything to you?"

"What? You saying that? 'I love you....' What does that even mean, Ny? Like you can just walk around saying that and it makes everything okay? You can screw a million women but say you love me, and that makes everything okay?" She was gouging at the bottom of his palm tree with a sharp stone. She figured it would only take her three weeks of monotonous hacking to get the thing down.

On the fourth day, at dawn, Ny was sleeping when Saffron decided to run down the beach and swim for it again. That had to be the way out, because the sea began to thrash whenever she went near it with thoughts of escaping.

Saffron got up and sprinted for the shore. She raced so fast down the beach that a plume of sand rose behind her feet. She raced even faster, stomped through the shallow beginnings of waves, then dove into the warm, salty water. She swam as fast as she could. When she broke the surface, she could hear the gurgle of water in her ear, and Ny yelling for her to come back. The waves had already begun to roar, as she figured they would, but she plunged on — stroke after stroke, breath after metered breath. She looked back over her shoulder, couldn't see Ny, and looked straight ahead. She stopped swimming. She choked on some water that had slipped into her gaping mouth. Her face went gunmetal grey, and her eyes bulged from their sockets. She was in a wave, a wave so big that, when she turned herself awkwardly in the water, she realized she was about four stories over the beach of the deserted island. She began to panic as the wave pushed her higher and faster. She became tangled in her long hair. By the time she started screaming, it was already too late. Far to her right she saw the wave begin to curl and come for her. She screamed again as the curl scooped her up, and the water roared in her ears. She was dragged under, then BOOM – she was spit out. Falling, falling, falling towards the perfect, white sugar beach. She smacked down face-first in the sand, every bone in her body crunching on impact. The wave retreated and left her body like a sack of blown glass.

She coughed and hacked, trying to remove the impossible amount of sand that filled her mouth and throat. She lay still, her mouth hanging open, hoping the sand would just fall out of its own accord. Every bone in her body was broken, she was sure. She couldn't move.

Ny raced to her side, half running, half flying; he was perfectly meticulous, as always, and unharmed.

"Don't touch me, Ny. I'm broken!" She meant to scream at him, but only managed a pathetic moan. Her eyes widened in fright, afraid of the pain she would feel when he moved her.

His eyes gentled as he looked upon her, and skimmed her body with a loving, nurturing look. "No, Saffron. No, no. Look, you are just fine. Move yourself, you will see."

And Saffron realized she *was* okay. Her bones weren't broken! There was no pain!

Saffron turned to look up at Ny, her grey eyes swimming in tears.

How could you, Ny? How could you make the waves do that to hurt me and trap me here.?

"How could you, Ny? How could you make the waves do that to hurt me and trap me here?"

Ny didn't speak. He averted his eyes. He was hiding something from her. Typical. Then, a forlorn look washed his features. *Ah, Saffron, I am not doing this to you. This is your mind, those waves the matter of all that you are.... You cannot escape by running away....* He wondered if the moment had come. Could he finally move to her now? Could he scoop her up, hold her, and claim her once more? His smile was sad. "You have always been a runner."

Saffron stiffened.

Ny held back, barely. He was so close to her now.

She sat up, her mouth hanging open in wonder. Why didn't she understand before? She looked at Ny. He saw the look in her eyes and became frightened. She sat there, drenched, her long hair, the hair he adored so much, hanging in wet clumps about her shoulders and back. Her lips were full and red, her grey eyes bright and penetrating. Her cheekbones were high on her heart-shaped face. He had loved it, he had loved the way she worshipped him, lived for him, and died for him. It was why he always came back for her. Why he always wanted her around, lifetime after lifetime. He had been with a million whores, homemakers, and adoring virgins — but he always came back for her.

Now she realized why — because her adoration for him endured. Impossibly, in all incarnations, Saffron always lived to lay her eyes upon Ny's perfection...at any cost.

Above all else, Ny absolutely lived for adoration. He got adoration from all of those other women, but their lust, love, obsession – whatever it was that held them to him — eventually, always waned.

But this was not the case with Saffron. He gave her a sheepish smile.

She closed her eyes in disgust.

He chucked her in the shoulder. No, Saffron went right on adoring him. She was his constant electrical supply when the batteries ran down on the others.

Saffron opened her eyes, stared at the cloudless blue above her and sighed. Then her look changed. A fresh look of hope washed across her soft cheeks and tired eyes, like a long-awaited breeze on a stuffy, hot day.

Ny watched the light of recognition ignite Saffron from the inside. He froze.

I have complete control. I only have to sustain the effort.

"I have complete control. I only have to sustain the effort."

Ny's arms went limp when the wind whispered her thoughts in his ear. Her voice was so sweet, soothing. So deceptive.

I have complete control.

"I have complete control."

"Very good, Saffron." Ny sounded flat and irritable. "So you finally realize you can control everything in your life. But, what will you do with this new-found knowledge? Ha! That is the question. How long before you give up and let your cravings take over for you?"

"I will walk away from here, Ny, from you. I don't *have* to run. Running never worked because I didn't have to do it. I'll wake myself up now, and get on with my life. I'll stop regretting and feeling guilty." She pointed a finger at him. "And I'll stop being afraid." She stared hard at him. "I'm getting on with my life – this is it, now."

It was the same lesson she had learned when dealing with Jethin. Did it apply to all of life's difficulties? How had she forgotten the lesson so quickly? How often in life would she have to remind herself that she was the captain of her own ship? Would she forget to remind herself? She rolled her eyes and stood up. "Yeah, you're hot. Yeah, looking at you right now — even though you tried to murder me..." her eyebrow arched, "...murder me repeatedly — I'm still attracted to you. But I don't need you."

Ny scoffed.

"And I'm going to walk away." She pursed her lips and turned away from him. She started to walk away. The sea was quiet as a lake at midnight.

He yelled after her, "In time, Saffron, you will come back to me!" He stomped his foot in the soft sand. "You cannot deny me!" He watched as her hair shortened to the length she had cut it.

She never turned around.

It's time to wake up.

"It's time to wake up."

The ocean pulled back.

It's time to wake up...

Palm trees and cypress began to tip over like stage props.

C'mon — wake up, wake up, wake up.

The seabirds shimmered away. Everything faded, till she was surrounded by blackness. A new sound floated to her ears — an alien sound from far away. She finally identified the blips and bleeps as hospital monitors, and grew excited because she knew it meant she was almost there. She opened her eyes with tons of effort because they felt grainy and weighed down by a bag of cement. Without turning her head, she saw her mother in a chair by the bed. Audrey was reading a book. A headache ice-picked at Saffron's temples, the fluorescent lights pulsed and slapped at her eyelids. She felt like she weighed three hundred stiff pounds. "Sorry I took so long, Mom." Her voice was croaky.

"Oh, hi, Saffron....I was just about to find out if Sofia runs off to the Caribbean with Eduardo!"

"No," Saffron grunted, and with difficulty, pulled one of the monitoring cords out from under her butt, "she doesn't. She wants more out of life than electric eyes and a nice ass."

Audrey beamed as she stroked Saffron's soft, shoulder-length hair, "Ah...I see."

A silent tear rolled down Saffron's cheek as she looked into her mother's love-filled eyes.

Suddenly, Audrey leaned forward and let her head fall on Saffron's stomach. She began crying silently at first, but soon couldn't control herself and began sobbing openly. She soaked the bleached, hospital-issue sheet as she clutched blindly to grab at her child. She stood and gripped Saffron by the shoulders, leaned down on her elbows before her body could collapse, and cried some more.

Audrey smelled fresh and beautiful to Saffron, her citrus perfume the most beautiful memory, her many bracelets a soothing, cacophonic symphony. Saffron ran both hands through her mother's tousled hair and whispered, "Ssshh, ssshh." It was all she could do to console her. "Ssshh, ssshh."

Derek came running into the room already honking and blubbering like a sea lion. Saffron looked over at him and smiled. If the shock of seeing Saffron sitting there, awake, wasn't enough — he was further perplexed by the look on the girl's face, and the strength in her features. There was something else, too. He studied her through his tears and frowned.

Audrey turned and crumbled into his arms, but still his eyes were on Saffron's face. He had seen a face like hers before — in artist renderings of saints, in movies of heroic underdogs. He read about such gazes in works by Shakespeare and Plato. A chill ran through him. Saffron appeared wise beyond her years. She exuded a strong confidence, and blessed him with a smile that said *all will be well, we have nothing to fear*. "Jesus Christ," he breathed. She looked...*old!*

"Derek, why are you looking at me like that?" Saffron forced out in her hoarse, just-out-of-a-coma voice. She tried to hack to clear her throat. He was making her nervous. He looked like he had just been struck by lightning. "I'm okay, you know."

Derek didn't move.

Saffron began to panic. Just a little. "See, I'm awake." She was stating the obvious, but all the same, it seemed to do the trick.

Derek snapped out of the spell that held him, a smile started on his lips. He reached for Saffron's hand. "Don't do that again, Saffron. No more going into comas. Dilly girl."

"Yeah, okay, Daddy. I promise."

They all held onto each other as tears of relief streamed down their cheeks.

Chapter 4

Several weeks passed. Most of the hubbub concerning Saffron finally quieted down. Audrey was improving with each day, and finding an outlet for her pain through her art. With Saffron home safely, Audrey could relax and mourn her mother. The piece she was working on was of a black lake at midnight, the full moon hanging above, and a beautiful goddess — radiant in her happiness — sitting in a small, glass boat and floating towards a distant beach. The painting made Audrey smile; she had no idea what inspired it. She had never done a painting like it before. It was so otherworldly and dark, and she had never felt such a fire within to complete a piece, either. Maybe, she mused, her talent was taking her in a different direction — a new beginning. She thought of her mother often as she painted and listened to the ethereal sounds of R. Carlos Nakai's flute. Sometimes she was brought to tears, but more often it brought a smile to her face as she thought of all of the funny things her mother used to say and do. Audrey remembered one time, when they could no longer deny the Alzheimer's, how she and Derek had gone over to her mother's house. It was the last week of November and they had helped her string Christmas lights. Two days later, New England experienced an unbelievable streak of several very warm days. When Audrey, Derek, and a disgruntled Saffron had visited Grandmother that following Saturday, they found her in the middle of taking the Christmas lights off the bushes — frantically working to remove them all. With all of the warm weather, Grandmother assumed it was spring, and was embarrassed that she hadn't taken her lights down after Christmas.

Now, in the waning light of the afternoon, Audrey smiled and continued to reminisce as she stroked the canvas with a fine brush — a shade of rich cognac for the eyes of her Asian goddess. Saffron asked if the painting could be hung in her room – that she would hate to see it sold, and would treasure it forever. Audrey was so touched that she couldn't stop the tears as she hugged her only child to her chest and rocked her slowly for a long, long time.

Markis was gone. He had asked Saffron to go to New Mexico with him, but quickly backpedaled when he saw all the color drain from her face. "On second thought — better not — you'll lose your job at the Chicken." He couldn't believe it — after all they'd been through, she wouldn't relent.

***

Saffron sat on her panda, on her chair by her window. She watched the stars. There was one that flickered green and yellow. If she wasn't so lazy, she'd get Derek's binoculars and look for the supernova just discovered by the handle of the Big Dipper. Derek told her the star had exploded over 200 million years ago. A cold thrill ran down her spine at feeling so small.

The wind changed direction, and brought a faint noise with it that made the hairs on the back of her neck stand on end. She sat up straight, craned her neck, and looked towards the sea. The noise grew louder. It pitched lower and became a moan. Then the moan turned into a cry of such wretched grief, that Saffron knew instantly — *she* was down there. "OMG, lady – you're kidding me, right?" Her muttered statement held none of her usual cockiness. She stayed perfectly still for several moments, leaning out the window as she considered. She shrugged, brought her head back in, and stood up tall to stretch her back. She walked to her bed and grabbed the quilted satin jacket that hung over the footboard. With minor stair creaks, she was down in the kitchen in two minutes. She slid her feet into her flip-flops, took the flashlight off the shelf, gripped the handle on the screened door and stopped. She raised her eyes to the ceiling and took a deep, cleansing breath before stepping out into the night.

She flip-flopped through the wet grass, buttoning her jacket as she walked across the front yard. As she made her way along the path to the cliff over the ocean, she continued to take deep breaths of salty, sea air. She had to remind herself to blink as her eyes dried out in the howling wind. When she neared the bluff, a sudden gust of wind screamed past her ears. She faltered. The dark of night suddenly felt too close. The green and yellow flickering star was behind black clouds – she was cut off from the universe; and the here and now was so constricting she had a difficult time breathing. She heard another strange sound, a whine, and felt the sudden press of something wrong. Fear turned to anger as she berated herself for being out in the dark searching for a dead woman.

What if Jethin was around? He had left her to die and she wasn't dead. Would he come back to finish what he'd started? She heard another cry. The woman was taking *forever* to jump tonight. Saffron forced herself to move. She straightened her shoulders and held her head up. *This is the new you,* she reminded herself, *you are going to become the new you by 'sustained effort.' You're going to go help that woman. Now.*

She rounded a low hill and a mound of scrub-brush. Several yards ahead, the woman cried out as she walked along the cliff, very close to the edge. Saffron pushed forward, looked down at her feet and counted her steps as she walked. The wind-shriek hurt her eardrums, and the saturated sea air was soaking her hair into clumps that hung over her eyes. Between the sound of the wind and the high tide that was bashing the sea against the boulders below, Saffron had to hold her ears. She would have to yell to be heard above the din.

The moon shone bright through the body and clothes of the small, ghostly woman. It cast a phosphorescent tinge on the dark rocks all around her.

Saffron cupped her mouth with her hands. She swallowed the lump in her throat and took one last, deep breath. "Stop!" Saffron cried out so loud, her voice cracked. She rolled her eyes. She had meant the word to come out strong, commanding. It was nothing more than a hysterical bark that fell limply at her feet. She tried again, louder, and forced her voice deeper. "You...don't...have...to...do...this!"

The woman didn't acknowledge Saffron. She continued along, at a slower rate, dragging her feet — as if her ghostly weight were too much to bear. Suddenly, she stopped and faced the sea.

Saffron's entire body was jitter-dancing. This was it, the moment when the woman would finally jump. She looked over one shoulder, then the other. Of course, there was no help coming her way. Why had the woman stopped walking? Was the jump going to happen now, or what? *Oh, Christ, lady, right now? I am* not *ready for this....*

The woman's chest heaved as she sobbed, the tears streamed down her cheeks. She looked out across the sea, reached out with one hand — her eyes wide and frantic, her lips pressed. Whatever illusory thing she was reaching for remained unseen — she let her arm drop. Then without warning, she slapped a hand to her temple, raked at her hair, and started howling.

Saffron stumbled back a few steps, her eyes and nostrils flaring in primordial response. *Get out of here — run, RUN!* But she didn't run. She even took one step forward — it was all she could muster. Never had she been exposed to someone else's raw pain like this woman's. She felt like she was intruding – like she shouldn't be seeing this. She looked back at the path that had led her there, and longed to run back. *You have always been a runner.*

It was the way the woman was quietly weeping that made Saffron turn and face her once more. *You can do this.* She needed to get the woman's attention, and quick. From several months' experience, Saffron knew time was running out — the ghost woman would soon jump. Saffron shook her whole body. She cracked her knuckles. She lowered her head and looked up at the ghost from beneath her brows, then walked straight at her. Her gait wasn't as confident as she would've liked – she was erratic and jerking, as if she were a marionette – but she was charging forward, for Pete's sake. Fear, she figured between rapid breaths, dashed all hopes of grace. She stood right beside the ghost, looked at her chalky face – and gasped.

Through the ghost's head, Saffron saw the rounding flash of a far-off lighthouse. She craned her neck and got into the face of the ghost girl, moving as close as she possibly could without teetering over the edge. Both girls — one dead, one alive — were now on the precipice, inches away from indifferent boulders, jagged rock and ravaging sea.

Saffron was almost nose-to-ear with the ghost when she yelled, "Hey!" The wind blustered through Saffron's hair and pitched her towards the cliff's edge. She stretched one foot out quickly to widen her stance and keep her balance.

The ghost didn't respond.

Saffron screamed right at her again, with such force she tasted copper in the back of her throat.

Nothing.

Saffron slumped. What could she do? It's wasn't like the ghost was ignoring her. Saffron could tell — the ghost was far away. Even though the spirit girl with the raggedy dress and hanging arm was right there – her consciousness was a hundred years gone. "I'm so sorry," Saffron muttered, but the greedy wind took her words and swallowed them. She put her hand over her mouth and finally let herself cry as the ghost girl's pain sucked her in.

The ghost had been staring down. She seemed terribly mesmerized by the turbulent waves. Suddenly, she gasped. Her head shot up.

Static prickled the air and left an acid tang on Saffron's tongue.

The ghost girl's head swiveled around on her neck. She looked straight into Saffron's eyes.

Saffron cried harder. "Oh, I'm so, so sorry." She fought the urge to run with everything she had in her. She struggled not to be consumed by the bottomless, edacious black eyes that threatened to overtake her as they studied first her body, her hair, then eye-to-eye. Saffron almost buckled under the heavy scrutiny. She held her hands out to the ghost in a placating manner. She whispered, "You don't have to be like this."

The spirit didn't blink, but her glance shifted almost imperceptibly from Saffron's eyes to her lips, as she watched the words form.

"You don't have to suffer anymore. You're like, suspending yourself in time, or something, and you don't have to. Look at you, in agony – you don't have to feel like that! I know what I did back then was wrong, but you don't have to suffer now."

The ghost blinked once.

Good, Saffron thought. She can hear me. She can understand me. "I can.... I can.... I can *feel* your pain! I want to help you. I need to tell you — you are...dead. You don't have to be like this anymore. You can get a new life. A better life." Saffron grimaced. "And I won't be in it. You don't have to worry about me screwing up your life again. You should go now – you'll be so much happier...."

The ghost raised an eyebrow. Her lips parted as if to speak, then closed again as she continued to stare silently at Saffron.

"Look, don't ask me how I know all of this. But you can trust me this time. You need to.... Whoa – whataya doing?" Now Saffron held her hands out to stop the ghost.

The girl had stopped listening to Saffron and had taken a step towards her. If the ghost girl had any substance, they could've touched noses. She was staring past Saffron, over Saffron's right shoulder, at the forest. Her tears had mercifully stopped flowing and the expression of unmitigated torture had lifted at last.

Saffron saw the tiniest pinpoint of light reflected in the girl's eyes. The light grew larger, until her pupils were no longer black, but two great mirrors of light. Saffron spun around. What was that? What was out there?

The ghost moved through Saffron to get to the forest.

It was a sensation Saffron would never forget. First, she felt all the air being sucked out of her body. Then she felt the girl inside her, and every emotion the girl had ever felt filled Saffron's soul and poured out of her skin. Then Saffron smelled cut green grass, and hot sulfa, followed by the scent of roses in full bloom — their perfume hot from the sun. After the ghost had moved all the way through, Saffron almost lost her balance at the loss of the soul that had just occupied her body with her. She wanted to crumple into a useless pile, but struggled to hold her skin and bones up. When she finally collected her strength, she ran after the girl, but she was becoming too hard to see. Before the ghost was swallowed by the forest, Saffron heard a whisper, in her right ear — "I just wanted you to know." Then, the girl vanished.

Saffron stopped running and stared at the darkness. She shivered and crossed her arms over her chest. She looked over her left shoulder, out at the ocean. She looked back to the spot where she had last seen the ghost. "Huh."

Chapter 5

*T*he magic is gone.

Saffron sat on her blanket by the edge of the sea, getting ready to
pick blackberries from the overburdened bushes.

The magic is gone.

She repeated this to herself several times to see how the realization
made her feel. And, as it is with the passing of many personal things,
she felt on the one hand, sad because she knew she would never
experience anything like that again. On the other hand, she felt great
relief that it was finally over, because most of the time, it was just too
much to bear. She was no longer a shining beacon for all the freaky
magic things in the world. No more naked gnomes, catatonic ghosts,
smelly gremlins, snotty unicorns, and best of all, no more damn
fairies. Good riddance. She didn't go to see movies anymore, but had
read about Jethin in the newspaper. Last February, he was employee
of the month.

It had been one full year since she sat here last, completely alone,
shaded by the pines from the pulsing August sun. This had been a
pleasant summer, if a little uneventful. Coco came over a lot.
Sometimes, she went to Coco's crazy mausoleum of a house and
laughed to herself every time she remembered that on the night she
first met Coco, she assumed the would-be stripper lived in a trailer.
Another reminder that you never can tell what's really going on until
you experience it. She and Coco like to make their own jewelry, and
their sales weren't too shabby. Markis had called a couple of times
from New Mexico. But their conversations were dull and heavy with

unsaid words.

Now, she sat alone, basking in the sun and suffering through a healthy dose of loneliness. Coco was in the Bahamas. Saffron no longer felt the same comfort in solidarity as she once had. Audrey was thrilled with the new Saffron — just yesterday, Saffron had received an acceptance letter from the state university. She was undeclared, but the locks were off her bedroom door and she was going off to college.

She felt the heat from a shaft of light beating down on her head. *Damn!* She had forgotten the sun block. She rifled through her pack, beyond the sweatshirt, the extra socks, the journal, the stationery and envelopes, bits and pieces of beads, earring cards and wire, and dug way, way to the bottom. There was no sun block, only a pair of tights.

"Whatever works," she grumbled. She pulled the waistband of the tights over her head, the legs dangling off the back, leaned on her elbows and shut her eyes. She'd told her mom that she would be right back with the blackberries, but the sun was making patterns on her closed eyelids and the birds were chatty – she wanted to stay forever.

***

Audrey stopped wiping a dish to squint out of her kitchen window. Somebody was making his way up the drive and he was pushing something. After a moment, she realized who it was and a sunny smile came to her face. But why was he pushing the motorcycle up the driveway? She laughed. Maybe he was trying to surprise Saffron — he didn't want her to hear the bike. Saffron wouldn't have been able to hear a herd of elephants tromping up the drive because she was tucked in the woods. She might as well be a million miles away — the tall pines and vines of the woods blocked all noise from outside its perimeter.

Audrey continued to watch Markis as he panted his way up. She giggled. Wowee, he sure was hot! If Saffron married him, Audrey would have the best-looking grandchildren on the East Coast. She sobered as she thought; *I could be a Grandmother before I'm forty.* She yelled out the window over the sink. "Markis, come in by the screened door out back. I'll pour you some lemonade."

Markis parked the motorcycle, and then met Audrey on the large, granite step before the door. He drank the lemonade in five gulps and wiped his mouth on the back of his sleeve.

Audrey motioned him in. She went back to the sink and resumed dish-washing. "How was New Mexico?"

"Yeah, it was great. I'm gonna ask Saffron if she wants to move there when we get married." He winked.

"Uh, huh. Well, she's out in the woods. She forgot her sun block; will you take it to her?" She squeezed out her sponge and wiped the counter. "If you follow that trail there, out back through the grass, you'll find another path through the woods. Keep on it and you'll find her."

"Thanks for the drink. It's nice to see you again." He plopped the heavy glass down on the wood chopping board by the sink, and turned around to make a mad dash for the woods.

"Ah, Markis?"

He skidded to a halt and faced Audrey.

"For future and significant reference, please — I really don't want to be a granny before I'm forty." She felt very satisfied with the way his cheeks blanched. That should set him straight — for a little while, anyway. She let him go with a wave.

He ran out back, jogged and leaped through the tall grass, sprinted through the forest, and finally found Saffron, alone, sitting cross-legged on an old sheet. She faced the ocean. Her eyes were closed.

He stopped short. He was still many yards away from the clearing, and he stood still to watch her as his heart squeezed into his throat. She was so beautiful. He adored the curve of her waist under the fitted halter top; her lithe, pale arms; her long, graceful neck; and little pigtails. But what the heck was on her head? Were those *pantyhose?* He smiled — only Saffron.... She could wear some old bowling shoes, hospital scrubs, and those pantyhose on her head to complete the outfit — she would still be a goddess. He shifted the weight of his backpack and slowly walked towards her. A dry twig cracked beneath his boot.

Saffron turned, alarm washing over her features. When she realized it was Markis coming up behind her and not a serial killer, she became even more distressed and ripped the tights from her head. "Oh, my God! What are you doing here? I didn't know you would be back already. Why didn't you call? I don't wear tights on my head that often — never! I never wear tights...well, not on my head...."

Markis sat down very close beside her and bumped playfully into her side, and held his knees to his chest — just as she sat now. He could smell her — baby powder. He leaned over and bumped her again. "I don't mind your pantyhose." His voice was low and thick.

"They are not *pantyhose,* Markis." Her voice was high and nervous. She snorted. "They're *tights* — not *pantyhose.* Who says 'pantyhose'? That's just weird. I missed your graduation when I was in the hospital..."

He turned a little to look at her. Graduation, of all things? What was she going on about? Then he saw how she was biting her bottom lip and felt how she was quivering, sitting there beside him. She wouldn't look at him. He sighed, turned his entire body, and moved to encase her, so that one of his long legs was behind her, and the other long leg was stretched out across her thighs. He put his palms on the ground, lifted his butt and moved right into her, hugging her close.

It was like hugging a statue.

Saffron felt the heat rise in her cheeks and fought to control the shivers that raced through her body. She could hardly believe this was happening. So much time seemed to have gone by since she first started wanting him, so much time when she had convinced herself that he would never want her as badly as she wanted him.

Now, the coast was clear. For once, finally, there was nothing, no one between them, no one moaning and lurking about. Well, not that she could tell. Not even her insecurities were there — they were gone with the ghosts.

He relaxed his hug and smiled. He'd give her more time, but not much. Today was the day — he could feel it, smell it, taste it. Today was the day. "I brought you some stuff...from New Mexico." He reached behind him to lug his pack into her lap. He put one arm back around her and wrestled the pack open with the other hand. He pulled out a brightly colored Native American blanket and gave it to her as he nuzzled her ear.

She held it in her lap and said nothing as her eyes welled up. It was an exquisite throw, handmade, with naturally-dyed threads of earthy browns and creams, and shot through with electric fuchsia, teal, and sunshine yellow. Saffron smoothed the blanket, then hugged it to her chest. "Thank you," she whispered.

"My uncle's family makes these. They sell them through consignment shops – even in Albuquerque and Taos." This trip to New Mexico had changed him. He loved staying with his uncle's family – eating traditional foods, hanging out on the farm, everyone one packing up and going to the hot springs at dawn.... He would never forget how he stood on the edge of the desert every night and watched as twilight slowly covered the land, and how the pain inside him would not ease as his grandfather sat on the tailgate of the pickup and played song after breathy, mournful song on his wooden flute. The ancient sound wrenched Markis' heart. He knew what it was about — this ache that plagued him, and rooted itself deep inside. When the first cries of the coyote came, he wanted to howl, too. He wanted her, he wanted her, he needed her. He told himself that, when he returned east, he would go get her and never let her go.

Now, he watched Saffron put the soft wool on her cheek. He took a deep breath and held it as she rubbed the blanket round and round. She was making him nuts, absolutely nuts. Did she know that? "Saffron – please...."

Saffron looked up, startled at the pleading in his voice. He unwound himself from her and crawled around to face her on hands and knees. He leaned forward and kissed her on her swollen lips. He pulled back a little to look in her eyes and saw trepidation, but also encouragement, so he knelt in front of her, grabbed each tiny pigtail, and pulled her close to kiss her again. This time he took his time about it and was more insistent. Saffron's eyes fluttered when he opened her mouth with his lips, but soon enough, her eyes shut again. Her heart pounded so hard in her chest that it hurt. She broke the kiss and gasped for air.

He sat back on his bum, stretched his legs out and covered both of her legs with his. He used his heels to coax her closer to him while she flushed five different shades. He placed the backpack between them and fished around in it one more time. "And this...*I* made for you myself. My dad taught me. Can you believe that great big guy actually does this as a hobby in his spare time?"

Saffron held out her hands to receive the gift. It was a mirror. It was round, and on one side, it had a crescent moon etched in it. The moon looked like frost.

"My father does designs — owls, people, fantasy stuff — but I just started with the crescent, so I wouldn't screw it up."

"Markis, this is beautiful! You did a great job!" She flipped the mirror over and over, then held it up to stare at her reflection – and was startled. There she was, Saffron, but different. Her cheeks were rosy and her grey eyes were bright under the fringe of long, rusty-red bangs. The baby curls that escaped her pigtails played around the skin of her smooth, heart-shaped face. Gingerly, she touched her cheek.

"Am I going to lose you to that mirror, Narcissus?"

Saffron let the mirror fall onto the blanket. She got out from under Markis and jumped to her feet. "Markis, you are so awesome! You are the best person in the entire world! I cannot believe you're here, like, right now. I cannot believe you brought me these beautiful presents."

Markis stood too, and grabbed her wrists as she spoke.

"And I cannot believe you like me...."

He was looking at her again – *into* her. His stare was intense.

She blushed and looked away.

He pulled her to him and willed her eyes back on his. They stood there in silence, looking at one another, as the waves crashed below, and the gulls wheeled high above. A gentle breeze blew a wisp of Saffron's hair across her lips. Markis brushed it back. Suddenly, Saffron jumped as if she'd been shocked. It was weird, what just happened to her — like when a plug fits into an outlet. As if a surge of electricity blasted through her.... It even hurt. She leaned into him and held on. "Markis?" Her words were muffled as she spoke against his t-shirt, which smelled of Markis and fabric softener.

He cleared his throat, but couldn't get the huskiness out. "Yeah?"

"I need to sit — something weird just happened. Maybe it's the heat. I dunno. I just need to sit...."

Surprisingly, calm, cool Markis seemed equally flustered. "Yeah, okay." He reached down, grabbed the new blanket, shook it out and spread it on top of the thin sheet. He held out his hands to help her sit down.

Saffron watched him all the while – his new frown, his ear tugging, the way his jaw was clamped — something had just happened to Markis as well. They sat quietly for a moment, not touching, side by side. They watched the seagulls dive below the cliff, past their line of sight.

Saffron didn't look at him when she asked, "Did something really...really...*sharp* just happen to you — in your head?"

Markis exhaled heavily. "Yeah." He smiled. "It was weird, but kind of cool. And don't take this the wrong way, but being with you is awesome....and a little scary. And whatever is going on now is a good example of 'a little scary'." He reached over and tugged on Saffron's pigtail. "But I love it — being with your scary self." He shifted a little closer to her and turned around so he was facing her. "Saffron...."

She looked at him. Blinked.

"I need you." He cleared his throat. "Right now." He dipped his chin, looked at her from just under his long lashes. "Know what I mean?"

Saffron reached for his neck as she lay back, pulling him with her. They didn't start slowly, and they weren't gentle — each grabbing at the other like a starving fiend. He yanked his t-shirt over his head with one hand, and pulled her beaded halter top up with the other, unhooked her strapless bra with his forefinger and thumb, and fumbled at the button on her jeans — as adept as a six-armed Hindu god. She pulled at his hair, already moaning in little bursts.

Snap.

Markis turned his head away from her so quickly, she was startled out of mid-kiss. "Markis?"

He was looking out at the ocean. On his face, he wore an expression of awe mingled with fear.

The shock sensation she had felt moments before returned, and with it came a dark pressure that blanketed her from head to toe.

Something was coming.

Something was getting nearer. Something that she couldn't see.

But Markis could see it — his eyes were glassy and staring at whatever it was. His eyes focused as it came closer, skimming across the waves.

"Markis?" Saffron's voice trembled.

Markis shrank back. His eyes moved with the nothing until he was staring straight up, as if someone was standing there, towering over them.

Still, Saffron saw nothing. But she could *feel* it now. Feel *him*.

All at once, Markis went limp. He crumpled down on top of Saffron, his hot chest against hers and her askew bra. The undone buttons on their jeans gave a little clink when he fell. His eyes stayed open and staring.

Saffron, chin on her chest, looked at the top of Markis' unmoving head. Then she slammed her fists on the forest floor. And slammed them. And slam, slam, slammed them. Above her, the tops of the pines swayed. She screamed. "Ny — !" holding on to the last syllable until it sounded like blood gurgling in her throat. Then she screamed again, receiving no response but the keening of the gulls, the roar of the breaking waves at the bottom of the cliff, and the buzzing of cicadas.

Chapter 6

"**M**arkis?" No movement. "Markis?" She looked back over her shoulder at the space he had been staring. There was no one there. Yet, she felt someone there. She shook Markis harder, rocked his entire body back and forth. He wouldn't wake up. She felt for his pulse with clammy, shaking fingers. She couldn't find anything. But what did that mean? She had never felt for someone's pulse before – maybe she was doing it wrong. She feebly shook him again. She tapped his shoulder and stared at his frozen face. She got up, fastened her bra, and was on her knees in less than two seconds. She put her ear to his mouth. No breath. Panic slammed into her like a throat-punch; it whitened her already pale skin to parchment. She jumped to her feet as the color rushed back to her face in a mottled-red rage. "Ny!"

With a click and a boom, sound burst back into the universe. Animals scurried and chattered — their small squeaks, hoots, and whistles chorused throughout the woods, blending with the waves and wind.

"Ny!" Saffron crumpled to a sitting position beside Markis' stone-still body. She slapped the blanket as angry tears spilled down her cheeks. It was no use. With the return of the noises Saffron had felt a change. Ny wasn't here, and neither was Markis. She took two deep, shaking breaths, forced her eyes shut and concentrated.

Li, where are you? Come here.

But she couldn't keep her eyes shut, couldn't concentrate. A sob heaved up from her chest and poured out. She covered her eyes with cold, sweaty hands, and tried again — breathing deeply, in and out, in and out.

Li, come here.

It took almost half an hour.

But then, they came. She saw them, hastening across the sea, floating towards Saffron like winged specters, glorious and shimmering. A whole flock of them. Saffron was not impressed.

The fairies touched down, spry and delicate, one by one, until they stood before her, still as statues except for their fanning wings. Li walked over to the blanket where Saffron crouched over Markis' body. The fairy looked down at Saffron with compassion, her porcelain-perfect skin glowing as if she were a Christmas ornament. White hair like spun-glass filament blew across her lavender eyes, fringed with white lashes. She moved the hair back over her shoulder with very long, very slender white fingers. The other fairies stood two yards behind her, as if loathe to move any closer to Saffron.

Saffron wasn't fooled by Li's pitiful glance. She knew Li too well by now. Knew her well enough to know Li probably knew all about Ny's plans. Saffron looked away from Li, her eyes burning into Markis' staring eyes.

"I did not know, Saffron. I do not know everything that Ny thinks." Li's voice was feathery-soft, like a voice from a far and hazy dream.

"Is he dead?" Saffron's eyes blazed as she crossed her arms across her chest and waited for the fairy to confirm.

Li knelt at Markis' side and touched him. She adjusted his body to a position that appeared more comfortable, smoothed the hair from his forehead, then touched her fingertips to his eyelids to shut them. She straightened his clothes. "No, he is not dead." She held his hand. "A fairy cannot kill. You know this, Saffron."

Saffron snorted. "They can cause accidents, can't they?"

"He is not dead, Saffron."

"But his soul isn't here, is it?" Saffron's nostrils were fixed in a permanent flare.

"No." Li's face looked properly concerned. "Do not lend free rein to your wrath, Saffron. You are hurting yourself. It does Markis no good."

For a moment, Saffron held to her countenance. Then, the mask of anger cracked and there below lay Saffron's fear – naked for all to see. She brought her hands to her face and rubbed her eyes. "Li, we need to find Ny, and fast. I can't go back home and tell my mother I left Markis' body back on this blanket!"

Li stared at Saffron's hands as she flung them around in hysteria.

"Li...." Saffron warned, hysteria peaking in her voice. Why did Li look worried?

Li stood holding her elbows close to her body, and still, wouldn't look Saffron in the eye.

Evening was coming on. Saffron shivered in the typical, New England, August breeze, which had lost 30 degrees in five minutes. She never expected to be out here this long. Her mother would come for her soon, assuming she and Markis were getting it on.

"Saffron, when a fairy chooses not to be found, he *cannot* be found."

"Wha...?"

"Ny can hide anywhere on Earth."

"Yeah?" Saffron didn't see the problem.

Li held her hands out before her. "The Earthrealm is not the only realm to search. There are other places, other realms. Hundreds of concealed lands. Sanctuaries of which you know nothing. They are on

Earth, but not of this time. They are through doorways you cannot see. To search them all...you would need more than your lifetime. Li looked forlornly at Markis. "We must take his body. We must move it to a safe place where no human will find it. We will hide it for safekeeping, so no one will come along and bury him."

Saffron's hand was over her mouth. "No." Her voice was weak. She didn't know what she was saying 'no' to. 'No' to Ny kidnapping Markis. 'No' to Markis' lifeless body. 'No' to a burgeoning problem so horrific, so impossible to solve.... She just didn't know. "Oh, my God. What have I done?" Her eyes flashed to Li. "What have *you* done?!"

"Blame will not find Markis. We can search, Saffron. I can take a troop with me. We can search. But you must understand we may never find where Ny has taken the soul of Markis."

"No." Saffron moaned. "Why do you guys act like this? Why won't you just stop? Why are you so twisted?"

Another fairy stepped forward — a male. He looked like a tree. His skin was literally tree bark. His head was almost owlish, complete with large, pumpkin-orange, glowing eyes. "Fairy claims fairy games." He crossed his arms over his chest (trunk), and looked down his nose at her.

"Yeah, okay. Not too effen creepy...." Saffron muttered as low as possible. She stood up and positioned herself on Ly's other side so she would be out of sightline of the total-weirdo owl man.

"If by chance we do find him, it may be years from now. We can return him to his body, but he will go home to a place that is there no longer. People that are there no longer. He will not be able to live normally in your world again." Li lowered her head. "Markis is not the first child taken by fairies."

Saffron stood rigidly and held her breath. *This can't be true. This is insane.* She sighed heavily. "I can't go back to my house without him. Are you listening to me? Tell me where to find him. You must know *something*."

"No, Saffron, no. *You* cannot find him. You cannot cross over into those worlds."

Saffron looked incredulous. "Well, how did Ny take Markis into those worlds? If *I* can't go into those worlds, then Ny couldn't have taken Markis there...."

"Ny took Markis' *soul,* Saffron."

"Then take my soul, Li." Saffron's eyes popped wide as she quick-shrugged. She leaned down and patted the lump that was Markis' body. "Stick my body wherever you're sticking his."

"No, Saffron!" Birds squawked and rushed from the pine tops, as if her words were wind that blew them all away. "You do not try to understand!" She looked as if she would stamp her foot, but the graceful fairy did not. "If it takes a thousand years to find Markis' soul, then we shall count ourselves lucky!"

Saffron shrugged with false bravado. "Doesn't matter. This is my fault. I can't just pretend this is not happening. I need to find him. He would come for me...."

"What about your family, Saffron? Your beautiful mother...?"

Saffron stood up, crossed her arms over her chest, and locked her steel-grey eyes onto Li. The fairy's overly large pupils, thinly ringed in violet, were as disconcerting as ever — especially contrasted with all of those white lashes — but Saffron spoke firmly. She shook her head slowly as she spoke. "You don't care about my family. You just want me to hurry up, get old, and drop dead, so I can return to you in the fairy world. Then maybe we can plan another great reincarnation adventure together, right? Maybe if I was *four,* I could appreciate your dire need to play house with me, but as we're talking about somebody's *life* here, I think you're just going to have to wait to play with me again."

Li's features tightened, making her face look like white crystal. Tears pooled in her eyes, but did not spill over. Confusion and anguish mingled on her face while she reached a finger to lift a tear away. She stared at the perfect dome of glowing, fairy liquid that shone on her fingertip. She continued to look at the tear as she spoke. "How could you say such words to me? You should not say such words to me." Her hand fisted to clutch the tear in her palm. "You do not know what you do."

"Li, store my body with his. I *will* search for him." Saffron's voice started to crack. Though she wanted to be strong, the fairy's misery was washing over her, filling her head and chest with a clutching blackness that brought such weight, Saffron found it difficult to continue standing.

"As you wish it, Saffron, but I will not let you go alone." Li turned away from Saffron and brought her hands up to cover her face.

Chapter 7

Saffron stood stiffly with her arms clutched about her. She stared at the trunk of an old oak standing several feet to her right. Its clinging vines reached up and swirled around its massive trunk, desperate for the sparse sunlight that was peeping between sections of canopy above. Moss grew on one side of the oak, a sprinkling of pale mushrooms at its base.

The fairies milled around Saffron in silence, quickly preparing to carry the body of her friend. Her boyfriend. They weren't sure how many of them it would take to fly him away. They were accustomed to escorting souls, not an entire human body. The weight of his flesh was considerably more than his spirit. They wanted to be quite certain that they wouldn't drop him mid-flight.

With glassy eyes and stoic expression, Saffron turned to watch the fairies. Her entire body moved as one fixed unit, as if she were a statue and was unable to swivel her head. The fairies' movement was fluid, hypnotic; or, maybe she was in shock, and that made their actions seem surreal, almost fuzzy, as if a sudden wind could blow the whole scene away. Their transparent wings were threaded with gold, silver, and bronze veins. Some had skin that sparkled. Their hair shone bright blonde, brunette, black and every color of the rainbow — even colors that Saffron had never seen before. Some of the fairies cast frowns in Saffron's direction, and this was finally what shocked her out of her complacency.

Frowning? She had never before seen a fairy so disgruntled. Well, Li and Ny could put on a good act – those two were almost campy –

but these frowns.... These fairies were in pain. They looked sad...and afraid. Why were they looking at her like that? Saffron's face flushed hotly. Bitterness seethed. What had *she* done? She wasn't the troublemaker here — it was one of their own, for God's sake, had *always* been one of their own. She was not the one who flew *herself* away one fine, warm August night to the Fairyrealm. She was not the one who kept the contact. After she'd been to the realm, twice, she had had enough and asked *specifically* to be left alone, to remain in the Earthrealm, and never be witness to their weirdness again — to never experience the creeping unease that crawled through her skin while she was among them. And...she was not the one who *stole* Markis' soul! Saffron narrowed her eyes and glared at one particularly belligerent female, a fragile beauty with transparent skin, her hair also transparent, like a clutch of rice noodles. She looked a lot like Li, except her entire body was roped in thick, red veins. The fairy whipped her head around, giving Saffron her back.

They finally figured the best way to carry Saffron was to have her stand and sit back on their arms. So, the males reached across and grabbed hold of one another, gripping each other's forearms. Saffron sat down on the shelf of their arms, totally mortified. They instructed her to wrap her arms around their necks. With a whump, whump, of their giant wings they flew off the ground and hovered several feet in the air, testing their strength and questioning their endurance for the flight to come. They seemed satisfied that they could make it and proceeded to lower her to the ground.

As she hopped off, she watched the fairies struggle with Markis' limp body. And winced. Every time they thought they had a good way to carry him, an arm would fall, or a leg would bend at an odd angle. Over and over they forgot to support his head, so it lolled around as if his neck were a licorice rope trying to support a grapefruit. Saffron squeezed her eyes shut. If they didn't start taking better care, they were going to break his neck! Finally, they thought they had it…only to have his body slide out from their arms like a greased watermelon.

Saffron rolled her eyes. "Hey there, mighty magic people — why don't you just go down to the fire station and ask them for a stretcher?"

Li nodded to one of her comrades. That fairy disappeared in a burst of light — leaving a whirling, swirling cloud, like a glittering dust mote. The energy in the swirl pulled at Saffron and stung the roof of her mouth, much like the sensation left after she had inhaled water.

Li looked to see if any ships were passing by. They didn't need human witnesses. The others dispersed. Some walked to the edge of the bluff to stare out at the ocean, and some settled in groups under the shade of the trees. Their ill-contained hostility cast a pall, and every once in a while, one would throw Saffron a furtive glance. Only Li stood by Saffron.

Saffron had her arms locked over her chest. "So, why do they all hate me — not that I care."

Li sighed. "They do not 'hate you,' Saffron. They are very distraught. We are all paying for what Ny has done. We are paying in the very worst way. Our home, Saffron — it is not what it used to be, what it always has been."

Saffron had been ready to counter anything Li said, ready to scream, 'This is Ny's fault- not mine!' However, she held her tongue at the hitch in Li's voice, at the sadness that poured from the fairy and clung to Saffron's skin like a thick mist.

Saffron cracked her knuckles and crossed her arms over her chest again. She scrutinized a wasp that banged along the ground, made to look a bumbling drunkard by the cold air. *What in the world was Li talking about now? Why would their entire world be changed because Ny took Markis' soul?* The wasp landed on Markis, his wings flexing slower and slower. Markis seemed smaller to her — helpless and sad on the Indian blanket. A pine needle drifted down from the canopy and settled in his dark, curly hair. "How's he going to get that stretcher over here — carry it around on his little, solar-bulb backside?"

Li smiled her indulgent mother-to-child smile. "It will change size when he changes size. He will have no trouble carrying the stretcher."

"Why can't you guys just do that with our bodies then?"

Li's eyes went out of focus — a great cumulonimbus cloud covered the sun and was reflected in her great, black orbs. "The human body does not change at *our* will."

Twenty minutes passed before Saffron finally saw the glow of an orb wending through the woods. The multi-colored male fairy appeared in a burst of energy, much like the one he had in which he had left.

"Did no one see you?" Li was wringing her hands.

The male fairy held the stretcher out to Li. His coloring was like a flame — bluish feet that gave way to fire-orange around his midriff, and mellowed into a warm marigold up around his neck. His head and hair were white, absent of all color — even his eyes were white. His smile was sheepish. "As a winged-child, this was my first time beyond our realm; I found it very...disconcerting." He gave Saffron a sideways glance.

He told them he had appeared behind a Dumpster at the fire station. A brilliant, sparking cloud snapped and popped as he descended the last two feet to the ground and materialized into his seven-foot self. There was a yard to his right with four boys sitting in a clubhouse. They stopped bashing their action figures long enough to gawk at him — the brightly colored man with wings and a white head. After a few moments, he stepped out into the open and walked towards the firehouse. Four men were sitting at a card table, drinking Gatorade, and bantering over a game of hearts that had gone terribly wrong. They ragged each other until one of them spotted the fire-colored fairy coming towards them. When the fire-fairy was close enough, he waved an arm and dulled their senses. As he walked by, they watched with glassy eyes and slack jaws. He found a stretcher, quickly slipped out of the firehouse, and passed the men at the table whom he thanked profusely. One of the men slowly lifted his hand in response; he was already starting to come out of the funk. The others still sat there listlessly. The fire-fairy took refuge behind the Dumpster, and disappeared. The men stared at their cards for another five minutes.

Li put a finger to her lips. "I hope the card players' sense of primeval masculinity stays strong, and that they will be too ashamed to admit to anyone that a fairy cast a spell on them — a half-naked male fairy." She knew male pride was common, and hoped it was enough to hide their deed on this day.

The fairies, as gently as possible, maneuvered Markis' body on the stretcher. Four fairies, one at each corner, flapped into the air to test the weight. Two more were requested to fly underneath, their arms stretched above them to support the rails on each side. Saffron settled onto the joined arms of her escorts, then gripped their necks into the crook of each of her elbows.

With a *whoosh*, Saffron and her escorts rose and flew quickly to catch the six fairies carrying Markis' stretcher high into the clouds.

Saffron felt her hair blast back from her face and form itself to the sides of her head as they sailed upwards. When they came beside Markis, the two males slowed their flight, and Saffron was able to open her eyes without her eyes tearing in the harsh wind. They flew straight up into the sky. Saffron watched the earth below her become smaller and smaller, until finally it was just a jagged puzzle of colors — brown and green, blue and pewter. Taking her body along for the ride was most uncomfortable compared to flight as a soul. She felt the bones of the fairies' arms dig into her rump, and imagined how silly she looked as her cheeks flapped in the blast of passing air. It was getting colder, too. As they climbed higher, higher and higher still, it felt as though the temperature was dropping ten degrees for each passing minute. Saffron took in a deep breath and started to cough. The coughing turned into a fit.

The fairy on her left looked sidelong at her. "No, Saffron, you must calm yourself. The air is thinning now. You must take very small, metered breaths."

Saffron nodded, her eyes wide with fright. Her teeth began to chatter. As the breath wrenched from her and escaped her body, she felt her chest tighten, her throat constrict. She needed to suck air in so badly, but couldn't. She felt panic ooze into her pores and shock her bones. *Where are they taking us? Don't they realize our bodies can't take extreme cold? I can't breathe! They're going to kill us. I should say something.* Saffron looked at her escorts, first one, then the other, while the air screamed past her ears. She didn't say a word. She looked at them again, and the fairy who had spoken to her turned his head momentarily to stare back at her in question. Again, Saffron said nothing. *They can't stand you right now, you know that. They probably want to kill you.* She ground her chattering teeth in frustration and fought to stay awake. The cold was now numbing her so much, she felt her body give way, and struggle for sleep. And then she stopped breathing. Suddenly, nothing was clear to her. She was surrounded by a muddy haze, and all she could hear was someone screaming "Ow! Ow!" Then she felt her heart leap into her constricted throat and she began to dry-heave. In a few short seconds, she could breathe again, but still, her heart choked her. She heard different screaming now — the screaming of the wind past her ears and understood what she heard before wasn't, 'Ow!' but, 'Down!' from the fairy on her right. And that's where they were taking her — down. They nose-dived like a many-bodied kestrel, and plopped her onto the forest floor. She landed like a heap of long, pale limbs and wind-plastered hair. She tried to sit up, but fell back down with a whump.

Li's face appeared in Saffron's line of vision. "We cannot take your body that high — it will expire."

Saffron's voice was croaky. "Oh, Christ, you're brilliant." She winced and rubbed her frozen arms.

"You must come out now."

"Wha — come out of my body?"

"Yes, just like before..."

"Yeah, well, this is a little weird you know...." Saffron looked around at her captivated escorts. They were smirking.

"I do not understand, Saffron."

Saffron ground her teeth. "It's the difference between undressing alone in your room and undressing on the beach!"

"Saffron, we have all seen you...without your body on."

"It's just *weird*. Can't they turn around or something?"

"Saffron, I am afraid I will never understand your fears — but very well." Li looked at the others. On silent cue, they turned around in unison.

"It's not a *fear*, Li...anyone would feel weird about this...."

"Yes, very well, Saffron; they are turned. Please commence."

Saffron huffed. She closed her eyes. It took a couple of minutes before she stretched with the pull on her skin and on her throat, arched as it went through her chest, and held her belly at the tug in her gut. Her whole body melted with warmth and she sighed as her soul left her flesh.

There was more hubbub as another stretcher was acquired to carry her body. More figuring as they got it on the stretcher, her arms and legs flopping like a ragdoll's, then they were up and away.

Li held her hand out to Saffron.

Saffron frowned as she placed her hand in Li's. The frown disappeared as soon as Li touched Saffron's skin. Through her smile, Saffron said, "I might be smiling now, but I won't be too happy once you let go and you're not pumping this happy juice into me...."

"Then, child, be free, and enjoy your short time with happiness."

Saffron tried to force her grin away — she could be happy without Li's help — but she couldn't stop feeling euphoric. Damn fairy.

They shot straight up over the ocean, and soared until they met the escort transporting Saffron's stretcher. Saffron watched her lifeless, waxy face and billowing red hair. She turned her head to look at Li. "Does it irritate you that I call you a fairy?"

"Why would this affect me negatively?"

"Because, you're Fey — right — or whatever...?"

Li smiled. "You may call me fairy, fey, friend, sister, Sidhe or Eeslu — as long as you call me." She winked.

Saffron tried to push a disgruntled voice through her perma-grin lips. "Hmph!"

They stopped soaring straight-arrow up, and were now flying on a more diagonal path. They flew across the sky until they reached a massive cloudbank as big as an island. They stopped in midair, and slowly landed on the cloud.

Saffron gave a small, mousy shriek. Maybe *they* could stand on clouds, but her body sure as hell couldn't. She let go of Li, her smile dropped, and she flew at one of the escorts holding her body up on the stretcher. She grabbed his arm. He looked at her oddly as she stared back at him with defiance. He laughed and pretended to drop the stretcher.

She screamed, "No!" and jumped on him like a monkey, trying to clamp his arms still. Her eyes were wide and terror-filled.

He pressed his lips and wiggled to get her off.

She hiss-whispered, "No.....no....nonono...," as he successfully unhooked her and began to lower his corner of the stretcher. Saffron lunged towards the next fairy, jumped on him, and wrapped her legs around his hips. She flung her arms around his neck, and with her face less than an inch from his, she stared dead into his eyes and firmly said, "No! Do not put this stretcher down."

He chuckled too, squatted, and lowered the stretcher as she clung to him.

She was so busy covering her eyes with grief, that she didn't notice they had lowered Markis and took his body off the stretcher. He now slumbered on the undulating cloud.

The fairies watched Saffron, some with amusement, some with irritation — others in pure amazement as she grasped for one of them, then the other, clinging like a gluey monkey.

The transparent fairy, with eyebrows raised, turned to Li and, without moving her lips, asked if Saffron really was her eternal soul mate.... Li waved the fairy away, then flew to the male fairies' aid as Saffron was very close to turning into a clawing, snarling beast. Li landed on the cloud and stood.

"Saffron." Saffron had one leg on top of a fairy's shoulder and both arms wrapped around his head. "Saffron." The call was calm, patient.

Saffron stopped struggling and looked under her armpit, down at Li.

"You can stand on the clouds, Saffron, you will not fall through. Even within your body, we would not let you fall through the cloud. This is an enchanted cloud. It has been so long before the time of the winged children."

Saffron thought about it. Even if she *could* stand on the clouds, she didn't *want* to stand on the clouds – it just wasn't right. What if there was a weak spot in the enchantment? Who really safety-tested these things anyway? The fairies had said themselves, they weren't used to dealing with actual bodies. So, what did they know? She'd give herself a heart attack standing around, waiting to slip through. She looked at her pathetic, unknowing body on the stretcher and felt sorry for it.

"I assure you, Saffron; you cannot fall through these clouds. They are enchanted, it is impossible."

"Crap." Saffron felt incredibly stupid. Slowly, she unwound herself and slunk to a sitting position on the white puff as it rolled like suds across and under her. Her escorts walked a safe distance from her, the clouds swirling around their ankles. One of them rubbed at his neck and rolled his eyes.

Saffron looked at Markis. A great wave of sadness fluttered up from her chest and sat in her throat, feeling as if it would strangle her. Tears welled in her eyes as she reached hesitantly to touch his black boot, his leg in his jeans, and finally the soft skin of his arm beneath the cloth of his t-shirt. She ran her fingers through his wavy, dark hair and smoothed it back from his forehead. A prayer vibrated through her mind, a desperate plea for his long, sooty lashes to lift off his cheeks and let his chocolate eyes cling to hers. No such luck. The guilt and shame that smothered her was becoming unbearable. Her tears came quickly as sunlight reflected off of them and blinded her with piercing light. *Oh, my God, how long is this going to take me? How many realms am I going to have to search for his soul? How could Ny be so awful? How could a fairy kidnap somebody's soul?* She threw herself on Markis' chest and sobbed. She sucked for air and found she couldn't breathe, only hiccup and gasp like a beached fish.

The fairies backed away from her and the two lifeless bodies. They didn't want to be touched by her sorrow.

Li knelt beside Markis, and adjusted first his legs, then his arms, then his head. She gently lifted Saffron's tear-streaked face and whispered to her that it was time to go, that there was no time to waste. "Saffron, you must leave your tears with your body. Position your body into its most restful position, so it can be well while you are away."

Saffron's brow furrowed as she meekly accepted Li's order. She was suddenly disoriented. Lay herself out? This seemed like she was preparing her body for her own wake. It was creepy. She put her body into the fetal position, one hand tucked under her head, fitting herself into Markis' side.

"Close your eyes and help us take you, Saffron."

Saffron looked doubtfully at the lifeless bodies. "Are you sure we're safe here?"

Li said nothing at first, then, "Who would harm you on an

enchanted cloud?"

"IDK — a bird with a huge beak looking for eyes to eat?"

Li's tinkling laugh. "Oh, Saffron; no bird flies this high. You are quite safe from the birds – both bone and metal."

Saffron shrugged. "Our bodies just look so exposed." Her body was clothed in the beaded, native-looking halter top and skinny jeans. One bejeweled flip-flop dangled on her big toe. She put it back on her foot, and brushed the red bangs from her eyes. Then, without realizing it, she brushed the red bangs from the forehead of her conscious head too.

"Let us be away from here." Li whispered.

Saffron stared at Li as the fairy spoke. For the second time, an odd thought occurred to her — just the tiniest unstitched thread of a thought that niggled at her mind. She pushed the thought aside as she held lightly to Li's hand and felt herself fly away over cloud and sea, mountain and desert.

***

It was very late in the night when Ny arrived at his destination. No stars, no moon, just a dark dome of sky blacker than hell. He held Markis' hand firmly, pulling him along like a stuffed puppy. Markis could see, but he was so confused that he thought he must be dreaming, and so went wherever Ny took him in quiet acceptance. He did not heed his grandfather's words: a dream is never just a dream — but a journey. If he had known what was really happening to him, he could have fought. But he was in shock, and thinking it was a dream was easier on his mind. Like life, he was content to let it all happen.

Ny cleared a low hill, and flew over a magnificent city of multi-tiered buildings with floret tops — every one of them etched and carved with a design almost indiscernible in the dark. They flew up to a castle, and raced up the outside wall of a tower as cold air rushed past their faces. Ny landed without a sound on an open window ledge, sat on his haunches on the cold, thick stone, still holding Markis' hand.

There Markis hung and stared, dangling from Ny's hand like a well-loved teddy. Ten stories down, a squat man clacked across the cobblestones with a wheelbarrow of muck.

Ny spied her in the massive bed, beneath a fur blanket, knowing her to be naked and already sensing his presence. His whispered words – both a little bit seductive and a little bit foul — came out of his mouth as beads of light and flew across the room. They landed on her lips, then worked their way down under the blanket.

She moaned — deep and guttural — and moved her legs under the covers. Suddenly, her eyes shot open. Horizontal pupils focused on Ny as he sat grinning, tottering on the window ledge. She sat up without using her hands, an instant fluid movement which caused the blanket to fall from her chest and expose six scaly breasts.

Ny whispered again. The balls of light careened straight for her breasts and caused her to squeal when they made contact. She bared her white teeth at him. "Come."

"It is my intent."

She arched one fine eyebrow. "Then move away from that window. It has been too long. Where have you been?"

As she spoke, Ny jiggled Markis in order to hang him up by the shirt on one of two iron hooks just outside the window. Markis gazed quietly at the moat below his feet. He heard Ny move away from the window ledge. For a moment, there was silence. Then an awful groaning started, followed by begging and stunted shrieks. Then came the howling and slamming — primal sounds which raced down every corridor of the castle, waking the inhabitants therein and causing them to lunge for the earplugs they kept at the ready. Some of them shivered in revulsion, as they knew for a fact, no one was in the room with their mistress, and they wondered what she did to herself to cause such a melee.

Chapter 8

Saffron and the fairies alighted on the mossy grounds of the Fairyrealm. She gawked as her heartbeat quickened — the Fairyrealm *had* changed — just as Li had said. What was once green with vitality now looked yellowed and grey. Sickly. There were no water pixies flitting about, the trees were silent, the song and voice of the woodland creatures — natural and unnatural — had vanished. Saffron stared down at her feet as they sank an inch into muck. The entire place looked...flooded. The bottom of Li's fine, filmy skirts hung heavy in the water.

"Why?" Saffron finally forced out. "Why all this over one messed up thing a fairy did?" She scratched the back of her neck. "...And why water?"

"With his continued deeds, Ny changes our world – weakens it. Good energy is being lost; it is being sucked into the abyss that Ny has left behind when he left this world." She swept her hand as she turned in a full circle. "This is how we know he does not hide the soul of Markis in this world." She pointed to the engorged stream. "What Ny has done, no fairy has ever done. What Ny has done goes against the laws of nature."

"Well, who's punishing *you* for this?"

"It is not a punishment. It is a tip in the balance."

"Who's got their finger on the scale?" As always, Saffron was creaking and screeching under pressure. "Li, who's *doing* this? It's...." She looked around with wide-eyed fear. "It's — what if it gets deeper? Is it going to get deeper?" Saffron's hand slapped to her gaping mouth. "Oh, my God! Did G*od do this?*"

Li sighed heavily as she helped a toad that was struggling in a too-deep puddle. Her wings fluttered — together, apart, together, apart — as a nervous person taps his foot or wrings his hands. "I have never met the entity who watches the scale...." Li sat with a humph on a nearby log. "We cannot rid ourselves of this water. We have tried. Energy seeps from us as from a wound that will not heal. And still the water does rise."

Rise? Rise where? What? Over their whole realm? Saffron flinched. "Oh, my God! Then leave! Go somewhere else!" Saffron panicked for them, since upon quick, roundabout inventory — she noticed neither strain nor concern on behalf of any of the fairy faces, just a wistful sadness.

Li looked at Saffron as if she were an circus oddity. "You suggest we run away? We will not take flight — this is our home. Even ten leagues submerged, this will yet be our home."

Saffron gasped. "You'll *live* under water?"

Li nodded. "Yes, and we will not see the sun, except as a blur through the water. We will travel above land nevermore. Will become human nevermore."

"But why?" Saffron didn't let Li answer. "Oh, my God! Oh my God — are you going to become *mermaids?*"

Li gasped. "Saffron, we cannot *become mermaids,* we are winged children!"

Suddenly, Saffron felt sheepish and incredibly stupid. Then she wondered why she should feel stupid? This whole conversation was stupid! How should she know fairies wouldn't become mermaids under water? They seemed to be able to do anything they wanted. Why stand around then, while these waters rose? Why couldn't they do something to save their world? Didn't they have magic? Couldn't they do anything? If not, *who* was stopping them?

Li simply shrugged in response to Saffron's mental muttering. "Land out of water will no longer be our domain." She waved around to indicate the others. "This tribe of fairies will exist under water. There are other tribes that exist as such." Li shrugged. "One or two maybe."

"Really? Well, what in the world did *they* do to deserve that?" Saffron pulled her foot from the muck and smelled the stench of sulfur as it sucked free.

Li looked at the fairies around her and licked her lips. No fairy responded to her in voice or glance. "They...ate humans."

Saffron was in the middle of removing her other foot from the muck and walking to a boulder when Li spoke. She lost her concentration when Li said, 'ate humans,' and tipped right over as her mouth made a perfect 'o' in horror. She thrashed about in the water and scrambled to sit on the boulder, dirty water streaming down her arms. "Ate humans! Are you shitting me?" She rubbed her hands all over her face and screamed, "You're all freaks!" She drew her feet up to her bum and put her head between her knees. "I can't take this. I'm going to lose it. Really, I'm going to go insane...." She slapped too hard at a passing fly and almost toppled off the boulder. She jumped off the rock and stomped around. "No. No. No. No. No! Go ahead; tell me why in a million years a fairy would ever *eat* a human." She slapped at some more flies that came buzzing around her head. With both arms flailing, she turned around and around and swatted.

The fire-fairy came forward and pointed at Saffron. She shrank away from him and stilled. He said, "She does ask, 'why,' too much, sister. We do not have enough time for 'why.'"

"Saffron, no fairy has had contact with them since they went under."

Saffron grimaced. "Li, I've known you long enough in this life to know you're avoiding my question and are hiding a better answer...."

Li cocked her head sideways and studied Saffron. "Do you really not understand, 'why'?"

Saffron rolled her eyes. "That's why I'm asking." She had started to shake. She had been so filled with joy the first time she had come to the Fairyrealm – that was so long ago. Now, every single time she came back, it sucked the joy from her. She could feel its greedy fingers digging into her heart, pulling at her, wanting any little bit of happiness she held inside.

"Saffron, we — you and I — live in the Earthrealm."

"Yeah."

"There is a balance of souls in the Earthrealm..."

"Yeah."

"There are now two souls missing from the Earthrealm. One that has chosen to leave; one that was taken."

Saffron frowned, stared at Li. *What about fairies eating bodies?*

"No soul can leave the Earthrealm without consequence to the balance."

Saffron forgot about fairies eating bodies. She stopped breathing.

"We must restore balance."

"Man. So that, each-of-us-is-special stuff isn't just a bunch of crap?"

"No, it is not. In so many words, that phrase was formed at the dawn of man. Each of us is essential."

Saffron felt weak. She wanted to sit down and stay down – forever. But the lot of them were standing about in the pool of tepid water, among drowning ferns and floating pine needles, and she didn't want to be the only one having a breakdown.

"Come — let us ready ourselves for our travels. We do not have time to sit here and banter of things that cannot be changed with banter."

"Li, wait...."

Li looked expectantly at Saffron.

Saffron suddenly had nothing to say. She pulled at the beads on her halter top. "I've been thinking. I mean, I know we're friends and all, you know — soul mates — but you seem like the head honcho around here, like people depend on you, you know. You need to stay with your people in their time of need." *Crap, crap, crap — as if she's going to buy that, moron.*

"Saffron, you do not want me to go with you?"

No. "It's not that Li, I just think...you're needed here. I can go by myself."

"You most certainly cannot go by yourself. Saffron, you will need to search over one hundred known realms, never mind the realms you stumble upon that are, as yet, unknown. And in most of these realms, the peoples use magic. It is only your ancient culture, Saffron, that still refuses to use magic. There will be times when you will only be able to temper magic with magic."

Saffron swallowed with difficulty. *'Temper' – she means, 'fight.'* A cold bowling ball sat in her belly with that thought. *But still, you're not coming, Li. You're not going to hang around and manipulate me like your little dolly anymore. Nice try.*"

Li cocked her head and stared at Saffron in wonder. Then she looked down and twiddled the golden cord that held her dress under her bust.

Saffron watched Li with suspicion. *Oh, man — is she reading my mind again? Does she know what I'm thinking?* In a flash, Saffron's emotions swung from hesitant guilt to anger. *Then, she shouldn't be reading my freaken' mind if she doesn't want to hear bad things! It's my mind — she needs to get out. Get out! Get out! Get out!* Saffron glared at Li.

Li looked back, innocently. "I know who can help you, Saffron. In fact, I think you will enjoy their company."

Saffron's anger drained and left her limp. Enjoy 'their' company? How could she have been so nasty to Li? Still Saffron stood quiet now, didn't even attempt to say anything to mend the tear she could feel forming between her and Li — this being that she had traveled through life with for hundreds of thousands of years. Still, she couldn't search for Markis with Li. She knew — she needed to be the leader in this search party. If Li went with her, Li would instantly take charge. That's just the way Li was. Saffron wasn't sure if she let Li take charge or if Li quietly bullied her way to first position. Saffron couldn't think of any of that right now, all she knew was that she had to do this without Li. She cleared her throat, and forced herself to stand up straight. "Can I meet them now?"

"Of course. Kuzih, could you fetch the twins?"

Saffron had seen Kuzih before. She was stocky — more of a cherub than a fairy. Her eyes were big and blue, her ringlets were short and fat. She had a very sweet disposition, even in the bleak time that had so recently settled upon them. Kuzih could still find reason to giggle and smile.

Soon, there was a commotion in the wet forest. In the tangle of mildewed growth, just beyond Saffron's sight, somebody screamed like a girl, then somebody else gave a Tarzan howl. There was three seconds of silence, then a burst of sound as a tow-headed boy, younger than Saffron, jettisoned from a bush. He must have been shoved from behind because he came tripping and sloshing through the muck, and landed on his face with a splash. He screamed like a girl again, and got a mouthful of muddy slop and drowned weeds for his effort.

There was something strange about him. Saffron leaned in for a closer look. There was something between his legs. He had a huge.... "Oh, my God." Saffron turned abruptly, faced away long enough for the boy to get up, sluice the mud from his legs, and pry a coconut out of his shorts.

"Wha...?" He gazed innocently at Saffron. "It's just tropical fruit." Saffron wrinkled her nose in disgust.

Another boy came bounding from the tangle of brush and howled, "Ha, ha! I am the veektor!" He stomped by his identical brother. Splash! Splash! Splash! — and shoved him in the shoulder. His brother leaped forward and shoved him right in the middle of his back. That second twin tripped forward and bumped into Li. They were dressed in grey lederhosen made of the softest leather, long-sleeved white shirts that billowed, wool socks pulled up to their knees, and brown hiking boots. They looked like they were going to a casting call for 'The Sound of Music,' except, Saffron thought, that didn't totally describe them either. With the way they pushed back their sun-kissed golden curls from their foreheads, and walked around with a confident, laid-back stance, they were almost like *surfer dudes* in lederhosen.

"Oh, luscious of all fair, winged children, what does thou desire?" The boy tilted his head and blinked his long, fluffy eyelashes while gazing rapturously into Li's own heavily narrowed eyes.

"Would you boys like to go with Saffron to find Ny?"

"Why us?"

The more ornery of the two looked so suspicious, he made Saffron paranoid. She scrutinized Li for any signs of a lie in her answer. Not that she could ever tell when the fairy was lying.

Li said nothing.

The other boy was ogling Saffron — one long look up, one long look down. He walked over to her and said, "Hey mama, what's up?"

Saffron jumped back from him, "Eeew!" as if he were a giant slug. "You're kidding, right?" Li stared steadily back at her. Saffron flicked her hand at the boy to get him to back off. "Oh, this is insane!"

He was only as tall as her elbow — short for his age.

"Oh, yes. I can see you three are going to get along just fine. Saffron, this is Wo." Li shoved the mud-eating boy before Saffron. "And this lovely man is Tai." She pulled Tai *back* from Saffron's face, he was staring at her like she was prime rib, and an ice cream sundae splayed in offering. "Wo, Tai — my friend Saffron needs help searching the realms for Ny and the soul he has stolen. If you could escort her on her journey, read for portals, use magic when required — that would be a big help in getting our realm back in order."

Wo, the one whose suspicions started early on, was still calculating. "How long is this going to take?"

"What does it matter; where are *you* going?" Tai muttered. There was pain in his voice, a weariness that humbled him — Saffron liked him a little better.

Kuzih ran up to Li, her round cheeks red with exertion. "Here it is." She handed Li a rolled-up bit of leather. It looked old and extremely used. The edges were frayed and, it appeared, bitten-off in some areas. Some spots around the middle were smudged and indecipherable.

"You know," said Saffron, "you should take that..." she indicated the weary, ancient-looking map, "...to Kinko's and get it copied before it falls apart completely." She nodded knowingly at her wise words.

The three fairies hunched over the map looked mildly annoyed. They ignored her.

"Come, Saffron — let us review this map of the known realms with Wo and Tai."

The four of them squished and squashed over to the large boulder where Li lovingly laid out the map.

Saffron strained to peer over Tai's shoulder, as he stood right in front of the map, hogging everyone's view. Li took him by the shoulders and pressed him aside.

Saffron moved closer, stared at the map, and sucked her breath. "Oh," she mumbled, "*that's* why you can't take it to Kinko's."

The picture on the map — the map itself — wouldn't stay still. The crude, wavy lines that indicated ocean or water, rolled gently. One-dimensional clouds moved across the top.

"Watch," Li breathed, and called out, "The Opleenrealm!"

Every line on the map shifted all at once, except for the clouds (which momentarily remained still). Then suddenly, there on the map, lay a land full of very few roads and very many ponds.

"That, Saffron is how you summon a realm on a fairy map." Li smiled down at her serenely, with a little bit of haughty thrown in for good measure.

"Li...I don't know how to call out for a realm on a fairy map...because I don't know the names of *any* realms." Saffron sniped.

Li reached out to rub Saffron's back, and smooth her hair. "The twins, Saffron, they will summon the known realms for you."

For the next hour, Li pointed to certain realms where she felt Ny might have taken Markis. She also pointed out realms that the three should avoid, or at least, save as the last possible option. She warned them that although the fairies knew of these outer realms, no one fairy knew much about any of them.

Saffron huffed. "Well, what if we search one realm, and Ny is, like, always one realm ahead of us? What if he's always one realm behind us? I mean, it's not likely he's just sitting somewhere, right? If he's always on the move, how the hell are we supposed to find him?"

Tai snorted. "Yeah, right. He's in one spot. Lazy ass."

Li looked deep into Saffron's eyes for a very long time before she answered; her large black pupils held Saffron frozen in time and space. The fairies that were around them stilled, as silent as a ladybug slumbering on a leaf. "Saffron, it is easier to try, than to prove it cannot be done." When she blinked, a low buzz of animation came back to the glade. "Now, Saffron, even though you do not have your human body in tow, it does not mean you are invincible. There are ways to destroy a soul — two that I know of.... There may be more ways in these different worlds. You must stand guard for yourself; always be ready so as not to be taken, destroyed, or misdirected." Her eyes shifted over to stare at the twins who, after the map reading had stopped and Li's words of wisdom began, had splashed off in a sudden fit of boredom and were now tossing a bleating wood elf back and forth like a flailing-limbed football. Wo dropped the elf on the last pass, and before Tai could grab him beneath the muck, the elf jumped to his feet and shook his fist as Tai descended upon him, made a grasp for him, and narrowly missed. Then, before Saffron could blink, the elf disappeared into the murky water and was gone. Li sighed, "Take care of my mischievous little friends."

Saffron frowned, *this better not turn into a big ol' babysitting expedition; I have enough to worry about. If they can't take care of themselves, what good are they?* She crossed her arms over her chest and glared at the two who were now, side by side, swinging from a tree limb by their knees and crossing their eyes at her. "Yeah, well, I'd love to stay and chit chat, but I have a friend I have to go look for."

"A moment, Saffron, a last word, if you please...." Li beckoned Saffron to her side as she drew an object from her gossamer robes, which fluttered in the restless wind that stirred the entire forest. "This is a timepiece." It was a metal ball engraved with odd symbols. Li popped open the small globe and held the palm-sized clock before Saffron.

Quite near, lightning touched down and momentarily bleached the woods. Only seconds later, an ear-splitting crack of thunder shook the earth. Saffron clutched her arms around herself and frowned; this whole scene was getting too creepy. She locked her eyes on the timepiece and forced herself to concentrate, just so she could get the hell out.

It appeared to be even older than the parchment, with a bronze face and silver back that had blackened with time. The etchings in the metal, which were exquisitely detailed and abundant, had all been just about filled in by the build-up.

"It will tell you how much time has gone by in the world you know as your home. It will show you the minutes here, the hours here, the days and years here...." Li let her voice trail off. She didn't point out the section that counted off the decades, and the other section that kept track of the centuries — not after the look of horror that crossed Saffron's face.

When Li said, 'the years,' Saffron felt her chest clench like it was in a vise. She raised her hand to her mouth as if to stop her heart from popping out. Then she took a deep, forced breath through flared nostrils and said, "No, Li — it won't take years. I'm telling you right now — it will not take years." She gritted her teeth and stared at the fairy. "My mother and Derek, Coco — they're all going to be looking for me. My mother is probably wondering right now, this very second, if Markis and I are 'getting it on' in the woods. She's going to come storming through the woods to find me pretending to be berry picking. If this takes twenty-four hours, even if we're gone for two days, I'm going to have a hard enough time explaining myself, but that's fine — I'll deal with it. But Markis and I *cannot* go missing for years!"

Li smiled sadly. "You know, you may be right. Now that I ponder, I am sure that Ny wants you to come after him — he will want to be found. Maybe it will not take so long as I originally feared."

Saffron grabbed the timepiece from Li's hands. Li gently took it back, grasped Saffron's wrist, and wound the long, golden cord trailing from the piece around and around again. The timepiece itself fit through a finishing hole and, voila, Saffron had a new necklace or bracelet she didn't care much for.

"And who will be in charge of this?" Li stretched out her long, lithe, white arm. In her palm was a small, flat, circular piece of glass."

Saffron looked down her nose at the piece and pulled her head back like a nervous horse. "What is that?" She clasped her hands behind her back.

Wo snatched the glass piece out of Li's hand and put it up to his eye, securing it between his eyebrow and his cheek. He squinted his other eye. "That's a monocle, Luv. All the better to see you with!" He pinched Saffron in the rear-end.

She squawked and slapped his hand away.

"That…" Li affixed a chain from the monocle to Tai's lederhosen bib, "…will enable you to see a portal." She stroked Tai's hair and bent to kiss him on the tip of his nose. "Please behave. And although you can communicate with your brother telepathically, please have respect for our Saffron and speak out loud."

Tai started to slosh away. Wo looked at Saffron and tilted his head, indicating she should follow.

Li wrung her hands. "Remember — though most realms have the energy to support magic, you must guard against it. Magic is not…legal — it will not be accepted without backlash…."

"Yeah, yeah — we know," Tai grunted without turning around. "Confucius say balance in all things, yeah — can we go now?"

Wo blinked and slapped a wet frond out of his way. "Who's this Confucius?'

"It's this dude, a proclaimer that the humans are all rabid about."

Saffron wrinkled her nose. "Confucius is dead — he died, like, a million years ago…?"

Tai shoved her in the shoulder. "Duh!" But he didn't look too sure of himself now.

There was genuine worry in Li's voice when she yelled, "Saffron, you must sleep. You must rest your soul from time to time!" Saffron could hardly hear Li because Tai and Wo had linked arms, and were already flying her away.

"Why do I have to sleep?"

"Oh, we'll tell you later, babe. Shet your yap, now." Tai winked at her.

"No. You tell me right now!" Saffron spat, and tried to yank her arm from Tai's grasp. The twins ignored her.

"Crap!" Wo did not fit the majestic and enchanting title of 'fairy' or 'winged child,' when he said, 'crap.'

"What?" Tai howled with laughter at Wo saying, 'crap.'

"Where are we going, Tai?"

"Hell, man, I don't know — I thought you knew!"

Wo sighed, "Turn around everybody, we're headed back."

"What? ....Oh fantastic! How are *you* two supposed to help me search 'several hundred realms'?"

"Keep your panties on lady — we just need a starting point."

Saffron glared at Tai. He was *so* rude!

Several streaks of lightning ripped through the sky behind him, casting him in an eerie light.

Saffron instantly felt nervous as he shrieked like a maniac.

They landed in front of Li. She answered their question before they asked. "The caves in New Mexico."

"Come on, Daffy Saffy," Tai sang out and grasped the belt loop on the backside of Saffron's jeans.

Wo gently took her arm. The trio shot into the sky.

"Wah – what? What the hell are you doing?" Saffron was spitting-cat-mad as they gained altitude.

"I am whisking you away, oh, great lady, to the portal of your dreams!"

"Listen, ass — you're not carrying me from portal to portal by my belt loop! And why the hell are my jeans going up my rear if I'm only a soul. Why can I still feel this? Why can I feel everything? This is so aggravating!"

"Now, now, Luv — calm down. Of course you can feel everything. Your soul is working on autopilot. You don't need your body to experience physical sensations — you've got the *memory* of your body within your soul. It's kind of like 'phantom pain', you know, when people lose a limb — an arm or a leg — they swear they can still feel pain in the missing limb."

"Ah, yeah — I was told this already! I was also told it would go away! When is it going to go away?"

"When are you going to let it go?" Tai yanked her wedgie higher. Saffron roared.

The wind pressed Wo's baby curls flat. "Be careful, Saffron. It's not safe to hold onto these memories of physical feeling. If you think someone has chopped your arm off, you'll really lose it, if that's what you believe."

"And by the way, Saffron," Tai elbowed her hard, so that she went sliding into Wo, "we aren't going to make you feel all dopey like the fairies did on your other rides to our realm. It takes energy to give you such a comfy ride, and, sorry but, I'm using all of my energy to get around — no cushy, cushy, here." He smirked.

Wo shrugged and continued to fly her straight ahead.

"And why did you call me that stupid nickname? How do you know that name? Don't call me that *ever* again!"

"Saffron, we know *a lot* about you!"

Tai's smile was so ugly, Saffron was afraid Ny had broadcast their filthy relationship for the whole world. Had he? Saffron wanted to shrivel up and die. She looked over her shoulder at Wo.

He nodded and raised his eyebrows twice in confirmation.

She wasn't too thrilled to be strapped to these arrogant little punks. Maybe she shouldn't have complained and just done this with Li. Who knew there could be fairies more annoying than Mother-Hubbard-loving-smothering, Li? "Great." She lowered her eyebrows and sulked all the way to New Mexico.

Chapter 9

They arrived at Bandelier National Monument half an hour later, as the sun was setting. They landed on ground that ran along the top of a red clay cliff. Two hikers were coming along the path, straight for them. The hikers startled Saffron. She gasped, then hurried to back out of their way as they came tromping by in their expensive hiking boots, the woman limping as if she had a nasty blister.

"They don't know you're there, Saffron. Man, are you ever jumpy. The humans in the Earthrealm cannot see us." Tai flicked her shoulder. "Well, most of 'em anyway."

"How am I supposed to know that?" She wanted to hit him, so badly. "*I* could see you when *I* was in my human body," this came from Saffron in a 'nah, nah' sing song voice.

"Well, I guess you're special then. Watch this...." Tai jumped five feet in front of the hikers. Suddenly, his soul appeared to solidify, wings and all. The woman hiker screamed and pointed straight at Tai while grasping at the shirt of her companion. By the time the man looked up, Tai had disappeared. All the man saw was empty space. "What?! What is it?"

While the woman began to gush about the angel that was just *right there*(!), Tai walked away from them and flipped Saffron the bird. He grumbled as he walked past her, then started down the path that would lead them into the valley. As Tai passed Wo, he poked him in the shoulder then screamed out in girly glee, "Oooooh! An Angel! Hah, my foot!" He held himself while he laughed; as if the force of the hilarity would topple him off the edge. "I *love it* when they call us, 'angel'."

"Should we scale that cliff ?" Wo pointed up.

Tai knew in general where the cave was, but not exactly where it was. Li would have known exactly where the cave was. Why wasn't she here taking care of this redheaded Banshee? His soul was relatively new — he was only one hundred and fifty years old after all — and his insight, as well as Wo's, was somewhat limited compared to the ancients. When Li volunteered them for this quest, he was all for it. After all, they had never lived a life outside of the Fairyrealm. They had taken some tours, of course, but had never lived a life in any human realm.

But now, he wondered, was this girl always going to be such a pain? Didn't she ever smile? Did she never *ever* stop complaining and being altogether a total drag? He knew her soul was just as old as Li's, maybe even older, why should she regress so much in human form? Again, these were questions Li would have answers for, but he had none. He likened becoming human to intoxication — souls regressed into dimwits.

Tai and Wo decided not to scale the first cliff. The three of them formed a single line to move down the narrow trail, first Tai, then Saffron, then Wo. Tai looked up at Wo as they passed each other on the switchback — Wo was a little irritated, too. When they first landed, they mentally agreed that they were done carrying Saffron. If she wouldn't give up her earthbound inclinations, then she would walk. He huffed; she was about as stupid as a fish jogging in water. They could travel faster by flying, but they assumed it would be some time before they could convince Saffron that her soul could fly — so convinced, so stubborn was she, and smug in her assumption that she was incapable of flight. Tai thought that Saffron would not allow herself to believe she could fly. The twins were not going to carry her about like the queen of Sheba. Their journey, at the outset, would be slow. And what did he care about time? Nothing. She was the one bitching about rushing, and here she was – walking when she could fly. A smile tickled under Tai's tongue. He struggled not to laugh as a fantasy formed in his little, black, mischievous heart. Saffron wouldn't learn new tricks very quickly. She wouldn't let go of her old memories without a fight either — her kind never did. With any luck, her soul would remember — in crystal-clear detail — what it would feel like to get a big fat blister on her toe. Tai let the smile fly free for a moment, then frowned. No, she had better not get a blister — he would have to listen to her complaining, probably for days, or until her soul assumed enough healing time had passed and the wound vanished.

They arrived at the bottom of the canyon. There were only a few tourists left, milling about the dry, dusty, canyon floor. They were over at the far end of the long cliff, about to end their day's sightseeing. Wo, Tai, and Saffron gazed up at the red rock cliff in awe. From where they stood, it looked as though hundreds of holes — some as tiny as pin pricks, some as big as manhole covers and bigger — were either carved out of the rock or formed naturally.

"Once, hundreds of years ago, some of these holes were the *homes* of the Anasazi people." Wo turned his head to inspect the canyon that opened wide around them, then he looked back at the cliff and spoke again. "This cliff is actually the lava from an ancient volcano. A river ran through here, eroding the lava and creating this cliff. Since this lava is not as hard as rock, the people were able to scoop it out and create their homes. See," Wo pointed to a hole, about the size of a car door, that had to be at least three stories above them, "even that was somebody's home."

Standing in the shadow of the cliff, Saffron gazed up at the hole that Wo pointed out. She wondered how mothers took care of toddlers up there, how often did they walk out the front door and fall off the cliff? Quickly, she looked down at her feet; just thinking of living up there was giving her vertigo. "How do you know all of that, Wo? Are you, like, a history buff or something?"

Wo stared at her in confusion. "I asked the trees...."

Saffron's eyes flashed. *That's right; the trees are conscious....* She looked nervously around her and saw a short tree several yards up on the cliff. Its limbs were long and gnarled. It had leaves at its branch tips and leaned sideways from being pushed by the endless winds that roared through the canyon. She had a sudden vision of the tree – a twisted face in the center of its trunk — uprooting itself and walking towards her. She shivered and decided to never carve or otherwise hurt another tree again.

They walked farther along the path and, as they made their way down and around corners, more and more holes appeared in the cliffside. Leading up to some of the holes were ladders made of trees, placed there so that the tourists could inspect the insides of the caves.

"Why are we just walking around here?" Saffron stopped suddenly and narrowed her eyes at the twins. "You don't know where it is, do you? I was worried that we might not be able to find Markis once we got beyond the portal, not that *you wouldn't even be able to find the portal!*"

"Of course, we can find the portal!" Tai snapped. "We just need time to concentrate and we won't be able to concentrate if you keep up your bitchin'! What do you think the portal is? An amusement park ride?" Tai started to shriek like a strung-out circus ringmaster, "Come one, come all; come vampires, come werewolves, come all black witches and wizards, come aliens, come psychotic humans who, for some reason got their mental wires crossed and are able to see magical things! Come into the flashing portal! It's right here! It's right in front of your face! It's easily accessible to you all, so you can go right through and pollute, annihilate, conquer, destroy, and enslave the outer realms!" Tai had been throwing his arms around as he screamed, but now they finally hung limp at his sides as he breathed heavily and shot daggers at Saffron with his bulging eyes.

Saffron sniffed. "Angel, you have an attitude problem." Then she yelled, "Just put your damn spyglass on and *hurry up!*" Then muttered under her breath, "Angel, my ass, that stupid hiker thought she saw an angel — try ungodly, beastly twerp!" Saffron was suddenly crestfallen. *My God, is that what people see when they think they see angels?* Saffron eyed Tai in horror as he picked his nose and concentrated intently on his find. *Angel!* "Blek, he's so freaken' gross."

"I heard that!" Tai made some kind of gesture at her with his fingers. It didn't look very nice.

Saffron whipped her head away from him and stared forward.

Both twins turned their backs on her and scrutinized another section of cliff. This part of the cliff was cut into more deeply by the long-since-dried-up river. The nook was so deep it appeared to be in perpetual shadow. There were a number of holes within it, and it was on these that the twins concentrated.

Several yards away, Saffron sat on a smooth, flat rock, and was suddenly startled by the scream of a hawk. She shaded her eyes with her hand to search for him in the deep, azure sky that was void of clouds from one end to the other. Before she could locate the bird, she heard a strange twitter, and looked down to see a squirrel with odd, pointy, black ears as it streaked past her. She picked up a smooth pebble and rolled it back and forth between her hands.

So, this was where Markis came from, where he went to live every summer. His father was Irish, but his mother was Native American. When they had all met at the movie theater, Saffron decided it was his mother that Markis most physically resembled.

Her back and neck began to ache. She curled up into a ball, rested her forehead on her knees, and wrapped her arms around her shins. *This is insane. How am I ever going to do this? I'm never going to find him.... What if it really does take a long time? But it's not like I can go back without him – I'd die of worry and guilt. I have no choice.* Slowly, she rocked herself back and forth.

The hawk screamed again and startled her. She shaded her eyes and looked up.

"You don't have to block the sun from your eyes like that, you know." Wo had flown up beside her. It's just your memory tricking you to feel the pain of the blinding light. If you let yourself, you'll feel all kinds of physical sensations, but they won't be real. You could feel a whole range of physical reactions or you could feel nothing — it'll be your choice. You could concentrate; you can learn to not let yourself feel the physical. It would probably be best for our journey...who knows what will happen to us?"

Saffron scoffed, "You know, I just don't get that. It's ridiculous!"

Wo raised his eyebrows. "Just try."

She took a deep breath, huffed it out, and concentrated. *I will not let the light blind me. I will not let the light blind me.* Slowly, she lowered her hand, looked up wide-eyed at the sky...and yelped when the direct sunlight shot her straight into her eyeballs and speared the back of her brain like a pulse of fire. It caused an instant headache. "Ahhhhhh, now I'm blinded! I've got spots in my eyes!"

Wo stared at her, looking very embarrassed, not being used to such human drollness. "There's something else. You need to learn how to make your body appear solid."

Saffron shook her head as she ground her fists into her eyes. What did *that* mean? She hugged her arms to herself and rubbed them hard. She felt the hug, her elbows pointing into the palms of her hands, the fine down as she rubbed her forearms. She shook her head again. "I *am* solid. I can feel my arms. I'm sitting on the ground; I can feel the pressure against my butt."

Wo crouched down and made Saffron's eyes meet his own large, dark pupils. He held out his hands, beseeching her to understand. "Saffron, that's your memory again. You are feeling the memory of what is most comfortable to you. You need to have the ground push you from below and you need to feel your body beneath your hands, so, you do. But really, it's just a memory." He pressed his lips and shrugged. "Actually, that rock is so hot right now, you would've jumped off it with your human body...."

"Nuh uh."

"Oh, yeah. I'm serious."

Despite the dry desert heat, a sharp chill raced down Saffron's spine. "What are you trying to say? You mean my soul, right? I'm a spirit now — I know that."

"But there's more to it than that. Really, Saffron, that doesn't mean much to you, does it? 'A soul' — I'm trying to tell you what that means."

"Then tell me!" she snapped. She knew it wasn't his intention but he was making her excruciatingly edgy.

Wo frowned and scratched his temples with both hands. He wasn't cut out for this — explaining the laws of his world to a mind that was incapable of understanding. "You'll need to learn how to solidify yourself. When you do, you'll be like...like a movie."

Saffron's eyebrows shot up. She focused over his left shoulder and spoke in a far off voice. "A movie."

"Well, to other people, you'll be like a movie. Yeah..." he nodded fervently, "this is how I'll explain it to you. I'll tell you how others will perceive you." He clapped his hands together once and looked at her intently. "You'll be like film. Once you learn to be solid, that is. People will accept your existence because they can see you and touch you. Like an actual piece of film, you'll have substance. But there is another way in which you are like film." He faltered; he was afraid this next would further disturb her. "Like a film being played," he poked on slowly, "people will see you in front of them – they'll be able to see you just as they can watch a person in a movie. BUT! If they touch you, it'll be like touching the character on the screen — they won't be able to feel your tears, your heat.... If you bleed, they would not be able to tend your wounds. Do you see what I mean? They will feel nothing but the solid shape you put on for them."

Saffron didn't react as he expected. She frowned, but she did not appear shocked. And she didn't throw her usual hissy fit. She was still looking over his shoulder at some hikers that had stopped and made a picnic for themselves — two girls about Saffron's age. One of them sat on a horse blanket, wiping sweat from her brow with a handkerchief. Saffron began to sweat. She squinted at the desert sun as it hung over the trench, casting half of the cliff wall in dark shadow. She wiped her brow with the back of her arm. "Why will I be like film?"

Wo fell back to the ground. "This is what it is to be a soul. I don't know how to better explain. You'll just have to see as we go along." *Why.* He had no idea why! "Now, when we go to these realms, the inhabitants — they'll think you....they'll think you're a ghost. You must trick them; you must show them a solid front. You are going to have to learn to concentrate and summon a solid appearance. We wouldn't want the hostile locals calling out their wise men to exorcise us, now, do we?"

Saffron shrugged. "Who cares if they do? I can run okay. I'm not in bad shape."

Wo stood up and looked down at her. His eyes were soft and patient. Exercise, exorcise...for the love of trees, he had a long way to go with this one. "If we scare the inhabitants of these realms, we may be chased out before Tai and I can feel the land properly for our missing boys. Their magic can cause us pain, Saffron. We'll feel their incantations like an electrical shock. Ever been electrified?"

In fact, Saffron had been electrified, and she winced at the memory. When she was a toddler, her mother was always hiding the car keys out of reach. Saffron wanted those car keys in the worst way. One morning, Audrey left them on the counter by a cooling loaf of bread. Saffron was four. She had grabbed one of the kitchen chairs and hauled it to the counter to get at the delicious-smelling bread. Her fat, baby body made the chair creak as she quickly pulled herself up to stand on the seat. But what was this? Keys! Keys or bread, bread or keys? Saffron snatched the keys and wobbled up the stairs to her room. She tried the keys in the keyhole on her antique bureau. She tried the keys in the metal buckle on her overalls. She tried the keys in her doll's mouth. She looked at the electrical outlet. *That* hole was just the right size. After that, Saffron only remembered a loud pop and her mother slamming into the room and screaming. Now, Saffron had a healthy fear of electric shocks.

Wo clapped his hands again, making a sharp, crisp sound to snap her from her memories. "So now, Saffron, concentrate and imagine yourself solid."

Saffron blinked several times, frowned, and concentrated. "Okay, whatever you say." She closed her eyes and held her breath. She scrunched her eyes up tight and puffed up her cheeks.

"No, no, Saffron. You don't have to asphyxiate yourself; just concentrate."

Saffron groaned and tried again, breathing this time.

And this time, Wo saw a change come over her — a subtle sign that only he could recognize. He fluttered his wings and rose slowly in the air. He watched, amazed, as Saffron struggled harder to clearly define her lines.

Suddenly, a rock larger than a man's fist sailed through the air, right at Saffron. It went through her body and landed with a dull thud just behind her, scaring off a small lizard that had been sunning his leathery body. The girls on the horse blanket looked up from their Snapples.

"Hey, Wo! Aren't you teaching that chick to become solid yet?" Tai was standing on a ledge on the cliff, several stories up, and screaming down to them. Tourists strolled leisurely all around them, unaware. "Next time I throw a rock at you, lady, it better bounce off!"

"What the hell?" Saffron shrieked and jumped to her feet. The mirage that had almost become her solid body shimmered away. "You could've killed me!"

"Oh, gimme a break, you moron!" His monocle fell out as he chucked her the bird.

Wo rolled his eyes, then landed beside Saffron and took her hand. "Come on; let's go. He's more than his usual cocky self. I think he must've found the portal." He tried to lead her along, but she yanked her hand from his grip and used it to shield the glare of the sun. She was shaking, and there was murder in her eyes. "You do know he's an ass, right? I mean, why do you hang around with him? He's such a jerk." Then she mumbled something about 'throwing freakin' rocks.'

Wo stopped walking and spun around. "I would never leave him. He's part of me." Wo looked up at the ledge to find Tai dropping wildflowers on the tourists' heads.

Every time he threw one down, a tourist jumped in shock and looked up at the empty cliffs. He howled with glee. "Hey, ya see that? That dude's gonna go home and tell everyone the spirits of ancient Indians were showering him with flowers!" He cackled as he rolled off the cliff. He stopped in mid-fall and fluttered back up to his ledge. He almost choked when he landed. There, towering above him, was an Indian spirit, hands on his hips, staring down as cold and still as a tombstone. Tai stayed down where he was, hands and knees in the dirt, and muttered, "Sorry." The Indian vanished before he looked up.

One corner of Wo's mouth turned down. "Ass, that he is."

Chapter 10

They were spinning. Spinning from belly, to shoulder, to back, to shoulder, to belly — and tumbling forward head over heels. Saffron retched, dry-heaved and screamed. Tai kept yelling for her to 'shut the hell up,' and Wo was chanting low, like a yogi. Everything was grey and loud and shiny. Saffron could feel her film self rippling like a skydiver in accelerated freefall. Suddenly they shot out into wide open air.

They crash-landed in the middle of a dusty, broken street. The deserted buildings that surrounded them on all sides were smashed in and half burned. There was dust and dirt everywhere, and debris slapped around in the wind. The whole place looked war-torn. As a matter of fact, the war was *currently* in session.

Saffron heard the rat-tat-tat-tat of an automatic weapon. Instantly, she stopped moaning over her bashed behind and jumped to her feet. She looked around and saw squat buildings — broken and vacant, signs full of holes, junk flying about — all washed in a dirty, sepia light. The twins flew in the air like hummingbirds, and looked around with disbelief. They didn't care if the inhabitants could see them, and they didn't care if the inhabitants could see they were flying. They were ready to *flee*.

"Oh...." Was all Wo could say as he took in the destruction.

Not one of them noticed the man crouched behind the pillar over in the shadows. But, he had certainly noticed them. He stared at Tai and Wo as they fluttered on the wind — the same wind that carried the sounds of weapons, the click-clack of spent shells, and the smells of acrid metal and burning flesh.

The man watched the girl with the puffy red hair stand in the middle of the street. She seemed confused, lost, and as beautiful as a porcelain doll. She didn't fly like the two boys in the weird pants. Her expressions alternated between fear at the sounds of gunshots and annoyance as the twins buzzed like flies around her head.

He grumbled to himself as he ran his hand up over his forehead, dragging thick, dark hair back from his temples. What to do? Leave them there to get shot down like ducks, or prod their ignorant behinds to shelter? There was another explosion but the boys still hung suspended, their wings vibrating like busy bees, and the girl still stood there, gawking.

Finally, *he* couldn't take anymore and stood, ready to move forward towards the girl. Then he stopped himself and crouched back into the shadows. He'd be an idiot to run out there. He waved his hand at her, and hoped she would see him out of the corner of her eye. But she just stood there, like an animal that has never seen the sun. She'd get struck down any second now.

They were slaughtering everything in this land — men, women, children, and livestock without preference. He was baffled to frustration, *why* was she just standing there? She had appeared from nowhere. They had materialized in the air, and tumbled onto the street. By *now* you'd think they would have figured out that they were in a hostile place and would take cover!

He stood again, groaned, then bent over with a concentrated frown and moved forward. He skittered over to her, crouching so low his knuckles grazed the ground as he moved, a rifle slung across his back.

Saffron watched, stunned as the man came out from behind a very

Roman-looking pillar and moved towards her. He was lumbering through the haze like a pre-historic human. Did the people here not know how to walk upright? Was her tenth-grade science teacher correct in stating one little change in the environment and Man would not have mastered bipedalism? She watched him gimping along and felt bad for him. Her eyes widened as she quelled the urge to pat his head. She bit her bottom lip and stared at him. The twins looked down on him from above as they hovered, and cast doleful glances at their surroundings.

"Fireball, I don't know where you just came from, but let me welcome you. Welcome! Now — get down, take cover, or get shot in the head!"

Saffron stared down at him without blinking. The twins stared at him some more. *Was* that how they walked in this realm?

"Aaahhhk." The man grasped Saffron's arm, looked at her in shock, and started pulling her towards a house with its rear-quarter caved in.

The moment he grabbed her, she suddenly snapped awake and began to make hissing and growling sounds. "Hey...HEY! Get your hands offa me!"

He threw her arm back at her side and absently wiped his palm on his torn pants. "Okay, little bird. Fly away — go die." He saw her eyes flash and her nostrils flare like she was a bull seeing red. In fact, the look she gave him was just like the look the invaders gave just before they gored people — the invaders that were swarming in the shadows all around them.

Saffron wanted to punch him right in the mouth, right now — this crouching man she didn't know but suddenly despised, all the same. She despised him because of another "man," Jethin, who had very recently told her the same thing — to go die. Saffron was quickly on her way to becoming bitter towards men. Her future rolled out before her eyes: she would be an old woman and live alone with her ten cats — like a properly disenchanted old lady.

The man caught movement out of the corner of his eye. It was off to the right, behind a creaking door that barely hung on its hinges. This time, he grabbed Saffron around the waist (and gasped in shock again), and carted her off. Her feet dragged as he took her inside the broken house across the street. He assumed her flying pets would follow her.

A single bullet grazed past Wo's ear, and, as he looked around in confusion, Tai quickly flew after the man who had taken Saffron.

Wo followed quickly. "Wow!" He was beaming. "I've never gone to see a war before! Hey, Saffron. Look at you, you're solid!"

Tai gave Wo a cocky grin. "Wo, you're all giddy and stuff — look at you. I think we've failed our undercover operation in this whack-job realm. You got anything ta eat?" Tai rubbed his belly as he stared expectantly at the man. "Puppies? Kittens? Bunnies...bwahahahaha!"

The man looked around the house at the smashed pottery, shot-up walls, tipped-over furniture and blood-spattered floor. Then he looked deadpan at Tai and said nothing.

Saffron smiled when she realized Wo was right — the strange man had gotten his hands around her and had carted her around like a sack of grain! Too thrilling! Wo watched her reaction and flew over to her. He clasped her hands in his as he beamed. She grinned back.

The man narrowed his eyes and looked at all three from under his lowered brow. He was trying to save them from being shot and one of them was asking to eat baby animals, and the other two were rejoicing, because *she was solid*.... This war had turned his brain to mush – only delirium would explain this scene. He lowered himself to the cracked, wooden floor strewed with broken things — photo frames, crockery, papers, and a doll that lay ripped and face-down in a grey puddle.

Saffron sat, too, and swallowed hard as she hugged her knees to her chest. Pleasant shock flew from her ribs like a released dove and was replaced with a knot of frightened shock. There was blood on the floor. It was lumpy and congealed. Now that she had focused on it, she couldn't take her eyes away from it.

The man spoke. "Sorry I was rude out there; I really thought you were going to get it. You wouldn't *move*. You're a stubborn gal, aren't you?"

"You're a classy guy, aren't you, telling people to go off and die...." Saffron stared at the man, then looked away in disgust. Disgusted at him for what he said, and disgusted at herself for not wanting to look away from his eyes when he looked at her like he was looking at her right now. Behind the fall of dark hair, and behind the dirt on his face, she'd captured and held great, big, hazel eyes that dazzled like kaleidoscopes. Geometric shards of green, blue, and yellow shimmered in different tones, depending on the way he tilted his head. She realized she was leaning towards him and puffed out her cheeks as she moved away.

"What's going on around here, anyway?" Tai poked his head out the window, then whipped it back in when a bullet zinged by. "Oooo-we! Testy!" He laughed whole-heartedly. These Neanderthals couldn't hurt him with their pop guns.

"If you mean, what's the war about — I can give you two versions. The invaders say the war is about their alien, who, they claim, is the one, true leader and should be revered by all. The people of this land say their alien is the one, true leader and creator and will hold on to their beliefs and their system of worship — they will not be bullied. Blah, blah, blah.... The real fight is over power. The real fight is between bunches of men acting like spoiled three-year-olds because the boy on the other side of the play-circle has more toys — toys neither party really cares about — but toys that both parties don't want the other to *have*. That is why the rest of us get to be shot down to drown in a pool of our own blood."

Saffron was still staring at the man, but forced herself to look at his dirty hands, not his eyes. His feet were drawn up, his hands dangled over his knees. "Do you guys, like, believe in God?"

The man had been looking out the broken window, but now he locked his eyes on her again.

As soon as he did, she blinked, and looked up to meet his gaze. She felt her spine melt away.

"There are no such things as gods, hothead. There are only aliens and this mess of a world they created. Pfft, gods — there has been no serious talk of gods since ancient times." He studied her as if she were a criminal. "Where did you come from anyway?"

"From Earth."

Wo sucked his breath in and stared horrified at Saffron.

Tai slapped his knee. "Wow, Saffron — your mouth is like, padlock-tight, isn't it? Why don't we all just go back now? This is our first realm, and we've flubbed it royally. Do you really think we can survive with our record?" He looked from Wo, to Saffron, then back to Wo. "C'mon. This is ridiculous."

The man's eyes had widened — he sat up straighter. "The Earthrealm?" His rough voice was barely audible. He let his hands drop to the floor with a thud while he looked away from Saffron once more.

Saffron couldn't believe this. The twins told her none of the beings they were to meet would likely know about Earth, that Earth was a totally sheltered realm, as the humans contained within were not ready for *the truth*. That they would likely kill themselves off in fear of the unknown, rather than believe — so they were kept sheltered. But, Saffron could tell this man was well aware of Earth. 'The Earthrealm' as he had put it. She watched him pull his fingers till his knuckles popped. He looked devastated. Her voice was hesitant. "You know about the realms?"

Tai's voice filled the inside of Saffron's head. "Shut up." She slapped at her ear as if to catch a mosquito.

The man didn't say anything. For a long time, no one spoke. They listened to the guns and the screams, and the sound of the fight fading, as if it were moving off to the next block.

Finally, "What are you doing here?" The man croaked the sentence out, still staring at the wall, ignoring Saffron's comment about him knowing about the Earthrealm.

"I...I'm searching. The soul of my boy...friend...was taken by one of their kind." She pointed towards Tai and Wo. "I need to find him." She was mumbling again. "It's my fault he's gone." As an afterthought she blurted out, "Their world is being destroyed. It's my fault — though I didn't know it — and I have to get those souls back to correct the balance."

The man snorted. "What balance?"

"The balance of souls to nature," Saffron quoted.

Another noise of incredulity from the man. "That's just an old fairy tale. People realm-hop from here all of the time – it's no big deal, and it doesn't upset the balance between souls and nature." He gave her a chastening look.

Saffron's cheeks burned as her eyes widened. Her mouth dropped open. "Duh! Look around, dude, your world is about as balanced as a see-saw being ridden by a fat man and his right shoe!"

A loud crack, followed by a deafening crash, caused her to slam her mouth shut and push herself tightly into the corner. Then a bomb exploded far off in the distance, but close enough to make them all to jump.

"I can help you," the man said quickly.

"Saffron," Tai flew to her side, "I don't think we need any help." He gave her a warning look and shook his head.

"I don't think we need any help," Saffron repeated to the man.

"Oh, I see. So, you all have experience you need to go realm-hopping?"

Wo shot a frantic look at Tai. Tai frowned and shook his head. "The help we need isn't from you. We need Saffron to shut her yap."

Saffron scrambled to her feet. "You two were the morons that left your wings exposed!"

The man scrutinized Wo, then glared at Tai. He smirked. "Say, boys, does your gal here know the danger she's in, traveling with you?"

Wo groaned. Tai spit in the corner, then narrowed his eyes on the dirty man.

Saffron shrugged. "We've been briefed about how dangerous the other realms can be...."

The man looked sly as his eyes roved back and forth over the fairies. He nodded at Saffron. "Ah, yeah – have you been warned of specific danger? Of danger because of them?" He thumbed Tai and Wo.

Saffron frowned. "Why? Just because I'm with them?"

The man kept looking at the twins. The twins remained silent.

Now, Saffron looked at the twins. "What's he talking about?"

Tai slapped his leg. "Yeah, it's true, okay? Bet you wish you hadn't pushed Li away like you did, because now you're with two mostly inexperienced fairies. And everyone knows, most of the world despises fairies."

"What?" Saffron whispered. A shower of bullets whizzed outside. She ducked automatically.

"Fairies have the most powerful magic and other beings are jealous!" Tai puffed out his chest with pride.

"Because fairies steal souls — the souls of infants." The man added with an eyebrow raised.

"Because fairies have the best kind of magic." Wo put in softly.

"Because fairies antagonize and cheat." The man said bluntly.

"Well, well, Sir — you are just as prejudiced as everyone else — would you like a medal?" Tai flew to the window, which encouraged a sniper to rip into his ghostly form. He wouldn't turn around. He vanished just before the bullets sailed through him and peppered the already-deteriorating wall.

"Prejudiced?" How bad could things get?

Wo patted her hand. "Pretend we're in the Deep South in the nineteenth century." Wo pointed to Tai then to his own chest. "We're black and you're the pink virgin we're dating — simultaneously."

Saffron gasped. That bad. Instantly, she panicked. "Well, how are we supposed to get around with everybody hating you...us?"

Tai shrugged, kept his back to them. "Pretend we're something we're not," he mumbled, "like people always do in this instance."

"Oh." Saffron's voice had grown small. Inside, her blood gelled and began to quiver.

"C'mon, now, boys — be truthful. People don't despise you for the color of your anything. As a matter of fact, in this instance, the prejudice is justified because your actions are real." The man leveled hard eyes on Saffron. "In the Earthrealm, fairies are revered. At one time, on a green island, they were even put up on the same pedestals as gods — but not outside the Earthrealm."

Tai whipped around. "Get off it, drama queen. We'll cover our wings, solidify our bodies, curb our magic — we'll be fine." He looked to Saffron, his eyes hard. "We'll be *fine*."

Saffron hugged herself. *This is for Markis. Your body is safe, far away. No one can really hurt you. Just remember that, no one can really hurt you unless you believe they've hurt you. Well, you can get electrocuted... And what else? Nevermind that — you need to find Markis. You can't go back without him.* She nodded empty-eyed and vacant, like a bobblehead doll.

"You need me," the man pressed, "for when a fairy just won't cut it. Others can find your fairy wings. Others can smell the rot of your stinking magic."

Tai sniffed. "We are winged children."

"By any name, you will cause harm to befall her." He stepped beside Saffron, his large, powerful legs hip-width apart, his arms folded across his broad chest.

Saffron cocked her head sideways, looked at him out of the corner of her eye, and grimaced. She moved two steps away from him. "And why do you want to come with us, anyway? So far, this isn't exactly fun, you know." Saffron crossed her arms over her chest, hoping to appear tough, but her jelly-legs betrayed her.

The man smiled a real smile for the first time since she'd met him.

A long, slow, bone-melting smile crossed his chapped, but lush, lips. It brought softness to the dirty lines of his face. The wrinkles of worry cleared from his wide forehead. Saffron found it hard not to smile with him. Then he looked around at the shambles of the home where they were taking refuge and, as he did, his smile, as slowly as it appeared, all but disappeared.

"There is nothing left for me here....so why not a little adventure to take my mind off things...."

Saffron sucked in her breath. "This was *your* home?" She took another look around and saw what she failed to notice before — not only was there blood on the floor, but there was blood spattered on the wall and hair strands sticking to it. It was long hair, brown, and glued in place by the blood. Its unanchored ends blew around in the swirling wind.

Everywhere, things were broken. Her eyes skittered over the floor, taking in cracked walls and shattered glass. Something caught her attention. It was a boot – and it was still on a leg. She sucked her breath deep through her teeth.

The others were looking out the window. They weren't arguing anymore. The man stood with hunched shoulders and an impatient scowl. Wo looked mildly concerned. Tai flickered between interest and feigned boredom. What did he care for the barbaric needs of Man?

Saffron swallowed hard and looked back at the leg inside the boot. As the leg inside the boot was on the floor across a doorjamb, she imagined that the rest of the body was just around the corner inside the room. She hoped. She moved slowly to her hands and knees, mesmerized by the leg in the grey, woolen sock inside the crusted and worn brown boot. The pants were also brown, but of a darker shade.

The cuff was raised high up on the leg. High-waters, she thought absently.

She crawled slowly towards the leg. It didn't move. On her hands and knees, she moved across the filthy floor until she was a foot away from the boot. She stopped. Her heart was not back on the cloud — it was with her now, choking her, and throbbing in her throat. She moved again.

The moment was surreal. Later, she would ask herself — *why, why, why did you do that? Why didn't you stop? Why did you have to look at him?* But now she didn't question herself. She moved forward on impulse and a need to see what lay around the corner; she had to see what was attached to that leg. Her nose was close to the boot now. She caught a whiff of soiled, wet leather. At least, her memory summoned this. Actually, the boot smelled strongly of the kerosene he lay in when he was struck down.

Saffron's hair brushed over the boot when she rounded the corner. There was more blood. There was the shiny, wet gore of partially exposed intestines. There was fine, soft hair that stuck fast with blood to his young, unlined face. Saffron wished with all her might that she could retch. She screamed, then gagged, and screamed again.

Quickly, the man left the window and slid over to her on his knees. Once again, he grabbed her about her bent-over waist, and dragged her back across the room to the far wall.

She held her hand over her mouth and dry-heaved again. It wouldn't matter; she was incapable of throwing up — no matter how badly she wanted to. She wanted to purge herself of that sight, somehow. She wanted to blast it from her mind by blowing it all out. Then she vomited. Dark yellow burst from her lips and dribbled down her chest, reeking of acid. She looked at Tai in shock as she swiped her face. He looked away in disgust, then flitted to a window on the opposite side of the room. Saffron cried bitterly as the bile began to fade. "Who *is* that?" she moaned.

The man watched the vomit disappear into nothing. He looked over at the unmoved leg in the grey sock in the brown boot. "Well, let's see. Tonight on the news, in a land over the ocean, the reporters will say: 'Fifty died today in a *skirmish* in Ackerlon.' So, hmm, let's call him...32. How's that sound?" He clamped his mouth shut and stared at the leg. He had spit out the word 'skirmish.' He hated it when they used that word. It was like 'tiff,' 'rift,' and 'kafuffle.' A belittling word that shed no light on the reality of the bloody violence of battle. *Skirmish.* He kicked a glass bottle clear across the room.

Saffron looked back at the leg in the boot. A dead man. A dead *boy. Lying in the room with them.* His soft face didn't look old enough to shave. He looked younger than she was. She swiped at her tears with the back of her cold, plastic hand. 32.

She was about to tell the man what she thought of his stupid and disrespectful "number 32" comment when she realized she had the man figured wrong. He was being sarcastic, not careless. She clamped her gaping mouth shut. The man was angry. She watched his teeth clench and release behind his cheeks. She wanted to touch his face, hold his jaw in her fingers and make the clenching stop. Then she became supremely embarrassed and looked down. Markis was her boyfriend. Her abducted boyfriend. What the hell was wrong with her? "How did this kid get here?"she whispered.

The man snapped out of his brooding and took his eyes away from the leg. "I brought him here. He was standing by the house next door when someone ripped into him. After the dust settled, I sneaked out and dragged him back here."

Saffron held herself tight with her arms. "Why?"

The man looked at his blackened fingernails. "Because he was somebody."

Saffron sighed. She thought again of the man snarling, 'Fifty dead. Skirmish." Those were terms she heard at least once a week back in her own realm on the evening news. Shame coated her. Until right now, this second, she had been one of hundreds of thousands, one of the millions, that processed those words with little more thought than she would give for a produce sale in the Czech Republic.

But now she could look Number 32 in the face, and see he was much more than a number. He had been something to someone somewhere, and now he was lost to those people. Tears flowed freely down her plastic cheeks. *Fifty Dead...Buy One Get One Free. Fifty Dead...Dog Show at the Palladium.* Saffron watched a crooked, broken frame swing on its bare wire from a loose nail on the wall. Its glass was broken. Through a fuzz of grief she realized the man beside her was in that photo, smiling. "I can't believe you lived here. This is so terrible." She was sputtering.

"Not mine. This was my brother's house. My brother, his wife, and his child. They're dead." His tone was flat.

Suddenly, a bomb exploded just across the street, starting a fire in the little store that crumbled there. A short scream burst from Saffron's lips. She could feel hysteria mounting, feel her mind pulling away.

"We can't stay here." The man clutched her hand. They stood together, Saffron and the man, and for a moment they stood face to face. Neither one flinched as they stared at each other. One last tear rolled down Saffron's cheek. He reached to wipe it away. He slid his thumb over her skin. As soon as he touched her cheek, he froze. He frowned and backed away from her.

"What's going on with you? I feel no heat when I touch you. I noticed that earlier, too, when you first came here, and I grabbed your wrist. I can't even feel your tears — there's no moisture! And you threw up — but where is it now? And not that I want it —but where's the smell of it? Where's the smell of you? I can't smell your sweat, your hair, your skin — nothing...."

Tai laughed. "Poor you, Dude — but do you really want to smell this stinky girl?"

"Shut up." The man and Saffron said it at the same time.

Tai pouted. "I wanna leave now. Why are we just hanging around here?" He flew to the ceiling and began scratching symbols with a charred chair leg.

Saffron's eyes were round and full of sadness. "I'm like a movie." She shrugged. "That's what I was told anyway."

"Yeah...." The man could only gawk at her. He didn't know what to think. He had heard some strange stories, had seen some strange things in his life, but nothing like this! Was this girl dead? He shuddered.

Saffron saw the shudder, saw him back away from her, farther yet, and saw distaste dance fleetingly across his features.

He composed himself a second later, but not quickly enough.

He's repulsed by you. The thought jangled loud and clear in her mind. Now she realized Wo's apprehension in telling her about her new state. Why he expected her to be more upset than she had been. Wo knew people were going to be repulsed by her. She couldn't help the wave of self-pity that swiftly pressed on her.

The man watched the girl crumble, knew he was the one who crushed her. He felt awful. But what could he do? He had never met a ghost before — he couldn't help his reaction. And he'd never been turned on by a ghost before either; it made him a little queasy. He felt a renewed surge to lay his previous offer on the table — trim it up nicely so they couldn't say no this time. "I know the portal out of this world, and when we get to the other worlds, I will recognize the signs that will lead us to those portals...."

Tai looked down at him. "We can find portals, we got this...."

"All we need to do is ask the trees." Wo cut in, then frowned up at Tai, who was in the middle of scratching out a really nasty phrase in the language of the winged children.

The man focused on Wo. "But what will you do when there are no trees around to ask — when you are in the middle of a barren desert, or lost in a land as desolate as the moon?" He was not being smug, but matter of fact. "I can help you in those realms —even when the portals are hidden; there are always clues. I know the signs of portals. I...." Suddenly, he clamped his mouth shut. Then quietly he said, "I just know."

"Oh, ho, ho!" Tai sang, "What have we here?" He finally left off with his graffiti. He narrowed his eyes at the man and looked him up and down.

The man decided for all of them. He waited for the gunfire to cease, then tugged on Saffron's hand. "Let's go." This time, he didn't release her.

They crouched and skittered out the front door and ran for cover in an alley. There they crouched again, and waited for the moment when they could run.

"What's your name?" Saffron whispered.

"Orji."

Saffron balked. "Your name is *Orgy*?"

Unaware of Saffron's shock, he nodded and slowly craned his neck out to search the next bend. All was quiet — no ptt, ptt, ptt, of gunfire, only dust pluming in the empty street. He was getting ready to tell them to run when Saffron spoke again.

"You cannot be serious!"

Orji looked back at Saffron over his shoulder. Sweat ran down his face in rivulets, streaking the weeks-old dirt that had collected in the creases on either side of his nose. He wondered, not for the first time since meeting her, if he should really be going with them, or leave well enough alone. How desperate was he to get to the Earthrealm? She was an odd duck, questioning his name and all, what was wrong with his name? "What's wrong with 'Orji',"?

"Well, you know....aahhh....lots of people....you know...." Awkwardly, Saffron wiggled her fingers and started to entwine them feverishly, as if they had a will of their own.

Orji stared at her in wonder and confusion, tilted his head, looked away, then cast another confused, sideways glance. "Look, *Saffron* — if we don't get out of here, we could get bombed, and if you're lucky, you'll only lose a couple of limbs, then bleed to death slowly, just long enough to make fun of my name for a few more minutes — sound good?"

I don't think that threat will work buddy, he reminded himself, *not on Little Miss Ghost, here.* But then Orji saw Saffron's expression drop at his words, and he realized it *did* work. She might be a ghost, but she was still afraid of the same things as everyone else. *Why,* he wondered, *why?*

Saffron hung her head, properly ashamed, and said nothing.

There was a vacuum of sound — all weapons were silenced for a moment.

Orji whispered harshly, "Run, run!" They sprinted for a house much like the sad, dilapidated house of Orji's brother. They waited again, this time in complete silence, then ran for a store with a shattered picture window. Through the course of the afternoon, they alternated running and hiding, hiding and running, until they found themselves on the edge of a forest. A forest filled with red-barked trees that towered six and eight stories high. The sun had since sunk in the sky, and they waited with quick breaths on the edge of night.

Saffron eyed the forest and gnawed on her bottom lip. "We're going in there, aren't we?"

Orji spat, then responded. "Yip."

Saffron's shoulders slumped. "Of course." The trees loomed above her. The gouges in their bark drew out deformed faces with bulges and squints. She looked at Wo. "I know this forest is enchanted, I can feel it. It's stinging my nose. But, you're enchanted, so you can navigate us through here safely, right?" She was doubtful.

Wo's answer was not heartening. He ran his hand over his mouth and tugged his bottom lip. "Yes, this forest is enchanted, only...." He looked at Tai in a funny way. It was a quick look and not filled with confidence.

Tai, who was suddenly captivated with the tops of the trees, made no comment.

Wo chucked Saffron on her plastic shoulder. "Time for another analogy! You know how in the Earthrealm you have your town — it's small, cute, and an all around not bad place.... Then you have Taos — beautiful, mysterious, charm of the old west.... And how about Paris — cultured, a center of fashion...."

Saffron's frayed nerves made her impatient. "What's your point?"

Wo scratched the back of his head and wiggled his nose. "Well then, this forest, in comparison to those places, is a town in the inner-most part of the poorest city in a third world country and it's two a.m. and we're a bunch of naive churchgoers entering with nothing but a ham strapped on our heads and hundred dollar bills taped to our naked, sorry asses."

Saffron shut her eyes.

Tai laughed. "Wo, you're Analogy King! Honestly, I've never heard so many analogies from you in the hundred-plus years we've spent together!"

Wo frowned at his brother. "I'm just trying to explain things to her so she'll understand on her own terms."

"Yeah, whatever, keep going. You make me laugh." Tai fluttered up and down, up and down. "Gods, you people are slow. Can we pick up the pace?"

Orji went to ruffle Saffron's hair, but it didn't move until she realized what he was doing, then it gave way under his hand. But, by the time it gave way, he had stopped rubbing, because her hair was so stiff. The softness he expected to touch was one-dimensional and cold. He looked away from her and tsk-tsked the twins. "Come, come now — it's not that bad. How dramatic you two are! Don't scare the poor girl! Let's go — our portal awaits. We'll just get there, and go through, and be done." He smiled a great big, cheesy, put-on smile. His lip twitched. He scrunched his face to pretend it hadn't.

Saffron shook her head. "We haven't even checked this realm for Markis...."

Tai slapped her up the back of the head. "Good God, let's go. He's not here."

"How do you know?" She swiped at him, but of course he moved out of reach.

Tai ground his teeth. "There are no fairies in this realm."

"Why?"

Wo poked Saffron in the back. "Sshhh...just keep walking."

As one, the group proceeded, lifting their feet high to tromp the prickly, marsh-like grasses that bordered the fortress of trees. The grass was anchored in black moss that was as puffy and spongy as marshmallows. The silence was thick around them and pregnant with an unknown menace. Wo and Tai whispered to each other above Saffron's head. Their flapping was loud as they lifted up and down in the air.

Saffron wished *she* could fly every time being grounded made her weary. Orji grabbed her elbow when she stumbled on the clumps that seemed to suddenly appear and disappear under their feet. Before Saffron could stop herself, her right leg landed deep in a hole that had suddenly formed, causing her to trip face-first into the murk.

Orji sighed as he helped her up and steadied her. Then he sighed again and lifted her up into his arms.

Saffron couldn't look into his eyes when she said in a flat tone, "You don't need to carry me." But she didn't protest any further.

"Say there, Orji, that's very noble of you, to help the girl, but what you don't know is that this here girl has left her body behind; it's only her soul you support." Tai landed in front of Orji and Saffron and crossed his arms. "If she were so inclined, she could concentrate and find that leaving her physical expectations behind will greatly lighten her journey...and yours."

Orji frowned. "Wha...?" Did that mean she wasn't a ghost? He let her slide out of his arms. Her feet landed with a squelch. He slapped a spider that crawled on the back of his neck and looked at her. "You're not from the Earthrealm, originally? You're not...*human*?"

Saffron lost her balance, caught herself, tottered a little more, then squatted to keep from bumbling. "Yes, I'm human," she responded quietly as she rubbed her knees.

"Are you, ah, dead?"

Saffron winced and squinted up at him. "NO! Oh, my God, no! I'm just — separated from my body."

"Oh, right. Of course." Orji looked thoughtful for a moment then said, "You know, boys, a big part of being human is being physical. Do you know what that's like? I mean, can't you understand why it may not be so fair that you wish she lose that...?"

Tai bristled suddenly, his thin, froggy-fairy skin turned brick-red. The black marshmallows around his feet started to smoke and bubble. Wo flew down to stand by his side. He patted Tai's arm consolingly. Tai was as stiff as an iron rod. "I don't need you to preach to me about what it's like to be human!"

Orji had jumped when Tai started yelling. He halted in the black moss that was starting to turn to muck. He looked back at Tai with his eyebrows raised as he waved the putrid, burning-sulfur smell away from his face. Seeing a look in Tai's eyes, and in Wo's, he decided to say no more.

About a quarter-mile inside the trees, the muck, murk, and grasses stopped, and they found themselves walking on flat, clear forest floor.

"I don't *know* why!" Tai hissed at Wo. They had been bickering quietly to each other up there for the last several minutes.

Saffron's head snapped up after she brushed at the last bit of slop that clung to her calf. "What? What is it? What are you talking about?" Her voice was starting to strain. Something about this forest put her completely on edge. It was dark, it stank like wet, moldering things, and it just felt *wrong*. Elusive thoughts trilled down her back, running their legs like millipedes.

Tai turned his venom on her. "Stop slapping at that muck on your leg? De-solidify! It'll disappear!" He kicked at empty air as his wings hummed to keep him aloft.

"Hey!" Saffron spat. "Get off my ass! I *want* to be solid! Didn't you spend the first part of this day bitching at me to get solid?"

He swooped down and yanked the clock on the golden chain over Saffron's head. He looked at it, squinted, mashed his lips, frowned and moved his mouth like he was counting. "It's been three days since then, Yoch." He dropped the clock into the pocket of his lederhosen as he enjoyed Saffron's silly facial expressions display.

She gasped. "What?!"

Wo landed beside Saffron. He looked at her with great big, green eyes. He knew her temper could be changed with a subject change. "We always navigate in a strange forest by talking to the trees."

Saffron, confused, looked at Wo and nodded. She scratched her head, trying to figure out what he was going on about now. "Oh, and these trees can't talk, right."

"No, that's not it." Wo shrank a little and looked nervously at the closest tree. It had to be at least four *hundred* feet tall, and all dark and gnarled. "These trees can talk. They just...*won't*. They won't talk to us."

"The trees are...," Orji coughed behind his hand, "...prejudiced. Looks like you need me already."

Tai scoffed, "Don't bet your sweet bippy. *You* won't be our savior. These trees don't like you, either!"

Saffron looked sideways at the big, ugly tree. She had a fleeting image of it moving, lifting its roots, and crashing towards her, limbs outstretched to grab her. The thought twanged a chord in her gut, and filled her with primal terror.

"It's all right, boys," Orji squinted in the direction of the tree, but didn't quite look *at* it, as if he were avoiding eye contact. "I know where the portal is all the same." He lowered his voice. "Just keep your head down, keep quiet, and follow me."

"How come you know where this portal is?" The twins had told her portals, in any world, were not common knowledge. It was how the worlds persevered, remained untouched by outside forces. Those who knew of a portal's existence kept the location a closely guarded secret.

Orji stiffened. He didn't answer.

Saffron struggled to keep up with his long-legged strides, and fumbled for a way to rephrase. "I mean, I heard that no one...."

Orji held up his hand to stop her from saying more. He whispered, "Really, Saffron, we shouldn't be talking." He looked up at the treetops. "We'll attract....undue attention."

Saffron crossed her arms over her chest and hunched as she walked. Her eyes scraped back and forth, back and forth. Good thing it was impossible to pee her pants, because she was so nervous now that if *anything* were to jump out of the brush, she'd lose bladder control. She stopped walking because she had just confused herself. *No, that's not right. I can pee myself. Everyone can see me pee myself, too. I could be totally embarrassed. But! The pee won't actually be REAL. So I wouldn't really pee myself, but everyone would still see that I did. Hmmm.*

She had to talk. She *had* to. It was the only way to take her mind off things. "What's in here?" No answer. She jabbed Orji in the ribs.

"Ouch!"

"What's *in* here?"

"I heard you the first time! Don't you know what *ignoring* is? Be quiet!"

"What's in here?"

Orji thought his eyes would pop out of his head. He spun sharply and halted all at once to stare at her. She was unbelievable! Wouldn't she shut up even to save her own soul?!

"What's in here?" Saffron held his eyes and asked quietly this time. She didn't know why she was pestering him this way. What did it matter *what* was in here? Whatever it was, it couldn't hurt her, not really. The trees could scratch out her eyes, tear her limbs, vampires could suck her jugular, werewolves could eviscerate her, a swamp thing could smother her, every little fairy and goblin in the world could bite at her ankles — what did it matter? Tai and Wo would simply carry out what was left of her and teach her how to imagine it back.

A quick pang of shame shot through her. Orji. Orji wasn't a soul — his flesh could be ripped to pieces. He *could* die. She grimaced. *Well, he knows this forest. This is his land. He chose to come in here; he knows the potential consequences.*

Orji couldn't look at her when he finally answered. "They say soul-stealers live in here."

Up went Saffron's hands, flailing above her head. "Of course," she snapped. She felt hysteria crawl up her throat with tickly legs.

"Come on," Orji whispered, "we've got a ways to go....just keep quiet."

Wo and Tai looked at each other. Instantly, they transformed into small balls of light. They looked around, they felt with their senses. There was no one in here, no one they could talk to. They had never experienced this in a forest before. Never had they experienced this feeling of doom, hostility, and concentrated hate.

The trees were outraged at the audacity of the trespassers. They recognized the essence of the one — he belonged to *her* — but they had given only *her* permission to pass, not him.

Saffron, Orji, Tai, and Wo walked on for hours.

Saffron obsessed over the fact that if something were to chase them, they would never be able to run out of these haunted woods — they were so, so far in now. How much time had passed in the Earthrealm? Her parents and Markis' parents must be searching for them by now. And what was Tai talking about — it had already been 'three days.' He was just being an ass. Wasn't he? And when did she start referring to her home as "The Earthrealm?"

Sometimes, as they passed certain trees, its razor-sharp leaves would flutter, as if a sudden breeze came to lift them. But this couldn't be, since none of the other trees fluttered. Saffron wondered at this phenomenon, but kept her head low, and her eyes averted. She had been silent for a while now.

Wo and Tai realized what the trees were doing — they were shaking with rage. Wo and Tai had never known a hostile tree; it was very unnerving to them.

Suddenly, Saffron heard a scuffle behind one of the trees, just to her right. Her eyes widened as she locked them on the area where the noise had come from. The others were unaware that she had stopped to stare; they were all walking a few feet in front of her. Tai and Wo were busy communicating with each other in silence, and Orji was focused on their journey, the path to get the hell out.

Saffron saw the shadow of....something. It began to move out from behind a tree. Impossibly, her eyes widened some more and her breathing became shallow. The shadow grew as whatever it was slowly made its way around the base of the immense tree towards her.

It moved, ever so slightly, into a beam of errant moonlight and now Saffron could finally see what it was.

A man — a hairy, beastly, hunched man with yellow eyes and yellow teeth.

Saffron screamed, spun on her heels, and ran. Orji caught her hand as she sprinted by him, and inadvertently, she got yanked back and fell flat on her rear. She scrambled up immediately and grabbed his shirt. "It's *over there!* Just behind that tree!"

Orji still gripped her wrist, and his fingers tightened, like a vise, as he scanned the area she had pointed out. He didn't see anything. He looked harder, his eyes penetrating the shadows, searching hard, hoping to see nothing. "What did it look like?" he whispered, still keeping an eye on the area.

"A hairy man. A really ug-" Saffron caught herself just before she said 'ugly.' If it was debating on whether to kill them, it didn't need to be insulted. "A hairy man —yellow eyes, yellow teeth."

Wo swung his head around, his eyes revealing the tiniest bit of alarm. *Kelpie?* He asked his brother without saying a word.

How the hell are we supposed to know? Tai's voice rang in Wo's head, *nobody will talk to us!* Tai wasn't taking this insult lightly at all.

All at once, there was a crashing from behind the tree they were studying. They all heard the noise this time, and instead of running, they remained rooted to the ground where they stood, petrified with fear.

Saffron nerves started to pop. "Oh shit. Oh, my God — Ohmigod!" She realized she had feet, and although they weighed a thousand pounds each, she forced herself to move them.

Suddenly, a flash of white came bounding out from behind the tree. It galloped towards them, to the middle of the open expanse in which they stood.

Saffron was ready to run now, and would have, if the thing — a beautiful white stallion — had not walked right up to her and put its nose to her hand. He nuzzled her gently. Saffron felt her fear drain away. She tilted her head to the side and reached to rub his thick, muscular neck. "Ooooh," she crooned. The stallion bowed down before her, one foot outstretched, encouraging her to mount him. Saffron's lips were in a frozen 'O' of surprise and pleasure. She moved to get on the horse.

"Saffron!" Tai hissed. The horse swung his head sharply and glared at Tai in warning, steam drifting from his flared, velvety nostrils. The warning was from one magical creature to another — the consequences of disobeying the beast Tai could only guess at — but he didn't want Saffron harmed, so he backed down.

The beast's eyes turned from melting chocolate to yellow flame.

"Don't do it..." Tai muttered under his breath. He knew better than to say any more than this.

They, all of them, had already been defeated. She was on the horse's back. It appeared she hadn't heard Tai at all when she turned at the waist to face him. She smiled angelically. "It'll be okay, Tai, don't worry." She was mesmerized by the horse's beauty — its powerful body, the intelligence in its soft golden eyes. Saffron gripped his girth with her long legs. Beneath her, with raw, animal force, the horse galloped all at once into the thickness of the trees. They were swallowed by the shadows.

The horse ran faster. They shot past trees and brush, and through the different depths of blackness. Saffron felt the wind on her face, heard a howling in her ears. She looked up to the sky and saw the full moon pouring down on her from between the tops of the trees. She screamed like a wild thing, as if she were a creature of the Darkrealm herself, her vocal chords exploding with a frenzied strength.

Wo, Tai, and Orji still stood where they had been left. The hairs on the back of Orji's neck stood on end as he heard Saffron's voice fading on the wind. There was something carnal about her howl. He shifted uncomfortably. "What *was* that?" He rubbed his face vigorously, dragged his hair back off his forehead, where it stayed plastered by sweat. He shook himself, trying to rid himself of the trance that the stallion had somehow caused.

Tai frowned intensely. "Kelpie."

"Well, where is it taking your Earthrealm girl?"

Wo walked away as he answered, in the direction in which Saffron had disappeared. "He's going back to his river. That's where they hang out, and that's where he'll take her."

Tai looked at Orji. "She did see a man, like she said she did. Sometimes Kelpies show themselves as hairy men and sometimes," he looked at Wo's retreating back, "sometimes they take the form of a young horse." He sniffed the air. "There has to be a stream or river around here somewhere, he wouldn't have strayed too far from that. We'll have to track them ourselves, I can't ask the trees."

Orji snorted. "So that's your great fairy magic, huh?" He waved his arms around and yelled, "Ask the trees! Ask the trees! Where's all your power now, boys?"

Wo shrugged. "We all need somebody to lean on."

"Ahhhk!" Orji punted the sizable, dried-out branch lying by his foot ten feet across the clearing. He nodded as if he ran into this sort of thing all the time. He grimaced as a thought ran through his mind — something about Saffron. He thought of her cry of wicked pleasure. "What's he going to ah, *do* with her when he gets her back to his place?"

Tai shook his head at Orji and motioned for him to follow. They caught up with Wo and climbed awkwardly through scraggly brush and over the slimy roots of trees. After a while Tai said flatly, "He's going to try and drown her."

***

The horse ran to the edge of a large, sluggish river. Saffron was smiling vacantly —absently running her fingers through his coarse mane, and luxuriating in the feel of the stiff hair between her fingers. She screamed again, so filled with dark pleasure, that she forgot all space and time — even herself. All she knew was the feeling of raw power beneath her, and the blanket of black that cocooned her.

The hairs of the horse's mane began to twine around her hands. Round and round her fingers. As if it was alive, it wound and clung about her wrists, binding her closely to the stallion's neck.

Suddenly, Saffron's feeling of sweet oblivion lifted and dissipated. She realized she was riding a horse — bareback! She had never been on a horse. She and her mother kept a farm, with alpacas — and you don't ride alpacas. Or cats. She only had alpacas and cats. She struggled hard to remember if, in fact, there may have been other animals —but she couldn't remember. Still, she was almost positive she had never ridden a horse. And this horse — this was not a horse she knew. Her scalp tingled, her hair stood on end, and fear came rushing coldly into her belly.

The horse threw its head back and whinnied, almost screeching, at sensing her fear. Then, suddenly, he took off in a full gallop towards the river.

"Wha...?" Saffron saw the river coming for her — felt the might of the galloping horse beneath her. Aghast, she finally realized the horse's intention. She started to scream. She only had time to scream twice before she was dragged beneath the cold, murky water.

Orji, Wo, and Tai heard the screams. They were very near the river now, as Wo and Tai had long since grabbed Orji by the armpits and were flying him along. He was a big man, muscular, not terribly tall, but nowhere near short. The twins struggled visibly with his weight. They worried about the kelpie. There were worse things than death. They found the river, dropped Orji like he was a pile of large limbs, and rushed towards the black water. They saw the hoof prints pounded deeply in the soft dirt of the riverbank. They looked hard into the black liquid as the wind picked up and marsh grasses whipped their unfeeling skin. The sky was a strange green-black here, pricked with the intermittent flashes of fireflies.

Deep down in the water, Saffron panicked. She could hear nothing but her own struggle — muffled in the pitch-black liquid around her. She held her breath and pulled frantically, trying to free her hands. The more she struggled with the bindings, the more they grew and slithered and tightened. The horse was repeatedly jumping off the riverbed and slowly landing on the muck. Over and over again. Saffron felt his girth and power as he forced his way up, then drifted down, and forced his way up again. She felt her eyes pop from her sockets as she held her breath. And then, she couldn't do it — she just couldn't hold her breath any longer. She pulled hard at her hairy restraints — each time with less strength and less effort. She stopped throwing her head from side to side and looked down. Shock jolted through her body. There, just below the horse's dancing feet, were bones — bones and skulls.

The horse came down again. His hoof drove easily through one of the skulls — cracked it like an egg shell. He picked his foot up and kicked off the clinging remains.

In horror, her mouth popped open of its own accord, and her last breath came rushing out. Water came rushing back in, filling her mouth, her nose, her chest. She tasted copper. She was afraid to die. Still, she expected to die now. She ceased her struggle and waited. She looked around. Everything was blurred. There was water in her nose, her mouth, her lungs. She felt the water move over her body as the horse did his slow jumps up and down. Nothing.

The horse stopped jumping and turned his head to stare back at her. His golden eyes glowed hotly in the dark plumes of agitated water. He sniffed, bubbles rose from his nostrils. The fear she was bursting with a moment ago was gone. The fear of human death — that he relished above all things — was no longer here. Confused, he pawed restlessly at the breaking bones, satisfyingly brittle beneath his hoofs.

Suddenly, Saffron realized something. She wished her hands weren't bound so she could slap herself in her head. It was physically impossible for her to die — because her body wasn't physically there. *Now what?* She stared back at the horse and shrugged. The copper sting in her nose and the metallic flavor of it just — vanished. The pressure in her chest left just as swiftly.

The horse hoof-bashed a couple more skulls and threw his head up and down. He brought his big nose around and stared at her with his yellow eyes.

She stared back. There were a few beats of stillness as they considered each other. Ghostly bits of debris rained past them and settled on the broken bones. Saffron could now hear the water-muffled shouts coming from above. The horse looked away from her and hung his head.

The hairs began to untangle themselves from her wrists and from around her fingers. The horse bucked her off his back. Saffron remained in a sitting position and floated gently to the floor of the river. The horse turned to face her. In a haze of liquid and moonlight, he loomed over her, staring down. Suddenly, he morphed, and turned back into a hairy man.

He had rat-small eyes, and wrinkled skin that was humped and bumped with warts. He took hold of Saffron by her bicep, his massive fingers encircling her arm completely.

Her fear returned, and caused her to hyperventilate large bubbles of water that floated delicately to the surface. She pulled away from him and with impossible slowness, began to swim away — fearing every second that he would reach out and snatch her back.

She felt his hands grip both her ankles. She screamed. She knew she shouldn't be afraid — it wasn't rational to be afraid — still, she hollered and swam frantically, as he held firm to her legs. *Now is a good time to NOT to be solid!* But she couldn't change. Under the stress of the moment, she could not concentrate, could not bring the change about, and remained a solid thing for him to entrap.

His hair and fur floated about his body like dark seaweed. He pulled her back towards him, and held her in front of himself like a rag doll. He looked her in the eye, his own eyes glowing. He put his hands around her throat and began to throttle her. Saffron's hands flew up in response as she tried to pry his fat fingers free with her own nail-bitten, slim fingers. She clawed at his wrists as he choked her. Then, she realized again — quicker this time — that he couldn't choke her. With every last bit of nerve, she forced herself to calm down. She went limp and stared at his jaundiced eyes as he strained even harder to kill her. He gave her two more good throttles, then *his* eyes filled with fear. In an instant, he changed back into the horse and galloped away through the murk of the water, silently crushing the path of bones beneath his hooves.

Once again, Saffron found herself drifting to the bottom of the river. She didn't want to move. She sat on the pile of bones thinking about what had just happened —what actually just happened to her, Saffron Keller, agoraphobic of the Earthrealm.

She sensed movement above her, looked up, and saw Tai.

He was sitting like Buddha with wings, his arms and legs crossed, as he drifted down through the water. He landed with a slow-motion POOF beside her. He gave her a look that asked, "Are we there yet?" and waited for her to respond.

She frowned, her eyes grew wide. Then, she barked at him like a harpy — the noise warbling and blurbling in the water. She slammed one of the skulls with her fist and pushed off from the bottom. When she broke the water's surface, she whipped her head around to look for the other two. She found Wo and Orji sitting on the opposite bank. Fireflies had clustered on Wo's wings and were blinking on and off as he slowly fanned them.

Why were they just sitting there?! Her fury lit up like a neon-red haze around her. "What the hell are you doing? It was trying to *kill* me!"

"Stop with the bleeding heart, Saffron; we're exhausted from carrying Mr. None-Too-Light, over here. Give us a break."

Saffron continued to tread the black water. She stared at them as moonlight glittered the water around her. She couldn't believe this was happening. "What the hell..." she whined. She slapped the water. "It was painful! It *felt* like I was *drowning*! It really, really hurt!"

Tai broke the surface just next to her. He rose up out of the water with a splashing of wings and a shower of drops. Before he could speak, Wo chucked a handful of gravel at them. "Yeah, and whose fault is that?" he spat and hung his head.

"What is your problem? Why are you sitting there like a rag? You big baby!"

"Saffron," Wo spoke quietly now, "we aren't like you. We aren't out of our bodies. We're *fairies*. Different rules apply to us. We needed to solidify to carry Orji, and the carrying was hard. It drained us of our energy. At home, we could manipulate energies to strengthen ourselves — but here," he glanced around nervously, "I'm afraid we've already attracted too much attention. I can't go waking up everything that slithers and crawls in this forest with our magic. We need to *get out of here*." He enunciated this last, but whispered it, so it took a few seconds for the words to float across the river to Saffron.

"And, yoo-hoo," Tai smirked and waved at her, "There are other *things* in that river, do get out, will you?"

The skin on Saffron's face tightened. She drew her feet up underneath her and kicked them out again to propel herself forward. She put her arms out in front of her and pushed her way through pink and green lily pads to get at the shore. All the while, she waited to be grabbed by the ankle, wrist or hair, and yanked back down into oblivion. As soon as she was close enough, Orji hauled her out across the slimy bank.

"So, Fireball, what happened down there?" Orji liked the way her shoulder-length hair darkened and smoothed around her face when it was wet.

Saffron shrugged. "It tried to kill me. It like, tied me up with its mane that was alive and then it turned into a man and tried to choke me."

"Ahhh." Orji nodded and opened his eyes wide — like people do when they're placating inmates.

"Then it was weird; I....I think it got scared of *me*." Saffron swiped her hair back from her forehead and wiped the water from her nose with the back of her hand.

"It was scared of you. It assumed you were a ghost, one of the dead." Wo stood up and offered Saffron a hand.

"But I thought you said she wasn't a gh...."

Tai flew off the ground and clapped his hand to Orji's mouth. He hissed low in Orji's ear.

"Now, now, now — don't go giving away all of our secrets to our neighbors.... Why do you think you're not dead yet?" Tai looked around, jaw clenched, to see if any of their lurking onlookers understood what Orji almost spilled. He waited for a change in the air. He knew they were everywhere, in every last shadow. It was good that the creepy-crawlies thought Saffron was a ghost — it was their best protection against further attack. From most things, anyway. Nobody liked ghosts. Nobody liked such a vivid, in-your-face-reminder of death. Not any race, species or creature.

Orji closed his mouth and Tai removed his hand. Orji looked over his shoulder at a suspicious-looking clump of brush. "Let's get out of here and find that portal."

"Yup," chimed Wo, "I don't think so." He pointed across the river where there were dark, black shadows moving. The shadows didn't go very far or very fast, but seemed to be milling around the edge of the river.

"What's that noise?" Saffron whispered, her voice straining. It was a low keening mixed with a guttural rumbling. It droned louder and terrified her.

"They're moaning...." Wo craned his neck to see better. "They're communicating with each other and aahh, here they come now."

Saffron saw how the mass of shadows broke apart and formed hundreds of beings. They left the river bank and started to cross the water.

Wo clapped his hands. "Okay, let's run."

"What are they? What do they want?" Saffron shrieked as she spun around to run for the trees.

"Just run!" Tai yelled.

The twins rose in the air. Orji grabbed Saffron's hand and half-dragged her as she sprinted over fallen, moss-laden logs and around large rocks. They ran blindly as they left the weak light behind, and the forest thickened around them. Saffron ran quicker than she could ever remember running in her life, her heels kicking up at her rear-end, spurring her faster. Soon enough, Orji's breathing became heavy and he grunted as he pulled her over the spongy earth and sodden branches.

On cue, she suddenly became short of breath, too. She heard moaning. They were running impossibly fast, yet still, the moaning was closing in on them. Tears streamed down her cheeks. She tried to think if this was a dream. Could she wake up? Her mind was so muddled with fear, she couldn't even remember why she was here, how she got here.

Suddenly, Orji yanked her to a halt. She looked up at him in confusion. He pointed straight ahead, in the direction in which they had been heading. She strained hard to look into the darkness. All at once, she saw them — more shadows, blacker than the forest pitch, moving in on them from that direction.

She started to make little yelping noises deep in her throat.

The shadows moved closer still.

Tai, Wo, Orji and Saffron were back to back, facing outward, watching as the shadows enclosed them.

On unspoken cue, Tai and Wo raised their arms. They didn't know what kind of defense to use against these things, but they were going to try. The noise the shadows made grew stronger, more manic, as if they were drugged cultists moving in for the kill, moaning for blood.

Saffron gave out three high-pitched, blood-curdling screams — and that's when it happened. At first, she didn't know what happened. All she knew was that suddenly, Orji disappeared from her side — his shoe hit her in the temple as he disappeared. Then she felt Wo leave her back — his wings bopped her head forward — then, he was with her no more. Suddenly, she felt pressure in her armpits. It hurt, like that time when she was five and she lost her footing on the jungle gym. She fell down through the middle of it and her legs got caught up by the bars. She was saved from a crash, but was reeling with pain. She winced; something just as hard as those bars was under her arms. It yanked her up, up, up, hauled her at the speed of the wind. Suddenly, the pressure left her arms, and she was flying through the sky, a cart-wheeling projection across the canvas of stars. Then the bars clamped around her biceps and thighs. The pinching hurt for only an instant. Soon enough, she was flung again into open air, then caught once more by the pinching grip. As she flew up towards the moon for the fourth time, then did a free fall back towards the leafy *top of the trees,* she understood — it was the trees.

The trees had bent over, and with their branches acting like arms and hands, managed to pluck her, Orji, Tai, and Wo from the ground, away from the shadows, and now were tossing them like rag dolls through the air from one tree to another.

Saffron saw Orji, several yards away, just tossed again, up over the canopy. He spent an eerie hang-time in the circle of the full moon before he dropped like dead weight down, down, down. She saw Wo, then Tai — arms, legs, and wings spinning head-over-heels. They were screaming, and looked like turtles who were trying to right themselves so they could fly. But they never got the chance — the trees were always grabbing too soon.

They must have traveled for miles, tossed by the trees. Saffron grunted and screamed like an animal. She felt like she was going to lose her mind.

Finally, the throwing stopped. She crashed to the forest floor. Orji, Tai, and Wo lay sprawled around her. She looked up and screamed again as the biggest tree of all loomed in front of her like a New York City skyscraper. Crashing and groaning it leaned forward and reached for her. With many small twiggy fingers, it grabbed her up and brought her to a big hole in its center that looked just like a gaping, black mouth.

She couldn't breathe, couldn't scream, and couldn't blink, as she was moved towards the mouth. There was only fear and a wish for death to save her.

The tree shot her through its hole. She fell into total blackness. Falling and falling — too stunned to scream, she fell further into a space of wide-open, cavernous blackness. She landed not too heavily on a hard, smooth surface. She started to slide down. She picked up momentum, and slid as if she were on a smooth, dry, water slide, barreling around curves, up on the left, then up on the right, down, down, down.

Suddenly, she saw a light ahead. She came upon the light quickly, then was launched into open air, and finally landed with a slam on a gravelly floor. The blare of rushing noise inside her head stopped abruptly. Complete stillness settled on her.

She rubbed her arms gingerly and was surprised to find no marks there. The tree branches hadn't hurt her at all. A jagged line, the mouth of the cave she was in, was just in front of her. Dazed, she got up and lurched towards the cave opening. When she looked out, she saw blue sky, purple flowers, and the beautiful radiance of the sparkling sun. Behind her, she heard Wo's giggles heralding his arrival. He plopped out of the cave wall onto the exact spot where she had just been. Tai followed, then Orji.

When Orji landed, they all fell silent and stared at him.

He was laughing, so thrilled to be alive, then looked up to find them all staring at him. He chuckled once more at their solemn expressions. "What?"

"Look at your arms," Wo whispered, "Your legs, your *face!*"

Orji looked at his arms and his face turned ashen. He was covered in blood and torn flesh. Purple bruises were already beginning to swell everywhere. Blood dripped from his chin. "Hmm, come to think of it, I can't move this arm." He smiled and pointed to his left arm. Then he passed out.

Chapter 11

"*O*h, my God!" Saffron ran over to Orji's broken body, but was afraid to touch him. She hovered over him uselessly, and pulled at chunks of her hair. She knew she shouldn't move him — she remembered that much from her first-aid class. He could have a spinal injury. But she didn't know what else to do. She looked at Tai and Wo. They shrugged.

"We only use magic to heal. Healing by magic is not always possible, not always *allowed*." Wo looked outside the mouth of the cave. "And we don't know where we are."

Tai sneered at Saffron. Did she expect *them* to do something about Orji? There was a reason they left Saffron's body where it couldn't be harmed, and this was that reason. Couldn't she *ever* figure anything out? "Do you know how much energy it takes to heal a wound?" He pointed at Orji. "Never mind this! It takes extensive magic to heal bones. We don't know if this realm supports such magic. And even if it does," he looked at the patchwork of wilderness outside the hole in the cave wall, "we don't know where we are — what kind of attention we'll attract. Since he can't run, we'll be trapped if somebody or some*thing* comes after us."

Wo nodded. "We have to get rid of his body as soon as possible."

Saffron's mouth dropped open. "Then you're okay with him going with us?"

Tai snorted, "Of course! This guy just saved our souls!"

"What? What did he do? What happened back there?" Saffron fell to her knees beside Orji and smoothed the hair back from his forehead. That's what her mother had always done for her when she was sick. She missed her mother rubbing her forehead, her back.

Wo hugged himself as if to keep from spinning out of his center. "The tree swallowed Tai and me last. It talked to us, finally, just before it dropped us in. It told us it 'was the man' who allowed our souls to be saved. It said that the man's kin used to bring it a magic potion. The potion had allowed it to grow strong and tall — that tree was the *king* of the forest! It told us the name of the potion...." Wo frowned. "Now, what the heck did it say?" He brightened. "He said that Orji's kin used to bring the potion for it from another realm. The tree called it, The Miracle of Growth. No, wait — that's not it. Growing Miracles – yeah, that's it."

Saffron squinted. "Miracle-Gro?" She jumped to her feet. "Hey! That's from *my* realm! *Our* realm, Wo!"

Wo nodded and shook his finger at her, "I thought so. I thought it sounded familiar."

Saffron slowly lowered herself to the dusty, rock floor. She fiddled with Orji's shirt and wrinkled her nose as she dragged her fingers through a clump of gelled blood. She smeared the stuff back onto his shirt and thanked God she couldn't smell it. Then she smelled it. She forced herself to look away from him. So, someone in Orji's family had been a supplier — an outer realm drug dealer to the trees. She sensed there was something criminal about him.

"It also said," Tai strolled towards them, "that *she* had not been around in a long time and they needed more Miracle-Gro. It asked us to retrieve some, bring it back."

"Back!?" Saffron whined.

Tai flared his wings. "Yes, back! And I agreed — what would you have me do? 'Oh, please Mr. King of the trees, please lower us immediately so that we may be swallowed up and exist as moaning shadows for the rest of our lives'!"

Saffron ppffftt him. "Can't we just forget it and not go back?"

Tai turned his back on her and muttered, "I gave him the word of the winged children. Fairy word. It cannot be broken."

"Oh, that's just great." Saffron put her face in her hands. Then she slapped her thighs and looked down at Orji — at his deeply-gashed wounds and quick-forming bruises. "Well, can't you do *any* magic?" She walked to the opening in the cave and poked her head through the slit in the rock. "I mean, it doesn't look like there are any settlements for miles. We're in the middle of nowhere!" she yelled over her shoulder. "It's all woods down there." She came back from the entrance. "It's so cool-looking, too — purple leaves!" A rip in Orji's pants caught her eye. It was a long, wide, and jagged tear. Saffron gulped. It exposed the top half of his right thigh, almost revealing his family jewels. "And, we need clothes, too." She squeaked out, "Orji needs clothes."

Wo looked at Tai and shook his head 'no.' "There are no winged children in this realm. I wouldn't do it."

"How do you know there are no fairies here?" Saffron slapped away a couple of flies that were swarming around her head.

Tai was swatting too; there were more around him. "It's an essence we have and can detect. That essence is not here." He shrugged. "Just go ahead and see what happens, Wo."

Wo raised an eyebrow and gave Tai a doubtful look. "Do you honestly think we'll get away with it?" He hunched his shoulders and fanned away a fly with his wings. "Why are there flies around us?"

"You're asking me? How the hell should I know? And why are they around Saffron? None of us is food for them."

"Oh, gross! Hurry up and do something?" Now Saffron was slapping and darting about the cave to get away from them. "Why don't you know if you can use magic?"

"We're not gods, you red-headed sea banshee! We don't know *everything!*" Tai dry-heaved and spit a fly out of his mouth. He bellowed and stomped. "What the hell is going on with these flies?"

"This isn't our realm, Saffron; your guess is as good as ours," Wo put with more tact. He slapped flies off of his arms and pointed at Orji. "There are no flies around him and look at him — he's literally a bloody feast!"

"Well, ask the trees if it's okay to use magic...." Saffron smacked her ear.

Tai stomped to the cave entrance as he wrapped his wings around his body to shield himself from the flies. He looked like a cocoon made out of a map with green and glowing roads. "Trees," he shouted, "is it okay if we use magic in this realm?" He leaned forward, poked his head out of his wings, and theatrically cupped his hand behind one ear. "Thank you!" He turned to face Saffron, and in a flat voice — "They have no idea. What's your next big idea Queen Know-It-All?"

"Get off me, you sad excuse for a mosquito." Saffron kicked gravel in his direction.

Tai's face turned purple. He shot his finger out.

"Tai, no!" But Wo was too late.

Saffron felt a zap of electricity stab her forehead. She reeled backward and grabbed at her head, knowing it must be completely burned. It wasn't. Instead, she felt on her scalp, smooth, wriggling tubes, and heard the hissing of snakes. She wailed louder than a police siren when she felt the snakes moving smoothly and coolly between her palms. Her head bobbed and weaved from side to side, forward and back, as the snakes swayed round her head.

"Eeew," said Wo, but was clearly amazed at Tai's fine example of mid-level magic.

Tai looked at Saffron's snake-ridden head in awe, clearly proud of himself.

"Turn me back!" Saffron screamed as she saw a triangular head hover out of the corner of her eye. "OhmyGod, turn me back!" The snakes were shooting and springing out from her scalp to catch the flies that swarmed around her head. They were held back, of course, and lunged harder with each consecutive try, till Saffron could feel them pulling at her scalp as if they were her real hair being roughly yanked by ghosts.

A noise caught Wo's attention. He ran to the slit in the cave wall with Tai close on his heels.

"There's our answer to 'should we use magic here'." Tai whispered and began to back away from the mouth of the cave.

"By the stars," Wo hissed and clutched at Tai's arm as he backed up with him.

"What? What?!" Saffron wailed as the snakes dipped to her eyes and nose and ears and tried to sniff her with their darting, pointed tongues.

Now Tai and Wo were clutching each other. They turned as one to stare at Orji's bloodied and broken body lying on the rock floor, barely clinging to life. They looked back at each other and gasped.

Saffron saw the look, knew what it meant, and forced a measure of calm to replace the rush of dread that currently ruled her. Someone had to take control. She moved like a be-snaked, bobble-head doll to the opening in the cave wall and looked outside.

But before she saw a thing, she heard it: the rush and flow and click of tiny things; the burr of wings and the clack of a billion insect legs. She looked over and saw them come out from behind an impossibly low cloud. She looked down at a dark mass crawling up the mountain towards them. The darkness of a million bees and flies, hornets and wasps, the blackness of a million ants and crickets, of fleas and beetles.

Saffron stumbled back from the opening and ran clear to the opposite wall of the cave. Now she had nothing to say. She stared wide-eyed at the twins. The first wave of insects crawled over the floor and along the wall of the cave, headed straight for them.

"What do we do?!" Saffron flung herself across Orji's body. She slapped at the ants that crawled up her ankles and across Orji's face. Her snakes picked them off one by one, but not fast enough. As a patch of flies began to sip at her eyes, a beetle got past the snakes, and crawled into her ear. She screamed. She dragged the beetle out with her pinky and smashed it on the rock floor with her fist.

The twins slapped at their orifices as the insect world tried to inhabit their brains. They, too, screamed like lost little girls.

Outside, the buzz and drone of billions of insects grew louder, came nearer.

Saffron slapped at the flies on her cheeks, smearing Orji's blood everywhere.

The twins ran to Orji and Saffron, grabbed each by the arm, and flew them out of the opening of the cave, banging Orji's head on the way through. They hung suspended in air for only a second above the forest of purple-leaved trees. The sun glared white-hot in the baby-pink sky and framed the black cloud that was almost upon them. They remained motionless save for the hummingbird buzz of Tai and Wo's wings.

Suddenly, the twins shot straight up, dragging Orji and Saffron with them, up through pink sky and fat, puffy clouds. At one point — Saffron wasn't exactly sure when — the buzzing stopped. They soared higher through the clear and quiet air.

Tai and Wo hung on to Orji and Saffron for dear life. Saffron slipped out of Tai's grasp only once, but Wo snatched her back up by the snakes. Nobody said a word until they finally reached the outer edge of the enchanted cloudbank. From there, they walked and flew for short bursts, until they reached the spot where Markis and Saffron slept peacefully. Tai and Wo lowered Orji's body next to Saffron's, so that she was between Orji and Markis.

"Hmmm," said Tai as he stared at the three, "how apropos," and then he collapsed on the cloud and closed his eyes.

Wo and Saffron did the same. Only Saffron lay awake and stared at the clouds that floated above. She didn't know what Tai meant by 'apropos' and she decided she didn't care.

She cleared her mind and watched the clouds, pretending they were an endless chain of ghost ships. She didn't want to leave these clouds, didn't want to go back to land, and would never in her life want to see a swarm of insects. There was no noise —not even the call of a bird or the rustle of the wind — even her snakes lay so quiet, she quite forgot about them.

Tai passed gas.

Saffron sat up, ramrod-straight, "Oh, COME ON!"

"Sorry, lady, did I ruin your heavenly moment?" Tai and Wo started in a fit of giggles. Wo laughed even harder and turned on his side to curl up in the fetal position. Apparently, fairies recovered easily from near-death experiences.

Saffron groaned. "You know, you can be in the most perfect place in the world, and if you're not with just the right company, that place can get real ugly, real fast!"

Tai let another one rip.

Saffron ground her teeth. She held her breath and counted to ten. Gross, vile, little things. "Hey! Be quiet a minute, listen — why did that happen with those insects? There were so many of them! God, they were trying to crawl into our heads! Why were you two so afraid?" Her breathing and her temper were even now, as she conducted wisps of cloud with her hands. One of the snakes seemed to want to cuddle against her cheek, so she let it.

Tai drilled his finger into his ear to make sure there wasn't a bug in there.

Wo sat up. "Well, now we know why no magic is used in that realm – it attracted the insects. Uck."

Tai snorted. "Yeah, they wanted to make a meal of us, of our essence. They could've destroyed us, you know. Never heard of such a thing! He gave Orji a sad look. "Nothing like the power of wings to deliver you!" He held his hand out to Wo for a high-five. "Good job, dude." He turned his head to the sun, closed his eyes, and let the clouds roll under him and massage his back.

"Well, how did they find us anyway? I've never seen anything like *that* in my entire life either!" Saffron rolled over on her side and stared at Markis.

"What...*that?*" Wo thrust a lazy hand out. Pshaw. "That was nothing, really. Just something cooked up by the inhabitants to counter fairy magic. An alarm system, a counter-curse, a warning. Doesn't take much to mobilize all of the insects within a hundred-mile radius. Bugs don't exactly have a strong individual will, you know.

Quite the contrary — their group-mind-existence makes them perfect for a curse such as that. I'll have to remember that. Very ingenious."

More of the snakes on Saffron's head began to stir, and like children – one is sweet, but several are whiny – they began to hiss, sway, and pull her head around. "Yeah, man, and you ARE going to fix this, too!" Saffron pointed to her head in disgust.

Tai giggled, eyes still closed. "You so deserved *that!*"

Behind the twins, on the slowly undulating mass of white, Orji moaned. "What kind of white-out blazing hell am I in?" He opened his eyes and squinted at Saffron. Then did a double-take. He pulled his head back a little and winced. "My worst fears *have* been realized; I'm in hell and the devil herself has come to destroy me." His eyes were weary — he was truly afraid of Saffron and her snaky head. He was *very* afraid of the pain in his ribs that caused his breath to be short and wheezy. He was *very* afraid because he couldn't feel either arm or one of his legs. The other leg burned as if it were frying in a pan, and his head throbbed so loudly he could barely hear anything else. He couldn't move. He tried to move his arm and a sudden, high-pitched scream blew out of his mouth.

His obvious pain set Saffron off, and she began to cry again. "Oh, you morons, please — please help him."

Tai and Wo flew to Orji's side. "Now that he's awake, we can." Tai muttered.

"We'll see later if you would actually call what we're about to do, 'helping'." Wo whispered.

Orji's eyes bugged out. The skin surrounding his eyes pulled back, revealing a large amount of white.

Saffron wanted to hold his hand, but was too frightened. What if he died? She couldn't take it. Didn't even want to be there. She wrapped her arms around her knees and looked away from him.

"Start with an arm," Tai muttered, "you go first."

"Thanks a lot." Wo frowned.

Tai shrugged his shoulders and fell silent.

Wo placed his hand on Orji's arm, then yanked it back as if it burned. "Shouldn't we place him under a spell? Something to comfort him so he doesn't even know what's going on? That's what they do in hospitals."

"Dude, if you want to mess with his mind, go ahead. I'm not gonna even *go there*."

Wo scratched his chin roughly and squinted hard in thought. Once again, he took hold of Orji's arm and began to mutter soft words.

Saffron could hardly hear him, but she knew he wasn't speaking English. He wasn't even speaking *Earth* as far as she could tell. The words were more fluid, as if a river of of sound ran from his mouth and passed under a full moon and over rocks of diamond before reaching their goal. She was amazed to be thinking such a thing, but these were the thoughts that filled her head as the alien words trickled on, syllables she couldn't repeat, not even one, not if she tried. She relaxed, sat still, and watched Wo work. She was lulled into a meditative state, seduced by his every utterance, pause, and sigh.

It took a very long time.

When Wo was done, Tai sat back in exhaustion and relief. "Wow, man, you did it. You totally did it all on your own."

Though Wo looked pitifully fatigued, a pink glow suffused his cheeks and a bashful smile spread across his lips. Pride brimmed in his eyes. "Thanks."

"How do you feel, Orji?" Saffron didn't look directly into eyes.

He sat up slowly. "Okay, I guess." He looked at the blue sky and patted the clouds that cushioned him, grinning like a small child atop a plume of cotton candy. He grinned at Wo. "Thanks."

Wo knew he meant 'thanks' for everything — for flight, for lounging on clouds, and for fixing him. He ducked his head and smiled back. He rubbed Orji's shoulder.

"Dude, we can't have that happening again. We're on a clock here." Tai spoke quietly as he patted the pocket that held the golden clock.

"Dude," Orji intoned awkwardly, as if he didn't feel comfortable with the title, "We can't have that happening again because...that *hurts!*" Orji walked around feeling himself, running his hands over the length of his body, up and down his arms and legs, as if to be sure everything was back in line.

"Great!" Tai stood and rubbed his hands together. "See those two over there? That's Saffron's body and the body of her friend, that chap who so unluckily found himself stolen. He's our mission. Find his soul, put it back in his body, end of job."

Tai put his hands on his hips and looked at Orji until Orji looked back. "And what'll you be getting out of it, hmm?"

They both turned around when Saffron said, "His name is Markis."

Tai looked confused and forgot about his question to Orji. Orji gave a little smile to Saffron and nodded as he pointed down. "Let's go, then."

"Right," said Tai, "Now, we need you to go lay down with the other bodies so we can draw your soul from your flesh." He gave Orji a hundred-watt grin.

"Okay...I guess," Orji replied uneasily. He strode to the bodies and glanced down at them, momentarily feeling the same way Saffron had of laying herself out at her own funeral. He ignored his sudden queasiness. After all, the little guys had just saved his life, had just healed his entire body quite nicely. He had to show them a bit of faith. He lay down and closed his eyes.

Tai began. He tried to pull Orji's soul, but it wouldn't come. Wo moved alongside to help. They tried together — again and again — but Orji wouldn't lift. Tai remained unusually calm and tried a few more times. To no avail.

"Hmm," Saffron mused as she strolled over, "*I'm* able to do it relatively easily." Her superior air was abundant and annoying.

"That's because," Tai turned slowly towards Saffron and delivered the blow that would shut her up for awhile, "Your *will* is so *weak*.... your self-preservation is so defunct...." He narrowed his large black-pupil eyes at her. His wings pumped like he was pumping his fist.

She walked away, blushing from ear to ear.

Finally, Orji was able to clear his mind completely, give into the fairies' call, and separate himself from his body. "Hey....whoooeee!....hey, that tickles."

Saffron wrinkled her nose and looked over her shoulder at the newly separated soul. From the noises he was making it sounded like Orji was having a one-man orgy.

Tai and Wo chuckled over Orji, as if he were their child discovering things for the first time. He made his wounds vanish — the trifling scratches that remained — and in the end he looked sharp and all cleaned up. "Incredible! I just imagined my arm was clear of scrapes and BAM! It felt better! It really did! Then, kapow! kapow! kapow! —bruises, gone, gone and gone! Incredible!"

Saffron listened to his glee and his shouts of joy. She wanted to chuck him the bird. How come she *still* couldn't keep the sun from blinding her? Why was it so easy for Orji to control his physical memories? Why was her will *so weak?* As the hours wore on, her black mood intensified. She didn't find any fun in the outfitting Wo proposed they do.

"Let's do the magic we need up here, so we can return to the cave — we need that portal." Wo clapped his hands.

"Fine with me. Who cares if we can't use magic?" Tai shrugged most assuredly. "I'm excited! This will be like a *real* adventure. We'll have to be creative, that's all. Put it this way, if humans can live more than a day without magic, we sure as hell can clear a couple of realms."

Saffron shot him a dirty look. "Then why do you all want to become human if you think we're so stupid."

Tai sneered back. "It's like wanting to be reborn a rock, you know? To be able to live a life with little-to-no brain capacity. Like vegging out."

Saffron 'Yughhhed' in disgust. She wouldn't talk while they were choosing clothes for themselves, so Orji ordered up her garments instead.

He played with her like a doll. First he had her snakes removed and replaced with her own beautiful, lush red waves. "Her hair's too short – make it long!" Then he commanded Wo to zap different items on her — outrageous things — hoping to bring a smile to her scowling face. He didn't know why she should look so angry and sad at the same time. He couldn't bring her around, so he became serious and chose items he thought she could really use while they "roughed it" in the upcoming realms.

He insisted on leather pants, confirming out loud that they would wear well in rough terrain and be good camouflage. Secretly he loved how they hugged her rear-end, as if they were her own second skin. He ordered a dark-green, gauzy tunic that was fitted to her every curve

– again, the green would help camouflage, and the light gauze for fewer encumbrances. He had a big smile on his face now. She looked like a girl from his realm. Like a luscious treat of a girl – with a bad attitude.

Saffron finally spoke. Actually, she let out a strangled scream and a slew of vicious swears as hers arms flew up to cover her chest. Tai had zapped the tunic in place and nothing else. Saffron looked down to find, most horrifying, her breasts could be seen clearly through the sheer fabric. "What are you doing?" she screamed at Tai.

Orji flinched involuntarily and snapped his eyes from Saffron, to Tai, to Wo. "What? What?! What's going on? What's the matter, Saffron?"

"You *know* what's the matter," she spat as tears of dreadful humiliation formed in her eyes.

Orji searched Tai and Wo again, who remained quiet. "Miss, I really don't know what the problem is." He felt bad for her, he really did. He could see her shame, but didn't understand it and was starting to feel irritated by her accusing eyes. "Well, that's enough of that. You..." he pointed at Wo, "tell me right now, what is wrong here?"

Wo blushed. "The girls...in the Earthrealm..." he looked at Tai, who broke out into a snorting nose laugh. Wo turned his back on Tai and kept his own face very solemn. "The girls in the Earthrealm don't expose their chests like that." He rolled the words out quickly, one attached to the other, then clamped his mouth shut, completely affected by Saffron's obvious embarrassment.

Orji looked over at Saffron, where her arms crossed her chest. "Is that so?" he breathed, "Intriguing."

Saffron slammed him with a look of fiery hostility.

Orji flinched as if physically slapped. He had never heard of such a thing in all his life — a woman so afraid of her own body. "Well, Milady, you are going to have to finish dressing yourself, then. Seems I've done a bad job."

Saffron was tempted to change the whole outfit, but something caught her up a split second before she gave the command. She wasn't sure what stopped her, but she wanted these clothes chosen by Orji, and she berated herself for such a crazy thought. "I don't think I should wear these pants...I don't want to run into the other realm PETA people. The animal protectors," she explained and shivered.

"But you should wear lower garments that are fitted all the same. Anything else may feel cumbersome or get snagged." Orji looked very serious.

"Aren't they just a movie like the rest of me?"

"No, Saffron." Wo shook his head. "We're getting these clothes from somewhere, so they're real. The only clothes that are 'movie' are the ones you left your body with. ...I could put those back on you...."

"She can 'think' them on her damn self, Wo...." Tai kicked at the clouds.

Saffron shrugged like she could care less. "Nah, I'll keep these." She was running her hand down the side of her waist and leaving off at her hip. She couldn't believe the watery, silky feel of the fabric. She sighed.

Orji licked his lips.

Saffron narrowed her eyes and considered Orji for a long time. "I'll take some jeans then, and some riding boots. Hopefully I'll look acceptable in the other realms. And give me a damn camisole or a tank top under this..." She fluttered the hem of the tunic with one hand while her other arm stayed firmly across her breasts. She huffed. "And a utility belt. Am I the only one with practical sense around here?" She looked hard at Tai, who obeyed her without interest, and zapped her a camisole *and* tank top, knee-high boots, and a worn utility belt that didn't look any more Earthrealm than the gauzy top did.

The twins held steadfast to their lederhosen.

"You can't wear your lederhosen! You'll attract attention...like we need that!"

"Not changing my lederhosen." Tai flicked his hand under his chin, like he was an Italian mobster.

"You look stupid. Are you going to walk around with surfboards, too, *Dude*?" Saffron frowned and shook her head.

"Saffron, we'll just pretend we're your kids or something. If we have to. Kids dress funny — we could pull it off. We don't need to argue about this. Our wings, too, we could pretend we're kids that like to play dress-up." Wo stood in front of her to break the connection between her laser beam stare and Tai's laser beam stare.

Orji chose dark-brown pant-like things for himself of another odd fabric. It was almost like muddied tapestry. Then he ordered up a snug sweater. The sweater was black, and it rounded nicely over his chest and biceps. It made his dark, curly hair darker, his hazel eyes brighter. He wore boots as well.

Saffron stared at him and absently wiped her fingers across her lips. "You should have a t-shirt under that."

"A what?" Orji lowered his eyebrows, but he was smiling.

Saffron huffed. "Wo, give him a t-shirt."

Pzzzzt!

"Ah, yeah — the t-shirt goes *under* the sweater..."

Pzzzzt!

Tai and Wo looked at Saffron, who was ogling Orji. Wo cleared his throat. "I think capes would be a good idea."

In the end, they all agreed on capes. Capes for the twins to hide their wings. A cape for Saffron, who liked to cover up at night — much to Tai's irritation because she wouldn't truly get cold, he reminded her. She ignored him. And a cape for Orji, who had never seen such a thing and thought he looked positively amazing in the yards and drape of fine cloth.

Saffron sized them up. "Oh, lovely. Now we look like the average household of circus performers." She yanked off her cape. "Gimme a backpack to carry this thing in."

Tai and Wo stared at her.

"A bag. You know? A bag with straps that you put on your back and hook your arms through?" She jumped when she felt sudden weight on her back. She let the bag slide off and brought it in front of her to check it out. "OMG...this thing looks like it came out of the Family-Von-Star Wars-Trapp wardrobe." She shook her head and shoved her cape inside it.

They conjured some gear they thought would be useful: Saffron insisted on a box in which to keep the monocle safe, a box of waterproof matches, gallon-sized Ziplocs (she had fun explaining *them* to the non-worldly winged children,) wigs, and pieces of gold.

Orji laughed. "I see you've done this before." He insisted on a little metal thing he called a laipet and nothing else.

Tai insisted on bubblegum.

"What the hell for — you can't even taste it!"

"Why do people start to smoke when it tastes like shit? Because it looks like fun!" He motioned for Saffron to kiss his ass.

Wo insisted on a collection of herbs in a small, velvet satchel.

Saffron didn't talk to the others as they descended from the clouds. With crisp breezes and a canopy of stars, they glided back to the cave. Orji judged, by the height of the moon, that it was near midnight when they returned. All they had to do was approach the part of the wall that they had been shot out of to feel the portal pulling on them. As a be-backpacked group, they took a step forward and were suddenly sucked into blackness.

Chapter 12

Saffron shot out of the black hole and into another cave, much like the one they had just left. She landed on her hands and knees, and looked up to see the twins come screaming through the opposite side of the cave, through the narrowest rocky slit. They were laughing as they collapsed at Saffron's feet, breathing as if they had just run a marathon. Outside, diffused light the color of a pink and golden dawn made everything glow. Saffron smiled; yesterday's rage dissipated like a dandelion puff in June.

"Oh, man, Saffron; we flew here like the wind, *like the wind*!" To demonstrate, Tai zinged back and forth in the cave, pinging off the walls like a fly trapped between windows.

Wo jumped up and spun around. "You are not going to believe this.... I'm out of my mind — I can't stop smiling!"

Saffron frowned. What was up with them? Her cheeks would ache if she smiled that much. She pulled her cape out of her backpack and laid it on the pebbly floor to sit. The twins were afraid she was going to get hurt. That's why they badgered her to give up her physical sense. She could understand that. But she wasn't ready to give herself up. She wanted the idea of sitting comfortably on a rocky floor. Didn't her soul depend on those things she filled it with? Well, she wanted to comfort herself, fill up with it. The twins had no more experience with humans becoming souls any more than she did. What if they were wrong in telling her to alienate her physical self? "What's going on? How long have you guys been here?"

"Dude, we've been here for like, hours!" Tai did three cartwheels across the floor, scattering stones and causing shiny, copper-colored, bat-like animals to flit from the dark ceiling of the cave.

Saffron hugged her knees and watched the giddy boys. She felt buoyant here, like three thousand pounds had lifted off of her shoulders. She couldn't help but smile at their antics. Their exuberance washed over her like afternoon rain in late summer's heat. "So what is it men; did the sun rise? Is water running downhill? Did you finally realize that you *are* crazy?"

"Better!"

"Definitely, better!" They either ignored her wry humor, or missed it completely —being in an obvious state of bliss and all. The twins looked at each other and wanted to bust at their smiley-mouth seams. Fairy essence blew off of them in tiny puffs of silver, like thrashed flour. "We found her," they proclaimed as one. "She's here!"

She? Who? What? What were they gushing about? If it was a *she* that they found, obviously it wasn't Markis — and with that thought, her spirits sank. So who was *she*? Maybe, *She* knew where Markis was! Saffron sat up straighter, dying to hear the news. "Where is She? Did She tell you where He is?"

Now the twins' excitement waned. They stared at Saffron in dumb confusion.

"Wadaya mean, 'He'?" Tai looked at Wo. Wo shrugged.

They heard Orji whistling outside the cave just before he emerged through the bright rift in the rock. "Mornin' folks; looks like a land where we can walk among the people —wings covered, that is." He shrugged to the twins, "And...we can hold our heads high, be ourselves, as long as we wear these...." With a silly, lopsided grin, he pulled from behind his back four strings of what looked like Hawaiian leis, except that instead of flowers strung about the loops, there were hard, brown balls. Here and there, bits of straw stuck out of the balls.

Saffron wrinkled her nose and jerked her head back in defense — as if the leis were about to jump out at her. "Oh c'mon, what *are* those?"

"Well, take a guess Saffron — you're a sharp girl, what do they look like?"

"They *look like* cow shit....but what are they?"

"Bovine balls is right, my lady, and here are yours."

Saffron pointed her finger at Orji, "You better just back the hell off...!" She stumbled as she walked backwards.

He advanced on her, lei stretched before him.

Suddenly, Saffron could smell the cow-poop necklace as he taunted and slung it around her head. She wrinkled her entire face and quick-waved Orji away from her.

The twins started whooping and clapping like lottery winners, with tears in their eyes and everything.

Orji halted. Saffron stilled, too, and turned to face the twins. Orji laughed at them.

They spoke quickly to each other, yet, they seemed to totally understand each other. They just chattered on like blue jays. Finally, they forced themselves to calm down, and volleyed their comments.

"Oh, my God," Tai whispered in awed reverence, "to me, this meeting...it's almost holy...."

"Do you really think this tribute is to *Her*?"

"This is unbelievable...."

"They *worship* her — she could have *anyone*, and she chose us!"

Saffron's eyes flashed as she took in the twins and their outlandish comments. *They're insane. Psycho fairies. What else is new?*

Orji had no idea what they were talking about, but the dialogue was so hysterical that he laughed and laughed until he started to cry. "I don't know what's going on, but don't stop. Whew!" He wiped his eyes and collapsed to the cave floor. He gave one more half-hearted chuckle, hysteria exhausted, and rested his head on his pack. He grinned over at Saffron, who scowled back at him, sending him into another fit of giggles.

Saffron thought he looked silly — that big man giggling like that.

"I'm wearing mine! Gimme it, I'm wearing mine, right now!"

"Here! Me, too!"

The twins flew to the spot where Orji had dumped the leis. Each fairy took particular care in choosing. Tai picked the one with the biggest balls and Wo picked the one with the most straw. They lowered the leis over their heads, and grinned like fools who had just won first prize.

"Whatever makes you happy, boys — I'm taking a nap," Orji stretched and put his hands behind his head to cradle his skull.

"No, Orji, no! We have to tell you all about Her! She is *so* amazing. Get up!"

"Little winged child, you don't understand. This soul thing.... It makes you tired in a weird way; I'm so tired right now, I feel like I might not exist soon...."

Tai pouted. "Orji, your demise due to exhaustion doesn't happen *that* quickly...pshtt – what a lightweight!"

"Come on, we'll take you to Her. She said she'd love to meet both of you!" Wo clapped his hands with glee, and when neither Saffron nor Orji made any sign of going, he begged for their compliance with his eyes. He looked so positively pathetic that Saffron felt bad, and stood to follow him.

Orji jumped to his feet and said, "Hold on a minute, miss, you forgot this."

She turned in time to watch a petrified lei fly at her face. She squealed with disgust and side-stepped the thing a split-second before it made contact. It dropped with a dull thud to the floor.

"Oh, Saffron.... I've been out there — every single person in this realm wears these. If we come upon any townspeople and you're not wearing this, you'll raise suspicions. We don't know how they'd retaliate.... I've snuck around the outskirts of town. Not *one single person* was without their cow-plop jewelry — it's probably the law." Orji's jaw was set and his stance was solid. He waited for Saffron to pick up the lei and lower it over her head.

Wo and Tai waited impatiently at the mouth of the cave, jittering from foot to foot, but said nothing.

Please," Orji said gently, "I would not be wearing this right now if I were playing a trick on you. I'm dead serious; they're all wearing these out there." He pointed out the cave entrance and stared at her with big, serious, ink-pool eyes.

Saffron shook her head. She rubbed her temples, and took a deep breath. She stared down at the lei. She let out the breath in one long stream, reached for the lei, swiped it off the dusty floor of the cave, and dropped it over her shoulders.

"There," said Orji, "was that so hard?" He had a sly smile on his lips.

Saffron pushed past him and stalked to the opening of the cave. Orji quickly took two steps back and blocked her path at the last second, still smiling. "How old are you?"

Saffron lowered her eyebrows and spat, "Nineteen."

"Really."

Saffron looked at the ground. Orji looked silly with sparkly eyes. Rough man like that with sparkly eyes. Silly.

He reached to touch her hair.

Saffron looked up and slapped his hand down. "I'm twenty-two."

Orji guffawed. "I don't think so honey; you talk more like a fifteen-year-old."

Blood made hot with indignation rushed through Saffron's body and bloomed on her cheeks.

Orji smiled wider.

"Well, Pepere, how old are you?"

Orji lowered his head and looked at her mischievously from under his brows, which he raised and lowered in quick succession like a letch. "I'm either twenty-five, twenty-nine, or thirty-two."

Saffron gasped in disgust, shoved him out of the way, and blundered forward.

Orji stood perfectly still, and watched her as she and her swishy hips hurried away. He rubbed at his mouth as if to wipe away his stupid grin. His face hardened swiftly and surely, like stone.

A quick glance at their surroundings told Saffron that this realm was much like the Earthrealm. However, she noticed right away, there were no birds – she heard no chirps or peeps – just the croaking of a million frogs. They were hopping everywhere. Saffron, Orji, Tai, and Wo scaled down the short mountainside and made their way through a field of wildflowers, neon frogs, mud-colored frogs, white frogs, black frogs, black-and-white frogs. With wide, glassy eyes, the frogs watched the four pass. The leaves on the trees were oddly shaped, and were more blue than green, all sheltered beneath the lime-green sky.

"How far are we going?" Saffron huffed and puffed and waved irritably as tiny frogs with wings bumped about her ears.

"Saffron," Wo replied with a little frown, "you don't have to get all worn out and huff and puff like that — that's another one of your physical memories — don't let it hold us back. Concentrate. Stop breathing hard. Pick up your pace — there is no time for your physical bindings. Do yourself a favor — don't think of yourself as human for now." Wo kept walking.

He didn't see how Saffron stopped dead in her tracks, how her eyes misted with tears, how her shoulders sank. "But I am human!" She swiped at her eyes. "And what does it matter, Wo? You guys are going to get winded sometimes, get physically exhausted — just like when you were carrying Orji. So, why can't I get winded, too?"

Tai made a 'gerrrrff' noise, that meant, 'I'm going to throttle you.' "You don't *have to* get physically tired. Are you going to just let it happen anyway, and hold us all up? This is *your* quest...you're being a brat!"

Orji's jaw moved back and forth behind the skin of his cheek. He lowered his head and looked like a bull seeing red. He stopped beside Saffron and looked at her with a question in his glance. "C'mon, Saffron. Huff and puff, hold your breath — I don't care. Let's get going. We'll meet Miss Wonderful, then head back. I need my beauty sleep so I can move on to another realm."

Saffron's eyes flashed. She watched Orji stalk through the grass. He used his large fingers to pull his hair back from his forehead, but some of it bounced back the second his hand came down. He was in the same predicament as she — wasn't he? Then why had a light sweat started on his brow? Maybe he would claim he imagined this on purpose — sweating was such a studly thing to do. He wasn't breathing heavily, though. Why was he so good at being a ghost? She shuddered. Why did she think about this so much? Why did it bother her? It was only temporary — this ghost life. She would find Markis, get her human body, and be done with it. Why did she contemplate this existence when it was temporary? She wasn't aging, so it really was no big deal. *Buck up, baby.* Saffron took a deep breath, stood up straight, and held her chin in the air. She wouldn't let these insensitive morons annoy her. She spun away from Orji, and stomped quickly through the rest of the field, down to a stream where the twins waited impatiently.

They weren't alone. They smiled from ear to ear, and frantically waved Saffron over, as they pointed to 'the friend' and patted her rump. Their friend had been taking a leisurely slurp from a rushing stream, and as Saffron approached the three with her mouth hanging open, 'Miss Wonderful' lifted her head from the water. She stared indifferently at Saffron with large, brown eyes, and proceeded to chew her cud.

"You must be kidding." Saffron tripped on a granite-hard tree root, looking awkward as she caught herself and put her hands on her hips at the same time. "Really, what exactly is this? I mean, you want to get it on with a cow – really?" Then she muttered, "Effen fairies."

Tai stared at Saffron with murder in his eyes. Orji snorted and looked away. He looked like he was trying not to laugh.

"Why did Orji and I have to come down here? We need sleep, remember? We don't want to exhaust ourselves and vanish because of your damn cow!"

Suddenly, the cow turned and bullet-stared Saffron in the eye.

Saffron tipped her head sideways, ever so slightly, her hands dropped from her hips. Her jaw unhinged so she looked like a Neanderthal.

The cow pawed the earth and snorted.

The hairs on the back of Saffron's neck stood on end — was this cow going to *chase* her? The cow had stopped chewing, stopped swishing her tail, and was *staring Saffron down* — as if she understood Saffron's insult!

Saffron straightened up again and narrowed her eyes — she wasn't going to let some otherworld cow bully her. She had already been through too much to be bullied by a heifer. Her lip came up in a sneer.

Miss Wonderful charged.

Saffron squealed and ran for the blue-leaved trees. She grabbed at a forked branch, ran her feet up the trunk of the tree, flung a leg over each side of the branch, then pulled herself up with her stomach muscles and did a sit-up to reach the branches above her.

Meanwhile, Miss Wonderful had her cloven hoofs on the tree trunk, and was snapping at Saffron with large, square, yellow teeth.

"Call her off!" Saffron screamed.

Tai and Wo still stood by the edge of the stream — they hadn't moved an inch. Orji stood by them, and took in the entire scene with naked wonder.

"NOW!"

"Saffron, she's not our dog. She does what She wants — She follows Her own will." Tai crossed his arms over his chest.

Wo, who usually cut Saffron some slack — at least more than Tai — spoke very rigidly. "You are so lucky She agreed to meet us out here, away from her subjects, because you probably would have gotten us chased out of this realm!"

"What is *going on here!*"

Wo spoke so quietly that Saffron almost didn't hear him. "It's obvious isn't it? We're in love. Against all odds, we've found our soul mate." His eyes *were* love-filled — they darkened with sorrow when he looked back at Saffron. "And all you can do is make fun of us.

Thanks a lot."

Saffron gasped in horror. "Well, how the hell do you fall in love with a cow? This is ludicrous! What — you took one look at her sexy, jutting, rump bones and went undone?"

Tai hawked a loogie in Saffron's general direction. "You know what your problem is, Saffron? You just can't let it go, can you.... You can't stop being a crass human for one minute!"

Orji cleared his throat. "Now, now – I didn't nominate Saffron to represent our race. Watch yourselves now...."

Saffron sniffed and looked down at Orji. "You're human?"

Orji smiled. "You need me to prove it?"

Saffron scowled and looked back at Tai. "What are you babbling about? I *am* human!"

"OBVIOUSLY!" Tai stalked towards the tree where Saffron had, by now, climbed as high as she could go.

"All right, hens, this has gone on long enough. Tai, Wo — Saffron is insensitive...."

"What do you mean *I'm* insensitive...!"

"....and maybe if she could shut up for five minutes...." Orji shot a look at Saffron.

She huffed and closed her mouth.

"....then, you could explain to both of us what it is that's going on here." He held his hand out to Wo, encouraging him to speak.

Wo waited a few more seconds to make sure Saffron was really shutting up, then spoke. "When we met Her, in this very same spot, it was just like a fairytale. We were the poor, young woodsmen going about our business in the forest, when we happened upon a beautiful princess drinking from a stream."

The cow had come away from Saffron's tree, had plodded over to

Wo, and was now gently nudging him. "Hey," he whispered with a smile, as he lovingly stroked her warm, chocolate fur. "Even before we looked into her eyes, when we first saw her bent over the water, we got this little thrill that fluttered through us — you know — like this electric zing.... And, all we knew at that moment was that we had to stop what we were doing —we had to go to her, we had to meet her, we had to be near her.

"Then She looked at us. First one, then the other, and smiled at us."

Tai nodded with a faraway look in his eyes.

"She s*miled* at you?" Saffron gave a hiccuping laugh. She felt very near the edge again. She had the urge to start howling. She didn't know if it would do any good, but she just wanted to start screaming and never stop.

"Enough!" Orji warned, and pointed at her without looking at her.

"When She looked at me, I started to feel woozy. I lost all sense of time and direction and balance. I just floated there, in empty space. No, not empty — She *was* the space.... I was surrounded by Her, touched and soothed by Her." He lay his head on the cow's back and sighed. She lowered long, thick eyelashes over her big, brown eyes.

Tai laid his head on her other side and breathed softly, evenly. Frogs jumped past their feet, heading into the stream for the evening.

Saffron sat silently on her bough and contemplated the issue. This was no joke. They really loved this cow. She felt an inkling of jealousy, and realized she had really, finally, lost her mind. But she couldn't get past the expressions on their faces — serenity, peace, and ecstasy.

"Okay, fine — you love the cow. I have to admit, it's pretty obvious that you're not faking here...but what do you mean 'we'? Are you *both* in love with the cow? How is that ever going to work? Have you thought about that?"

This time, Orji did nothing to silence Saffron; he watched her intently as she spoke, then turned when she was finished with a look of complete confusion. How *did* one share a beloved cow with his brother? He glanced at Wo and Tai — they were frowning.

"So, what's it going to be, boys? How's this going to work? We can't hang around here forever, you know — you promised to help Saffron on her journey." He dropped his chin and looked at them as if he were an inquiring professor glancing over his spectacles.

Tai scratched his head and muttered incoherently. Wo stood quietly with his shoulders down.

Tai kissed the cow on her nose and announced, "We're taking Her with us."

Wo awoke from his stupor and broke into joyful song.

"No! NO. NO. NO! She'll slow us down!" Saffron was salivating.

"YOU are slowing us down, humanoid! You are slowing us down because you're too stubborn to listen to us!"

"My God! You two are morons! Idiots! We won't get anything done with her around — you can't realm-hop with a cow!"

"Wah, wah, wah — shut up!"

"Hey," Wo sputtered, "You got to take *him!*" he pointed a shaking finger at Orji. "We just want to take our love with us too."

Saffron kicked the tree branch in front of her. "Orji is *not* my love. And it wasn't like he was *my* pick, or anything — *my God*!" Her face was as red as her hair.

"Fine," Tai yelled, "You got to take *your god* with you — fair is fair, we take Deva."

Saffron flung her arms around like a toppling windmill. "He is *not* my God — I didn't say that!"

"You don't have to say anything...." Tai hovered off the ground and advanced on her.

Saffron white-knuckled the two branches on either side. "You're *fairies,* aren't you ashamed to be acting like this?"

"Like what?" Tai hung right in front of her.

Orji couldn't listen to any more. He took off his manure lei, dumped it unceremoniously into the reeds, then turned around and headed back to the cave. When he got there, he sat outside on a little, rock lip and watched the frogs fly around in the heliotrope sunset. After an hour or so, Saffron, the twins, and the cow paraded across the field below. He sighed.

Saffron scrambled up the rocky incline and, when she was at his feet she said, "The twins say they won't go any farther without her." She tossed her head in the cow's direction. With the sunset behind her, her hair was alight with red and pink fire. Her highlights twinkled, like golden fire on a crimson red sea. Her eyes looked tired, beaten. "And I can't get very far without the twins, so I guess we're all one big, happy family now." She looked sheepish. "Furthermore, we realize how much help you've been – what with the tree-gang thugs — and don't want to go further without you." She raised her eyes heavenward. "And, I want to apologize for my recent, annoying behavior." She shrugged. "There....."

"Sorry!" Wo called up.

"Sorry!" From Tai.

Orji smiled at the twins and looked back at Saffron, who stood balanced on a rock just beneath his feet. "Come up here, Fire."

She frowned. "What...?"

"C'mere," he crooked his finger and gestured for her to come up on his level, "I wanna touch your hair...."

"What?" Her cheeks colored — two perfect, red pancakes. She looked down at her silly adventure boots. "No. Stop that."

He yelled to the boys, "Good enough! Welcome, cow; I'm sure you'll find this group...tons of fun. Chaps, did you pick up a scent while we've been lollygagging here?"

Wo and Tai exchanged guilty looks. It was Wo who spoke. "He didn't go through here." A brush materialized in his hand — an ornate brush, detailed with gold filigree.

Saffron, who was looking at the fairy boys over her shoulder, jerked in surprise and quickly scanned the area for attackers.

Wo proceeded to groom his new girlfriend. "Deva says they haven't had Fairy in this realm for over two hundred years. We have, by the way, caused quite a stir — the inhabitants know we're here. They don't know *exactly* where we are, but they've already grabbed their torches and pitchforks, so to speak. They are, at this moment, searching for us with murderous intent." He placed a kiss on Deva's nose and patted her head.

Quite clearly, Saffron saw Deva smile.

"So that explains why you've just used magic — again — because there is no use in hiding it since we've been exposed.... But why, oh why, Mister Brilliance, did you have to use it just now? For, you see, the fairy exhaust has alerted the people of our EXACT whereabouts...and here they come!" Saffron had started her comments softly enough, but by the time she finished the sentence, she was shrieking as she watched crudely-dressed people lurch out of the trees like zombies. They most assuredly were armed for attack with axes and bows. Orji jumped to his feet, Saffron started screaming down to the boys to 'run!', and Tai and Wo hopped circles around Deva.

"What are we gonna do? We can't drag her up the side of the mountain!" Wo started running for the mountain base. He shouted for Deva to run with him.

She mooed disconsolantly and galumped after him.

"Stop, Wo – STOP!" Tai flew in the air and landed in front of Deva and Wo. They both crashed into him. Tai hopped up and yipped as he watched the gangly inhabitants closing in. "We can make her smaller – put her in our pockts."

Wo screeched, "I don't know what that will do to her! Only we alter our size!"

Tai grrrrrrd, "We can't discuss this here. Fine, help me carry her up the damn mountain."

They groaned and strained and almost dropped her, but finally got Deva up to the narrow slit in the cave wall.

"Ohhhhhhhhhh! She'll never get through *that*!"

Tai shoved her from behind. "Go, Deva! You can do it! Oomph. Gooooo!" Wo shoved too, and they managed to get her in — just barely.

Saffron, Orji, and the boys grabbed their packs off the floor. Wo stuffed some treasures in his bag. From this realm, he had collected a purple rock, a sundried spotted frog, and a handful of orange grass. They headed for the back of the cave and the portal. As soon as they got there, fiery arrows started pouring in from the outside.

Wo warned Saffron with a stern finger, "Don't presume you're dead and drop if an arrow hits you — it will take us forever to get you to come 'round, and we don't have that kind of time. We have to remember, Deva is still flesh and blood, and we don't want one, tiny hair on her pretty head to be harmed in any way."

They stood by the wall that they had shot out of, but this time they did not feel the portal pulling them. They stepped closer to the wall and still, no pull. The hole was there, they could see it, like a puzzle that is clear only when you've been shown the answer — but it was quiet and as energy-less as any other cave hole. One by one, they climbed into the tunnel. Orji went first, then Saffron, Tai, and Wo.

Deva bellowed like a laboring musk ox.

"Wait!" Wo cried, "She doesn't fit in the hole!" Wo looked back at Deva. He momentarily considered shoving her in.

"Oh, here we go." Saffron muttered as she turned her head in the darkness and peered behind her. "I told you this was a stupid idea!"

Her words floated down the tunnel. Tai and Wo pulled ugly faces and mimicked her without a sound.

Tai and Wo climbed back out of the tunnel. Tai put a hand on Wo's shoulder. "We have to do it."

Wo chewed on his thumbnail and looked forlornly at his love. "But, what if she gets hurt? What if it doesn't work right on her?"

Tai blinked. "We have to do it, Wo."

Wo put his hand on Deva and shut his eyes.

In a pop of fairy flotsam, she was suddenly a tiny cow standing on the dusty cave floor.

Wo knelt down. "My darling, are you okay?"

Deva shifted from side to side and smiled up at him.

Wo closed his eyes and gave quiet words of thanks.

The voices of the outraged natives were coming closer.

Tai scooped Deva up, magicked a boxy pocket on the front of his lederhosen bib, and gently lowered her inside.

The exhaust from all that magic was so great, it came rolling out of the mouth of the cave like a big, dragon belch. It made the people sneeze and scratch at their eyes as they entered the cavern's confines. But try as they might, they couldn't identify — among the fifty or so choices — the hole in which the group had disappeared with their beautiful goddess.

Inside the tunnel, Saffron discovered she was just a wee bit claustrophobic. As she crawled the smooth, inclining floor, she tried to take her mind off the pressing darkness by annoying Orji with questions.

"Why are we taking this tunnel again? We've already been to this realm. I'm not in the mood to retrace our steps. We're not going back to that fricken' forest, are we? What's the point of this? Can you hear me? Isn't there another portal we can use? Can you hear me? You have no idea what you're doing, do you? That's why you won't answer me. Can you hear me?"

Orji gritted his teeth and continued to crawl. The cold stone slid under his palms. His hands moved – one, two...one, two — mechanically, one after the other. The tunnel was as smooth as marble. His knees started to ache a little, so he consciously dismissed the pain.

"Hey, do your knees hurt?" Saffron was stalling. Her voice sounded farther down the tunnel than it did before.

"Get over it, Saffron!" Tai was close behind her.

"Concentrate, Saffron. Just concentrate." But Wo was much farther behind them. He had hung back for a few moments to make sure the natives didn't discover their tunnel.

"Hurry up, Wo. They won't find us now. Li said the portals have ways of camouflaging themselves. Let's go." He pulled on Saffron's ankle and made her scream, which made him smile.

"ORJI!"

Orji recognized hysteria when he heard it. "What *is* it, Saffron?"

"Oh...thank God. I can't see you. Why are you leading us back the same way?"

He stopped crawling and waited a couple of minutes for her to catch up. She did, finally, and as they were in complete darkness, she didn't know he had stopped until her head bumped into his rear. She screeched again, sounding like a terrified piglet.

Orji winced as he dropped to his elbows so his large hands could cover his ears and block the piercing sound as it bounced off the confines of their quarters. Since he didn't prepare himself, he thought he could actually feel his eardrums split. "Hello, Saffron."

"Orji, you scared me! Why are we stopped? Where are we *going*!"

"We're going to the portal, Saffron. Most portals are like street intersections. When we get to the middle of this portal, there will be a choice. We will be able to choose to travel one of four ways. We've already come from one, and searched another, so now we know we'll have two choices out of four to pick from."

Saffron pushed at his rear to get him moving. "Huh. How will you know which one we came from?"

"I looked, Saffron. When we passed through here yesterday, I watched where we were going, so I'd know where to go when we returned."

Saffron's voice became edgy. "We were barreling down this tunnel, Orji — how could you possibly have paid attention to what was going on?"

"I looked, Saffron, I looked. Trust me."

Saffron grunted. "Well, good thing you're driving — I have no idea what's going on with these portals."

Orji smiled. "You'll learn. As we travel, things will become more obvious."

Tai's voice startled them. They hadn't heard him crawl up behind Saffron. His green eyes glowed like a cat's in the darkness. "Can we move a little faster here?"

"Just waiting for you, slow-poke," Saffron smirked.

Orji sighed. All Tai and Saffron ever did was bicker. He crawled on. Finally, the tunnel became larger and larger until it was big enough for the group to walk. After they had walked a mile or so, a light began to glow up ahead — just a pinpoint at first, but eventually it became brilliant and large enough to engulf the entire space. Now that Saffron could see the walls of the tunnel, she gasped in shock. From the cold, hard feeling under her hands, she had imagined the tunnel was marble. But, the tunnel wasn't marble at all — it was smooth, clear glass. "Ooooh, this tunnel is made of glass — look!"

"Nope," Orji yawned. "Not glass — diamond. Flat, polished diamond."

Saffron stumbled forward, completely enchanted. Suddenly, they stood on a threshold, a cliff that hung over a deep, black precipice.

"Let's see," Orji stroked his chin and confirmed with Tai, "We came from there, right?"

Tai frowned. He looked at Wo. Wo held Deva in the palm of his hand. He raised her up to give her a kiss on the back of her neck. He studied the direction in which Orji and Tai pointed.

Saffron looked to where they pointed also. She saw nothing. Well, she saw more cave. Not smooth like their diamond tunnel, but a brown, rocky, normal, and very large cave. The cave had no ceiling and no floor. When Saffron looked up, she saw only a black hole. She looked over the edge of their cliff and saw more of the same. She looked back in the direction in which they were still pointing. She had no idea what they were seeing.

"Yes, that's right." Wo finally agreed. "Yes, we've already been there."

Orji looked, considered their travel options. A slow, devious grin crept across his face. "Well, boys, I'm sure you can imagine which way *I* want to go — but I don't want to insist. Please, let me know how you feel about it."

Tai was confused for only a moment before he realized which path Orji was suggesting. He snickered. "Well, I insist you insist on that portal."

Saffron frowned. They were up to something. Something not good — she could feel it. They were all behaving like mischievous children again, and she was quickly becoming annoyed. "What are you laughing about, Tai?"

"Is it okay with you, Wo?"

"Oh sure, why not? We have to keep checking until we find them. Why not that way, right?"

Tai clapped Wo and Orji on the back. With his arms around the two, all three turned to smirk at Saffron.

"What?" she snapped. They were *so* childish.

"Oh, it's nothing," Tai chimed innocently. "It's just that, *that...*" and he pointed straight down the maw of the black hole, "...that is our next path."

Saffron refused to do it. She refused to give them what they were fishing for. She refused to scream and cry and object. She refused to give them *anything* that they could enjoy. She forced her features to harden into what she hoped was a poker face. She took a few short moments to get a total grip on herself. "How do we start on that path?" she questioned evenly enough.

Tai's smile slipped — just a little bit. "We jump!" he hissed.

Saffron was about to gasp, but caught herself in time. She held her breath to keep from flinching. "Fine, I'm about to jump off of that cliff, so if you're playing games with me you had better let me know now, before I start...free falling."

Tai got his smile back full force. He heard the pause before 'free falling,' and it was enough to titillate him. He nodded slowly and held her eyes. "Yes Saffron, yes. We have to jump!" His wings flapped lazily, back and forth. He knew she wouldn't do it. She'd start bawling and crying any minute now. Then they'd waste more time while she sniveled. More time for him to taunt her in her misery.

"Fine." She assumed a snooty air, "I'll go first, then, since you're holding us up with your theatrics."

Orji watched her closely. They all did. Her face contorted as she struggled for a look of nonchalance. Her hands were fisted into balls, her arms held ramrod-straight at her sides. Her shoulders were held back, her chin high as she eyed the hole.

Saffron's mind was reeling. She broke through the inner screams of hysteria to calm herself. *They wouldn't let you get hurt. They wouldn't let you step off the edge unless it was safe. Trust them, even though they're toying with you. They wouldn't let you get hurt. Step off.* She stepped to the edge. She looked back over her shoulder at Orji. His eyes weren't mocking her as she had expected. They were soft and encouraging. He gave her an almost imperceptible nod. Saffron allowed herself to fall forward even as she held his gaze.

Tai was quite perturbed. "What was all that about?"

Orji shrugged, "Looks like our lady is made of more than we had imagined, hmm?"

Tai grunted and flew down the hole after her. Wo flew down, too.

Orji took a running start and jumped from the edge with all his might, to see how far across he could reach, before he descended. He almost made it to the middle, then pummeled down like a rock. He fell so fast, he felt like he wasn't falling at all, but sitting still while a massive wind pushed past him.

Saffron could feel the fall, though. Her heart flew up her into her throat and sat there, strangling her. She was absolutely horror-struck as she shot through the empty space. She had enough time to think, which made her feel nuttier. *I'm going to die,* she thought. *And what really sucks about it is, I have all this time to think about it. I'm just falling and falling, and pretty soon, I'm going to crash and die.* She had more time, and soon remembered her current state of existence. *Oh yes, that's right — I'm not going to die. I'm going to crash on some surface, my body will turn to bloodied jelly, but I'll still be alive, and can remain there — as fully-conscious, bloody jelly. And I'll have to remain bloodied jelly until I turn myself right again.* She rolled her frenzied eyes. "How long is this going to take?" she yelled, then screamed like the banshee everyone assumed she was.

Chapter 13

They plunged into water. It was the first time a portal had led them to water, but here they were, plunging down several yards into a frothy, icy sea. This was their seventeenth realm. The handful of realms after they had met Deva were uneventful, save for a few small run-ins. They found no hint of Ny or Markis in those realms; no hint of fairy existence.

Saffron was blasted down into the depths of the water, and then, just as quickly, was thrust towards the surface like a cork. Before she came to the top, she panicked and thrashed her arms and legs around wildly. She felt a hand grasp her arm and pull her up. When she broke free of the water, she was face-to-face with Orji. He was howling with glee and spitting the water, fountain-like, into the air.

"Whoo wee! Wasn't that fun!?" His hair was plastered back from his face, the greys and greens of his hazel eyes sparkled brilliantly as drops of water fell from his lashes. He was very close to her, and his hand was still clenched on her arm.

She smiled at him and his manic glee as she pried his fingers from her bicep. She swam a little bit away from him, but looked back when his laughter came to a sudden stop. He stared at her, an expression on his face that she could not read. "Thank you. Thank you for saving me. I'm going to tread water over here now."

"Hey, it's no problem. Do whatever you want." He seemed a little embarrassed and turned away. He looked intently at their new surroundings.

"Get her up....get her up!" Wo was screaming at Tai.

"She *is* up! She's fine! Chill out, will ya!" Tai glared at Wo as he tread water with his two legs and one free arm. With his other hand, he held Deva aloft. She was bellowing softly, as befitted her still-small size.

Wo shot up and out of the water, droplets cascading from his flapping , wet wings. "Give her to me — before you drown her!" He reached down and gently pried Deva from Tai's fingers.

Tai gave her up so she wouldn't get hurt. "She was fine....I wouldn't let her drown, you know!"

Orji stopped playing spitting-fountain-head. "Why can't we all just get along!? Why don't you stop griping, and live it up, right? What we're doing here – it's called 'having an adventure.' So quit your whining and have fun!"

Nobody said anything. Tai and Saffron treaded water in silence and Wo crooned softly to Deva as he hung fluttering in the air. Tai flew up by his side and crooned to his love.

"Well, now, that's better. Silence is a great alternative."

Saffron, Tai, and Wo — united at last — glared at Orji.

Orji was very irritated himself, but refused to show it. When he was with Saffron just now, holding her arm and looking in her eyes — her bottomless, beckoning, naïve eyes — he thought he would go insane. For the very first time in his life, he felt that sensation of 'about to lose it.' Then he saw her eyes blink from welcoming innocence to hardened closure. When she swam away, it was unbearable. He felt himself being gathered up in a net she had unknowingly cast. When she swam away, she made a hole in the net, big enough for him to slip through and get away — save himself. Still, he swam within the net, confidant that he could get away at the last minute. Orji scratched his rough chin and chuckled.

It appeared to be dawn in this realm. A mist hung over the water, making it impossible to see farther than twenty feet in any direction. Wo licked the water from his lips and brushed the hair from his forehead.

"There," said Orji. He pointed to a place, a dark blur behind the mist.

"Do you know what it is? I mean, are we swimming towards a pleasure palace that will serve us a twenty course meal, or a slimy sea monster that'll gnaw on my girlfriend for dinner?"

Deva mooed. Wo stroked her tiny head with his forefinger and sang her a song.

"Doesn't matter, make a swim for it — we'll figure it out when we get there. I don't feel like treading water all day long."

Tai picked his teeth. "You could levitate."

"OMG! Do not start with that crap again! We can't levitate, okay? Shut up." Awkwardly, Saffron turned in the water so she was looking away from Tai.

Orji swam away from them. Something in the movement of his ghostly limbs, the push of water against him, the energy it took to cross the water, satisfied him. He pushed harder. Saffron was getting on his nerves, and he didn't like to be an irritated guy. He wanted her off of his mind. He was the first to arrive on the little beach. Tai and Wo had hung back to chatter quietly as they often did. As soon as he could, he touched down on the soft, sandy bottom of the sea. He walked forward until he reached dry sand, then collapsed.

Saffron collapsed beside him. The twins fluttered over. They all sat complacently on the beach with nowhere to look. Everything was shrouded in mist. Deva mooed and made them all jump.

"You know what?" Wo muttered, "No one will see our residue here, and the energy from it won't travel — the mist will work as a container. I'm changing her back to her usual size. She really hates being this size. It's been horrible not to be able to oblige her; she's such a good soul."

"She's a cow," Saffron mumbled.

Tai and Wo gave her dirty looks. Tai gently lowered Deva to the sand and then they each put a finger on her body. A sparkling cloud of chartreuse fought with the mist for air space, and then, poof, Deva stood before them, full-sized.

"Hey, Deva." Orji gave her the thumbs up like he would a good buddy, then hung his head between his knees.

"Hey, Deva, lookin' good..." Saffron chirped, "...especially if I had some tangy sauce!"

Deva turned around, raised her tail, and evacuated one foot away from where Saffron was running sand through her plastic fingers.

"Yeah, nice.... Nice girlfriend you guys have."

"Hell of a lot better than *Orji's* girlfriend," Wo whispered to Tai.

"What?" Saffron looked at them with narrowed eyes. "*What?*"

Deva snorted and smiled.

Saffron was about to press them when Wo cut her off. "Hey," he whispered and jabbed Tai in the ribs with his elbow, "..look." His eyes widened. "Look at that man."

Orji, Tai, Deva, and Saffron stiffened as they spotted the man through the mist.

He was strolling onto the beach with a surfboard, and soon caught sight of them. "Hallooo!" he called out, friendly enough.

"Stars above...," Wo whispered as his entire body went lax.

"What, Wo? What is it?" Tai frowned and stared at his starry-eyed brother.

Wo was totally transfixed by the man. He got up to follow the newcomer as he strolled on past them.

"Wait!" Tai yelped and flexed his wings as he reached up for Wo's slack arm. "Wo, where are you going?"

"Oh," said Wo. "I'll be right back...." Then he disappeared into the mist after the man with the surfboard.

Orji jumped to his feet and dusted the snow-white sand off his behind as he watched Wo retreat. "What's going on?"

"Your guess is as good as mine; what kind of realm is *this?*" Tai craned his neck, but there was no longer any sign or sound of Wo.

"He said he'll be right back." She shrugged. "So, he'll be right back." But her mutters sounded hollow with disbelief.

"C'mon, no use sitting around — let's check this realm out, and move on."

Tai wouldn't budge. He stared hard at the mist where Wo disappeared.

Orji spoke gently. "They just went surfing. This mist should lift soon, and after we check the place out a little, we'll come back here to collect him. Let him go."

Tai nodded and trailed slowly after Orji, who was followed by Deva.

Saffron got up, dusted her behind, and followed too, as Orji strode towards what looked like a building in the thinning mist.

It wasn't long before they found themselves on the main street of a bustling town. People passed them, gave them friendly smiles, and murmured polite greetings. Orji and Saffron were thrilled to be received as such, for once, as they appeared. No one mocked their clothes, sneered at their hair, chased after them because of their differences. The townspeople seemed genuinely pleased to see them. But the folks didn't hover. As polite as they were, everyone seemed very busy with their own affairs, and after a very brief 'hello,' each person moved on.

One woman stopped to pinch Tai's cheek, and coo at his cuteness. He smiled back at her, then wiggled his wings out from behind his cloak and stretched them wide. He was testing her, as Saffron had seen him do before, to see if the woman would shriek in horror or smile with dollar signs in her eyes at the discovery that the cute little boy was a freak. Tai enjoyed testing people by flashing them, which Saffron thought was a little disturbing. The woman did not scream or look greedy — she didn't flinch at the sight of his wings at all. She merely formed an 'O' with her mouth, and 'ooohed' and 'aaahed' like a good mommy when her child has done something amazing. She gave him one final pat and moved on.

Tai grinned like a fool in love. "Well, this is a nice change." The woman gave a friendly pat to Deva on her way by as well. Deva smiled with all of her teeth.

Orji and Saffron released simultaneous breaths of relief. Finally, they were able to relax just a little, after what seemed like an eternity. They looked around.

It was a hilly island. Almost like Greece. The walls of the dwellings that surrounded them seemed to be made of white stucco. They were igloo shaped; every building with a rounded dome roof. Most of the buildings were built into the hillside, and disappeared in the mist.

On the street, vendors sold food, toys, furniture, and odds and ends. Saffron watched as one man called out his variety of meats — sausages, chicken, turkey; all roasted brown and perfect. Saffron felt her mouth water — how she missed her body sometimes. If only to eat again. The vendor was a heavyset man with jet-black, oiled hair and a long, black, curling moustache. He wore a puffy-sleeved white shirt, a red vest, and black swashbuckling pants. He called out with a rich, deep voice. "Sausages here — git your sausages here! Flaming hot and juicy — freshly roasted!" He smiled at Saffron; she couldn't help herself, and grinned back.

The city was intoxicating. Just then, another man walked up to the vendor. They shook hands fervently. This new man was tall, lean, with wavy, blond hair and blue eyes. The two men chatted amicably for a moment, and then the blonde man stepped behind the meat cart as the curly-mustached man stepped away from it. The curly-mustached man saluted the blonde man, then disappeared into the crowd.

Hmmm, thought Saffron, *must be his relief person.* But almost immediately, she noticed *all* of the other vendors were being replaced by someone new. The original vendors took off into the crowd, and Saffron thought that they must work for the same big corporation and were probably relieved all at the same time.

They walked on.

Tai came to a sudden stop. "Who's that?" His eyes grew round and soft with amazement, like a child recognizing his reflection for the very first time. "Quick! Don't lose her." He sprinted forward, leaving Deva to moo at his sudden absence.

"Oh, c'mon," Saffron muttered, and placed her hand on Deva's head as they surged forward to keep up with Tai.

But Tai was already, suddenly, gone. He was lost within the folds of the ever-thickening crowd. "Tai!" Saffron shrieked. There was something odd about the way people disappeared around here. Although the land was beautiful (from what she could see within the mist) and the people kind, just the tiniest bit of anxiety started to cool her blood. "Tai!" she shrieked louder.

"I'll be right back!" She heard him answer. His call was exuberant, joyful, even.

Saffron stopped walking and let her hands fall limply to her sides. She frowned and looked at Orji. Deva moved closer to her side and Saffron patted the cow's head absently.

"What's going on here?" Saffron whispered to Orji.

"I don't know, but I'll tell you what..." he looked around at the smiling faces and laughing crowd. He breathed the fresh, sea air, and noted that the sun that had finally come out. The mist was almost dissipated. "...I'm not going to worry about it right now. Things are a little weird, yes — but very far from bad; that's for sure."

Saffron nodded slowly and looked around. She wanted to take his word for it, needed to take his word for it. Maybe she wasn't used to nice people and nice places. *Perfectly nice places.* Maybe she had been bitter for so long, she couldn't see a good thing without prying for its faults. She took a deep breath, then another, and told herself to relax.

That's when she saw the woman. She was standing at a vendor's cart, inspecting a small wooden object, and laughing with the sales clerk. The woman shook her head to nod in agreement with something the vendor said. Her long, chestnut-brown hair flowed and shook, like a silk banner as it rippled in the breeze. Saffron could smell the woman's hair, could feel it between her fingers, and felt it fall across her face as her mother read her a goodnight story.

She took off after the woman.

She was so close. *Wait, don't go,* Saffron thought, but said nothing out loud. The woman was still at the stand. Saffron could close the gap in a few quick seconds. She pushed through the crowd.

"Saffron!" Orji grasped her hand.

Saffron was snapped from her thoughts. She turned around to meet Orji's furtive glance.

"Where are you going?"

She saw the distress in his eyes, but realized, finally — he would find someone soon. He wouldn't be wallowing in his grief for much longer. She couldn't help him, anyway. She needed to go — go after her mother before she disappeared. "Orji, don't worry — I'll be right back." Then she pried her hand from Orji's desperate clutch and ran after the woman who had moved away from the vendor's stand.

When Saffron caught up with the woman, she was breathless. She tapped the woman on the back. She was almost convinced her own mother was about to turn around. But, no, when the woman turned, Saffron realized she was a stranger — someone who looked like her mother.

The woman smiled warmly at Saffron, then reached out to smooth a strand of hair behind Saffron's ear.

A warm, soft feeling started to flow through Saffron; it calmed her and washed her in bliss. "I...I'm sorry...." Saffron stuttered. She couldn't keep her eyes off the woman's hair — it was *exactly* like her mother's. It was the same length, shade, and texture. Saffron was convinced it must feel as soft, too.

The woman eyed Saffron with a twinkle in her eye. "Here," she offered Saffron a length of hair, "is it just as you remember?"

Saffron took the hair, in the middle of the crowded street, and ran it between her thumb and forefinger. "Yes," she sighed softly, then smelled it because she couldn't resist. Yes, the scent was the same. Saffron was beside herself with joy. Somehow, in this realm, all of her senses were back with incredible strength and such poignant clarity, that she wanted to weep. She could smell and hear and feel everything!

"Who was your woman?" The stranger cocked her head to the side. Her eyes sparkled, her lips curved into a soft smile. "She was your mother, wasn't she...."

Saffron nodded. "I know you...don't I? We have a past...?" Saffron beamed as she looked at the woman. She wanted to hug her, go home with her.

"No, Luv; we have never met before. But I will not begrudge you your mother. Come with me. Let me love you, comb your beautiful red hair, tell you bedtime stories, cook your meals." The woman gently pulled Saffron to her chest and hugged her.

Saffron closed her eyes and sighed.

The woman held her in the middle of the busy street and rocked her gently. As she rocked her, she sang in Saffron's ear, the very same tune Saffron's own mother had sung to her before she fell off to sleep every night as a child.

***

Wo sat on the beach with the man, who was waxing his surf board. While he worked, he explained what he was doing. The man lovingly ruffled Wo's hair, and talked about how they were going to go surfing togther. Then, later, they would go fishing and perhaps that evening, they could camp out on the beach — make a fire from the driftwood, and contemplate the constellations. Tomorrow, the man said, he and Wo would start batting practice. The man was exactly as Wo imagined his father would be. The father he had never met.

***

Deva stood alone in the middle of the crowd, mooing pathetically. The passersby said, "Oh, poor thing," and patted her on the head, and kept going. Deva was all alone. First Wo, then Tai, then Saffron (which Deva was actually glad of), and now, Orji.

A woman had made off with Orji. She was an older woman, whose hair had just started to grey. As soon as Orji locked eyes with her, he was gone. It seemed he never heard Deva call after him.

Now, Deva looked frantically around. She was about to cry big, cow tears when suddenly something caught *her* eye as well. A field — a field beyond town filled with luscious, green grass. She moved towards the grass like a hypnotized beast, her tongue lolling like a dog's.

***

The woman told Saffron to call her 'Mom,' as they walked into one of the domed buildings. "Shall we live here?" Mom asked.

Saffron looked around. It was a simple house — rustic kitchen table with mismatched chairs, old-world pottery strewn about, and plants everywhere.

"This is an odd place," Saffron said as she moved to stroke one of the clay cooking pots.

"Tell me, what was your home like?"

"Oh...." said Saffron, and struggled to remember. Her old home seemed so far away — her memories were clouded and wishy-washy. "I think it was a farm by the sea — but I can't remember much more than that...." Saffron sighed.

"Well, I think I have just the place!" The woman clapped her hands with delight, then rushed over and took Saffron's hand. She led Saffron out of the dwelling and down the street. As they walked, time seemed to warp around them. Everything would speed up and blur, as if someone was pressing a fast-forward button. Soon enough, they arrived at a dwelling that sat on the edge of the sea. "And, how is this?"

Saffron looked around, noted the furnishings were more contemporary — just like in her old home. "This is perfect!"

"Good! Then let's live here!" The woman rubbed Saffron's back, then told her to sit at the kitchen table. 'Mom' was going to make fresh-baked, chocolate chip cookies.

Saffron felt her heart swell, and her senses fill with a warm, mellow feeling. It was like love and deja vu and ecstasy all rolled together. The feeling washed away a little when she remembered, "I don't think I can eat them — I'm a ghost."

"Oh, that's sweet, dear. Don't worry — anything is possible here. You'll enjoy them." Mom laughed. "You'll enjoy them." She kissed Saffron on the forehead, smoothed her hair, and set about making the cookies.

Saffron looked out the kitchen window to the sea, and soon lost herself deep within memories of her beautiful mother and happy remembrances of childhood.

***

"Do you think this could work?" Tai had drawn up some quick plans to incorporate a double-sided fireplace in the half-finished mansion on the hill. All of the other guys on the crew gathered round to inspect the plans.

"Incredible! I think it'll work!" Some of the men clapped Tai on the back, and encouraged him to talk about the details.

Once in awhile, Guy, one of the guys, would interrupt Wo to tell the next dirty joke in his repertoire of never-ending filth — he couldn't contain himself — they were *good* jokes.

When Tai was finished casting his plan, the men cheered as one.

Then Sully said, "Shit; let's get started — these plans rock!"

Tai grinned and followed the men over to the other side of the house. They were a gaggle of sweaty, foul-mouthed, talented, overgrown children.

***

Orji sat with the salt-and-pepper-haired woman on a steep, rocky hillside that rolled down to the sea. He plucked a length of tall grass and worked it between his teeth. He turned to the woman and smiled. She grinned back.

"I can't believe it; you're just like her, you know. And I'm not talking about your looks only — you are *just* like her!"

The woman smiled and patted his knee. Then, once again, she looked down to watch the ocean crash and turn far below them. " That's the way it is in this place. We always find each other — somehow."

"Am I like someone you once knew?"

"Oh, yes. There has to be a pull between the two, or we wouldn't pair off. But, it's relatively easy to pair off, I believe. I've never been left longing for too long — not here. It seems I can find him in so many faces."

Orji was quiet.

"You remind me of my son. My son — just before he met that woman and changed into a person filled with hate and sadness. He left with her, you know — I never saw him again." She looked wistful for only a moment, then smiled and cupped Orji's chin. "Until now. How you remind me of him — the quiet confidence, the screaming cockiness!" She laughed and lovingly gripped the back of Orji's neck.

"So, what do we do now?"

"Why, we enjoy each other, of course!" She stood up and reached for his hand.

They walked along a curve of the steep, hilly path and chatted.

He didn't think of his friends, or the need at hand — he was entranced with this woman — who was the essence of his mother.

***

The next morning, Wo woke up to the sound of the ocean. The water lapped at the shore, while gulls screamed overhead and searched for breakfast. He crawled out of the tent and left the man — the father he always wanted, but could never have. The man snored like a lawnmower; it made Wo smile.

Wo sat on the beach and thought about the night before. He had ached as they watched the night sky — oh, to be an astronaut! The open universe! Fairies couldn't go into space any old time they pleased. Humans, who had no wings, could go into space – but fairies were locked within the planet's atmosphere, as if in a bubble. Wo wanted to be human. He wanted to be launched in a shuttle into outer space.

"Mornin'!" A man strode over to where Wo sat in the sand. The guy crossed his arms over his chest, and stared into the cloudless, blue sky. Then he glanced down at Wo, and said with a wink, "Lift off at 1400 hours — want to come with?"

Wo's jaw dropped. "What?" He was barely able to squeak out that one word.

"I'm going to the stars, son — you look like a budding rocket-man to me. If you want to come, there's an extra seat."

Wo jumped to his feet and followed the man off the beach.

***

Saffron sank her teeth into a soft, warm pancake. It was all buttered up and sprinkled with cinnamon and sugar. And there were maple sausages — her favorite breakfast. It was just as wonderful as those cookies 'Mom' had made. She had smiled with pleasure when she realized Mom was right — she *could* remember the taste of a freshly-baked, chocolate chip cookie! She had finished the cookie quickly, ate three more, and chased them with some cool, creamy milk. She could taste her breakfast this morning, too. Mom leaned against the kitchen counter, sipping hot coffee. Outside, the ocean bashed against the cliff on which the little house was perched.

"What is this place?"

Mom walked over and patted Saffron's hand. She sat down on the chair across from Saffron, sipped her coffee, and said, "It is the place of longing fulfilled."

"Who are you?" Half of Saffron didn't care who the woman was — she was just so happy to be with her, be near her. 'Happy,' didn't describe the feeling of pure joy that moved through her in rolling waves. It was like the first time Saffron finally realized Markis liked her – when she replayed the moments with him in her head — over and over — just to feel the surge of emotion jolt through her. Euphoria.

Then again, a little part of Saffron frowned on the whole thing. And, although it was only a tiny part of Saffron — it was persistent. This part of Saffron needed to know exactly what was going on here, because the whole realm was more than a little odd, and not being able to put her finger on the precise oddity made her all the more leery.

"It is the place lost souls and needing souls gather to find each other." Mom smiled and ran her forefinger around the edge of her mug, slowly, until a whoo-whoo sound started. She kept the pace steady as she traced round and round and round the edge.

"Why are you here?" Saffron bounced her knee and fiddled with her hair as she stared, starry-eyed, at Mom.

"I lost my child, my little girl. I'm looking for her." Mom stopped her finger and held her hands in her lap. She looked intently at Saffron, "you are like my little girl — red hair, impish grin...." Her voice trailed off. She walked to the window of the little house and looked out at the sky.

Saffron heard a noise, a ruckus outside. She walked to the large window which looked like something the seven dwarfs might have installed, and looked out.

Nothing.

She heard a giggle, then the gurgle of a baby. She poked her head out, and there below her, in a bed of petunias, sat a little girl.

The girl had copper-red hair and was digging in the dirt with an ancient-looking trowel. She looked up at Saffron and screeched. She threw some dirt.

Saffron was mildly surprised to find this squabbling baby all alone in the flowerbed.

"Look, Mom."

Mom turned from the window on the other side of the room. As she moved across the room, her skirt swished and lemongrass scented lotion hung in the air. Mom looked out the window, then down. "Ooooh," she cooed. She tweaked Saffron's nose. "I'll be right back...."

Saffron watched Mom make her way towards the smiling baby in the crushed flowers. She watched the woman pick up the baby, and kiss its sweet, chubby cheeks. She watched her whisper soft things in the baby's ear. She watched her walk away, slowly, down the lane.

She cried, "Mom!" then ran down the lane after the woman. Soon, Saffron found herself back in the center of town — in the crowd of souls. She searched. She searched for her mother. She searched for

Derek. She searched for Markis.

Suddenly, there he was – Markis. He called her over. She let out a soft cry of relief as she pushed her way towards him. But the throng of people had become too thick, and they were all walking in the opposite direction — milling slowly and impenetrably against her. "Markis...!" But he was no longer there; she had lost him too.

Someone tapped her on the shoulder. She heaved a sigh of relief — somehow, Markis must've come up behind her. She turned with a smile, frowned in confusion, then beamed with joy. It was her grandmother. Her mother's mother. "Grandmother?"

"Of course, Darling!" Her Grandmother's laugh tinkled like the bell sound of the wretched fairies. "Come with me — we'll make sure that frown stays upside-down!" Saffron nodded and drifted to the edge of town with her 'grandmother.'

***

Orji hurt his cheeks with smiling. He had to keep reminding himself that this woman was not really his mother, but he was ecstatic to be with her all the same. He questioned her on this.

"Oh, it's nothing really. Remember those moments just before you fell asleep on a restless night? Think of all of those times you thought of the past, of the people you loved, and of the feelings you had with those loved ones. That is what this world is —those feelings of longings fulfilled. The feelings of blissful satisfaction."

"But it isn't real — you're not really my mother. Why am I satisfied to sit here with you as if you were? Why do I have no urge to leave here?"

"Well, why is a memory so satisfying? Hmm? It isn't 'real,' is it? It's not the exact moment it happened. It's just the memory. But, oh, the powerful emotion that comes with memory. Here, my lad, your emotions are satisfied, purged. There are no hardships here — only the different levels of bliss." She patted his knee. "Just sit back and enjoy. Then, after a time, if you wish to find someone else — your father, sister, brother, lover — you leave here and go look for him or her. You can always find anyone here, and relive those days. Why, you can even live your dreams — work a job that satisfies you, sit by the ocean and dawdle the day away, visit a far away country.... You can find your mother again, too, in a different face. You can find your mother at a different time in your life as well." She laughed. "I don't know how long I've been here — a long time, I guess — I've found my son a thousand times. He is all I wish to search for."

Something, way down deep in the pit of Orji's gut, nagged at him. But he couldn't think clearly, and preferred to push it away, instead of drag it into the light of day and figure it out. He rubbed his eyebrows. "I came here with some..." He felt very confused now — he didn't even know what he was trying to say. He shook his hand, "some...people." For the life of him, he couldn't remember who they were.

The woman raised an eyebrow. "Interesting — I've never heard of one arriving *with* people — we've all come here looking for people. Hmm. No matter — if you need these people again, your mind will beg, and you'll find someone close enough to assuage your memory and fill your senses."

Orji nodded. "Okay."

***

So the days went on. Orji, Saffron, the twins and Deva moved from loved one to loved one, and from dream to dream. The Dreamrealm had set them adrift, and not one of them cared.

Chapter 14

Ny sat with his elbows on his drawn-up knees. The land around
them was brown and dry, a barren wasteland, void of life. He looked
behind him and watched as Markis slept at the bottom of the gilded
cage. He contemplated waking Markis up, for some companionship —
maybe to pick on him. He scowled. He was no torturer — he was a
lover! Why did Saffron drive him to do this? He disliked being here.
He was tempted to leave Markis here alone, and go out and have some
fun. But, then, he ran the risk of discovery. What a shame that would
be; he had worked so hard to never be found. He wondered if Saffron
would give up. He hoped so — that would mean that she didn't really
love Markis. That would mean that he could pay her another visit, rile
her up, and set the chase anew.

Chapter 15

Back in the Waterrealm, Saffron and Orji came face-to-face in the marketplace. They were both leaning over a stand of fresh, tropical fruit, sniffing at mangoes, when they bumped shoulders and looked at each other to apologize. But, before any words fell from their lips, shock washed over them and rendered them speechless. A wave of energy ran between them. It was so thick that it was almost tangible.

Saffron frowned as she stared at the strange man before her. The mango fell from her hand. The man was so...beautiful. His dark hair was wild and messy, his sparkling, hazel eyes, magnetic. She couldn't look away from him. Who was he?

Orji found himself in the same predicament. She was like a goddess, this woman before him. Her porcelain skin was smooth, flawless. Her hair framed her face in red fire, her eyes lulled him. He wanted to kiss her.

This meeting was odd. He had met many of his loved ones in this place, and had spent time with them all. But this woman was not like them – he knew the others when he met them. *Who was she?* This was like trying to remember the title of a song. He knew her name — it was right there on the tip of his tongue — he just couldn't spit it out. But he knew one thing for sure; this was a woman he had to kiss. He had to crush her against him and feel her and kiss her.

He dropped his mango as well, and moved to her. He placed his hands under her soft hair, at the base of her skull. Her eyes glazed and her lips parted. He watched her eyes. She wanted him, she seemed to be anticipating this moment — it was all the encouragement he needed. He leaned forward and covered her mouth with his, drawing her tighter and tighter into his arms.

It was true; Saffron had wanted this man to kiss her. More than anything, at that moment, she needed him to step forward and do exactly what he had done. And, just before his lips touched hers, she thought she would faint dead away with the intensity of it all. But when his lips touched hers, and as she pressed her body into his, she suddenly realized — there was no feeling here. Emotion aplenty. But feeling? No. It was like kissing plastic. Not like Mom and her warm cookies. Not like that girl who was the spitting image and temperament of Coco. This man was like no one she remembered from her past, and though she wanted him desperately, she couldn't feel him. She was so sure the kiss would tell her *something*. Then, suddenly, she had the most instantaneous, rudest awakening of her life. All at once, she remembered who this man was. Man, nothing — this was *Orji!*

"Saffron!" Orji spat her name out like a hiccup, because he, too, had a sudden rush of memory that tried to overwhelm his senses.

"Oh, my God, Orji! What are you doing!" Saffron pushed off of his chest and swiped at her mouth. She backed up a safe distance and eyed him warily. "Why did you *do* that?!" Did he *know* she didn't know who he was? Was he totally taking advantage of her? She crossed her arms over her chest and glared at him.

She tilted her head. Her alarm vanished. He *hadn't* known. He had no idea. She could see it in his confused and searching eyes — he was just as bewildered as she was. He looked sheepish as he ran a hand through his mop of hair. He glanced around the marketplace, as if searching for a distraction that could end this excruciatingly odd moment. His eyes settled back on Saffron. He winced. "I have no idea what the hell just happened here. I have no idea why I've completely forgotten you exist until this very minute. What kind of place *is* this? I mean, it seemed good. But no, it's not so good. Why does it make us forget reality and encourage us to live out altered memories?" He shook his head.

Saffron shrugged and looked at her feet. Her head shot up. "Wait a minute...." She looked around the marketplace as well. "We're not the only ones here. We came here with someone else. No...not someone...others....Right?"

Orji's eyes narrowed and he stared at a point just beyond her right shoulder. "Did we have a pet?"

Saffron nodded slowly. "I think so." She was thoughtful for a moment. "Did we have a horse? Like a miniature pony or something?"

Orji didn't look convinced. But he wasn't exactly sure she was wrong, either. "Yeah, I think you're right. I think it was a miniature horse." He tried to work that out in his mind, like a child who forces a puzzle piece into the wrong spot, just to have someplace to put it, and end the aggravation.

"But, there were others, too," Saffron pointed out. She bit her bottom lip.

Orji snapped his fingers. "Weren't they like dwarves or something? They had something...." He shook his hands in the air trying to come up with a word. "Something, about them."

Saffron leaned against the cart, sending coconuts rolling off the top. She picked them up absently, and put them in the pineapple bin by mistake. The vendor quickly retrieved the coconuts and put them back in the correct bin. He tsk-tsked Orji and Saffron, and encouraged them to move along, to have their conversation somewhere else.

As they walked away, a little unbalanced, Saffron slipped her hand into Orji's.

Shocked, he looked over at her.

Right away, she said, "Look, I don't think we should get split up again."

He nodded. He gripped her cold, celluloid hand tightly.

"No matter who you see, no matter what you feel...just hang on to me, okay?"

He nodded again, more vigorously this time. "You're right, you're right. We need to get out of here and get our wits about us. Let's just try to find our friends...what were they?" He rolled his eyes. "Let's just try to find them and get out of here."

Saffron stopped walking. "How do we get out of here?"

Orji shrugged.

"How did we get in here?"

Orji shrugged.

Saffron waved the air with both hands. "What are they? What are our friends?"

"They had something about them." Orji looked at the sky. "They weren't human." He watched a bird fly by, then dismissed it. "They had a thing...." He scratched his chin. "Like a horn or something."

Saffron perked up. "Yes, that's right!" She forced herself to concentrate. She stared at the ground. "But it wasn't just one...they had two things...one on each side...two horns...I think."

Orji tugged on her hand. "You mean like little devils or something?"

Saffron shrugged, comme ci comme ca. "Sure."

Orji smiled encouragingly. "Well, let's get to it then, shall we?

We're looking for two little devils and a miniature horse."

Saffron smiled weakly. But, since she didn't have a better idea, she began to search for two little devils and a miniature horse.

They searched the marketplace. They searched the shore. They searched the countryside. Many nights passed and still, hand in hand, they searched. They were approached several times, sometimes by people who "knew" Saffron, sometimes by Orji's acquaintances. They held fast to each other. Even when the desire to follow another was great, they held fast. Each relied on the other's will — the other's strength. They now believed that what they really needed, what they really searched for, could only be found if they stuck together.

On the morning of the fifth day, while Saffron considered a beverage cooler in a small country store (a store that could have been found in Arkansas in the late fifties), she found Tai.

She knew him instantly. "Look, Orji — there's one of our little devils."

Tai sat crouched behind a rack of beef jerky, firing spitballs at the woebegone clerk. He was crouching low on his haunches, rocking back and forth on the wide plank floor. He sucked in a gulp of air, and shot it out with such force, that a sloppy ball blasted across the room and, SPLAT, shot the man in his newspaper. The spit, already soaking into the thin newsprint, slightly marred an advertisement for the new "Turbo Bra." Tai wanted to whoop with glee — a direct hit! But he somehow contained himself.

The clerk didn't even blink, but kept reading. Just when Tai thought he would quit, (it was no fun shooting the things at people if they weren't going to react!), the clerk suddenly became animated, reached under his counter and retrieved an unusually large bat. He came screaming from around the back of the counter and crashed right after Tai. Tai laughed with evil merriment, fluttered into the air, and cruised right over the clerk's head and out the door.

Saffron watched wide-eyed. Wonder filled her as his wings flitted as quickly as a hummingbird's. She looked at Orji. "Told you we were looking for devils."

"Yeah right, horns/wings...what's the difference? That was an easy mistake." He grimaced. "My God Saffron, we could have been searching for little devils the rest of our days! We could've wandered around here aimlessly for the next hundred years!"

"Don't blame me!"

"I'm not *blaming* you!"

"Then why are you yelling at me like that? I don't care what you're *saying* — your *tone* of voice is blaming me! Why don't you just..."

Suddenly, her eyes filled with fright. She looked beyond Orji's shoulder, towards the front of the store. The psychotic clerk had given up on Tai, had spun about, and set his evil eye on Saffron and Orji. He gave a blood-curdling scream and headed towards them, his bat brandished high.

Orji and Saffron cut to the right, bashed down the baked goods aisle, and ran out the front door, leaving the ting-a-ling of bells in their wake.

They caught up with Tai on a dusty, tire-pitted road. He had a stick over his shoulder, a handkerchief tied at the end which held something round and heavy. Saffron took him by the shoulder and roughly spun him around. He stared at her indignantly for a good, long minute. Then his eyes widened in surprise as he croaked out, "Saffron?"

She clapped her hands with joy and yelled, "Yes, yes!" She took him in her arms and kissed the top of his honey-scented head.

Tai let Saffron hold him. In fact, he clung to her for dear life. "What's going on?"

Saffron shook her head and wiped at her tears. "We have no idea, really. Just hold on to my hand and don't let go. We know that much for certain — you mustn't let go."

Tai agreed easily enough, and slipped his hand into Saffron's. Saffron felt his heat, and a fleeting yearning whirled through her as she held tight to Orji. How she wanted to feel Orji's heat. She glanced back wearily at the little store, but the clerk didn't come out.

Tai swatted his hand in the same direction and sneered, "Ah, he won't come out, that worm. He's a serial killer. His thing is to act like a geeky little store clerk, then WHAM (Tai slapped Saffron upside the head — she shoved him back) crack people's heads with his bat." He snorted. "That's his thing. I've been watching him — him and countless others. Killers. I've been pissing them off, too! That's MY thing!" He remembered some of his zany antics with the killers of this world. He chuckled and patted himself on the back.

Saffron watched Tai carefully. His eyes were the darkest shade of moss and filled with misery. She assumed this world had not been so good to Tai, not nearly so fulfilling as it had been for Orji and for her. She wondered, "Tai, have you...found anyone here? Found any of your loved ones?"

Tai scrunched up his nose, looked at her as if her mind was gravely disordered. "I've found no one here, just been wandering around...annoying serial killers...." He scratched his head, looked away from her and into the dark woods ahead. His shoulders drooped.

Saffron moved to him and stroked his cheek. Then she inched closer still, reached around, and rubbed his back between his wings.

He leaned into her, just a little bit.

"I won't let you go again, Tai. I'm going to hold on to you and take care of you and everything is going to be fine, understand?"

Tai could have argued that statement, could have proclaimed his fairy superiority, but he didn't. He nodded and allowed her — just this once – to care about his welfare.

"Tai, do you remember who else we need to find?"

"My brother, Wo." It dribbled out of his mouth like water — even he was surprised at his knowledge and quick answer.

"We had a pet, too," Orji, reminded them. He pointed a finger at Tai. "I even seem to remember...she was your *girlfriend*. She's a miniature horse."

Tai's shoulder's hitched up together as he winced. This could not be! "I'm dating a horse?" He was incredulous. It just couldn't be! And yet.... "Whatever you say, man, I can't even think straight. I'll go with what you say." He looked around uneasily. "When the time comes, are we going to be able to get out of this funky place, or what?"

Saffron scrunched up her eyebrows. "I think that's something you do; you go into the woods and ask...someone."

"Trees!" Orji shouted. Tai and Saffron jumped at his loud outburst.

Tai's eyebrow shot up. He rubbed his lips together and thought. He nodded then, impressed with his own ability. "Let me give it a try here." He walked over to a large, leafy maple tree. It was bursting red in autumnal glory with a wide spread of leaves that shaded the entire lane. He stood silently before the maple and looked up into its canopy. He walked back to Saffron and Orji and grabbed Saffron's hand.

"Nope, sleeping. Dreaming about walking around, its roots like feet or something."

Saffron shuddered. How that image freaked her out. "Let's get going," she mumbled.

They decided to retrace their steps — the market, the shore, the country. One evening, they found Wo back on the beach where they had first lost him. He was sitting with Deva and they were watching the sunset. He had his arm around her; she had her head resting in his lap, like a dog.

Tai took flight and landed on his brother with an Apache war cry. The twins tumbled in the sand, laughing and screaming. They stopped wrestling, and Tai leaped onto Deva. He grabbed her neck, kissed her nose, and scratched her ribs. She fluttered her long eyelashes and mooed sweetly. Then he looked up and frowned at Saffron. "She's not a *miniature horse*, you simpleton — like I'd ever love a miniature horse! Sheesh!" He rolled his eyes and buried his nose in Deva's neck. "She's a ridiculous human, huh, baby."

Saffron bit her lip to keep from spewing fire. Let him make love to his cow — he was insane. "Let's get out of here. How do we get out?"

Orji grabbed her wrist, twirled her around, and grinned. "A portal — we need a portal!" His face contracted with swirling emotion — shock, confusion, shocked confused. Finally, his face became devoid of all expression. "And, I can find it! *I'm* the one who can find this portal because...." He looked towards the sun as it sunk into the ocean. "....because it's out over that water."

A huge grin spread over Saffron's face.

Orji smiled triumphantly and smiled down at her as she beamed at him. His eyes traveled over her lips. He opened his mouth to speak – then remembered their kiss.... What had gone wrong? Why had it felt like he was kissing a doorknob? Memories were still coming back to him about this girl. Slowly, but surely, he was realizing the position they were in. When he had met her back at the fruit cart, he was operating on pure instinct. He had looked at her, was struck by her raw, wild beauty, and decided he needed a taste of her. He had no memory of their previous encounters to stop his advance. But now, those memories were slipping back, and actively eating at him like a disease out of remission. With the memories came the irritation. He didn't *want* this girl. He was relieved kissing her was so unexciting — it put an immediate end to a situation that could have been even more embarrassing. What if they had gone further?

They found a boat abandoned on the beach. A little dinghy, really, in need of a scrape and a paint job. At least it was sea-worthy. There was some trouble getting Deva into the thing and settling her down, but, finally she sat, her legs folded under her. Throughout the process, there was nonstop bickering — Saffron wanted Tai or Wo to zap Deva into a miniature cow, Deva protesting vehemently that it was not necessary to change her size, so she wouldn't give her consent, and Orji grumbling under his breath.

Saffron sat beside Deva on a splintering bench while Tai and Wo flew beyond the bow, tugging the vessel towards the sea with an old, frayed rope. Orji was behind the boat, pushing with all his might. Finally, the boat parted from the sandy bottom and set adrift towards the sun. Orji jumped in and rowed with one pitiful oar.

"Which direction?" Tai was not thrilled to rely on the starry-eyed Orji. He wished there was a tree in the middle of this wide water so he could depend on himself. But, what if there were? The trees in this realm, so he had discovered, were as whacked-out as the people — no memories of anything constructive, just some emotional jargon and vague yearnings. He spat into the waves.

"Straight towards the setting sun," Orji said with confidence, then looked back and settled his eyes on Saffron. He had no idea what he was talking about, 'straight for the setting sun.' He laughed a bit maniacally — recovering his memories was grueling. This place had brought his mother back to him, and it was all the more unbearable because she wasn't real. As they floated farther and farther away from land, the blissful feelings lived-out there dissipated like fog in the sunlight.

Saffron and Deva frowned at Orji. He seemed...not too well in the head. Their woman's intuition had united them. They exchanged knowing looks. They huddled together and looked back at the shore as it drifted out of reach.

Chapter 16

It was as if they were pummeling down an outer-space, alpine slide
— whooshing around smooth curves and barreling down steep inclines
of clear, empty blackness. Upon their rude delivery into a field, they
streaked across rough grasses that made their teeth chatter.

"Will this ever get predictable?" Saffron moaned, and received only
a few grunts and swears for answers.

The trip from the ocean to this new realm had shaken them all.
They had been slowly floating out to sea, when, suddenly, their little
boat shot forward. As if caught up in a hurricane-force wind, they
were shoved towards the sun, then spun about in the water multiple
times before they were pulled straight up into the sky – boat and all.
After several moments – filled with screams, grunts, and moos – they
were here, in a field.

"Let's get out of the field, folks, and into that dense forest just over
there. We don't know where we are. Come on now, stealth mode,
everybody." Orji lowered his brow and looked furtively around as he
made for the forest with long, quick strides.

Saffron, Wo, Deva, and Tai struggled to their feet. They left the
boat sitting in the middle of the field and moved to follow Orji into the
cover of trees. Wo flicked his right wing several times, just like a
person whips his hand to get his elbow to pop.

This land didn't look much different than the Earthrealm in
summer. The trees were lush with green leaves. The sky was robin's-
egg blue and the gold field grasses waved whenever a breeze touched
them. They crossed a tiny stream that burbled clear, cool water – the

only thing that set it apart from Earthrealm streams was vibrant, yellow rocks that glowed and hummed as if electrically charged scattered up and down the river banks.   Saffron breathed a sigh of relief. That other world — she couldn't even describe it — had been too cockamamie for her.

They walked a couple hundred feet into the forest and came upon a slightly elevated spot covered in pine needles. It seemed like a good place for a temporary camp.

Back in their little boat, in the Dreamrealm, slow sailing had set Saffron nit-picking. She glared up at Tai till he could ignore her no longer, and finally, shouted, "What...?"

"What are you waiting for?" Saffron tapped her toe impatiently.

"Holy crap, crazy woman – what are you *talking* about?"

She huffed. "Tai, somewhere back there in mind-meld land, our packs disappeared. Don't you think you'd better get us some prep and props while we're safe? Who knows if you can use magic in the next realm!" She shook her head like he was the biggest dolt on the planet.

Wo held his hand up to Tai. "Don't say a word. Let's just do it. You know it makes sense."

So, Tai and Wo conjured up new cloaks for them and fulfilled wishes for various do-dads.

"Can't you like, summon up a yacht for us? A yacht with an engine? This slow-ass dinghy is going to sink and drown your girlfriend.... Saffron eyed Deva wearily.

"Yeah, sure — can you give me a thousand push-ups for *my* enjoyment, Saffron?" Not for the first time, Tai chucked Saffron the bird.

Saffron snorted and ordered her cloak be put back in the ether. She didn't want a cloak; she demanded a pashmina scarf — of alpaca

— just like her scarf at home. The scarf was eight feet long, three feet wide and the electric, magenta color of a Caribbean sunset. She ordered black jeans too, and a black, turtle-neck sweater. Under the sweater, was a black, fitted t-shirt, and steel-grey camisole

Wo and Deva tilted their heads together and smiled at Saffron's picks — the vivid pashmina, the impossibly soft, alpaca-fiber sweater and scarf, and the same tall boots she had had on since they changed back on the clouds.

Tai rolled his eyes. To him, Saffron couldn't be more ridiculous. He adjusted the hood of his new cloak around his head and sat regally at the stern as tiny waves licked the sides of the boat.

Tai and Wo had worked for a long time, redressing everyone, and filling their packs with what they argued would be the best stuff to have as they moved forward. For the final touch, Wo and Tai presented Deva with a thick blanket for her back, and a heavy gold chain on which hung a large ruby. They put it around her neck. She sighed with pleasure.

"Wait, Tai – where's our monocle?" Wo gave his lederhosen pockets a pat-down.

"I don't know, man. I don't know where the last several weeks of my life went, never mind that damned thing."

"Tai! That was ancient! Fairy-made!" Wo gave Tai's lederhosen pockets a pat-down.

Tai giggled. "Whataya doin'? Stop that!"

"Tai, we can't go back to the realm without that – they'll kill us!"

Tai shrugged. "They can kiss my ass. I was a zombie – how could I possibly have kept track of it?"

Saffron groaned. "Just stop your whining and make another one."

Tai and Wo both looked at her like she was a cross-dressing gnome.

Wo shook his head. "We can't just make something like that – it takes elders and ceremonies and gods present to conjure up one of those things...."

Saffron tsk-tsked. "You guys are in huge trouble."

"Yeah, if we ever get home." Wo magicked up a shiny, new oar for Orji to row with.

Orji grunted. "Yeah, a small engine was too much to ask for, right?"

Wo sighed as he continued to pull small necessities out of the air.

All of that magic had given off such a large plume, the dreamers on the far-off shore thought they were seeing an aurora borealis effect.

Now, in the new realm, the twins left, searching for signs of Ny or essence of fairy. Saffron rummaged through the packs for their tents. Deva was off a little ways, trying to find suitable munchies.

"Isn't it weird – you don't have to set up those tents at all...we could just sit here and let hurricanes pound us...." Orji was smiling. It was a wistful smile, but he was grinning — like usual.

"Tents wouldn't help us in a hurricane, anyway, Orji – I'm setting these up for appearances, in case anyone from this realm comes across us...."

"Yeah, I know. I know. I'm just amazed at how much we do for show, and how little we really need." When she reached for another tent pole he tilted his head so he could see better – her sweater fit so snugly to her waist.... "Saffron...."

She been bending over, trying to figure out which pole went in which hole.

"Will you stop fussing? I want to talk to you." Orji's voice came from close behind her; it was low and warm – as if he was touching her.

She shot up and stood pin-straight. She felt very alone with him, here. Her ears began to burn as she felt control sliding out of her ghostly muscles. This was way too uncomfortable. "Orji, shouldn't you be off to town – trying to find out what people are like...?"

He smiled at her and didn't answer.

"You know...like usual...don't you need to get going?" She pointed in the direction from which they had come.

"Why don't you come with me?" He was standing there, so innocent-looking. So welcoming.

Saffron was tempted. "Aaahh, no." She shrugged her shoulders and turned back to the tent in dismissal.

"Come on, Saffron. Come adventuring with me, live on the edge. There's lots to discover...." He walked right up behind her, clapped his big hands on her shoulders, and rubbed them vigorously. He bent down and whispered in her ear, "It'll get your blood flowing!"

Saffron jumped when he touched her and gave a little yip. When he started whispering in her ear, she moved away from him. It was embarrassing to be touched, knowing she felt wrong to others — as if her soul was diseased and contagious. What was up with him? He was in the same predicament that she was in — didn't he mind that he felt like a Ken doll to everyone else?

"Stop it, Orji!" She didn't *want* to go into town. She didn't *need* those people staring at her. There was no *reason* for her to subject herself to that when Orji could do it, and didn't care if people stared at him.

Orji looked thoughtful. "When I found you in the Dreamrealm, by the crate with mangoes, you were alone — all alone in a bustling town. You weren't all stressed out and timid then. Do you remember that?"

Saffron's hand flew to her throat as she fought down an eruption of shame. His words had brought the scene screaming back. The kiss. The kiss she had wanted, at that moment, more than anything in the world. The kiss that bombed so badly. She didn't want to think about *that*. After all, they were here to find Markis — that was the mission — not to get Saffron over her fear of townies. She made a noise of disbelief and shook her head. "I had no memories in that Dreamrealm," she replied with a superior, knowing air. "I didn't remember that I hate walking around alone. Now I remember. Now I don't want to."

Orji hunkered down, balanced his rear-end on his heels, and leaned his arms on his knees for balance, "Can't you find some strength in that? I mean, if you did it before, and did it well – can't you go into this town with a new mindset?"

She still couldn't put the right pole in the right hole. She threw both of the fiberglass rods to the ground and roared, "Orji! Just go, will you? I need to get *this* done!" She stalked away from him, over to Deva, where she proceeded to chastise the cow for her habitual eating.

Orji stood up, crossed his arms over his chest and stared at the back of her head.

She could feel his eyes piercing her skull, so she squared her shoulders and refused to turn around. She threatened to whack Deva's nose if she didn't stop eating. Deva head-butted her and sent her flying into a thorny thicket. Saffron screeched when she felt the thorns slice her. Deva went back to her very sweet, five-leafed-clover patch.

Orji walked away. Earlier, on the way to the forest from the field, he had noticed a path that led along the edge of the field in the opposite direction from their camp. He intended to follow this path now, and hoped it led to a town.

There was a buzzing in the air, not unlike the grating strum of cicadas in August. As the sun beat down on him, he made his way along a freshly-mown field. He breathed deep and willed the heavenly smell of cut grass to come back to him. Surely, there must be inhabitants close by. He whistled a tune and hopped over fallen logs. Pink butterflies floated about his head and clung to his shirt — obviously attracted by the shirt's dark red color. They soon formed a cloud around him. It wasn't too unpleasant — they weren't buzzing in his ears, or trying to take a bite out of him. But, they did make it somewhat difficult for him to see. Soon there were so many, he was stumbling along the path.

"Take that; you Daffrigits!"

A stream of liquid blasted Orji in the face. It smelled like vinegar, as if someone had just hit him with a torrent of pickle juice from a water gun. It trickled down his chin and soaked the front of his shirt. "Blah!" He grimaced and spat out the briny liquid.

The cloud of pink butterflies dissipated.

"What's the matter, there, you? You go out de house without your shnagu?"

The old man — no teeth, tattered clothes — was eyeing Orji suspiciously. At least Orji *assumed* the old man was 'eyeing' him. How could anyone tell? Instead of sunglasses, the old guy wore a curtain rod on his head – a curved rod, fastened into the hood of his cloak with a little curtain hanging from it that covered his eyes.

Orji found it disconcerting to talk to the man. He didn't know what feature to focus on when he spoke to the guy. He preferred to look into people's eyes when he spoke, that way he could read their true feelings; because the words people spoke were often not as true as the expression in their eyes. He cleared his throat. "I've misplaced my *shnagu,* actually." He shrugged and looked at the man's chapped lips. He winced and spit out more of the vile fluid. "Blek! What *is* that?"

The old man jerked his head back. He suddenly looked very nervous, as if he realized, too late, that he was with a crazy person.

Uh-oh — wrong thing to say, Orji. Now Pops is more than suspicious — good going. He spoke quickly. "My mother's recipe, you know, for that stuff...hers is not so...."

"Oh, gee — then you taint from round here, are yer? It's all the same round here, now, isn't it?"

"Yeah, you're right — I'm not from round here. I'm from the North...."

"Yah, yah, that makes sense — they talk funny from up de North."

Orji displayed his Village Idiot smile. He silently reminded himself to shut up. It was good advice that got him out of many dicey situations — *When in doubt, shut up.*

Alarm froze the features of the man with the walnut-shell skin. He pounded a beetle with his walking stick. He looked around – probably hoping for back-up. Suddenly, he mumbled something that sounded like a departing comment and skulked away. He turned his hidden face towards Orji to keep an eye on him from behind the veil. When he was a good distance away, he turned back and yelled, "You know, tis vulgar to walk around so, without your shnagu — take care thems don't pick up you! Tis disgusting what you do!" Now the old man was good and mad. He jerked himself around and stomped off down the path.

Orji was trying to sum this all up when he noticed something else that was very odd. As the old man stalked away, Orji was shocked to see the guy's bum – there was a hole in his pants big enough to expose the whole thing! Orji stood still, thinking, for several moments. He decided to walk on and inspect more villagers before he jumped to any conclusions and took on any changes.

Soon enough, he found the village nestled in a valley, looking like a conglomeration of tiny pyramids. From the safety of a bush he spied on the townsfolk. His fears were confirmed — like the old man, all of their backsides were exposed to the wind. He sat back in the cover of the shrubbery and contemplated his next move. There wasn't much he could do about the whole situation, but join them. With a shrug, he took off his pants. He withdrew a pocketknife and got to work. When he cut the bum out of the pants he saved the severed piece of leather to use as his face covering. He wouldn't be able to see through it, but he had no other cloth on hand, and no fairies to whip some up. He scratched around and found a pliable twig to use for the curtain rod. He cut two holes in his hood, one on either side of his face, and hung the tiny thing, rod and leather, across his eyes. It was completely awkward. He had to reach up every few seconds and adjust his handiwork. Finally, he gave up adjusting and cracked the stick, so it settled tee-pee-like on the bridge of his nose. It was the ugliest pince-nez ever.

When Orji was done fighting with the mask, he held his pants up to appraise that bit of work — it wasn't designer quality, but it would do. He slid the pants on, shivered as the air caressed him, and walked into the village. A smile spread across his face as he thought of Saffron, and what she would look like with her pants "altered." He walked along the town thoroughfare with his head tilted back and his eyes peering from beneath his 'veil.'

A plump woman greeted him as she passed. "Jolly-jolly," she said. Her tilted head faced him longer than was comfortable. But, she moved on.

He stumbled on a rock, caught himself, and kept going. He supposed he looked strange — but not too strange — and might be able to pull this off without alarming anyone. Next, a young woman passed, all the right curves in all the right places. He nodded at her, drawled a seductive, "Jolly-jolly," and then tried to control his grin as he snuck a look at her after she passed. His jaw dropped and he stared harder. *Oh, sweet alien gods, I sing your praises on this day!"* He was still grinning madly when he was shoved from behind.

"You okay there, bull?" A big, brute of a man stood sweaty and heaving before him. The brute man clenched his fist so his knuckles cracked. His veil fluttered lightly as he exhaled through his piggy nostrils.

"Yeah, I'm alright." Orji rolled his eyes. A thug was a thug was a thug, in any realm. "How bout you?" Orji was glad he couldn't smell — the man had a host of flies milling around his body.

The brute made no move, just towered like a redwood tree, and looked silly behind his delicate veil.

"Yeah, I gotta go." Orji would have loved to take a jab at the oaf, but they weren't done in this realm yet. He rolled to his right and disappeared in the thick and flowing crowd of the small city. The brute didn't bother to follow him. Orji moved awkwardly. Sometimes, he looked down to shuffle around various feet, his leather veil falling forward and allowing him a good view of the ground. Sometimes stuck his nose in the air and peeked out from underneath it. This method soon proved dangerous, as people gasped and backed away from him when they caught sight of his eyeballs.

He grew short-tempered and dreamed of jumping someone, dragging him into the woods, and taking the man's little veil. He was gathering more and more attention. Then, as if in answer to his unspoken prayer, he found himself beside a little shop that sold veils. He quickly moved inside. As soon as he entered, a short man approached him, and asked if he could be of service. The clerk eyed Orji at length. "Oh, my, my, my," the man bubbled, "of course I can help. What is this here, this shnagu, you're wearing currently?" The man bit his bottom lip as if to hold back a smirk.

"This veil wasn't cheap, you know, and it's all the rage up de North!" Orji sniped.

The smirk left the clerk's face. His cheeks turned a bright, siren-red. "But, of course, sir. Forgive me...I am not worldly, and would be forever in your debt if you would be so kind as to fill me in on all of the latest Northern fashions!" The clerk snapped his mouth shut, and stood waiting.

"I wish to shop in peace!" Orji boomed, and waved the clerk away.

"Oh, yes, sir! Yes, sir — whatever you wish!" The clerk was off with a flutter of his fine veil.

As soon as the clerk's back was turned, Orji grabbed a handful of veils from a nearby basket and, with the other hand, a clutch of rods. They were safely stuffed in his pants long before the clerk reached his desk and turned back towards the store with an air of snooty indifference.

Orji picked up an unusually sheer veil and brought it to the clerk. "What about this one — will this do?" Orji held the super-sheer veil before the clerk.

"Oh, well, yes. Well, she must be a fiery one to wear this! This is practically see-through! This, sir, is for a very racy lady. This is perfect for the intimate evening alone."

"Hold this aside then; I'll have my wife come try it on later."

"Most certainly, sir!"

Orji caught a glimpse of the price sticker; it had a lot of symbols on it. Must be why the clerk was suddenly so joyful.

"For you, sir, I shall hold it till closing!"

Orji strolled back outside. He casually made his way behind a large pyramid – it looked like a maintenance supply shop. He felt around in his pants for the contraband and fitted a veil over a rod. He forced each rod-end through the holes in his hood. Better already — he could see through the veil, and since the rod was thicker than the tree limb he had just used, it fit into the holes on his hood more snugly, and was not apt to fall down.

He took a moment to tamp down his indignant pride. He had never stolen anything before. But, they all had a job to do in finding this freak of a fairy, and he thought it a good idea to go out among the people – he always learned something important when he mingled with the natives. Saffron was correct in one respect — if they did find Ny in a certain realm, and needed time to rescue Markis, then they had better know something of the local culture and customs so that they had a better chance of blending and avoiding being found out as realm-hoppers. To be among the people in this realm, alterations were called for. He stuffed the remaining veils and rods into a pocket on the inside of his cloak and rejoined the crowds on the city streets.

Now, he was seeing quite a bit more than he had before. Men, in bottomless-butt suits relieved their bladders, just off the sidewalk. When they were done, they fastened their pants and walked on — as if they had merely stopped to smell the roses. Not one person in the crowd looked on as if anything were amiss. On a park bench, two mothers nursed their babies — breasts exposed, and eye-veils firmly in place. Up ahead, in what looked to be the city center, there was a very large wooden, wooden block bench — about twenty feet across and ten feet wide. About every four feet, there was a hole in the box, so half of each side held a row of five holes. It appeared to be a giant domino with ten dots on it — but this was no giant domino.

Orji realized, all at once, what is was, and although he considered himself to be a man who had seen it all, a man jarred by nothing — well, he simply couldn't believe this. He held his breath and winced. This "domino" was, in fact, a big bank of toilets. Passersby simply walked up to a hole, sat down (there were a few with reading materials), and got on about usual toileting activities. Again, not one person took a second to stop and stare, or even do a double-take. No one but Orji.

A ball rolled across the street and knocked into Orji's feet. It startled him out of his reverie. He picked it up, looked around, and saw two young boys waiting for him to return it to them. He walked the ball over to them.

"Hello, men, how are you?" The two veiled heads looked at each other in confusion.

Orji blundered on, "Jolly-jolly, boys! I'm not from around here. I was wondering if you could tell me why those men over there are peeing on that tree, and why those women over there have no tops on while they feed their babies?"

The veiled heads looked at each other again. Finally, "Whadaya mean?" The boy with the brown hair shrugged, "You gotta pee, you pee — you gotta feed the baby, you feed the baby." He shrugged again.

"Well, I think some people would say a man can't pee on that tree because it's not clean...."

"Listen buddy, if my dog can pee on that tree, then I sure as hell can — nature is nature right?" He took a step back from Orji.

"Well, why do the people wear pants at all?"

This time, both boys took a step back. "Well, you gotta kneel down sometimes...." Dead silence. "C'mon, Brint, let's go." The brown-haired boy clamped his hand on his friend's arm and quickly pulled him away.

Orji decided not to pursue the subject with anyone else – he made for a strange stranger. But he was quite sure these people would find the ways of *his people* off the wall at times, as well. He wondered how the old warmongers were faring. He wondered at the absurdity of the latest alien-encounter tales. One thing was for sure, he was going to miss those alien stories. Who knows, maybe in his realm, he was now a folk hero — a martyr, or at the very least, a celebrity. He knew without a doubt that the town's people would be spinning tales about his "alien abduction." Those that weren't dead. When they didn't find his carcass in the street they would naturally assume he'd been abducted by aliens. It would be a nice supplement to fortify their weak beliefs.

He approached an old man sitting on a park bench. As he sat down, the man smiled with very worn lips. His face was so steeped in wrinkles, Orji had trouble finding the man's mouth amongst the trenches.

The man croaked, "Heh-hee! What a day! Think they're still having crappy weather in Dazidukk? I hope so, those daffrigits! Hee-hee." He leaned back against the bench and entwined his bony fingers.

"Funny you should mention, Dazidukk — I came to ask for directions." Orji's mind was buzzing, searching for the different jumps he could make to lead the discussion to a nonchalant chat about portals.

The old man jerked forward. "What? Go to the Center Building, register, go through the portal...." He shook his head as if Orji were a naughty puppy.

For the second time today, this odd realm had taken Orji by complete surprise. All of the realms had been a little odd, but this one, this was *the* Oddrealm. He sat there dumbly. His Go-Into-Town-And-Spy mission was so easy, he was slightly annoyed. He wanted to have at least a *little* adventure. Saffron was going to be thrilled to hear that all they had to do this time was walk to the center of town, sign a paper, and walk through the portal. Orji's shoulders slumped as if he was deflating.

Just then, a beautiful woman walked by. He watched her pass, a feverish light growing in his eyes. He grinned. His grin turned into a huge, cheek-aching smile, and his eyes glowed beneath his veil with an evil idea. He sprang from the bench and giggled with glee as he headed back out of town.

As he jogged along the trail outside of the city, he took off his rod and veil. He came upon the twins. They were gliding straight at him. On the ground below, Deva bounded along like a puppy to keep pace. It was an odd thing, to see a cow bound. The twins seemed glum. They were shaking their heads, 'No.' Orji assumed correctly that they didn't find Ny and Markis.

"He didn't even pass through here to get somewhere else. This is getting annoying, but at least the trees are friendly here. The trees told us the portal is in town. All we have to do is register and walk through. It's not even going to hurt this time, can you believe that? Just walk right through to the other side." Tai scratched his head, then suddenly started flinging his arms wildly all about him, to scatter the cloud of butterflies that had gathered out of nowhere and were flitting about his head.

"Whoa, whoa, big fella! Here," Orji stood and moved two steps closer to the twins, well within their personal space, and stood quietly. In an instant, the butterflies broke up and flew away.

Wo looked sideways at Orji.

"Don't worry, my friend; I'm not moving in on your little heifer there — just clearing the butterflies for you. Some old coot sprayed me earlier with this foul-smelling stuff that repels..." he smelled his shirt, "...probably everything."

Tai snorted, "You don't have to tell me. Whew, you reek!"

Orji winked. "I have no idea what I smell like! Got some good news, boys...." He proceeded to tell them what he learned of the town, and even better, the plan he'd been cooking up in his head. "Of course, it'll help her get over her fears...."

"Orji, there are people with big coconuts in the world, even bigger than yours, who wouldn't do what you think you're going to get Saffron to do."

"She'll do it — go in the woods over there and fix your pants. We'll be along soon. Just don't make fun of her right from the git-go. We need to get her far enough into the city that she won't consider running back to the woods... We need to get to that portal."

The twins flew off , followed by their bovine lover.

"Wait!" Orji walked through tall, blue-green grass to get back to them. "You'll need to wear these too." He handed each of them an eye curtain and curved rod. "Poke the ends through your hood. Like this...." He showed the twins the correct way to wear the unflattering headgear.

Half an hour later, Saffron was ranting, raving, and screaming in the middle of the woods. Orji had told her that he had met the twins on his way back from town and they hadn't found Ny. He had also told her that she needed to prepare herself to go into town to use the portal. He told her *exactly* what she needed to do.

"I'm sick of this! I'm sick of weird people who do freaky things! I'm tired of you always telling me 'We have to, Saffron,' 'It's the only way, Saffron.' This is stupid and it's GROSS! Who walks around with their derriere hanging out?!" Then she screamed some more. After a while she threw herself to the ground, panting.

Orji said nothing during the entire tirade — in fact, he was speechless. Saffron had such *passion* in her — if only she would use it for good instead of hysteria. He waited a little while before he said, "Saffron, do you ever stop and think before you start screaming? The only reason this is a big deal is because it's a big deal to *you*. Nobody else out there in this realm, thinks there is anything odd about the way they dress. If you could give up your prejudices for one afternoon...."

"I am *not* prejudiced! I've got a poster of Will.i.am on my closet door!"

Orji made the wide-eyed, I-think-you're-a-lunatic face. "So?!"

"So...he's black." Saffron stammered.

"Saffron," Orji tugged at his ear lobe, "there are a million more things in the world to be prejudiced about than just the color of someone's skin."

Saffron's face turned purple with rage. "Don't you talk down to me! I know what being prejudiced is, and I'm not!"

Orji broke out into a big, toothy grin. "Good! Prove it! Stop complaining, stop making fun of and belittling things and people that scare you, and just do it! Let's go out into this realm, Saffron! Let's show everybody that we can hang bare-assed in the wind and not have a care in the world!"

"Very funny," Saffron sulked.

"Look at you, Saffron — I bet you'd look cute with your rump hanging out of your pants!"

"Oh, my God." Now, all the color drained from Saffron's face. She sat down hard, as if she had already cut the trap-door out of her pants, and wanted to hide her behind. That's what Orji had told her just now — the people in the town — they had *holes* in their pants...! Right where the bum is...! For convenience! "Why do they *do that?*" she asked miserably.

"I talked to some boys — this culture seems to think it's ridiculous to cover certain areas of their bodies – they don't want their functions hindered. Like the boy said, 'it's all nature'." Orji lowered his voice, gentled it to a lilt. "Saffron, we have to get to the portal and search another realm. Do you have any idea how much Earthrealm time has passed?"

Saffron shrugged, "Not *that* much time...."

Orji's shoulders slumped. She really liked to repress things. He didn't care how long this quest took — he had nowhere to be, and no one to miss him. Life was just one ongoing adventure. Now that these nice folks took his body to a cloud far, far, away — he couldn't age either. He was thrilled. He could see each and every realm — even if it took him 500 years — and he'd always be this same, young, strapping-hot guy. He smiled —what a world! But people missed this girl. And she missed them. He could see it in her sad eyes and ever-slowing reactions. Time meant everything to her.

"You can't look at me." Saffron mumbled.

Orji stared at her blankly. "What?"

Saffron sucked in some air and stood up tall. "You can't look at me."

"OH!" Saffron's meaning suddenly dawned on him. He brushed

his knuckle under her chin. "No problem — I'll walk in front of you." He looked as sweet as angel — one of the ones that set up shop below-ground.

"Okaaay...en oh — NO!" An uninvited image of Orji's naked butt floated to the surface of her consciousness. She tried desperately to beat the image down with hard-blinking eyes. "No! You will walk on the *side* of me — that's the only way I'll do it"

"Fine, fine. C'mon, I'll help you cut your pants."

"Oh, you wish." Saffron refused to make eye contact as she thrust her hand out, "Gimme your knife; I'll do it myself!" She turned and walked into the woods, ruthlessly swatting at helpless branches. "And don't follow me, either," she spat over her shoulder.

He mimicked her as he watched her walk away.

It was a long time before she emerged. The twins had sneaked back into the camp twice, impatient and rearing to go. Orji mouthed, 'No!' and waved them back to their camouflaged waiting spot. She walked super-slowly out of the woods and kept mumbling, "OhmyGod, OhmyGod...." with each footstep.

Orji experienced just the slightest pricking of shame when she finally stood before him.

She was so scared, she was shaking. Her eyes were dark with fear, her pupils dilated to two large, black spots. Her hands were at her chest and she wouldn't stop wringing them. She entwined her fingers so violently that her knuckles cracked. Tears welled in her eyes.

Orji had never seen anyone quite like this — unless you were to count that time he and his buddy were captured by terrorists. The terrorists threatened to skin them both alive. Orji and his friend had glanced over at a pile of bodies with no skin seeping fluids into the dirt in the corner of the compound. They knew the terrorists weren't kidding. At that point, Orji's friend had started to panic — to fall apart just the way Saffron was now. Orji hoped nothing *really bad* ever actually happened to her — she'd give herself a heart attack. She could probably self-combust. "Saffron," he whispered, and gently massaged her shoulders, "never mind — you don't have to do this...." He sighed. "We'll go at night — we'll break into the town building and use the portal." *What if there's an 'on' button and you have no idea what it is — or, how to activate it?* "Or maybe, we'll have the twins make you invisible. Don't worry, we'll figure it out."

Saffron swiped at her eyes and immediately resumed the hand wringing. "No," she said flatly, "I'm sick and tired of being a baby — I'll do it."

Now Orji felt like a real loser. "Saffron, you're not acting like a baby. This fear you have, it's...it's not your fault. I know I've been pressuring you to get over it — and maybe I've been wrong in doing so. I never thought it was your fault.... This fear you have — it's just something that happens to some people. It seems like it's terrible." He shrugged, "I was just hoping you could get over it, so you could have a little happiness in your life —breathe a little freer."

"I said, I'll do it." Again, flatly.

"Okay, then, here's your veil." Orji handed her the veil and rod. He swung his pack on his back. He had repacked the entire camp while Saffron dawdled in the woods. As it turned out, it wasn't a very big realm. The twins had scouted the entire world in a few short hours. There had been no reason to set the camp up in the first place. But they didn't know that at the time.

Orji helped Saffron adjust her veil, then carefully turned around and moved close to her side. "There. Neither one of us can see the other – although, I don't mind if you can't control yourself and need to take a peek."

Saffron's eyes became slits as she ground her teeth.

"No? Well, okay, but you'd be the first to complain."

Quickly, Saffron pushed her veil-rod back like a headband, and looked up into Orji's eyes. She had never considered his sex life before. What was he talking about — she'd be 'the *first* to complain'? What was he, some kind of man-ho? Her stomach did a little flip-flop before she got control of herself, and forced all considerations of Orji's past out of her head. Though it had been nice. For those two turbulent seconds she wasn't thinking of her poor hiney.... She closed her eyes and took a deep breath.

As they walked the path, Orji kept up a running commentary of all that he'd learned about this realm. Saffron wasn't really listening, but the drone of his deep, melodic voice soothed and comforted her. She was able to tune out her nudity and concentrate on his voice.

Soon enough, they came upon the twins, who pretended they were just getting back. Orji flashed them a look and gave a slight, almost imperceptible shake of his head.

They looked at Saffron, then back at him with evil hilarity in their eyes.

Orji pursed his lips and slashed his finger across his throat. His movement startled Saffron.

She looked up at him in confusion, wondering what he had just done with his hand.

Orji smiled warmly at her and shook his head.

Saffron looked straight ahead, prepared to zone out, and put her mind somewhere else. She ignored the breeze that kissed her rear.

The twins jumped in front of her. With their little butts a-jiggling, they sang and walked arm-in-arm down the lane.

Saffron made the throat-clearing noise that means, 'I'm eternally disgusted by you.' She looked down at her feet and ignored them.

By the time they reached the outskirts of the city, everyone was back to his or her old self. The twins kept passing gas — to them, nothing else in the world was more hysterical. Which made Saffron vicious, which annoyed Orji so much that he felt the need to antagonize her all over again.

"You know, Saffron," Tai stopped walking and turned to face her. "had you gone with the cape, instead of that stupid scarf, like I told you — you could have hidden your butt *behind* the cape without drawing too much attention. Too bad for you — you have that *stupid* scarf that just blows in the wind, flops around, and exposes *everything! Ha! Ha! Ha!*" He sneered at her ridiculous get-up. The fuchsia scarf lay over her head like a turban, with the veil-bar forced through it. She looked like a broad from the fifties, ready to get into her powder-blue convertible.

Saffron screamed. A white-hot, rage-filled, blood-curdling, murderous scream. She lunged at Tai.

Orji's hand shot out. He grabbed her by the hair and turban — it was all that he could reach.

Saffron, yanked back by her head, turned around to gawk at Orji — her eyes wild, her mouth almost foaming.

"Saffron, c'mon. Leave the VERY immature fairy alone. They don't hide themselves with their capes in this realm. So, even if you had one, you would still have to wear it like this." He gathered his cape and threw it over one shoulder to demonstrate. "There's something else I want to discuss with you, too."

He continued to talk, although Saffron wasn't really listening. She was staring at Tai, and willing the untimely destruction of his soul.

"Before we go to the portal, there's one little shop we have to stop at.... I promised the shopkeeper we would — he was nice enough to help us acquire these 'must have' veils and rods."

"What's the deal with these, anyway?" With much irritation, she adjusted hers for the twentieth time.

"I never did inquire; we'll ask the shopkeeper. We'll have to do it delicately, though. It would be like a stranger walking up to you in the Earthrealm and asking you why you wear underwear. So, tact, Saffron, tact. And, patience, Saffron, patience."

When they arrived at the first two large pyramid buildings, they peeked between them, down the alleyway, at the townies.

All along, Deva had followed solemnly, as Tai led her along with a rope. She stopped now and sniffed the air. The little hairs around her nose had gone completely white —she had aged considerably, hopping between this realm and the last. Tai and Wo knew she had aged. They also knew she had developed arthritis, and it stung her hip viciously.

Saffron didn't notice. "I can't do it." A harsh breath escaped her lips. "I can't walk into town like this."

"Saffron, it's no big deal. Tell yourself you're in a land where it doesn't matter. Just look around you, revel in this new society, leave, and never see these people again – it's not like they're gonna post your ass on Facebook...." Wo smiled at her, but he looked very impatient.

"Yeah, okay." She sounded as if she were about to start crying again.

"Here I go." Orji walked forward, into the dusty alley, and forward still, into the melee of shoppers. His cloak lay casually over one shoulder, his buttocks shone bright-white in the setting sun.

Saffron's eyes locked on his rear-end — in awe, in reverence, in primal fascination, and in disgust.

Orji stopped when he reached the crowd and waited for the rest of them. The twins came next — their wings concealed under their cloaks, their cherubic bums poking out of their pants. Deva gimped along behind them.

No Saffron.

"C'mon, Saffron — just do it." Orji whispered to himself.

Then suddenly, miraculously, she was there. Her face was drained of all color, but she was there. She looked up at Orji with the most pathetic, hang-dog expression he had ever seen in his life.

He nodded and patted her back. "You can do this, you know. In the end, you'll be disappointed because no one noticed you...."

She nodded back.

Hand in hand, they walked forward.

Almost instantly, the townspeople on every side of them stopped. 'Oohs' and 'aahs' broke out among the crowd. People started to whisper loudly and point.

They pointed at Saffron.

Everyone, *everyone* was staring at her. Fifty veiled faces were pointed in her direction. The crowd hushed as if their voices were swallowed up in a vortex, and for one whole minute, no one made a sound.

Saffron felt her entire world stop spinning and come to a crashing halt. With her gravitational pull gone, she teetered like a drunkard. "Ooooh," she moaned. "OOOhhhh...."

Orji caught her under the armpits just in time. "Saffron," his call was harsh. "Saffron — get up." Through gritted teeth he hissed, "I don't know what's wrong, but it ain't your purty rear-end — they haven't even seen that yet. Up!" He tried heaving her up, then whispered sharply again. "If you would just get a grip, and stand up, please —we can figure this out." He threw her weight from one arm to the other, trying to get a better grip. He grimaced at the crowd (although he believed he was smiling), "My wife —she's with child — and the heat is too much for her."

His words seemed to awaken the people. Some of them moved on in embarrassment, some pretended they weren't staring at all, and a small few held their ground and continued to stare in wide-eyed fascination.

When Saffron struggled to her feet, a length of her hair crept out from her turban and hung across her face. It glinted gold and red in the afternoon sun.

The crowd that still watched gave a collective sigh when they caught sight of the hair. Women brought their hands to their mouths, little children moved in for a closer look.

Orji watched the crowd watching Saffron's hair. "Well, I'll be a Daffrigit," he muttered. He took Saffron's hair and smoothed it back under the blinding-pink bindings.

Saffron stood shaking and looked at Orji with glassy eyes.

"No way, baby — you're not going to space out on me. You just keep that witchy hair out of sight, and we'll be okay. Perk up, Saffron, clear your head — we have a walk through town to make."

Saffron was trying to wake up — she really was. Even as she felt herself fainting, she had tried to stop it. But it tried harder, and pulled her under. The feeling was so sleepy and dreamy-drowsy — how could she resist? Then, she had felt so comfortable lying in Orji's arms, watching butterflies, thousands of pink butterflies, swirling around in the liquid blue sky. She leaned on him again.

"Nope, up...." He plopped her unceremoniously to the ground, then bent down to squat in front of her. "Saffron, look at me." His face was just inches from her own. He looked anxious. "This isn't the time to give in. You have to get through this...." He snapped his fingers in her face.

That was what did it — that and the fact that he had plopped her on the dirty, stony ground. "You don't have to be rude," she hissed.

Orji looked pleased. "I knew you could do it! And you let yourself go pretty far away too, I could tell. Good recovery!"

Saffron shook her head at the ridiculousness of the situation. She stood up, and reached to swipe the embedded gravel she imagined was all over her rear-end. She was doubly startled when she realized, all over again, that her ass was exposed and gravel couldn't possibly be embedded there, because her butt was like hard plastic. She groaned at the sea of buttocks that milled around her. These people had capes, for God's sake, and instead of letting the capes hang down their backs (like normal people, she thought), they had their capes flung over one shoulder, and strutted around like peacocks.

"When in Rome, Saffron...." Orji was gentle when he slid her hair back under her turban; then, he reached around to collect the tails of the scarf, and carefully draped them together over her right shoulder.

"Oh, how gallant of you, great sir," she muttered, and refused to look him in the eye.

He smirked. "This is too funny — one day we'll all look back on this and laugh." But just as he said that, he sobered. If they ever found Markis, he would be looking back on this alone — Saffron would be long gone. He looked at her. She was gasping and covering her mouth, trying not to look at the townspeople and their derrieres, as she had called them. She was high-maintenance. But he also saw how her face softened when a passing child smiled at her, and how she clenched her fists like a boxer, ready to take out a rough-looking man who shoved past Tai. He adored how she reached up to pat her head and check to see if that glorious red hair had tumbled out again. He loved how her lips always stayed soft and full, even when she bit the bottom one in distress. He made himself sick. "Let's get going," came out as a short series of grunts. He flicked irritably at his veil.

His tone snapped Saffron to attention. She was amazed at the way he could be crying laughing one minute, then back to his old grumpy self the next. "Do you have Troll in your bloodline?"

Orji ignored her and pushed a path for them through the crowd.

As they walked, Saffron tried her best to keep her hair under her long, slippery scarf. She had to motion repeatedly for the twins to catch up — they liked to lag behind and gawk at the crowd. When she wasn't paying attention, they liked to appear out of nowhere and pinch her bum, then jeer at her when she responded to their ghostly touch that she shouldn't even feel.

By the time Orji announced they were at the shop, Saffron was raging-bull mad.

"Alright, you little punks. You stay outside and keep watch." Orji pushed at the twins to keep them from crossing the store's threshold.

"What are you talking about, 'keep watch?'" Tai charged forward as if to force himself through the door.

Orji pointed at the street, "Goddesses with no pants on...."

Wo's eyebrows shot up as a woman, six feet tall and perfect, sauntered past. Her fluttering veil barely turned in their direction, but it was enough to give all three males in Saffron's party a start.

Deva bellowed and pawed the ground. She mooed so hard, the ruby hanging from the chain at her neck trembled violently.

"Oh, it's okay, baby!" Wo smoothed her nose.

While Tai and Wo fussed over Deva, Orji and Saffron slipped into the shop.

"Hello, sir — how are you this afternoon?" The clerk greeted them as if this were the first time he had seen Orji, which wasn't true — he had been waiting with ill-contained patience for his oddball customer to stop talking to those ragamuffins out there, and get into the shop. He had been waiting, poised to say those words, for at least five minutes! He had been waiting for the strange wife to come in too, so he could get on with business and over with business. They definitely weren't from around here — the wife looked almost *elfin*. And stars-a-bursting — what the hell kind of cloth was on her head, and *red*(!) hair? He clucked his tongue. "Is this your lovely wife, sir?"

"Yes," Orji took Saffron's hand and rubbed his thumb down her fingers as he continued, "Isn't she beautiful?"

Saffron gave Orji an ill-concealed look filled with malice as the clerk retreated to his desk. She snatched her hand back and rubbed it as if it had been burned. "Stop telling people I'm your wife," she hissed.

Orji imagined Saffron was giving him looks of disgust and rolling her eyes and all of her usual facial theatrics, but, thanks to the veil, he couldn't tell.

"Here it is, sir — the loveliest veil in the store for your loveliest wife."

Saffron rolled her eyes. People shouldn't try to lie if they couldn't do it well.

"Baby, I don't think we should invest in something so exquisite without you trying it on first, do you?" Orji's lips curved under his veil.

Before Saffron could answer, the entrance bell jingled. Saffron, Orji, and the clerk turned to see a young man come in. His hand came up in greeting, then he took off for the far right corner to peruse some wares.

Saffron reached up to yank off her veil. She wanted to try the other one on, quickly, and get the hell out. Why had Orji wanted to come in here anyway?

The clerk noted her intent, and let out a strangled, "Aaaaaggghhh! Madame! The dressing room is this way, Madame." He took her by the hand and followed his upturned nose towards the back of the store.

Why do I need a dressing room to try on this veil? I could just whip it on right here! Why do I need to try on this veil? She suddenly got the creepiest sensation that Orji was up to something but, since she had no idea what, she felt powerless to stop it. "What *are* we doing here?" she grated out.

Orji just smiled and held his finger to his lips. "Shhh, I'm helping you. We're discovering together...." He held the dressing room curtain back and gently pushed her in. "Try it on, honey."

In a huff, Saffron whipped her veil off and slid the new, tranparent veil over the bar, then put the bar back into the holes in her drooping turban. She smiled at herself in the mirror. This was more like it! She could actually see her face, and she could see through this veil without the thing aggravating her like the other one did. She came out of the dressing room, did a twirl for Orji and said, "Well, what do you think?"

"I think you're beautiful when you smile." He enjoyed it this time when she rolled her eyes. "Well, Saffron, it's truly beautiful, but let me make sure it's sitting on your head correctly. We'll have the clerk give his advice, shall we?"

Saffron frowned. Why in the world would they want the clerk's opinion on this? She wanted to tell Orji, 'No,' but he had already taken off. Saffron watched the other shopper as he made his way to the dressing room with a fistful of veils.

When the shopper noticed Saffron standing clear-veiled before him, he jerked to a stop and sucked in his breath. "Oh! Oh, I'm so sorry!"

"No, wait — it's okay — you can use it." Saffron thought he wanted her dressing room.

The man backed up one step, hesitated, then quickly cast a look over his shoulder.

Saffron watched the man look at Orji, who was deeply engrossed in conversation with the clerk at the counter.

The man closed the space between them — getting way into her personal zone.

Warning bells chimed in her head. Something was wrong here, but she still couldn't figure out what.

"Your eyes are so...so...mmmmmmmmmmm." He growled out 'mmmm' like a bear slobbering over its raw, fleshy dinner. His mouth curved into a friendly-neighborhood-pedophile arc, and his perfectly straight, white teeth came out to gleam.

Saffron blinked and looked at the wall. She looked back at the man. She thought the whole foot-fetish thing was weird — this guy was practically drooling over her eyes. Freakazoid.

"You want to see *my* eyes?" He panted the words.

Saffron crossed her arms over her chest and stared at him — hard and steely. "Whatever floats your boat, man."

Quickly, he lowered his veil, and stared at her with penetrating, dark chocolate eyes.

Saffron stared back at him. He would've been good-looking, if he wasn't *such a creep.*

He rolled his eyes and looked up. He was starting to breathe heavy. Saffron looked up. Was there a spider on the ceiling? What the hell was his problem?

"Ooooh, you're a tease!" He put his face right near hers and stared at her without blinking.

"Okay, that's it...." She was pissed. She *still* wasn't sure what was going on, but she *knew* that Orji had set her up. She heard the voices of Orji and the clerk as they approached. Saffron saw fear fill the perv's eyes just as he raised the veil again. He dropped the veils he had in his hand and fled the store.

Orji and the clerk watched the man scamper away. The clerk was confused, but Orji was trying to suppress his glee.

When they rounded a rack of veils, the clerk took one look at Saffron, sucked in *his* breath, seemed to quickly get hold of his reaction, and walked close-kneed over to her. "My dear, your husband is searching for a second opinion on the fit of your veil. May I have permission to approach and check the fit?"

Saffron waved her hands around in the air. What *was* this? "Yeah, whatever!"

He approached her slowly, as if she were a set trap. When he was about a foot away, she noticed how his breathing hitched and became ragged, and how he was trying to control his actions.

Orji was behind the clerk, wiping his eyes with his veil and covering his mouth to keep from laughing out loud.

"This..." the clerk fingered the veil lightly as he stared and *stared* at Saffron's eyes, "...seems fine." His voice cracked at 'fine,' so it sounded like he said, 'foyne.'

Orji erupted into a "Bwhahahaa" barrage and disintegrated with laughter. He was laughing so hard that he couldn't catch his breath.

Saffron finally realized what was going on. To these people, these cover-your-eyes-but-nothing-else weirdoes, she had just exposed herself like some exhibitionist. Images of kicking Orji in the head danced and twirled through her mind. But, she wouldn't give him the pleasure of laughing at another one of her outbursts. She clamped her mouth shut, marched back to the dressing room, and frantically worked her opaque veil back on the rod.

"Sir," she heard the clerk spit with disdain, "I don't see the humor in all of this —your wife needs to learn a little discretion, if you ask me."

Saffron's mouth dropped open. What was that clerk saying? That she was some kind of whore?!

"Hey, buddy, I know I've got the raciest, fun-loving wife – and I didn't ask for your opinion!" Orji hooted some more and walked towards the front of the store to wait for Saffron.

The clerk followed close at his heels. "You know, you can get arrested for indecent exposure around here!"

"Then call out the squads, because it's raining asses out there — arrest them all!"

The clerk 'yiped' and took a step back. "I'll thank you to leave my store, and take your street-cat wife with you!" Then he stomped his foot.

Saffron came charging out of the dressing room, rammed down the aisle, knocking veils and rods to the floor, and shoved through the store's front door.

"Buh-bye," Orji waggled his fingers at the clerk, then was off in Saffron's wake.

Saffron stomped past the twins, who jumped to their feet in alarm.

First, the townie had come charging out and, now, Saffron. They
didn't like it when they weren't the cause of the melee and pouted as
they ran after her. They pouted because they had to run, too – their
wings were getting itchy, being all cramped up and unflexed for the
better part of two hours. "What? *What!*" they nagged Saffron, to no
avail.

She kept walking. Her scarf drifted down from her shoulders,
floated behind her, and slapped at her buttocks. She stopped
suddenly and grabbed the wrist of a woman who happened to be going
in the other direction. "Please, which way to the town building?" The
woman pointed to a silvery pyramid about fifty yards to Saffron's left,
then yanked her wrist back from Saffron's desperate grasp and
hurried away. Saffron stormed all the way to the town building,
through the double inner doors, through the double inner doors, and
over to a large wooden desk, helmed by a short, dumpy woman.

The woman's veil appeared old and discolored by the sun. "Yeah?"
She barked out the word in a gravelly voice without looking up from
her tablet.

"Which way to the portal, please?"

"Up the stairs, down the hall to the left — the door with the portal
insignia." She crunched into what looked like tree bark and kept
reading as crumbs fell on her lap.

"Thank you." As Saffron charged towards the stairs, Tai, Wo, Deva
and Orji came skidding through the inner entrance doors. Deva
clacked and lost her footing on the smooth-as-glass stone floor.

Orji sprinted extra fast and was soon at Saffron's heels. "What do
you think you're doing, Saffron? Do you think you're going through
the portal without us?" He tugged on her hand.

She pulled it back and slapped his hand when he reached for her again. "Losing you in the portal transfer would be a blessing, jackass."

"Oh, good. We're speaking again. You'd be lucky *not* to lose me, you know."

He was so arrogant! Saffron could only stand there and stare at his veil.

He tipped his chin down; his smiling eyes peeked at her from above the rod.

Who the hell was he, anyway? Really. He was just some strange person she had picked up in some strange realm. For the very first time, she consciously realized she didn't know *what* the hell he was. He couldn't be human — humans were from the *Earth*realm.

Tai and Wo arrived on the stairs behind them. "What's going on?" They said it at the same time like twins on a commercial.

Saffron would have liked to assault them all at that point. She burned with humiliation. She turned away from them, mounted the rest of the stairs, and shot down the left-hand corridor. Suddenly, she came to a halt. There had to be over a hundred doors here, which of course was impossible — they were in a pyramid. And they were closer to the top of the pyramid than the bottom. It was impossible that the corridor was that long. Saffron groaned.

"Well, baby, which door is it?" Orji leaned on the wall and crossed his arms over his chest.

Saffron closed her eyes for several moments and forced herself to take deep breaths. She already needed him. Blek. He probably knew what the insignia for a portal would be — maybe the twins could have figured it out — but he already knew. She could tell by the way he was standing there. He was so smug!

She couldn't guess. Each door was made of glass – dark, purple, opaque glass, and each had a symbol on it. She didn't know what any of the symbols meant. She could go downstairs and ask toady-lady which door it was, but somehow, she imagined, if she asked that woman for any more help, she would probably get herself eaten. Besides, she couldn't raise suspicion — she was *supposed to know* what a portal insignia was.

Orji interrupted her thoughts. "A portal insignia, Saffron, looks something like a rod — like a staff with a hole in it. It has a slot at the top, like the eye of a needle." He flexed his muscles like Hercules. "See that, Saffron? See that brute strength? Go ahead, touch it — feel that muscle; it's hard as a rock!" He grinned.

She stood rigidly, glaring at him.

"C'mon — come feel my muscle — it's incredible!"

"How do you know that?" She arched one angry brow. "The twins told me portals weren't common knowledge — that it was dangerous for common people to have portal knowledge."

Orji feigned pain in his heart, and put both hands on his chest. "Are you calling ME common? Why, you little tart!"

"Orji, don't avoid the question. *Why* do you know so much about portals?"

As he walked away he said, "Come along, little fireball. Come feel my muscle."

One of the doors opened and a woman emerged. She had caught the end of Orji's order to Saffron, and now walked down the hallway with a smile. "I'll test that muscle, big guy!" Her gapped teeth were pearly white under her veil. She reached for his pumped-up arm with two greedy hands. As soon as she touched Orji's arms, she snatched her hands back in alarm. She wasn't sure what she had just touched — couldn't describe it — it *just wasn't right*. She walked away quickly, confused and concerned.

Saffron stopped in mid-stride, her face contorted with anger and dismay as she ranted, "Oh, brilliant, Orji — now you've set her off. I'm the only one who can touch you and understand you...have you forgotten?"

Orji's face brightened. "Really, now...!" He was still in full-fledged-cocky mode.

Saffron sucked at her teeth. "Oh, please. You know what I mean." She set off down the hall.

Orji watched her butt as he walked behind her. She had completely forgotten her trap-door was gone. "No, I don't. Please, tell me exactly what you mean."

Wo and Tai were still busy watching the other woman walk away. Deva back-kicked a hole in the wall and herded the boys on with her nose.

Saffron yelled back at the twins and Deva, "You, you, and you...NOW!" She pointed rigidly down the hall.

Deva yelled, "Moo!" and stomped her foot.

"Oh, *now*, you want us to go with you." Orji allowed her to pull his arm. He enjoyed it.

Saffron scanned the doors as they rushed past. They must have gone by thirty or so before she found it. The insignia was gold and looked exactly like a needle with a door at the top, where the threading hole would be. She released Orji's arm and pushed through the glass door. There before her was movement in the air like a quivering mirror. A man sat beside it at a very unofficial-looking desk. He was half asleep.

Saffron balked. She tried in vain to keep the fright out of her voice. "We'd like to pass, please." She held her breath and clamped her teeth. What if he asked for papers? What if they did some kind of physical check, like at the airport?

Orji and the twins shifted uncomfortably. Saffron could make a whole room ache with her energy. The four of them stood silent, their errant veils hanging at different angles of cockeyed. Deva snorted.

"Well, obviously — I didn't think you were food services." The man in charge hacked out a short, phlegmy cough, then indicated a sheet of parchment. "Sign that before you go through."

And that was that.

The gatekeeper didn't care about Saffron's nerves, the weird little boys, the big guy or the old cow. He wanted to go back to sleep.

This time through the transfer, they didn't experience a flying sensation or pushing or shoving — it was as if they were standing in one spot, and suddenly, painlessly, their bodies started to disappear, piece by tiny piece. After a time, the pieces all came back together. They were about to assume they had gone nowhere at all, when suddenly they heard someone trying to get their attention.

"Come, come, now — mustn't loiter in the portal all day! Handle your livestock and present yourselves! A man appeared in front of them, waving them on. He spoke in exclamations and, with his black suit and round head, he looked like an upside-down exclamation. He was not like the other keeper — he stood erect, pressed, and proud. As they emerged into the room, they found everything — the walls, and the few objects therein — impossibly, impeccably, white. They filed past the gatekeeper.

He started to splutter, his face becoming as white as the walls. "What? What?"

Orji heard the panic in the gatekeeper's voice. He crouched low, ready to be attacked. He whipped his head around to take in the whole room. "What?"

Saffron's eyes grew wide as she looked longingly at the exit door. "What?"

The twins stiffened and started pushing Deva towards the exit. They said nothing.

The gatekeeper waved his hands in staccato bursts. He waved at them. He waved at what looked like a viewing screen and control panel. "Only two and an animal! Only two and an animal registered!"

Silence.

"Oh, yes, yes." Orji clutched his belly in over-the-top, mad-cap hilarity. "I'll need to speak with you now, sir. He took the gatekeeper by the elbow and led him to a corner of the room where blinding white walls met blinding white floor.

Tai, Wo, Deva, and Saffron congregated by the exit door. They waited while Orji calmed the man — it took forever. With two more words they couldn't hear, he patted the very tense gatekeeper on the back. Finally, he walked away from the man, crossed the room, and said, "So, we'll be on our way now. You know you can't keep royalty waiting."

The gatekeeper nodded dumbly and never left the corner as they walked out the door.

"Thank you." Saffron mumbled. When they were out in the hallway, she breathed a heavy sigh of relief. She looked sharply at Orji, her lips opening to ask the question.

He put his finger to his lips and winked.

She stayed mercifully quiet.

Out in the hallway, the walls, the fixtures, the floor were all sparkling white. They passed people dressed in all white, who gave curt nods in greeting and rushed away.

"Do you think we'll have to dress like them?" Tai muttered. He really didn't want to give up his lederhosen and dark, mysterious cape.

"Nah," Orji whispered, "They get transients from the other land through that portal all the time. The people in the Oddrealm were mostly dressed in brown and grey, remember?"

Tai smiled, placated — his lederhosen were grey.

"'Oddrealm,' Orji?

"No one else gave it a name — so I did."

"Can we call it, 'Psychorealm?' Saffron nodded in encouragement.

"No, Saffron, I called that one. You can name this one." He honked her nose with his knuckles.

Deva mooed forlornly. She was getting hungry — hungry and irritated. She wanted to see the twin's faces. She hated the ghastly veils.

The twins stopped to console her.

Orji walked on; the suspiciously clean building was starting to make him edgy. He wanted out.

Suddenly, the lights in the hall dimmed, then glared powerfully bright. It hurt their eyes. The lights grew brighter and brighter, till Saffron thought she would be blinded. A noise started in the air, as if someone was approaching from far away with a vacuum cleaner. The machine-like drone became louder until it matched the glare of the lights in intensity.

"Oh, great." Orji moaned, but no one heard him over the noise.

Saffron covered her ears and screamed, "What's happening!"

Tai and Wo simultaneously yelled, "Disappear! Disappear now!" Then the three of them, Wo, Tai, and Deva vanished in a whir of clotted magenta mist. Orji had just desolidified when Saffron screamed.

"I can't Orji — I can't do it! Please! Don't leave me here!" And she couldn't do it —not fast enough, and not on demand. It was math class all over again, when her teacher made her go to the board to answer a question. She couldn't do it. Not even one plus one, not with the pressure on her. Her voice was ragged.

Orji could hardly hear her over the noise. And he couldn't see her at all because of the light. This light wasn't normal light; he couldn't just will it away. He felt for Saffron's hand and grabbed her.

They ran.

They ran down the hall, towards the source of the noise. Saffron's eyes felt like they were splitting with pain. Her eardrums popped as if the noise had made them explode. Saffron screamed in agony.

They ran closer into the sound.

"Why?!" Saffron screamed. "Why are we going this way?!"

But Orji couldn't hear her.

Then it was as if they ran *through* the sound, because suddenly, the piercing shriek was behind them, along with the glaring lights.

"Run faster!" Orji roared.

Saffron sprinted as hard as she could. She didn't turn to see what was behind them. People were coming out of their offices now, and staring in wonder at the two that fled past them — one, a girl with a veil-rod for a headband, and a man with a veil-rod bouncing under his nose.

Orji didn't really think they would make it, but he ran faster still, and practically dragged Saffron behind him. They raced down a white, marble staircase, across a wide, white-tiled floor that seemed to be growing white, stone columns. The columns were everywhere — an acre of white-tile floor with jutting white, stone columns.

Saffron and Orji sprinted through a white, arched doorway, and into the rainy night. They ran on. Saffron was, by now, almost hyperventilating and tripping on every fourth step. They crossed a street and trotted down a lane that ended at a half-dilapidated barn. The barn was white, of course. Orji shoved one shoulder into the barn door when it wouldn't give, and finally it sprung open with a loud creak and groan. They stumbled through the barn, bumping into things everywhere, until they reached a back corner, and collapsed together on the floor. Saffron turned her face into Orji's chest and began to cry. Orji stroked her plastic hair and whispered to her.

"I think the Portal Police are on to us." He shut his eyes.

Chapter 17

*O*rji's eyes snapped open. It was dawn and Saffron was awake.

She hadn't shifted in the least, but still, he felt that she was awake and lying patiently against him. He wondered what she was thinking. They had never had this kind of body contact before, and frankly, he thought it was pretty remarkable. He had assumed from the beginning that they would never get this close. Even though there was no physical heat between them, even though her body — which appeared so, so, soft — was only as pliable as a garden hose, he smiled. She was lying against him.

He couldn't smell her hair. His eyebrows knit into a tight, troubled frown. He loved to hold a woman like this and smell her hair. He remembered the previous evening, how Saffron had wept so bitterly, but when he reached for her, like the day they first met, he touched a living, wax statue. The tears did not come away wet on his fingers. There was no heat emanating from her soft-looking skin, and taut-looking limbs. He could have cried. They were lost moments — he could touch her, but he couldn't feel her.

He forced out an exaggerated cough.

Saffron shifted, and pretended to wake from a deep sleep.

"You're such a faker — I knew you were awake." Orji smiled and stretched luxuriously, while Saffron popped up and away from him.

She wasn't very nice when she said, "And I know you were sitting there, smiling, before you decided to go back to your usual troll-like ways!" She tried to stare him down.

The cocky look melted from Orji's eyes and he tilted his head.

"How did you know that?"

Saffron thrust her chin in the air, looking very haughty. Then she looked bewildered as she stared at beams of dusty light which shot through the broken barn wall, and highlighted a rusty, old wagon. "I don't know."

For several minutes, they remained silent, each lost in their own thoughts.

Saffron stole a glance at Orji as he concentrated on his twiddling fingers. His cloak was thrown off to the side, discarded without care into a pile of moldy hay. His hair curled slightly on his forehead, his broad shoulders stretched the thinning fabric of his shirt. A small flame grew in her belly, followed by a violent chill that rammed her so hard that she clutched herself for support.

Orji looked up and motioned for her to sit beside him. "The twins will find us eventually. Let's just rest for a little while and get a grip — okay?"

Oh, God, Saffron panicked, *What does he want now — to sit on that nasty hay and make out?* "I'll sit over here. I'm not sitting on that rotten hay." Her voice was weak and shaking.

Orji frowned. "Honey, do whatever you want — it makes no difference to me — I don't give a rat's ass...." He looked away from her, out to the land beyond the broken wall slat.

Saffron's eyes welled up with tears. She was determined not to let him see. She bit her bottom lip — hard — and tasted blood. She reminded herself not to taste blood. But it was there, the copper taste, all the same. She cleared her throat and forced her voice to be strong. "What the hell happened last night?"

Orji shrugged.

"Who were they? *What* were they? Can they see us right now?

Can they come find us in this barn?"

"They can't see us any old time they please, no. They would have to track us, wait for us. They'll have the portals here well guarded; you can bet on that. They're waiting for us at the portals....they never stray too far from them."

"What will they do if they catch us?"

Orji didn't answer.

He looked so deeply troubled, so desperate, Saffron didn't ask again. She assumed he was afraid of, and thinking of their immediate predicament. She was wrong.

Orji thought of his mother, and the way she used to smile at him. He remembered the way she smelled when she leaned over to kiss him goodnight, and how she liked to play her little wooden flute at sunset. Its forlorn whistle, in hindsight, seemed to proclaim the doom to come. In his mind too, Orji heard his mother screaming. "They'll kill us."

Saffron jumped, startled out of the funk she allowed herself to wallow in, the lazy place in her mind. "What?" It had been almost ten minutes since she had asked him the question, and in that time, since he never answered, she had forgotten all about it.

"The Portal Police," he looked her square in the eye with a sadness she had never seen — a longing she could not fathom. "They'll destroy us if they catch us. They have all kinds of weapons to get the job done — be you man or beast — it is simply their pleasure to destroy people's souls, from the inside out." He snorted. "Saffron, if I am to understand correctly, your realm still jails the body for infractions. Tell me, is this form of punishment working?"

Saffron thought about prisoners being let out because of overcrowding. She thought of states putting *billions* of dollars into building more and more penitentiaries. She shook her head no.

"Well, let me tell you what they've figured out in the Outerrealms. Some brainy person has figured a way to suck the soul from a body and completely annihilate it. Clever person. As you can imagine, crime is relatively low in many of these realms. 'Soul annihilation' is much more threatening than 'kill someone and we'll stick you in jail with benefits for a couple of years.' When a person's soul is destroyed...you can't come back —ever.

"But why would they destroy us just because we went through that portal?" She shook her head incredulously, and pointed at the barn doors. "They *let* us! We signed a paper!"

"It's the fairies, Saffron."

"What?"

"Only souls can pass through portals. Souls and animals. Nature. You can bring your potted plant through just fine. But those damn fairies are illegal. Nobody wants those damn fairies in their realms. It has to be them. I guarantee Tai and Wo didn't register on the gatekeeper's control screen — he must have alerted the police."

Saffron could say nothing at first, as thoughts buzzed and bounced around in her head, each trying to get to the top, but only succeeding in confusing her with their frantic urgency.

"I thought I handled it okay when the gatekeeper became suspicious. I told him Tai and Wo were granted permission to travel with a low profile, a pardon from the king. I told him they were on secret business for the king." Orji shrugged and raised his eyebrows. "I guess *that* didn't work."

Saffron frowned. "Why does this realm have an open portal and the others don't?"

Orji shrugged. "At one time, they must have made some kind of agreement."

"So portals are controlled by people who think they have the right to control them...? That doesn't seem right."

Orji scoffed. He actually *agreed* with portal control — he just didn't want to get caught. "With good reason, Saffron. There are too many crazy people in the world — in all of our worlds! Realm-hopping is illegal to keep the crazies from leaving one ravished realm and doing the same to another."

They watched a mouse-like creature scurry around a dark corner, fill its mouth with something, then disappear through a hole.

"It's important for the five of us to keep a low profile. We don't want to taint the realms we drop in on with our other-worldly ideas and footprints. Take my world for instance — we're at war. War is like a disease. If those warlords were to leak into a realm like this..." he pointed towards the barn doors, indicating the land beyond, "...those warlords would start war here — because that's what they do, that's who they are. They start wars everywhere and anywhere, hiding behind false justifications. Do these people deserve that?"

Tai and Wo came barreling into the barn, wrestling and kicking. Deva stayed out in the field behind them, swishing her tail at flies and pulling up clumps of green grass. With the passing, most of her face had gone white with age.

Saffron narrowed her eyes. "I'm so mad at all of you...."

Orji laughed. "Girl, what in holy hell are you talking about? Do you have a split personality or something?"

"Or something," she gritted out. "Why did you do that to me yesterday? In the store.... Why?"

"Oh, that." Orji waved his hand to dismiss her question.

Tai fidgeted and made little hops in the air. "Actually, I'd like to hear the whole story!"

"No — we don't have time for the whole story! I want Orji to tell me 'why,' and then we're not going to talk about it anymore. Hey, are Ny and Markis here?"

Tai snarled, "We don't have time to tell you!"

Orji grinned. "Yesterday was nothing — just a little lesson...."

"Who said you needed to teach me a lesson?" Her voice raised an octave — she was on course for a full-blown shriek. "I don't need any lessons from *you*."

He still looked pleasant. His voice was calm and level. "Sure you do."

Wo and Tai sat between Orji and Saffron. Their eyes volleyed back and forth as if watching a ping pong match. Presently, Deva came in, still munching. She moseyed over to stand between the twins and chewed her cud with annoying smacks. Every once in a while, her long, white lashes swept leisurely up and down, in a lazy blink.

Saffron waited for Orji to defy her.

"Look, Saffron. This was the point. That guy, that stranger in the dressing room, he was behaving oddly — correct? He was probably drooling, making weird noises with his throat. His pupils were probably dilated and he may even have been breathing heavy. Right?"

"Yeah, right! How could you do that to me?"

"Do what? Right then, at that point in time, you were in *complete* control. There was nothing wrong with you and you knew it. *He* was acting weird, *he* had the problem — and you knew it."

"There was a whole lot wrong, Orji, and *you knew* it! My eyes were *exposed*. To them, that's like a woman walking around with no shirt on in the Earthrealm! He thought I was vulgar!"

"That's it right there! Before you ever knew, all of that was going on — you thought there was nothing wrong with the way you were standing there. *And there wasn't!* Whatever he thought of you, was *his* problem. Why can't you see that?"

Saffron opened her mouth to speak. She opened and closed it a few more times. She looked like a fish out of water, gulping uselessly for air.

Orji's smile never wavered. "Nothing bad happened in that store yesterday, Saffron — you did just fine."

"Well, you didn't have to enjoy my little lesson so much." She pointed an accusing finger at him.

Tai felt like taking a bite out of that finger.

"You were laughing at me, Orji!" Saffron kicked the rusty, white tractor. Her hair was wild and full of straw. Her pashmina was tied around her waist to cover her bare bum. The others had their capes down to cover theirs.

"NO, no, no. I was just laughing — laughing in general. Hey, I like to laugh. Everyone should be so lucky. Saffron, you need to laugh more."

She nodded. "Maybe I'll find a lesson to give you — so I can laugh."

Deva groaned.

They all looked at her.

She groaned again. It was a deep and disturbing sound that came right out of her gut. She swayed. It looked like she was about to lean on Tai, but she kept going and crashed to the ground.

Wo screamed.

The twins fell to their knees, calling her name.

But she was already dead.

Chapter 18

She was in one of the highest turrets of the castle. In fact, it had taken her close to twenty minutes to walk up to this room. No one else was allowed to enter. It was her special refuge, filled with all of her books, potions and herbs. Rain fell in sheets past the long, narrow openings in the wet, slightly slimy stonewalls. With supple hands, she conducted the mist before her, to keep the image clear. Her fingernails or, talons — to be more precise — were painted blood red. They sliced through the mist, over and over again, always clearing the air to reveal the image of the human girl. Finally, she tired of watching Saffron sleep in Orji's arms, and let the mist hide the girl from her sight.

She didn't want to look at Saffron. But, since she was unable to see Ny, she looked at the human girl instead. It caused acrid venom to pool under her forked tongue. Over her long, lean, sinewy body washed the tantalizing urge to take one taloned finger, pry open Saffron's petulant lips, and breathe fire down her throat. She smiled pleasantly at the thought.

Chapter 19

They passed through more realms. No sign, no hint, of Ny and Markis.

The twin's pain at the loss of Deva was palpable. It cast a net of anguish over them all, and they drifted through many days like stoic ghosts.

One day, they landed in the most enchanting realm, and would later (tongue firmly in cheek) refer to it as the Perfectrealm.

They emerged at the very tiptop of a high, pointy mountain. Winter sun shone on their faces, but did nothing to melt the snowy mountain cap on which they landed.

"There are fairies here." Tai and Wo gave each other a high-five. Saffron jumped up and down while she clapped, and Orji winked at her, but didn't seem too moved otherwise.

"How do we get down from here?" Saffron had to yell to be heard above the screaming, wild, mountain wind that had been chiseling the peak for centuries.

Wo smiled and pointed a little to his left. A disc of blown-up rubber appeared, large enough to seat them all. There were nylon handles sewn into the rubber, a set for each being. A rainbow of sparkly, magic residue rose above the mountaintop like a question mark, then blew away in the next gust of icy wind.

Saffron gasped.

"I'm not walking down this mountain, Saffron. And since you won't fly...." Wo shrugged.

"Yeah, but, what the heck are we going to do with that? Why did you use magic to summon that wheel of death? Why don't you just transport us to the ground?" Saffron screamed as the wind keened louder, nearly piercing her ghostly eardrums.

"We. Need. To. Start. Having. More. Fun!" Tai looked skyward. "I love you, baby, but I have to let go of this grief!" Tai ran and jumped into the sled.

Saffron shook her head, turned to give them her back, and looked out across the land below. She realized that she was at the top of the very largest mountain she had ever seen or heard of. Most people never got a chance like this in their entire lives. She felt cold as she stood at a loss for words and frowned at her silliness. She had no idea how cold it really was — if she was in her body, she would've been dead already, frozen harder than steel, five minutes ago.

She shivered as she stared down at the forests and lakes. To the left, something glittered like a diamond. The clouds below began to drop snow. The fluttering white perfection, of the flakes bolstered her courage, for some reason. She whipped back around and said, "Whatever. Let's do it."

They barreled down the mountaintop at breakneck speed. Saffron screamed and cursed. Orji howled and choked on laughter. The twins were feverish with maniacal glee. The tube flipped several times, sending them crashing through the air and bashing into snowbanks and boulders. When they sailed into the tree line, several minutes after takeoff, the tube cruised into trees, sending bodies into flight all over again.

The tube met hard-packed ice. Saffron was shot up into the air when they hit another rock. While the others spun around and around inside, Saffron hung on to one of the nylon handles and screamed from the outside of the tube as she was dragged along. The others didn't help her in; they were having too much fun watching her fishtail behind them. Eventually, they hoisted her aloft, and continued to rush faster than the wind, for miles down the mountainside. It was over all too soon. The tube slid slower and slower until it came to a complete stop at the base of the mountain. Their laughter turned into grins and exhausted moans.

Saffron lay sprawled in the tube. She looked at the powder-blue sky, and the towering forest of trees that surrounded them. She sat up. Untouched snow carpeted the quiet land. She closed her eyes and raised her arms heavenward, in a luxurious stretch, then looked at the others in the tube.

Orji was lying on his stomach. He held her eyes and smiled at her.

She couldn't help but smile back. She rolled over to him — right across a grumbling Tai and squirming Wo, and landed on Orji's back. She placed her hands over his eyes, and kicked at his legs, while she screamed, "Ya! Ya!"

Orji clenched her thighs under his arms, and stood up, with her on his back. He growled like a bear.

Saffron, her hands still across his eyes, kicked at him and egged him on.

"Okay, sweetheart. But, if we run headlong into a tree, it's entirely your fault."

She made a 'pffft' sound. "What's another tree?"

He started to run — fast.

Saffron screamed, cried, and laughed all at once. When Orji was about to crash into a tree, she let him loose and fell to the ground.

It was too late for Orji — he ran into the tree anyway.

Saffron howled with glee.

Wo and Tai were disgusted by the two silly humans — as if they were two small children watching their parents share an amorous hug. That ride down the mountain was so cool — and those fools had to go and make everything weird.

Wo started to walk away, crunching in the sun-sparkled snow.

Orji walked over to Saffron and helped her up. The snow was falling harder. He brushed crystalline flakes from her sweater. A flake landed on her nose and stayed there, not melting. He brushed that away, too.

She gave him a smirk.

He shrugged and let her fall back down.

"Big baby!"

"You have snow on your ass."

Saffron jumped to her feet and followed the others through the woods.

Birds accompanied them as they walked. Deer and rabbits came to greet them from the thick, snow-covered brush. A gnome ran up to Saffron with a heavy, wooden plate of treats and warm cider in little, wooden cups.

Orji raised an eyebrow and looked at Saffron with a question in his glance.

"How should I know? I don't have the best track record with gnomes, so I'm just as surprised as you are...." She gushed over the little gnome and thanked him profusely —never had they been greeted so kindly in any of the realms.

It was a good day. They spent their time hiking out of the foothills, and onto flat, wooded terrain, which shone bright with snowdrifts and squat bushes of dark green ivy. Several creatures came to greet them and wish them well on their journey. By dusk, even Orji was completely entranced with the land.

All the inhabitants of the wood — enchanted and unenchanted — helped with camp preparations. Little green men, who called themselves, 'Tree Keepers,' promised to introduce Wo and Tai to fairy tribes, where they could question about their fugitive and abduction victim.

This was the most posh camp the four had ever experienced. They were encircled by trees. Sunlight streamed down and made everything glow. Saffron envied the rabbits who sat in the afternoon sun, and soaked in its heat. Each traveler had a tent of his or her own — tents made of bright-colored silk, like peony, daffodil, and periwinkle. Inside each tent were hordes of plump pillows and silk-lined blankets, all piled on top of beds that rolled when sat upon, as if they were waterbeds. Each individual tent was scented as well — vanilla, evergreen, and clove. Warm baths were had down the path, in a small pool that was fed by hot springs.

Saffron frowned; she couldn't feel the heat of the bath or smell the sweet tents....

"Watch yourself," Wo bit out. "We are guests here — show respect."

"You should take a bath in those waters anyway, Saffron. Maybe the ritual of it will soothe your mind — bring back memories." He moved an errant red curl off her plastic cheek.

Saffron gently pushed his hand away. "Aww, you just want to see me nekkid!"

Orji smiled and put his hand over his chest. "Ya got me."

In the evening, the camp was lit by hundreds of fat candles. The animals of the forest loved to play, loved attention, and vied for the traveler's audience. Elves, sprites, gnomes, and local fairies stopped by for a bitter beer and nuts.

Saffron and her friends were held in high esteem by the inhabitants, as if they were celebrities. It was a big change from being on constant watch for hostile beings. For once, they all sat back and enjoyed themselves.

They heard stories from the elves, about an ancient war fought against an evil that had come from within the earth. People, animals, and magic folk alike fought a bloody fifty-year war before they were finally able to overcome the beast. Now, for the last one hundred years, they had all lived together in perfect peace and harmony.

Orji was amazed. This was the very first and only realm where the inhabitants could say as much — that they were totally happy with each other and getting along. He was mystified. He wanted to know how this could possibly be. He asked them for answers —maybe one day he could go back to his own land and help end the murdering and plundering that was going on there at this very moment. He understood fighting for one's rights — but by the gods, he was sick to death of death

Saffron listened enrapt as well, for her Earthrealm could use the lessons of peace.

Tai and Wo agreed with everything the elves said with an eye on Saffron, and an 'I told you so,' air of superiority — as if she alone were responsible for the warring of men.

Saffron toasted a family of badgers, then begged off from the party and made for her tent. She was ready to sleep for a million years.

***

Orji sighed. What was he doing? What was he doing here, with this unhinged and bewitching girl? He watched as she bestowed a family of badgers with the most angelic smile. His heart leapt to his throat – he wanted to follow her into that tent in the worst way. What was he doing?

He had set out on this mission with one simple goal — to help the girl to help himself. His father hailed from the Earthrealm, and Orji needed to find his father's people. He knew the odds weren't very good, considering all the time that had gone by.... But still, he wanted to find his father's people — his people. Did he have half-brothers and sisters? He wanted to know! What he didn't want was to want this girl. It wouldn't take too much to lose her, and that was something he could not bear — losing another loved one.

It was the story of his life. Love somebody — lose them. Love somebody — lose them. He felt he was cursed — everybody he loved either died or disappeared.

He had been so silly when he met Saffron. He told himself she was the way back to the Earthrealm — she was just what he needed. Load of crap, he muttered to himself. He didn't need her to get to the Earthrealm. He had never needed her for that. Eventually, he would have found a different way. He needed her for something else entirely. Something he couldn't face then, and couldn't face now.

He thought back to that day. The day they had met. He saw her appear in the war-torn street like an incandescent light — her fiery hair flying about her head as if it were a live, whirling-dervish entity. High cheekbones; large, dark eyes. Long, graceful limbs. He had wanted her instantly. Just looking at her standing five yards away had heated his blood to a boil and it bubbled as it pumped through his veins.

He smiled wistfully. It wasn't quite like that anymore. With his body gone, animal urges were only a memory. It unnerved him. When he had been a complete physical man, he had placed great importance and great pride on his physical prowess. Now that it had been so long, he had to constantly reassess what made him feel proud.

He still had his strength. Sure — it wasn't in muscle, but in manner. He was a confident man, and wise enough to know that his confidence was his ultimate strength. He had his intelligence; that was power too. But, he had this other power surging in him — this constant pull for Saffron, and towards Saffron. It was something that grew stronger every day. He shuddered.

He couldn't toss her aside. No matter how he wanted to, no matter how she infuriated him — and she did — she infuriated him till he thought he'd rip his head from his shoulders. And it wasn't amusing that she loved someone else. Still, he could not leave the girl stranded. For the love of aliens, he was screwed.

***

"I'm going into town by myself." Saffron said this matter-of-factly, as if commenting on the weather. She didn't look up from her chore — she was going to start the campfire for breakfast. She laid small twigs one on top of the other, and acted like nothing out of the ordinary had just happened.

Orji, Tai, and Wo exchanged startled glances, followed by suspicious looks.

Orji ran his tongue over his teeth. "Saffron, you don't have to do that. I can...."

Tai jumped to his feet, spitting like an alley cat. "Yes! Yes, she does, Orji! Let her go. She needs to start pulling her own weight!"

"What?!" Saffron shrieked.

"What?" Orji frowned at the fairy. What the hell was in Tai's craw, now? Could they not rise on a beautiful morning, after a wonderful night with friendly people, and be happy with one another? Apparently not. As usual, Wo was quiet, but observant.

"Oh, you heard me! What the hell do *you* mean, Orji? Very nice acting, very believable confusion." He pointed a sharp finger at Orji. "You know exactly what I'm talking about." He threw down the stick he had been whittling since dawn.

The rabbits laid their half-eaten beets on a stump table and backed away. A deer and a fox sprinted away with their tails between their legs.

"Great! You ass! There go my first restaurant customers!" Saffron threw a whole bunch of sticks in the fire pit and scattered all of her hard, kindle-stacking work.

Orji sighed. "Tai, get it off your chest — but keep your anger to a minimum; you're terrifying our oh-so-generous hosts."

Tai spit on the ground. "AAaaaak! Just let the girl go, Orji!" He crossed his arms over his chest and grumbled low in his throat. "You're not helping her, you know. You aren't helping her with her irrational fears by coddling her all the time."

Orji was aghast. "I *do not* coddle her!"

Wo puckered his lips as if he was going to whistle, then rolled his eyes and looked over his shoulder at nothing.

Orji caught him. "What, Wo — you disagree?"

Wo winced and tugged at the base of his earlobe. He shrugged.

Orji commanded, "What?!"

Wo spoke very quietly. "You're letting your feelings for her stunt her growth. She'll never be able to grow if you keep sheltering her so."

Orji had cringed, and his shoulders shot up when Wo said, 'feelings for her.' "Aaaah! Shhhh!" Orji hissed. He looked around for Saffron, but she had long since disappeared. "Wo! Don't say stuff like that!" He frowned hard. He crossed his arms over his chest, and wouldn't make eye contact with anyone. "Because it's not true. And you know her —she'll take it the wrong way, do her 'high-and-mighty-miss act!

Wo giggled. "She'll do what?"

Orji shrugged. "You know — get all pompous and everything."

"Because you love her."

Orji looked downright downtrodden. He nodded. Then he shook his head violently. "No, no, no, no!"

Tai was completely miffed. He rolled his tongue around his cheek and glared at Orji. Then he looked around the camp. "Too bad, we're arguing about this for nothing." He swirled his finger around to indicate the entire camp. "She's already gone." He smirked at Orji.

Orji ignored him and stalked off into the woods.

***

Saffron marched through the woods. She passed the steaming bathing pool. She stopped and glanced back at its warm, beckoning waters. She shrugged. They weren't in a rush — may as well have a bath before the big trek into town. She stepped out onto a rock that hung over the pool. Water pixies shot down from the trees and offered to help her bathe by pulling off her clothes. Saffron squirmed and tried to push them away. "No. No, no. No, thank you."

Their laughing was like glass wind chimes as they persisted.

Saffron willed herself to calm down and graciously accept the pixies' help.

As soon as her clothes were removed, she slipped into the warm water, lay her head back against a smooth-contoured stone, closed her eyes and sighed. She only imagined the warmth of the water, only imagined the smooth, soft flow of it. She took comfort in the sound of the water and let its simple song lull her.

The pixies worked quickly and quietly. They brought large, cupped blossoms from somewhere within the forest, filled the cups with water, and washed her hair and face. They had no reaction to the odd feel of her – they just lathered her up. They told her what scents they were using and Saffron tried her hardest to remember the hot smell of lemon-grass, mint, and vanilla. Her eyes rolled back as she sank farther into the water. Tai and his demands that she drop her physical self be damned.

Someone was watching.

He didn't mean to — it was purely accidental that he had stumbled upon the maiden — the very nude maiden — enjoying her morning bath. On his father's land, no less. Had he not been so stunned by her exotic beauty, he would have questioned her without delay about trespassing this day.

As it was, being blinded by her beauty and all, he hid behind the trunk of a great old tree and watched her. He did not think it wrong, this spying, because he decided he was in love with her. After all, there was nothing wrong with watching your beloved having her morning bath. He would have her for his bride, he decided. He did not know who she was, or where she was from. But he did not care. She would be his wife — the queen of this land where she now trespassed — when the title was handed to him on his father's death.

He quirked an eyebrow. Where did she come from? The pixies attended to her as if they knew her. Yet, here he was, in the middle of his father's land, miles and miles from any human inhabitants. She couldn't be out here alone. Could she? Did she come out here with a man? Her man? Was her man close by? A frown formed on his face that deepened as he searched the silent woods around him. It didn't seem likely that there was another person about. He relaxed, for he saw no betrothal bracelet round her right wrist.

He had another thought. Maybe she wasn't human. Maybe she

was of the Enchanted, and playing a trick on him. After all, she was too incredibly beautiful. He pushed a wavy, auburn lock from his forehead and stared at her some more. Should he slay her?

He didn't care *what* she was, he wanted her.

Every girl in the realm wanted him — his title, his money — but finally, after what seemed a lifetime of searching, he had finally found someone that *he* wanted. Even if she was an enchantress, he could marry her — it wasn't unheard off. He just hoped her true form wasn't too incredibly hideous.

She was sponging her chest. He wanted to do that for her.

Saffron stood up and water streamed down her body. Sunlight accentuated and highlighted every wet curve. Steam rose and swirled about her, stroking her with possessive fingers.

The man couldn't move, couldn't blink. He watched as pixies flew in with soft, sun-warmed cloths to dry her. He held to the tree for support.

She dressed slowly, mesmerized by the songbirds flitting from tree to tree.

When Saffron was fully clothed, she continued her walk. After a time, she heard footfalls behind her. She spun around, expecting to find Orji stalking her. She wouldn't be surprised. She had seen the look on his face when she told them she was going to venture out on her own – he didn't like it.

But when she turned, ready to berate Orji for his hypocrisy, she was stunned to see a strange man behind her — an absolutely gorgeous guy, with hair as red as her own, leading an elegant, dappled horse.

The man smiled timidly, and gave her a half-wave. He saw the shock in her eyes, the naked fear at being alone in the woods with a strange man. He cut his wave short. He stopped walking towards her, so she wouldn't feel threatened. He smiled again.

She didn't move — just stared at him in total fear.

"It's okay," he said finally. "I saw you a while back, and I just wanted to talk to you."

A while back. A while back. Saffron tried to get beyond her fear to process this bit of information. A while back! When she was naked?! She took three steps back and held her hands out in front of her to ward him off.

The beautiful man took three steps back himself. The horse matched his movements. "No," he said, as he walked, "Please...don't be afraid. This is my father's land. My father is the king. I ride this trail every morning. I mean you no harm. I was just out on my regular morning jaunt when I discovered you back there. I don't mean any harm." He held his hand out in a placating manner. "Please, really," he shrugged, "I just wanted to talk to you."

Saffron didn't back away any more. She stared at the young man. They were in the middle of nowhere — he could attack her at any given moment. But, instinct told her everything was okay.... Her shoulders relaxed; she smiled at him. She didn't exactly make eye contact, but she looked just to the right of his dark eyes and said, "You can never be too careful, you know...."

He grinned and took small steps forward, anxious to close the gap between them. He stood tall and proud, and was heartened to see the smile on her sweet lips. He swept his hand before him in a grand gesture. "All of this is my father's. He is king of this land, and I am the king's son — Prince John."

Pleasant shock swept through Saffron's body. She scanned the land around them —the thick forest, the bright, rolling meadow up ahead, the outline of mountains behind them — *King! Prince! Yeeha!*

The look of pleasure on her face encouraged the young prince considerably. He quickly closed the space between them and stood not two feet from her.

She couldn't help grinning like a goof. Giddy jolts ran down her legs and made her want to pee. "Wow!" she gushed.

"My lady, even though we have yet to be properly acquainted, I am quite certain that will be rectified soon." And here he showed all of his teeth; his smile was quite dazzling. "I was wondering — would you do me the honor of being my guest at a royal ball this evening? My father is hosting the ball." His lips closed over his teeth, but his grin was permanent. "It is my father's intent to find me a bride at this gala event...."

Saffron placed both hands behind her back and squeezed her fingers, forcing herself to show some decorum. Her eyebrow shot up. "Oh, my God!"

"Indeed! Would you, fair maiden, allow me to escort you to the ball?"

Saffron took a deep breath and held it. She was about to accept, to scream 'Hell, yeah – that would be awesome!' when her smile faltered. She released her fingers, and her arms hung limply at her sides. Why in the world would she suddenly be feeling guilt right now — and over *Orji,* of all the ridiculous things. Why Orji? Why not Markis, her lost love? Why did Markis seem so distant to her — like the tiny shadow of a hawk trailing over a far-off mountain? It was almost as if Markis wasn't a real person, but a dream about a boy from childhood.

The prince noticed the not-so-subtle change that came over Saffron, and her deepening frown. Quickly, his hands swooped forward. He wrapped his fingers around the upper part of her arms. "What is it?"

"Oh, it's nothing." Saffron managed a weak smile. "It's just that — I have...I have a...someone...that I need to bring with me." She wanted to slap herself in the head.

The prince laughed. In his joy, he rubbed her arms with passion before he realized his fault in such a familiar display. He dropped his hands immediately. Ah! Her eyes blazed like faceted jewels! "Of course, you have an escort — it is only proper."

"Ah, yeah, that's right...."

"But, feel yourself! You are cold! Will you walk with me to the castle where I will have a proper invitation drawn up for you and your escort? Once there, I will find you a suitable fur, then escort you back to..." he looked at the empty woods behind her, "...to where you need to be."

His eyes met hers again — his were dark, like bittersweet chocolate.

"How gallant of you!" Saffron nodded her acquiescence. This was it — this was all her playacting in the woods come true! Although, when she played in the woods, the prince was always Markis....

There was no fairy dust now — just Saffron in her worn, black pants, mussed up hair, and nearly-flat chest. Yet still, this gorgeous prince that stood before her looked at her as if she were Venus just stepped down from her shell. No one had ever been so *immediately* entranced with her before. Pride swooped through her chest and raced to her head, making her feel slightly intoxicated. This was a moment to squeal about at a slumber party!

On a whim, she decided to enjoy this maiden-in-the-woods-meets-the-eligible- good-looking-prince scene for all its worth. She needed a break — and this would be harmless. After all, she liked the idea of a *prince* liking her. She wasn't about to fall in love with him — so she wasn't really cheating on Markis or anything.

A royal ball!

Talk about cloud nine!

Not only did the Prince take her to the castle to receive her formal invitation, but he also took her out among his people later that afternoon to show her around. Tears slid down her cheeks as she nodded to passersby, waved to workers in their fields, and patted the heads of small children with chubby, red cheeks.

This land, these people, were exactly out of a fairy tale. The mountain she had stood on top of yesterday seemed so close; it lined the back of the town — a natural, towering barrier against invaders. The people lived in a deep valley, green and lush. The prince told her, in high summer, eight-foot-tall grasses rippled in the wind. The grasses were a staple for the animals that the people depended upon for their livelihood.

Saffron and Prince John walked past a cobbler's shop, a bakeshop, a smithy, and stopped front of a tailor shop. They entered. A bevy of women rushed forward to address their needs. Prince John dismissed the women with a smile and a wave of his hand. He turned to look down into Saffron's eyes. She breathed deep — still hoping against hope to detect a hint of aroma from the scarlet silks that robed him, or the spices of his freshly, washed hair. She smelled nothing and her heart fell.

Prince John noticed. He chuckled softly. "Why so sad, my angel? Your countenance was pure felicity when we walked among my people — what is it?" Before she could answer, he held up his hand to answer his own question for her.

Saffron was relieved — she didn't know how she'd explain to him that she was sad because she was trying to get a *whiff* of him and failed.

"My dove, I know what is troubling you — I have figured it out. You do not have a gown for the ball this evening, do you?" He grinned widely, pleased with his intuitiveness. He hoped he impressed her as much as he impressed himself.

Saffron snapped up straight, as if she had just awakened from a long slumber. "Ahhh...." She looked around the shop at the half-finished gowns of jewel-tone silk. He was right about one thing; she *didn't* have a gown. Was he about to offer to buy her a gown for the ball? She faltered. That was nice and everything, but she doubted these non-magical seamstresses could make anything close to the spectacular piece that Wo could conjure. This was her big chance at a royal ball — and Wo could use magic here.... If Prince John bought her a gown from this shop, she would be so...*average.* The corner of her lip went up at the thought.

She shook herself and cursed herself in her mind. *You snotty little witch! A royal prince, a ROYAL fairy tale-like prince is about to offer you a brand new gown so you can attend his ball, on HIS arm, and you're getting snide about it?*

Shame, swift and sudden, slid down Saffron like a greasy sheet of muck. "I would love for you to purchase one of these fine gowns for me so that I may wear it to the Royal Ball, thank you."

The prince frowned in confusion. "Oh — of course."

Saffron slapped her forehead — which startled the prince so much, he grabbed her hand and stared at it, as if it had attacked Saffron's forehead of its own accord. He held her hand tightly and gawked at her.

Saffron, you ass, he didn't even offer yet!

The women slyly looked up from their stitching, embroidering, cutting and measuring. They cast the prince and the odd girl glances.

Then they sneaked looks at each other and rolled their eyes.

They didn't hide their looks well enough — Saffron saw them. She felt stupid. She sighed. "Look, I'm sorry — that was incredibly rude. I mean, don't buy me a gown. I mean — I'm not expecting you to buy me a gown." She put her hand on his chest. "But if you did, I would love it....but, you don't have to....but, I would love it....but, it's not necessary." She rolled her eyes.

He was grinning. "I can't buy you a dress today. It would never be ready in time for the ball. These dresses take months to make...." Still smiling, he narrowed his eyes and said, "Where are you from?"

"Another realm. It's the Earthrealm." She picked her bottom teeth with the nail of her pinky.

"Oooohhhh! That *does* explain a lot." He grasped her gently by the elbow and led her to the exit of the shop. Once they were back on the dusty street, he sucked at his teeth and explained, "Only, don't say that too loudly," He greeted a richly-dressed man in passing. When the man was out of earshot, he said, "It is illegal you know, to hop between realms, and as open as we are here..." he shrugged and raised his eyebrows, "...it's not exactly acceptable." He ran a hand up and down her arm. "So that explains this." He squeezed gently, as if he were testing produce at the market. "And this." He smoothed her cheeks with his fingertips. "Your flesh isn't...warm. And the texture is odd...like soft marble...if that makes sense"

Saffron had often wondered what she felt like to others. She thought she felt like plastic, like camera film. No one else made the comparison Prince John had made — not even Orji. She assumed none of the other realms *had* plastic or celluloid, and didn't know what it was. She also figured that was probably a *good* thing — seeing as how plastic wasn't biodegradable and all.

Still, perplexed as the prince was, he enjoyed himself immensely as he tested her flex — and pliability.

Saffron relaxed visibly, happy to have the strain of the secret of her origins finally out in the open. She liked her new friend, and laughed as he bent her hand back and forth. She was never good at colossal lies. She grinned sheepishly, "I won't tell if you won't tell!"

A slow, bone-melting smile crossed the prince's lips. His face was close to hers. "Agreed," he whispered. Then the amorous haze cleared from his eyes, and his smile disappeared. *And how, exactly, oh, Great Prince, are you going to bed your new enchantress?* Perplexing indeed. He cleared the thoughts from his mind, as glasses from a table, and troubled himself no more with such gibberish. Things always had a way of working themselves out. "Now, ahhh..." he put some space between them, "...*do* you need a dress, Lady, Saffron?"

"I actually have a gown back at camp that will do just fine." She giggled. *Airhead!*

They rode horses back to camp. They galloped through fields — the horses kicked up the fluffy snow — then slowed their animals to a trot to pick their way through the woods. When they arrived, Tai, Wo and Orji all stood at the same time. There was such an amusing collection of looks on their faces that Saffron couldn't help but laugh. Wo looked anxious, Tai had an air of disdainful indifference, and Orji leveled her with a sour frown. She dismounted her white mare and made introductions.

Tai and Wo received the prince with the reverence that people placed upon royalty — they quite enjoyed the "Royalty" game that humans played.

Orji greeted the prince with more than a hint of smugness, and with laid-on sweetness he said, "How wonderful to meet you, young prince."

Saffron frowned. 'Young Prince?' Why, Orji was, *maybe,* five years older than the prince. Five at the very most. Orji was *so* condescending, he probably didn't have any friends at all back at his old realm, Saffron assumed incorrectly. "Prince John has invited me to attend his royal ball this evening..." She paused for dramatic effect, but hurried on when she saw Orji stiffen and open his mouth — ready to admonish, no doubt. "...and I've told him I would love to attend...."

"Saffron," Orji growled.

"....and that my *escort,* Orji, would be attending also." She folded her hands across her slim midriff and smiled prettily at Orji.

A cocky grin cracked his hardened features. "So, I'll be your date." It was a statement, an Orji statement, full of bravado and finality.

"Ahhhh...." Saffron felt the upper hand sliding away.

Prince John frowned. This... *He*...was Saffron's escort? Prince John didn't like this one bit. This strange man before him, Saffron's *friend,* was a great bull of a man with chiseled features and brooding, possessive eyes. Nay, Saffron's *friend* was no longer welcome to escort her to the ball. But what could he do? He didn't want to risk Saffron's refusal to go to the ball herself.... His heart sank.

After several minutes of forced conversation, the prince felt he had spent enough time with Saffron's friends and bid quick adieus. He gave his stallion a click of the tongue to signal him on and took the reins of Saffron's horse. His emotions cartwheeled between excitement at his growing feelings for young Saffron and dismay at Orji's mere existence. There was something not right about that man, Orji. He kicked the stallion's flanks and drove the beasts harder. What bothered him, really, was the fire in Orji's eyes when Prince John emerged from the woods with Saffron. What also bothered him was the way the very air seemed to be sucked from the universe when Orji stood by Saffron's side. Prince John was a perceptive man; he knew what he had witnessed. It came crashing down on his head now. What bothered Prince John was that, most certainly, Orji was in love with Saffron.

But did she love him?

The horses were foaming at their bits. He kicked his steed again and raced home as if demons from hell were well on his trail.

Chapter 20

Saffron sighed deeply, flipped her long scarf back with flair, and flounced down on a large mushroom. She beamed at Tai and Wo (who returned unsteady smiles), then finally rested her eyes on Orji. There was no emotion on his face. She kept smiling at him anyway.

Orji felt his temper rise. What was she playing at? He was so enraged right now, he could feel himself placing his hand around her long neck and giving her a good throttle. But, suddenly the rage diffused, and in his mind his hands lingered on her neck, his fingers felt her soft, pliable skin. He rubbed his fists in his eyes. "What?" he barked out.

"Isn't it cool?" Saffron's question was breathless.

"*What?*" Orji grated.

"Oh, my God! A prince! A *prince* wants me at his ball! He *likes me!* Couldn't you tell?" she chirped.

Orji's brought his hand up to rub his mouth. What kind of response, exactly, was she hoping for by telling him this? "Are you insane?" Or thick, he thought, or psychotic.

"What?" But, she wasn't looking at him. She was watching the trees and the tiny fairies that flew through the limbs. They were decorating for the full moon festival that was to be celebrated, come evening.

Orji stomped off.

"Hey," Saffron yelled, "will you take me tonight?"

He yelled over his shoulder. "I wouldn't *dream* of letting you attend that ball alone."

"Oh, okay...." She fiddled with her scarf tassels.

Orji was halfway to the bathing falls when he stopped. He charged back to the camp.

Saffron was standing where he left her, still a little space-shot.

"Saffron."

She stared at him blankly.

"What are you doing?" He crossed his arms over his chest. "I mean, aren't we searching for Markis — the great love of your life? So what is it? You get a little bored on your mission, and that makes it okay for you to get funky with the area prince?" His voice had gone low and dangerous.

Saffron winced, then her eyes popped with rage. "Since when do you stick up for Markis? All you usually ever do is put him down! And, you don't even know him! How the hell is he serving your purpose now — you hypocrite!" She was shrieking.

Tai, Wo, and the gnomes they were telling dirty jokes to covered their ears.

"You didn't answer my question! What do you think you're doing?"

"*I*... am attending a *Royal Ball*...with a *friend*!"

Wo shook his head.

Tai shrieked with laughter and punched Wo in the side. "Saffron, that is soooo weak!" He snorted. "He's just a friend," he sang out in a girly voice.

"Oh, man, Saffron....do you know how tired that is? How old that is? How much of a bunch of *crap* that is?" Orji's eyebrows knit together tightly and one corner of his mouth pulled up. "You might be only twelveteen and all, but the lines you're just starting to use are as old as the hills. You sound ridiculous!" He mumbled as he walked away.

Saffron stamped her foot. "I am not a teenager!" Saffron turned to Tai and Wo to protest, but they raised their hands in unison, as if to stop her.

"I'm 28!" Saffron spat over her shoulder at Orji's retreating back.

He didn't turn around. He swatted his hand at her words as if they were flies around his ears.

Saffron turned back to the twins and opened her mouth to speak.

"No, Saffron! We don't want to hear it." Tai crossed his eyes at her.

Wo smiled at Saffron. "But, do you know what we *are* into — what's in our very blood?"

Saffron pouted, "What?"

Wo flung his arms out. "Dressing things beautifully!" He clapped his hands together and pointed to the fairies in the trees. "Our distant cousins up there are getting ready for the Full Moon Festival but we get to do you up for *A Royal Ball!* It doesn't get better than that. We're going to get you first prize!"

Saffron giggled. Wo's exuberance was infectious. "What? What can you do that will get me first prize?"

Wo waved her over. "Anything — beauty is the fairies' domain!" He elbowed Tai until his twin broke down and laughed.

"Well, I'll tell you," Saffron skipped over to them and whispered conspiratorially, "he wanted to *buy* me a dress....but...I knew — it would never compare to what *you* two could create!"

Tai patted her head. "Ah, Saffron, flattery will get you everywhere!"

Wo and Tai patted each other on the back. Should they use silver? Should they use gold, emerald, ruby, sapphire, or amethyst? Copper or Titanium? Should the magic be on the dress or in the air around her? Should they alter her features? No? Not even the tiniest bit?

What to do with that hair? And those feet – a size smaller there might enhance the overall appearance. Should they plump up her skeletal hips? My goodness, they hadn't even gotten into town in this realm yet! Was anorexic or pudgy the style? Or was it something in between? They'd have to check on that — body types were always all the rage, and you had to know which one was in style at any given moment, as the ideal was always changing. Maybe the women were all pumped up around here? Who was to say? They asked Saffron, and she confirmed big muscles weren't the current style here. How about hairlines — were the woman ripping at the hair at the crown of their heads to make their hairlines appear higher? Were the woman sporting eyebrows or tugging them off? Were the women stretching their earlobes, their necks, or fingers to enhance their beauty? Were noses, ears, or anywhere else pierced? What was happening with hair color around here? Was bathing in style or maybe just a little perfume over some pungent B.O.?

Saffron tried to answer the questions as quickly as they were thrown out to her. It was hard, though — she tried her best to remember everything she saw on her walk through town. Shortly, she became annoyed; she couldn't keep up.

"WAIT! STOP! Some of these questions are *ridiculous!*"

Tai and Wo ceased their chatter all at once. "Excuse us," Wo tried as politely as possible, "but we are not from this realm, Saffron, and we don't know the styles here. Were we preparing you for a Royal Ball in the Earthrealm, we wouldn't need to be asking most of these questions – we'd know from experience. As it is, we are not from this realm, and must rely on all that you have taken note of today. Our questions are far from ridiculous, far from ridiculous — beauty, in any realm, land, or universe is not the same. Beauty is not universal."

Saffron stood very still. "Hey, you can't seriously tell me B.O. might be in style!"

Wo snapped his fingers a couple of times to get her to focus on him. "Of course, we can. If this realm has decided, for whatever reason, that raunchy is the rage, well, then, you going to that ball clean-smelling is going to turn up a lot of noses...."

"No. I'm calling some shots here — I don't care what they'll say, there are just some things I won't do — stink is one of them."

Tai raised his brow in surprise. "Wow, Saffron, I never thought I'd hear such a bold statement from someone like you."

"What's that supposed to mean?"

Tai shrugged, already bored of the conversation. "Nothing — it's just not something I'd expect you to do."

Saffron scratched the back of her hand and decided to ignore him. She looked to Wo. "Look, there are some things I'm sure I want — if you could be so kind — and I don't care what the people say about those things. So, if you could...." She raised her arms up so they could begin their magical transformation.

Wo raised his hands as if to begin conducting. "Well, at any rate, what *were* the body types?"

Saffron thought hard. The people had been built like they were back home. Some tall, some short, some pudgy, some obese, some athletic, some scrawny. She shook her head. "It doesn't matter...I...I want...my own body."

Tai and Wo gasped simultaneously.

She had said it, had really said it, and had really meant it. She shocked herself.

Wo and Tai were shocked as well. They had learned Saffron's feelings towards herself — or thought they had. Now, on one of the greatest nights of her life — the night of the Royal Ball — she was confident in her *own* body?

Wo glowed with pleasure. "Very well," he murmured.

"But wait...!" Tai was curious. "Are you sure? Saffron, c'mon, this is a pretty remarkable statement coming from you."

Saffron shrugged. "It's just that, we've been through all of these realms, you know...and I've noticed that in each realm I've been looked at *differently.*"

Wo nodded like a bobble-head, "That's what I've been trying to tell you, that's *style!*"

"Yeah, yeah!" Saffron was excited herself. "Sometimes it was cool, you know...people smiled at me in some places — but then it sucked, too, because we'd hop into another realm, and those people would stare at me like I had hairy feet and smelled like manure. At first it bothered me — it bothered me a lot! Then I tried to please people, tried to alter little things to be more acceptable. But, that didn't work; we changed realms too often, too fast. Then, when we did hop somewhere else, there was always a new ideal. After awhile, I got sick of it — stressing out because I might not be what people wanted." She hugged herself and rubbed her arms vigorously. She was starting to feel embarrassed, exposed — she had *never* talked about herself so much.

Wo coaxed her on, "So, when did things change?"

She smiled, "I don't know." She shrugged. "It's not like the movies, you know — *the big change.* It's just something that happened along the way, all without my realizing it, until this moment. I guess I've been working on the change."

"You had to have been." Wo tweaked her nose. "A lot comes out of sustained effort."

Saffron sucked in her breath. "Yeah, that's what my Grandmother told me just after she died!" Saffron looked around as the fairies in the trees multiplied and worked more frantically. It felt like Christmas. "Only, you forget every once in a while, you know? You forget to sustain the effort. Then things don't change, and you don't realize why. You just...accept it. When it doesn't have to be that way." She shook herself from her thoughts. "I don't care anymore what other people want my body to be like. I think I know what *I* want my body to be like – so I'm just going to go with that. I'm most comfortable being who I've always been. I *want* this body."

Tai sniffed and patted at absent tears, then applauded slowly and loudly. He blubbered, "I need a hug." And pranced to Saffron's side.

She giggled and shoved him away. He landing squarely on his rear on the forest floor. He grinned back at her and reached to grab her calf, pinching it none too lightly.

"Ahhhhhhh!" She howled and jumped to the ground to wrestle him.

"Tsk, tsk, now!" Wo admonished and separated them, "Look, nightfall is approaching and we have work to do!"

Tai helped Saffron to her feet. "Okay, we're good with the body and we're — we're not changing hair color, right?" He eyed Saffron. "We're just styling it?"

Saffron smiled shyly and agreed. She would keep that fiery bush of a hairdo, and keep it with pride. "Just try to tame it somehow, dress it up. I can go back to being wild tomorrow." She addressed her answer to Wo, but he shook his head and pointed to his brother. "Right there is your master hairstylist — that's not my specialty."

Saffron was pleasantly surprised. "Tai? Really? Well, I wouldn't have guessed *that*."

"Hey, just because I'm incredibly stud-like and could rock any woman's world, doesn't mean I don't have fascinating hidden talents."

Saffron slapped a hand to her cheek, "You don't say!"

Tai whispered to Wo, "Can't I just give her a good beating before we start? No? Not just *one?*"

They worked.

Of course, they drew a crowd; you can't start doing magic as they were without drawing a crowd.

Saffron stood on the large mushroom. They had gouged trenches in the mushroom cap so Saffron could stand in them without wobbling. Tai raised both hands a-la-conductor, frowned at her in deep concentration, then began waves of magic that pulled and worked through Saffron's tresses. Several combs worked out the snarls, lotions and crèmes appeared to tame the frizz and add shine, and her curls and waves were encouraged to bounce higher. In the end, her hair was very big, very beautiful, and dusted with hundreds of tiny diamonds that twinkled like fire every time she moved. Tai crossed his arms and smirked at Wo in challenge.

Wo saluted Tai. He worked for the next hour, trying one color after another, all beautiful, but none perfect. He went back to antique gold for the third time. "This is it, isn't it? Gold for our golden girl. And I know what I can do with that...," he mumbled but didn't explain to anyone else. He kept working.

The forest animals, the fairies, the elves — all had ringside seats, and cheered or vetoed each change as it was made. Someone made batches of popcorn and passed bowls out to the crowd. Darkness was creeping in. Torches were lit and a runner was sent to find Orji. Orji had to come back, or Wo and Tai wouldn't have enough time to do him up. As it was, they were both feeling exhausted, their energy depleted on Saffron. They didn't have to go as crazy as they did, but it was the first time in a long time that they were allowed to do more than parlor tricks.

Finally, Saffron was done. She stood tall on the mushroom pedestal, seeming to float in the glittering fairy smoke that veiled the entire circle, as if she were an illusion —a magical princess standing in an immense snow globe.

Everyone broke out into applause. Saffron had to concentrate on keeping her happiness from swooning her right off the mushroom. She stepped down carefully, holding the hands of both Tai and Wo, while they hovered in the air. On her feet was a pair of finely-tooled leather boots to wear in the snow, and dancing slippers were tucked into a gold-beaded reticule for later in the evening. Saffron curtseyed to the mesmerized crowd and murmured her thanks. She smiled at Wo. "Can I see?"

Wo slapped himself in the head. "But of course, how could I forget?" He waved his hand across the air in front of Saffron until a shimmering started that turned into a mirror big enough for Saffron to see her entire dress in.

She gasped loudly, then lost her breath altogether. Her voice was filled with wonder when she spoke. "Oh, my God — this can't be." Tears filled her eyes, but didn't fall over and mar the swirls of gold dust that decorated her cheeks. Light, coffee-colored paint warmed her lips, and a faint, russet shadow curved on her eyelids and lit up her bright, grey eyes. Her tresses were curled and bejeweled, and her creamy skin was rubbed with gold dust.

She looked down at her dress.

It was made of golden silks – flowing, golden silks of several different shades, which spread out around her and floated on the air.

She squinted. There was something in the air around her — more gold — glowing and swirling wherever she walked.

Tai narrowed his eyes and glared at Wo. "If I had known we were allowed to enchant the air *around her, I* would have done something different with that hair!" Then he started to cough and gag. "Blahhh! Hack! Hack — for the love of nature, Wo — we have enough haze residues around here from all of that magic without you adding to it by giving her an orbital field!"

"Oh, shut up, you big baby. This isn't your moment." Wo didn't even look at Tai when he admonished him.

The dress was of medieval style, with a little room for fantastic embellishment —fairies would have it no other way. It fit to her upper body and was tied off under her chest with a golden rope. The rope was intricately woven and spanned her midriff, its tails hanging past her knees. Golden brocade bands surrounded her biceps, gathering the sheer sleeves close, but letting the fabric drop at her elbows. The ends of the sleeves were so long they nearly touched the ground.

Tai whispered to Wo. "Do you think it's too much?"

Wo shook his head. "Nah, who could ever have too much gold?"

Tai sighed. "How right you are, brother. How right you are."

Just then, Orji emerged from the trees. He took a short look at Saffron. His face never changed, never showed an ounce of the fire that suddenly welled up within him. But it was not her hair that fired him, not her dress, nor the golden mist that danced around her. He knew she was beautiful. He had always known she was beautiful. What caught him up and nearly made him lose his stiff countenance, was the way she looked at him — her starving eyes begging for his approval, as if his opinion mattered most. He could have kicked himself for his fantasizing. *She gave you no such look,* he admonished and forced himself to get control. He didn't even blink. He disappeared into his tent.

Saffron's smile fell and her shoulders drooped. As if it had been a wild party broken up by the cops, the music suddenly died, beings lowered their jubilant shouts to a low grumble, torches were snuffed, and everyone but Wo, Tai, and Saffron slunk off into the woods, leaving the camp with a completely littered, smoky, after-party ambiance.

"Well, obviously I don't look *that* fabulous," Saffron muttered and crumpled to sit on her mushroom.

"No! No!" Wo ran to her side and pulled her to her feet. "You can't sit in this dress, Saffron — it will ruin the effect. You're going to have to wallow on your feet this time."

Her frown deepened.

"I'm sorry. Look — who cares about him anyway? Who cares what he thinks?" Wo patted her back, but thought correctly that there was little he could do to console her.

I care, Saffron thought. A tear slid down her cheek and made an obvious streak through her gold-dust swirl.

Tai huffed. "Freaken' Orji." He hurried off after the lout, followed him right into his tent. Kaleidoscope swirls of fairy dust puffed out of the tent door, like someone was having a fight with an array of electric, cotton candy sugars.

Several minutes later, Orji and Tai came out. Orji was garbed in the strangest eveningwear Saffron had ever seen, but it wasn't unattractive. As a matter of fact, the more she stared at him, the more she liked the ensemble.

His pants billowed like those in an Arabian Nights tale, puffing out, then gathering close around his ankles. The fabric was decorated in

what looked like Chinese-style dragons. But they weren't dragons....
The pants were a darker gold than Saffron's dress; the 'dragons' were a
faint detail in crème embroidery. On top, Orji wore what looked more
like a medieval tunic, forest green with gold embellishment, and fitted
so very nicely to his wide shoulders.

Saffron decided to ignore his rude behavior and try to start their
evening off on a pleasant note. "That is a very beautiful outfit — how
did you think of it?"

"I gave Tai the details of my officer's robes — the clothes I wore at
court in my realm."

Saffron gasped. Officer? At court? She hadn't questioned him
enough on his past! She had tried, but he was never forthcoming with
answers. This display of his court uniform, surely, was inviting her
questions, right? Otherwise, why would he show her something so
personal? He could have chosen to wear anything....

Orji placed his hands on his hips; he looked very put out. "Isn't it
time we were going? I'm sure your prince awaits you with bated
breath, *M'lady*."

Saffron shook her head and her red curls bounced. *What a prick
you are, Orji!* She wanted to scream it in his face. Instead, she
ground her teeth and forced herself to be quiet.

Tai clapped his hands and startled everyone. "Well then, happy
couple — if you would be so kind as to progress to your chariot and get
this joyous evening under way, my brother and I can finally be rid of
your tiresome selves, and get down to business of interrogating
another tribe for our lost boys." He smiled a great, big, fake smile and
gestured at the caramel-colored pony that stood before them
suddenly, waiting to pull the golden sleigh behind it. The pony and
sleigh were decorated with lush, green garland and shiny, brass bells.

In the sleigh was a mink-lined seat and mink blanket for the riders' comfort.

Wo and Tai helped Saffron into the sleigh. She kissed them both on the cheek and thanked them profusely. They smiled, a little embarrassed, and with hands and wings waved her off. As the pony started to trot away, Saffron gave Orji one last disdainful look, then shot her nose in the air.

The pony had not taken ten steps, when suddenly, Saffron squawked and plopped down to the floor of the sleigh. She cursed loudly and repositioned herself on the seat after awkwardly getting up from the floor and shaking out the contraption that was her dress. She had been afraid of that. When the wagon had first taken off she had felt the silk of the slippery dress sliding across her plastic body, not hampered at all when it touched the cool, smooth mink. She held on with all of her might, but couldn't stay put, and fell off the seat five more times before they reached the castle.

By the time they arrived, Orji was howling with glee, and was only too happy now to play the perfect escort. He couldn't help it — there was nothing funnier than watching the Haughty Miss fall on her embellished ass, over and over and over.... He roared with laughter again, scaring the footmen that ran to receive them.

Before she knew it, they were inside, standing on the threshold of the most magnificent scene Saffron had ever seen.

At least *she* felt that way – Orji had been to hundreds of balls in his lifetime, and this looked much like any other I-can-spend-more-money-than-you affair. His eyes narrowed as his gaze fell on the young twit of a prince, who was below them on the bottom step of the sweeping marble staircase. The prince looked stupefied, staring up at Saffron, as if he had been turned to stone. Orji grunted.

Saffron found Prince John a moment after Orji had, and she gave him the most stunning, enchanting smile.

My wife, was all Prince John could think — it roused his senses — *my wife, my wife, my wife.*

Orji yanked Saffron's hand. "Let's go, Petunia, and get this greeting over with." He hoped to startle her out of that goofy grin and glassy-eyed look. It didn't work. Saffron practically floated ahead of him, right into the waiting arms of the prince. The prince didn't take her hand and kiss it as any normal boob would — no — he took her fully into his waiting arms and kissed her cheek. A blast of air roared up through Orji like a bullet train. He thought he'd choke on his fury right there. Choke and kill. Kill while choking. He descended the rest of the stairs and moved in behind her. He stood absolutely still, right behind her — so close, in fact, that her hair rubbed his face and the back of her dress pushed against his front. She didn't notice; she was so engaged with the splendor of the castle and the attention of the prince.

But, Prince John noticed. He wasted no time in inviting Saffron to dance, which successfully removed her from Orji's vicinity.

Orji ground his teeth and whipped his head to the side. He needed to stop staring at them. When he looked over his left shoulder, his attention was drawn to a gaggle of females that had been staring at him ever since he had entered. He looked away, breaking several hearts at once. If this had been another night, another realm, he would have had his fill of those girls — all of them — and, with the dawn they would have gone home happy. He stalked to the group of females and plucked one without consideration. He spun her onto the dance floor and kept pace with Saffron.

He didn't pay much attention to his partner. Her hair was all bouncy, blonde ringlets that dropped over her corseted, pushed-up chest. She smiled wantonly and forced Orji's gaze back to her own cat-green eyes.

"She is very beautiful." The woman motioned with her chin in Saffron's general direction, who was swinging by in the prince's arms and laughing with abandon.

"She's a pain in my ass." Orji grunted and swung his partner around, obstructing her view of Saffron.

"Aaah, then I'm too late — you're in love already." The bombshell shrugged and left Orji alone on the dance floor.

Saffron hoped Orji didn't notice, but she had her eye on Miss Jugs (so Saffron had instantly decided to name her). She couldn't believe it when the woman broke the dance and left Orji stranded. *Hmph — he must have pissed her off too!* Orji just had no clue when it came to women!

For Orji, the night dragged on like a torturous hell.

For Saffron, the night whisked by like an enchanted dream. Gone were the memories of Ny's harassment, gone were the feelings of guilt for her dwindling attachment to Markis, gone was the sorrow of losing her family and her life in the Earthrealm. She was happy — blindly and blissfully happy. Nothing could take away her enjoyment of this totally perfect evening.

They sat down to dinner, she to the prince's right and Orji somewhere down to the far, far, far left. Saffron saw Orji so far away, and giggled — she didn't know they *made* tables that were that long! The prince smiled at her chirping laughter and toasted their happiness. Saffron sucked on the bubbly drink in her glass that looked very much like champagne. She ate. There were platters of roasted game with wild herbs, candied vegetables and fresh snap peas, puffed pastry stuffed with meat and seafood (she hoped, but what did it matter to a ghost?), fruit-like things, followed by snowy white cake and creamed berries. And, of course, more bubbly stuff. The food did not excite her palate, nor did the bubbly drink quench her thirst. But the perfection of the evening filled her soul, and she was sated.

The prince stroked her smooth, cool cheek and stared into her eyes. He invited her out to one of several grand, sweeping balconies. It was adorned with hundreds of white candles and many vases filled with roses the colors of deep sunset — their petals dark orange, their tips tinged blood-red.

Prince John led Saffron to a black, marbled rail. Over the dark forest beyond, an unusually large full moon hung low in the sky. The prince took both of her hands and smiled down at her. "Saffron," he began, "I know I don't know you very well. I know you're from another realm, but I feel, in this short time, that we've grown to know each other — that there is something special between us, something I don't want to let go of...." He waited to see if she would say anything — maybe agree whole-heartedly, perhaps? He continued on when she said nothing. "You are so beautiful this evening! Your gown shines like the very sun! Your hair reminds me of raindrops, jeweled raindrops that I wish would shower me, also...."

Saffron searched for something intelligent to say. "Red rain is toxic – it's full of acid...."

"Pardon me?"

Well, that took him by surprise. Her next swift comment was a noncommittal noise. "Aaahh...." Her joy was snuffed like a lit candle dropped into a pond. The prince was taking this evening in quite another direction altogether. She gave him a small smile. "Uh-huh...." No great works of verbal art, to be sure, but she was absolutely at a loss for words. Was he really going to pop the dreaded question? Was he insane?

"What I mean to ask is...." The prince got down on one knee and held a ruby-red velvet box up to her.

Oh, my God – you're a moron....

"Would you agree to become my betrothed, Saffron of the Earthrealm?"

Saffron's eyes grew wide at the humungous blue diamond that seemed to catch fire when the moonlight hit it. It lay in an intricate filigree setting mounted to an equally ornate wrist cuff. She didn't know that it was possible to choke on air, for a ghost even, but she was about to prove that souls could indeed gag and die on oxygen. "Oh, hell no!" She slapped her hand to her mouth.

Prince John must have suffered from temporary deafness – he went ahead and locked the cuff on her wrist. His eyes glittered.

Orji stepped out onto the balcony, just in time to see the prince on bended knee before his redheaded devil. He was decking her out with a betrothal cuff — and Saffron was just standing there, letting him do it! Orji knew his eyes didn't deceive him — yet still, he couldn't believe it. His looked at Saffron – she was looking back at him. Her eyes *clung* to his.... She truly looked *desperate*.... Suddenly, Orji realized his fits of rage were all for naught, his unchecked jealousy good for nothing. He smirked at Saffron and wagged his fingers in greeting. Then he turned around and disappeared back into the ballroom.

Saffron moaned. Why didn't Orji storm over and demand to know what was going on? Couldn't he see what was going on?

Prince John cleared his throat.

Reluctantly, Saffron looked back at him. He had obviously been thrown by Orji's appearance; a single drop of sweat ran from his brow and rolled down his face. "You will marry me, won't you, Saffron?" His voice shook.

Saffron kept the offending cuffed wrist held away from her body. Her mind was screaming, trying to sort out just the right excuse — something to let him off the hook easily. She thought she had the perfect little speech concocted in record time. She opened her mouth and blurted, "Ahh..."

Prince John looked very confused. "Oh," was all he said and stood up. He looked back at her, tears in his eyes. "You will," he whispered.

Saffron winced. Great, he was crying. "It's....complicated — you're so hot and everything — you know? ...if this had been a year ago, I would have totally proposed to you first...the second I saw you...because when I say you're hot, I mean, you know..." She fanned herself wildly for emphasis, "...woooooweeeeee! But, I met all these people last year...these guys...and I'm so messed up, right now, you know...?"

"It's him, isn't it?" Prince John looked forlornly at the spot Orji had just vacated.

"Who?" Saffron looked at the spot, too, but had no idea what she was looking at. Then she realized who he meant. She balked, "Who...Orji?! Oh puh-lease! No." She shook her head vehemently.

The prince didn't say anything; he just looked at her with the saddest, most beautiful, puppy-dog eyes.

Saffron didn't say anything, either. She rubbed her eyes and felt like pushing them into the back of her head.

The two stood there awkwardly, not knowing what to do next.

The prince pushed her outstretched betrothal wrist down to her side. "You will marry me." There was victorious dominance in his voice.

Saffron arched an eyebrow and dipped her chin. *Why, you little....* She opened her mouth to protest.

"Yoo-hoo, Milord! Over here, Milord!"

Saffron's head snapped over to see what ridiculous person was calling Prince John like that.

The servant had ruddy, red cheeks, and a plump bottom lip. Her hands pressed gently to her wide girth. "Milord — do forgive the intrusion. But, may I borrow your little friend, if only for a moment?"

Prince John frowned. "And what, mayhap, would you be needing her for?"

"Oh, nothing but a little surprise for you, Milord...." Her voice was gentle, encouraging.

Prince John relented; it was the easiest way for both of them to part from this extremely embarrassing situation. The prince flicked his eyes to Saffron's for a mere second, then nodded in the direction of the servant. He turned to hang over the balustrade and would look at her no more.

Saffron frowned as she walked towards the servant. This was *weird* — what did the woman want? The servant waved Saffron on, encouraging her to pick up her pace. Saffron did so, not really wanting to take orders from someone she didn't know, but too bewildered to do otherwise.

"Thank you, Milady, now — where is that spicy bit of man you came here with?"

Saffron looked doubtful. Spicy bit of man? "Who? Orji?" Try *bastard troll* — that would be more precise.

The servant and Saffron swept into the ballroom to look for Orji.

More than half the ballroom had emptied out!

"Where did everybody go?" Saffron cried.

"Oh, here and there," chirped the servant. "Ah — there he is now." The servant pointed to a shadowed corner where Orji had a slender woman with jet-black hair in a fit of giggles.

Saffron sneered. How could that woman be laughing so hard? When had Orji ever said anything so funny? Snide maybe — but funny? *I know that moron, and he ain't that funny.*

"Good sir! Good Sir! Would you be so kind as to escort us? We have a surprise for the prince in the works and we need everyone's help...could you...*now*?" The servant's grin held strong. She clutched Orji's elbow and held fast to Saffron, then escorted them out of the ballroom.

The servant hummed in a high-pitched, tuneless way. It took one glance for her to decipher the situation between the young girl and the pompous stud — so, it took little effort for her to set about distracting them. "My, my, sir, that black hair – your friend seemed like a lovely woman — is she your wife?" The servant raised a jaunty eyebrow and feigned great curiosity. The seemingly innocent question set the redheaded girl off – just as she had hoped.

"Wife, my ass! Try ho, prostitute, lady of the evening, harlot...." Saffron strained for more terms, which allowed Orji an opening.

"Saffron, what's your problem? You don't even *know* that woman — how could you say such hateful things?"

"*You* don't even know that woman, Orji! How could you corner her like that – you looked like you were getting ready to jump her! My God! Couldn't you find a room? We're in a damn castle – there are a million rooms!"

"Hey, this isn't *my* castle, remember? It belongs to your betrothed," Orji jabbed a finger at the cuff around Saffron's wrist, "maybe you could ask him for a room. Get one for yourselves, while you're at it." Tiny droplets of spittle came flying from his mouth while he yelled, not unlike a dragon foaming at the fangs.

The servant was more than pleased. It was exactly the reaction she'd been hoping for. Now, they were too busy fighting to question their destination. They wound down shiny, stone hallways, past hulking, gilded frames, and over the fur hides of murdered beasts. They descended hundreds of circular steps – with Orji and Saffron hissing and spitting all the way.

Although they were behaving exactly as the servant had hoped, their high-pitched bickering began to get on her nerves, and she wondered, perhaps, if *they* got a room, their negative energy wouldn't be feeding foreign wars.

They turned into a low-ceilinged room brightly lit by torches that lined a great, stonewall. Before Saffron and Orji, there was an elaborate mural of green mountains brilliantly lit by an orange and yellow sun. It was the like the tapestries Saffron saw above stairs, except this painting was on wood, or something like it, and stood from floor to ceiling. There was a cottage in the scene. The cottage doorway was an actual hole, so that someone could walk through the mural and end up on the other side of the painting.

"Here we are!" The out-of-breath servant sing-songed, then motioned for Saffron and Orji to walk through the door-hole in the mural.

Orji stalked through without a thought, and Saffron was biting right at his heels, squawking and screaming like a parrot.

"Now, we'll be right back — don't worry." With those last words, the servant reached into the small room that Orji and Saffron had entered, and pulled a jail cell door closed with a resounding clank.

"Oh, great." Orji muttered and stalked to the door. Now that they were inside, they saw what the mural effectively concealed. A jail cell. Not one, but several jail cells that spanned the back dungeon wall — all hidden behind the cute mural. Orji roared and shot his fist between the bars. As soon as his knuckles met wood the entire enormous façade slowly toppled over and crashed to the floor with a woody slap and a whoosh of dust.

Saffron nodded absently and stared down at the back of the mural — it looked just like plywood. She brought the corners of her mouth down so low that her bottom lip pushed out in a pout. "Oooh, very effective."

"Well, these bars *won't* be very effective. C'mon, Saffron, liquidate so we can get out of here. I can't believe you agreed to marry that punk – you like it when he locks you up? I'll lock you up...." He flicked a cold, metal bar, then turned to Saffron and waited for her to clear her soul of substance.

"I *did not* agree to marry him!"

"Then what the hell are you wearing that for?"

"He just put it on me!"

"You just let him!"

"No, I didn't!"

"If it's on you — you let him!"

"Aaaaaghhh!"

"Yeah, like I said — you let him." Orji's nostrils were flared like a raging bull's. "It was *your* choice. You let him." He poked her in her plastic-like center.

"Don't poke me," Saffron hissed.

Orji poked her again. "Don't let me." He poked her again.

Saffron didn't move.

Orji poked her again.

Angry tears formed in Saffron's eyes.

Orji poked her again.

Suddenly, Saffron let out a long, rattling, murderous scream.

Orji sniffed. "So, you can turn into a banshee — but can you turn into a real, live ghost? C'mon. Hurry up."

Saffron turned away from him, swiped her eyes, and closed them to focus. She'd vanish all right — she had to get out, away from the castle, and away from Orji. She grunted and strained and concentrated, all with her eyes squeezed shut. After a while, she let out an exasperated breath. "I can't do it."

Orji huffed. "Saffron, now is the time — just do it so we can escape here before they come back." His last words were mumbled, "We need to get the hell out of this realm anyway — we've been here *way* too long."

Saffron closed her eyes and tried again. This time, she felt her shimmer. After several minutes, all of her solidity was gone and only the two-dimensional Saffron was left behind — her lightened soul.

Orji grunted and changed himself in a second – in a split second.

It happened right before Saffron's eyes, like someone turning out the lights. "Show-off."

"Jealous." Orji retorted, then held his hand out for hers. She couldn't exactly hold his hand, so she moved her hand into his essence until she felt the jolt of electricity, then she knew she had made contact with his soul — she knew they met where his hand should be. They stepped forward together, towards the steel bars. They had pushed halfway through the bars when, suddenly Saffron discovered she could move no further.

Obviously, Orji was having trouble, too — he was straining and pushing, yet could move no further. "What the hell is this?" he bellowed.

Saffron instantly lost her concentration and became solid.

Orji became solid, too.

They pulled, they pushed, they grunted. They reached for each other awkwardly, but couldn't connect to try and pry each other out. They tried some more. Then, completely frustrated and drained, they finally hung limply – half in and half out of the bars.

Somebody was coming. Down the damp, stone stairs, Orji and Saffron heard the almost imperceptible sound of a clothed footfall. Whoever was approaching began to whistle a cheery tune, and when his supremely tall and gaunt frame rounded the corner, he gave them a wink. He still had on his soiled whites — he appeared to be the castle chef.

Saffron returned a limp wave and frowned. Wasn't the cook even wondering why she and Orji were suspended in the *middle* of the cell bars? What was the chef doing in the dungeon? He acted as if nothing was amiss as he traipsed across the plywood and approached the door of the adjoining cell. He whipped out a key ring and commenced opening the cell. He didn't even seem to notice that he was walking on the big, overturned plank of wood!

What is he doing? He has no prisoner with him — what is he doing? Saffron craned her neck to ogle him a little better.

The chef engaged the lock — clink — swung the cell door open, then promptly entered the cell and proceeded to shut the gate and set the lock firmly.

Orji and Saffron stared at him, mouths agape. They blinked only once, in unison. The chef walked to the back of the cell, settled himself on a long, narrow bench, and produced a book from one pocket and an apple from the other. He found his place in the book, bit the apple, and wiped the juice that dribbled down his chin with his soiled sleeve. His eyes began to rove the page.

Orji and Saffron said nothing. They didn't resume their conversation and they didn't question the obviously-detained chef. They just hung there dumbly.

A short while later, a raucous bunch descended the stairs — their shrill voices bounced off the cold stone, their trilling caused Saffron to grind her teeth. Four women — four chambermaids to be exact, all howling and cackling like a murder of crows.

Only four, Saffron mused — she could have sworn there was going to be at least a hundred by the amount of noise they made.

They four stopped short when Saffron and Orji came into view. They burst into booming laughter. Out of the corner of her eye Saffron saw Orji flinch.

Just as soon as the women looked at the two oddballs hanging half out of the cell, they looked away, their beady eyes settling on the cook. They gave the chef low wolf whistles and fanned themselves dramatically. "C'mon, bad girls," he growled, "get ye ample behinds behind these bars where the likes of you belong." He hurried to unlock the cell, admiring their voluptuous bodies as they filed in, each giving him their own version of a seductive look.

Yuck, Saffron sniffed, *they ain't picky around here — are they?*

The group in the next cell made so much noise that Saffron and Orji felt comfortable enough to resume their quiet conversation. "What the hell is going on?" Saffron hissed.

"Baby, I have no idea." Orji wished he could run his hand through his hair, rub at his face in frustration, chew the calluses on his thumb — anything! But no, they weren't moving.

"Hey, at least we have no blood in our bodies. At this angle I'd be getting pins and needles right now." Saffron indicated her right arm with her chin. The arm was bent at the elbow, with her fingers reaching heavenward. Then she groaned as she felt the familiar weakness engulf her arm and assault her with thousands of tiny, electric pricks. She groaned. She couldn't summon the scent of the prince earlier, but she had to sit here and feel this phantom pain. It was all so aggravating!

Orji raised his eyebrows and smiled. "Yer feelin' that – aren't ya? There's nothing wrong with feeling, Saffron."

"That's where you're wrong — this particular feeling sucks."

Over the next half hour, more people — evidently the castle staff — came down the stairs, clacked across the fallen plywood, and let themselves into the jail cells.

The matron that had tricked them here in the first place suddenly stood before them. She was 'tsk-tsk-tsking.' "Aaahhh, so, you're enchanted then. Never would have guessed that — it's so...unlikely."

Saffron and Orji had a feeling the woman just gave them a smiling insult, but they weren't exactly sure. She acted so friendly.

"And nobody could release these poor souls?"

The dungeon was quite noisy now, what with the one hundred and fifty plus people who filled it. Only a few stopped their conversation to look at the matron. They ignored her all the same and turned away.

The matron sighed. "When I take your hands, move back into the cell and you will be released. No more of your wiliness — your type of magic won't work here — we're enchanted against enchantment." She gave a solid nod, and laughed at her wit — the sound cut short by a phlegmy, asthmatic cough.

"Wait!" Saffron shouted.

The woman, who was reaching for them, jerked her hands back.

She gave Saffron a tired look.

"What if we go forward — will we be free?"

Orji rolled his eyes and growled, "We would have been, if you had just done it, not announced to our captors that you were *going* to do it!"

The matron's eyes widened; she shook her head hard. "No, my friends — you do not want to be outside of this cell tonight. The other partygoers have been set out into the night — but you, we shall protect, as His Highness has shown special interest in you." The matron glanced at the betrothal cuff. Real fear had crept into her eyes. She cast a short glance at a high dungeon window. She could see the location of the moon from where she stood; it was high in the sky and gleaming full, though clouded over like a dead fish eye. She grasped their hands; Orji and Saffron stepped back into the cell.

Suddenly, they were both nervous. Rather, Orji was nervous, and Saffron was terrified. What was going on?

The woman let herself into their cell, locked the door, and turned to face them. She stroked Saffron's cheek. "You'll be safe in here — don't look so worried. I'm sorry I scared you, but you need to realize the depth of the situation, and right quick. It's almost time now." Saffron stiffened at her touch, so the matron took her hand away. "Come, let us relax. I will tell you the story."

"M, m, my friends, they're out in the woods — will they be okay? Saffron's voice was rising. "My friends! Help me, please — we need to warn them!" Her growing hysteria was starting to attract and upset the cellmates around them.

"Sssshhh," the woman soothed. "Are your friends nearby?"

Saffron shook her head no.

"Then they'll be fine. This is a curse on the royal family. We take care of them. They will not go into the woods to feed. We take care of them." Finally, she got Saffron to sit down. She put her arm around the frail girl's shoulders. Orji sat right next to Saffron, almost on her, and took her hand.

Saffron stared at the stone floor. Not far from them, a bear hide rested on the stones. Four people settled on it to play cards. "What do you mean, 'feed'?"

"It doesn't matter, Saffron, look...." Orji swiped his arm right through Saffron's midsection, then solidified once more. "No one can do us harm. Don't worry."

Forcing herself to be calm, Saffron repeated, "What do you mean, 'feed'?"

The matron licked her lips. "The prince...and his family...they 'feed.'"

Her words were cut short by shouting.

Saffron jumped.

"Cookies!" screamed the shouter. "Cookies and cocoa — line it up!" The hundred and fifty cellmates moved to the front edge of each individual cell and held their arms through the bars to receive their snack.

"Oooooh," cooed Miss Matron, and disappeared from Saffron's side for her gimme. A handful of men and woman worked quickly to give the others their snack, then locked themselves into various cells.

Saffron had noticed earlier that there were cell cliques going on. She and Orji were in cell three. If you counted across the back wall from left to right — the pretty, bitchy girls were in cell one, surrounded by droves of good-looking guys. In cell two, there were pretty, nice girls — surrounded by several guys, who were all varying degrees of geek, scary, or just plain odd. In cell four there were a handful of older gossips. Cell five — stoic men. Cell six — artsy types writing on the walls and performing bad a cappella for each other. Cell seven — acrobats or perverts — Saffron wasn't sure which, so she stopped looking over there. The wall rounded a corner, so she wasn't sure about cells 8, 9, and 10. She had the gamblers in her cell. When the matron was done with her cookies, she glanced longingly at the boisterous, bear-rug players. But she shook her head and made her way back to Saffron.

"My girl, I shall tell you the tale..." She looked away from Saffron when the boisterous, bear rug players hooted and hollered. Then she shook her head and made her way over to Saffron. "My girl, now, I shall tell you the tale of the cursed family..." Her eyes strayed to their farthest reaches. She looked so far over to the left, Saffron could only see the whites of her eyes. She looked like the chubby living dead.

The matron, cleared her throat, and visibly forced herself, once again, to face Saffron. "My girl...."

"Oh, can it, lady — I don't really care. Just tell me when we get out of here, then go play with your friends."

"Thank you, Miss! You know...if it was another night..." Her eyes glittered as she spied the lousy hand held by one of her mates. "...If it was another night I would have been happy to fill you in on monsters and death, and all that brouhaha, but, tonight, tonight is our championship game, you see, and...." She looked over at the players again.

"Just go!" Saffron bit out. She took the woman's elbow and pushed her off towards her friends.

"She didn't tell you when we can leave." Orji pointed out.

"Oh, I don't care!" Saffron almost shrieked.

"Of course you care — why do you keep *saying* that!" Orji stared hard at her. Did everyone in the Earthrealm say that? 'I don't care! I don't care!' He had never before met someone who *did* care so much — cared about *every,* tiny, little thing!

Saffron pulled her knees up to her chest and hugged them tightly. She teetered on the edge of the bench. Orji stretched his long legs out before him and raised his arms up, resting the palms of his hands on the back of his head. From their line of vision, the moon was just starting to cross the narrow width of the very long window above. Actually, it was more of a slit in the castle wall — there was no glass.

They sat in silence, watching the castle staff go about partying in their individual cells. Saffron shook her head — what a bunch of freaks. Hiding in jail cells while monsters roamed the castle. Devouring cookies, playing cards, exchanging gossip — she looked over at the perverts/acrobats — even doing the limbo, while *things* were feeding upstairs. What things? Feeding on what?

Saffron mulled over the evening. After awhile she said, "You know what?"

"Not really, I'm sure." Orji turned his head and smiled.

Saffron crossed her eyes and stuck her tongue out. "No really — listen." She took a deep breath. She was obviously struggling with what she was about to say.

Orji's cocksure smile faltered. Was she about to say something serious? To him?

"I'm just glad that you're here, that's all. I aahhh..." she lowered her voice to an almost inaudible whisper. "...in case you haven't noticed — we're surrounded by freaks. And, well...I feel *comfortable* with you. These people, you know, they're hinting that they're saving us from something terrible that's walking outside these cells, but I'm thinking, you know, they're kind of freaky themselves, and I don't feel safe, exactly, being shut in with them, you know, so I'm glad I have you. That's why I feel safe." She nodded, satisfied that she had explained herself to Orji well enough.

Orji nodded. He took her hand and patted it. "Are you trying to tell me you love me? Do you want to get married?"

Saffron snatched her hand back so she could slap him with it. The betrothal cuff slid around her slim wrist. "Ooooh!" She looked at him as if he'd been dunked in cow dung.

Orji smiled pleasantly, rubbed his slapped cheek thoughtfully, and relaxed against the wall. "Wanna do me a favor? Why don't you go ahead and take off that damn betrothal cuff...."

Saffron nodded, "Gladly." She looked for a clasp and couldn't find one. She flipped the thing around and around and couldn't find a catch or a way to get the thing off. She tried to shove it over her hand but it *shrunk* when it got near her knuckles and wouldn't slide off. "Shit. Are you kidding me?" She looked at Orji with a desperate pleading in her eyes.

He shrugged, took her wrist, inspected the bracelet and shrugged again. He dropped her hand. "So, was your ball everything you dreamed it would be?"

Saffron shrugged and hugged her knees harder. "It was — at first. I mean, back at the woods, it was, getting ready and all. The twins and the magic, and all of that — it was surreal. Then, when we got there, there were beautiful woman *everywhere*. In the Cinderella story, she's the most beautiful woman in the room.... In all the fairy tales, the main character is the 'most beautiful in all the land'."

Orji glanced at her. "Maybe, *to them*, you're not 'the main character'."

Saffron was folded up like a pretzel under her golden gown.

He looked at her face under the dusting of gold and swallowed hard. She was absolutely the most beautiful woman at the ball tonight — the most beautiful woman in this realm, the most beautiful in all of the realms that they had visited. He ached to reach out and free her curls from the confines of Tai's elaborate coif. "How do you know you weren't the most beautiful woman at the ball? People were staring — they probably thought you were the most beautiful."

"It was the dress Orji; they were staring at the dress." She punched at the garment puffing up in her face. "Look at me — I'm Viva Las Vegas La Cinderalita."

"Aaahh." Orji had no idea what the hell she just said.

"Put this dress on any one of those woman I saw in the corner, and *they* would have been the most spectacular girl at the ball. That doesn't mean that *I* was spectacular — it was all smoke and mirrors. She started to undo her hair; it fell piece by piece.

Orji smiled softly. Saffron, as usual completely wrapped up in herself, didn't notice his longing stare, or the quiet pleading in his eyes. He found it so seductive, this letting down of her hair.

"I was so excited to go to this ball, you know, like finally my wildest fantasy was going to be fulfilled, and I was going to be happy — just like the girls in the stories...but no — I'm just confused." She shifted and faced him. "Why is that? Why am I still so lost?"

"You've dreamed of this ball for so long, and so hard. Sometimes, Saffron, the destination is not as important as the journey, the arrival not as spectacular as the quest...." He waited for the words to sink in.

After a moment of thought, Saffron frowned. "Yeah, Orji, Steven Tyler already told me that...." She sighed.

Orji shook his head, completely exasperated. "Who?" His eyebrows crushed together in a severe frown.

"No, really," Saffron crossed her eyes, and waggled her head, "Confucius say, blah, blah, blah. Blah, blah, blah, blah, blah, blah!"

Orji pinched her arm. "You're a vicious little thing! Maybe if you listened, for once, you wouldn't be so miserable! You're not lost, Saffron – you just refuse to wake up!"

But she *had* listened. His meaning disturbed her. Was he trying to tell her that her travels with him were going to be better for her than finding Markis? Wasn't that what he was trying to get at?

The moonlight that filled the slit in the wall was suddenly snuffed out. Something had blocked the moon — something more than a layer of clouds. Something was filling the opening of the window far above their heads. Every single person in every single cell stopped talking. As one, they glanced upwards. No skirts rustled, no throats were cleared — the silence was pristine. Finally, the shadow moved and moonlight once again poured into the room. The crowd sighed all together, and resumed whatever it was that they had been doing.

Saffron locked eyes with the matronly servant woman on the bear rug.

"He is searching for you." Then, the matron simply returned to her cards.

Icy cold dread filled Saffron's veins.

Suddenly, a howl filled the night — a screeching howl, followed by the death squeal of a screaming pig. There was slapping against the windowless slot — a meaty slamming sound, and after the third thump, blood rained into the room and spattered on some of the people below. It oozed down the sides of the wall. The small crowd that received the vile shower hurriedly moved over to the far corner of their cell and continued to wait with apprehension. The meaty slams kept coming, more blood rained.

Saffron's eyes widened and slowly, slowly she turned her head towards Orji.

He took her in his arms and held her tightly.

The servant woman dropped her cards, begged out of the game, and came to Saffron's side. "Well, now — that was gruesome, wasn't it?"

Saffron gave her a dirty look and snuggled closer to Orji. He grabbed her up with ready arms.

"Now, Luv, you've no need to fear me. I may seem a bit off because I'm unaffected by this. I apologize. It's just that we've been through i'tall before. Over and over, in fact, and when you've seen it as many times we have, it gets old."

Saffron stole a peek at the macabre scene — the window dripping with fresh blood. "Why are we locked up here, anyway?"

"Well, if they get beyond the upper door, they'll never get through these bars, will they?"

Saffron blinked. "I have no idea, do I...."

"Oh, Luv," the matron tugged a piece of Saffron's hair, "you don't want to lay eyes on these creatures. No, it's best they travel around up there, do what they need to do and stay out of sight of the good folk down here." She nodded solemnly and looked up at the ceiling when something crashed.

Saffron jumped at the crash and gripped Orji's shirt. "What's going on, anyway?"

"Oh, it was a long time ago — a nasty witch, and a horrible curse. Seven generations, I believe, now." The woman drew a rag from inside her dress, blew her nose, then tucked the soiled thing back into the dark valley between her breasts. "One day, the prince of this land set out on his morning ride through the southwest woods. On that morn, he met a maiden by a stream. It was the middle of winter, and steam rose from the body of the girl as she bathed by the icy, cold waters. Her jet-back hair fell in piles around her delicate frame. A fine young lass was she, of such surpassing beauty, he begged her hand in marriage. She was much taken with the handsome young prince and instantly agreed."

"Whach ye piping about now, Merry?" One of her comrades had come over to see why she hadn't returned to the card game.

"Oh, just telling the pretty young vision here, about the curse."

"Shishe! Again with the curse? How many times can ye tell that old squash and drivel?"

Merry exploded into her phlegmy, hacking laugh. "Oh, Murto! It doesn't get old! Let me enlighten the young thing — she's nervous."

Murto rolled his eyes, annoyed at the delay in the game. He took himself away, grumbling loudly.

"Well, the young prince took her back to meet his parents — the king and queen. Not long into the meeting, it became apparent that the girl was not of royal blood — not one of the king's serfs, at that — but a forest dweller who lived alone with her mother and lived off the land in the middle of the great woods. The king nearly exploded with rage. His son knew he must marry royalty — what was he thinking — bringing the trollop of the trees before him." Merry shook her head. "In the old days, it wasn't like it is now. Now, the prince can choose to marry anyone he wishes. He can choose anyone, because of the curse that was placed on the royal family that very fateful day, seven generations ago."

Saffron fidgeted and moved out of Orji's arms.

Merry eyed them warily. What was up with these folks, anyway? That girl hopped back and forth like she was burning to be with him, but getting burned when she was — all that with the prince's betrothal bracelet around her wrist, too. Merry sighed, she knew folks, she imagined these lovers were just as out of it as any two fools in the throes. What a mess.

She cleared her throat and brought both pairs of stranger's eyes back to her. "So, the maid went home crying to her Ma, telling the woman of the prince who wanted her for marriage, but so easily gave her up just because his father had said no. The girl's mother, who — lo and behold! — was a witch, became enraged. She had never liked the royal circus, and now had reason to hate them. The royal family would not insult her, or her own, and get away with it."

Saffron shifted again. One golden-capped sleeve slipped off her shoulder, exposing a good bit of satiny skin. Orji found this to be completely delightful and willed himself to remember. Remember the rush of blood a man feels for a desirable woman, remember the tingle in the roof of his mouth, and the powerful surge throughout his limbs. He sat back, smiling a delicious smile, and staring at Saffron's bare shoulder.

Saffron had the sensation she was being watched, and fearfully, she looked out the blood-stained-window high above them. There was nothing there now. She looked around, frowning deeply. She turned abruptly and her eyes rested on Orji. He was in mid-drool. With a huff, she hiked her sleeve up.

"The witch worked for several hours, consulted many demons, and finally came up with a curse that would appease her rage. She boarded her sleigh pulled by three black wolves and, at dusk, raced across the ice and snow to the royal castle. She stormed through the gates, casting curses at those who attempted to hinder her surge for the king and queen. Finally, she stood before the thrones of the two, chanted her awful words, and raised her awful staff. When she pointed the staff at them, thunder cracked and lightning sliced. A torrent of hail rained down on the castle and smashed the stained glass windows." Merry was standing now, shouting the story excitedly, and waving her hands around with each expletive.

"Hey, Merry," shouted Murto, then spat on the cell floor, "Aren't ye forgittin twas during the reign of the sun when all of that be happenin? Twasn't hail breaking yon windows, twas moon rocks and spring chickens!" He was on his feet, mimicking Merry's drama. People all around them broke out into knee-slapping, howling laughter. Merry shouted not-very-nice swear-words at them and encouraged them all to shut their traps. It took several minutes for everyone to forget Merry and the strangers and go back to their business.

"Anyway..." she had lost her gusto for the story and quickly brought it to a close. "...from that day, till this, on the full moon of every month — the king, the queen, and their offspring would change. They would turn inside out. Yes, inside out, and so would their minds. Things, horrible things, they wouldn't imagine doing on a normal day, they would now do. So, each full moon we lock ourselves in here to avoid seeing them and..." she shuddered, "...avoid being eaten by them. Because, my beauty, that is what they seem to enjoy doing most with their horrible bodies pulsing inside out — they chase whatever living thing they find, and chew it alive!"

Saffron jumped back, back into Orji's arms, only this time he wasn't there to catch her, and she slammed into the wall. She searched frantically for him, and found him by the front of the cell, giving her a carefree wave. He had seen the whole thing, knew she had flung her body back, hoping to land on him.

She wrinkled her nose in mortified repugnance. "You mean the prince, *my prince*, the dude who just proposed to me a few hours ago, is out there," she indicated the dried-blood window, "chewing on things that are trying to run from him?"

Merry clapped her hands together, "Oh, my lady! He proposed! Did you accept?!" Several heads raised and looked over at them when Merry shrieked 'proposed'.

"Aaacchh! SSShhhh!!!" Saffron grabbed Merry's hand and shook her head, 'no,' violently. "Don't *tell* anyone, Merry!

"But, *why,* Luv — THE prince proposed to you! How wonderful! You should be screaming such from the hilltops!

"Stop it, stop it!" Saffron stared from under her furrowed brow. "Honey, c'mon...I am *not* marrying that dude — he eats things that are trying to run from him! And, he's inside out!" Saffron kept trying to wipe the gruesome image of pulsing organs and wet, bloody turned-inside-out skin from her mind. She prayed she wouldn't come face-to-face with that thing.

"Oh, pish!" Merry was becoming annoyed with Saffron's theatrics, her insults cast at their wonderful prince. "He's not *always* like that. Do you get your monthly yet, dear?" Merry eyed Saffron's tiny breasts with suspicion.

Saffron gasped and brought her arms up across her chest. Was the old chick *serious.* Her 'monthly'? Did that mean what Saffron thought it meant? Of course it did! Heat shot up through Saffron's cheeks and singed her ears. "Of course," she hissed.

"Well, Luv, it's a bit of the same, isn't it? *You* get a little monstrous once a month too, don't you? And more than a little bloody!" Merry clapped her hands at her own bit of humor.

Saffron walked over to Orji and slammed her hands on the bars by his head. "I can't stay here, Orji. I need to get the hell out. These people are whacked!"

Orji leveled narrowed eyes on her. "Know what I was just thinking?"

Saffron rolled her eyes and looked away without answering.

"No, really, Saffron, listen — this is an important observation."

Saffron looked back at him and tapped her foot to let him know she was in no mood.

"Have you realized, Saffron, honey, that you have absolutely the worst taste in men?"

Saffron froze.

"It's true. That one out there — he's feasting on still-warm pig entrails and the other one — what did he do?" Orji squinted his eyes, feigning great concentration. "Ah, yes, I remember now — sucking the necks of frigid, young virgins wasn't it?"

Saffron shook her head slowly, a warning sign that she was about to haul off and clock him.

"And the one we're tailing now – what is it? Took the soul of your high school sweetheart. And your high school sweetheart — didn't he take off with another man?" Orji smiled.

Saffron surprised him by smiling back. "Now, Orji, if it were true that I only date monsters, don't you think I would have gone for you a long time ago? After all, *you* are a great big, hairy beast!" She slapped the bars. "I want out of here!" This time, she screamed. Mostly, everyone ignored her. They were used to the breakdowns of newcomers after the fourth hour.

"Yeah, okay, let's go. You know, I was really enjoying being trapped in this cell, but, you're right, dear, let us adjourn." He swept his hand forward to indicate 'ladies first,' then waited for her to walk.

She locked an icy stare on him.

"My lady, let us away!" He swept his hand forward again, smiling. "Move your arse my love, let us go forth!" He tried to sweep his arm forward again, but Saffron grabbed it in mid-swing and flung it down like a child throwing a log.

Orji grabbed Saffron's head with both hands and smoothed her cheeks with his thumbs. "Saffron, my spoiled little child, we aren't going anywhere until these people let us. So, get a hold of yourself, go lay down on the bench, and sleep it off. If you go to sleep, tomorrow will come faster." He beckoned her. "C'mon. Let's go lay you down." He led her to an empty corner of the cell, settled himself against the wall, then encouraged her to lie down and put her head on his lap.

They awoke at dawn, along with most everyone else in the dungeon. Some hard-cores had stayed up all night, including all of the gamblers. Orji had stayed up for some time, watching them bicker over their game. At some point, he had drifted off, his hand resting lightly on Saffron's head, the other on the curve of her back.

Saffron was slow to sit up.

All around, people were yawning, snorting, clearing throats, rubbing at their eyes, and popping the kinks from their backs. There weren't many conversations — just a lot of grunting, groaning, and avoidance. Everybody looked as if they'd partied hard the previous night, and were now ready to scurry to their private holes and sleep it off.

Saffron was genuinely pleased she couldn't smell the scene; these people looked like they *reeked*. Cold, morning sunlight barely limped into the dungeon — a wide expanse of the room was still mostly in dark shadow. Saffron just wanted to get out and leave this realm. Leave it far, far behind. She snorted. *With my luck, the twins*

probably picked up a trace of Ny in this realm, and we'll be stuck
here until the next full moon....

Cells doors started to bang open. Saffron's shoulders slumped in relief, and a smile crossed her wary lips.

"Are you ready?" Orji's deep voice by her ear made her jump. She looked at him shyly and nodded. She felt like an idiot. What must he think of her? Searching for the love of her life, but crawling into his lap like that. She wanted to tell him that she wasn't using him. Because she wasn't — at least, she didn't *think* so. She frowned and looked up at the ceiling. *Am I using him?* She hugged her arms across her chest and followed the river of folks out of her cell, then joined the flood of people slowly making their way up the stone stairs.

Orji saw it in her eyes, in her posture. She regretted last night.

Saffron tripped on her tattered dress as she climbed the last step. She started to topple forward and, just before her face met cold, hard cement, Orji caught her by the back of both arms and pulled her back into his chest. Saffron breathed a sigh of relief and looked up into his warm smiling eyes. He pushed her back on her feet, albeit gently, and removed his hands from her arms.

They bounced back to camp in the sleigh pulled by the caramel-colored pony. Saffron slid off the seat almost immediately, swore, and sat on the floor of the bouncy thing for the rest of the journey. Orji didn't mind, he enjoyed watching the way her chest popped up with every jounce. Her low-cut ball gown was a refreshing change from the black turtleneck and concealing scarf.

Soon enough, they arrived at camp. Tai and Wo had already packed up — Ny was not in this realm.

"Tell us!" Wo sprinted to the sleigh, grabbed hold of the reins, and petted the caramel pony.

"Uh," Saffron grunted and waved him away.

Orji got out of the sleigh, then turned and extended his hand to help Saffron up.

Tai sauntered over. "Saffron, why are you sitting on the *floor?*"

"Aaaahh!" Wo's hands fisted and slammed to his chest as he eyed Saffron's torn dress with utter misery. "What happened to my dress!!"

Saffron looked down at the frayed edges of gold. "Oh," she replied despondently.

"Last night was a flop, boys, don't even ask." Orji clapped them both on the back. He looked around at the clean camp. "Do we know where we're off to?"

Tai sat on the large mushroom, placed a walking stick between his knees, and resumed whittling. His wings fluttered in the breeze. "We met someone who's seen Ny."

www.ingramcontent.com/pod-product-compliance
Lightning Source LLC
Chambersburg PA
CBHW030021180626
46810CB00001B/146